TUNERS

TUNERS

by MATT HOWARTH

The Merry Blacksmith Press

2015

a shorter version of this novel was published in digital format
in 2000 by Howteck Industries

For information, address:

The Merry Blacksmith Press
70 Lenox Ave.
West Warwick, RI 02893

merryblacksmith.com

Published in the USA by The Merry Blacksmith Press

ISBN— 978-0-69247-572-0
0-69247-572-9

THIS TALE BEGINS several generations removed from the end of civilization as you know it. At this point, how *the end* occurred is immaterial. By the time of this tale, mortal villains have been forgotten; the only *blame* that is remembered falls upon the concept of *technology*.

Now: by dark waters.

Grahum Palma was not comfortable being a tiller of the soil. Besides the fact that the soil was a stubborn partner in the task of farming, Grahum had never possessed an affinity with growing things. His interests lay more in the *whys* of how things grew, leaving the *hows* to his brethren.

Many things had he learned by simple observation. When a question arose around the Palma farm, it was usually brought to Grahum, thereby provoking a deep jealousy and distrust in the Tribe's answerman. Several times, that self-anointed individual had publicly challenged Grahum's advice, resulting in a state of mutual animosity between the Tribe's hierarchy and the Palma farm, much to the detriment of the rest of the Tribe, since Grahum's insights had made the farm the region's largest crop producer.

Normally, Grahum Palma was not overly vocal regarding his knowledge. He preferred to spend his days wandering the woods, sometimes even venturing into the dust hills that surrounded the Tribe's lakeside encampment. At night, he would survey without criticism the handiwork of his brethren, then immerse himself in the emotional care of his immediate family privately within the confines of their meager log cabin. On communal occasions, he was wont to remain in the cooking areas, avoiding the queries of his curious neighbors and thereby sparing the answerman further embarrassment.

Standing nearly two meters tall, Grahum towered over most of the members of the Tribe. Like them, he was tanned by the sun and wore comfortable weave shirts and loose hide pants. His shoulders were still broad with the power of youth which had not fled him as he entered into middle-age. His hair, once long and strikingly blonde, had browned over the years and was beginning to show traces of gray. A mild vanity induced him to keep his hair cropped close to the skull; he often further hid this gray with a gaudy yellow bandanna worn in cap fashion.

A stranger would have imagined Grahum harbored little intelligence behind his rustic face and vacant blue eyes, but then few strangers visited the lakeside village and the Tribe all knew not to be deceived by Grahum's faraway look.

Today, Grahum was sharing a small portion of his secret knowledge with Rett, his youngest manchild. They strolled far beyond the territory of the Palma farm, following an ancient asphalt road that weather had reduced to little more than a path frequented by hunting parties as it wound through woods and field.

Despite the region's unfriendly soil, woodlands stretched far to the south, separating the Tribe's farms from the dust hills. The trees were not unhealthy, but they were uncommonly brittle, growing barely higher than three meters. Their leaves were a hearty breed, larger than a man's hands-breadth and almost as thick, spread in solidly overlapping sheets to collect the meager sunlight that fell to earth. Harsh shrubs clustered at the bases of the gnarled trees, making the forest an impassable nest of needles and dried twigs. What animals lurked in the woods were few, small and furtive; even fewer birds made their homes in the trees. Keeping these creatures away from the Tribe's fields was a constant problem, the crops being the diet of choice for man and beast. While the bestial denizens of these woods were numerable, they were too puny to suffice as a food source for humans. Hunters for the Tribe were forced to range further north, beyond the deadly marshlands for meatier animals to stock the Tribe's larders. Only the foolhardy would risk eating any creatures from the lake.

Gesturing to a rare clump of violet flowers that grew by the side of the path under a lean of oak trees, Grahum instructed Rett in the curious medicinal properties of the bloom's pedal, carefully elucidating the methodology recommended to produce the correct dosage. The boy nodded, feigning an intense fascination for the man's words.

In truth, small Rett longed to be back on the farm, indulging his cunning in means of avoiding work and torturing his eldest sister, Nitch. The boy did not reflect his father's physique or mental inclinations. He was slight, almost winsome, with a tousle of dark brown hair with a predilection for curling. His hands and feet were large, gratefully not grotesquely so. As with any boy of eight, his attentions were devoted to roughhouse antics and climbing everything in sight. Enduring his father's meandering lecture was not high on his daily itinerary, but at least it provided him with a frequent exemption from the sweaty labors of farmlife. Much to the boy's disappointment, Rett's father was aware of his errant attention and often quizzed him regarding his instruction.

Rett didn't understand why he should care about the things his father struggled to teach him. The boy perceived little connection between these lessons and the lore of tilling the fields of Palma farm. The farm was life, not these secrets his father spoke of.

Everyone has secrets, mused small Rett as he impatiently toed the pebbles at his feet. His father had secrets. The Tribe's answerman had secrets. Even his sister, Nitch, had secrets. *Well,* he told himself, *so do* I.

As the father further extolled the medicinal values of the purple blooms, his son's mind wandered across the countryside, back through the forest to the ruins that lined the shores of Oogolah Lake, where lay *his* secret. He and Dayf Murlo were converting a crevasse into the ultimate stronghold: a fortress that would serve them well in upcoming clashes with the Volvo brothers. They had spent days clearing the deep fissure of all debris, and days more discovering a series of small tunnels that ran deep beneath the ancient ruins. Actually cracks and gaps between the jumbled slabs that comprised the ruins' outer regions, they seemed like *tunnels* to the two boys, perfectly scaled to their diminutive frames and eager curiosity. They'd found secrets far beneath the ground where certain tunnels spilled out into strangely rectangular caverns. Useless secrets, though. Useless—just like the stuff his father was talking about now.

What Rett truly wanted to learn were the ways of *war* so he could defend his fishing hole and favorite climbing trees from the Volvo brothers. But all of Rett's attempts to coerce his father to teach him how to fight had ended badly. Grahum Palma had exploded into a long speech about pacifism and coexistence and tolerance and compromise. So heated grew the speech that the force of his father's convictions had undermined the actual beliefs he was trying to instill in his son. The boy respected his father's passion, but the *reasons* for that passion routinely bored Rett numb.

Defending his fishing hole from the Volvo brothers—*that* was reason for passion. If they didn't back off, Rett knew that a *war* would be required to drive them away. He and Dayf were prepared for that possibility; now all they needed was to learn how to conduct such hostilities. Alas, neither his nor Dayf's fathers were willing to teach them *this* knowledge. Apparently pacifism was a trait vanguarded by most of the adult members of the Tribe.

Sweeping his long arms to indicate the nearby treetops that lined the rough path, Grahum inquired if his son knew why plants grew toward the sky. *This* was a subject that captured Rett's interest—it involved trees, which were fairly integral to his favorite past-time of climbing. He paused, asking his father to explain this facet of nature.

Not six words into his discourse, Grahum halted to observe the approach of a figure on the path. A stranger! And one coming from the direction of the dust hills. Still only a silhouette beneath the trees' shadows, the figure walked along the path in a strangely stiff manner, causing Rett to wonder whether the man suffered from loose bowels brought about by some dietary deficiency.

"Hail," he waved, startling the traveler.

After a momentary hesitation, the stranger plunged his hands deep into the pockets of his dark garb, then proceeded to run toward Grahum and his son.

As the figure came closer, the haze of distance fell away to reveal the stranger and his even stranger attire. He seemed to wear a black body-suit, achieved by winding a ridiculously long scarf about his torso, neck and lower face.

"Boy," Grahum spoke sternly to Rett, worrying the child with his suddenly strict tone, "You run back home—right now. Everyone you see, you tell them Quiet Men are coming."

The boy hesitated, disbelief thick in his expression. "Aw, Paw, ain't no Quiet Men. They's just boogie men what Grammy uses to scare us to sleep at night."

Grahum turned on his son, savagely grasping him by the upper arms, almost lifting the child from the path. "You *go*, boy! You go *now!*" he yelled, "This is *no* game!"

Releasing the boy, he shoved him back along the path. Rett stumbled, confused for a second before his father's furrowed brow scared him to flight.

Once certain that his son was off toward safety, Grahum crossed to the trees beside the path, searching for any loose branches that could be utilized as a weapon. The Quiet Man was closing the distance between them with alarming speed and unnatural silence. His gait was quite unnatural as he ran with his arms stiff at his sides, hands deep in some pockets.

As the stranger reached Grahum's immediate proximity, the farmer turned, brandishing a stout wooden limb over a meter long. He attempted to strike the Quiet Man over the head with the branch, but his blow slid clumsily off the stranger's shoulder. In a sudden instant, the dark clad figure was upon him. Empowered by momentum, the Quiet Man's frail weight knocked Graham to the ground, where the pair rolled, grappling at each other with clawed fingers and tanned fists.

Their tussle placed Grahum on the bottom as they struggled near the edge of the path, sharply cracking his head against an upthrust slab of concrete. Grahum's vision swam as he groped to retain consciousness. By instinct more than intention, the farmer let out a pained cry.

Hands flying to clutch his ruined ears, the Quiet Man rocked back from atop Graham. It was apparent that some cruelty had mutilated the stranger's ears, leaving only infected scar tissue crusted about the canals that led to the eardrums. The stranger twitched in obvious agony, falling upon the ground to roll away.

Shaking sensation back into his head, Grahum clambered to his feet, searching for the lost branch. At the edge of his peripheral vision, he saw Rett far back along the path. The boy had halted, peering back at the struggle with the curiosity of youth. Grahum yelled at his son, waving him to flee. This gesture was the father's undoing.

A noise-maddened Quiet Man descended on him from behind, savagely striking the back of Grahum's head with a blunt object he had pulled from beneath his scarf-wrapping. The stranger viciously pummeled the farmer with the uncooked potato until Grahum sank stunned to the broken asphalt path.

Standing over the unconscious farmer, the Quiet Man shook his fists at the sky. He shook his shaved head about as he commenced to prance about his fallen victim. The silence that accompanied his dance was disturbing, for clearly a brutal passion drove the stranger's lunatic actions.

With an quickness that bespoke a cruel purpose, the lunatic crouched down to wrench open Grahum's gaping mouth. Into this maw, the Quiet Man plunged the potato, driving it deep into the farmer's helpless mouth. He worked intensely, shoving it deeper and deeper until finally the farmer's throat distended with the lump of its mass. Only then did the dark figure resume his mad cavorting, arms flung to the late afternoon sky.

Far down the path, Rett watched in horror as the boogie man of his Grammy's bedtime stories murdered his father in broad daylight. A terrible nightmare had clawed its way from the land of sleep to attack his father. How could the denizens of Grammy's horrific bedtime stories be walking about in daytime? The small boy's body trembled with considerable convulsions, his mind tormented by terror and disbelief.

He took a hesitant step toward his father's body, but fear won out, turning him to wildly flee. With a sudden gasp, the boy rushed squarely into the dark figures that had appeared behind him. Two Quiet Men barred his way, clutching at his thrashing arms. Close enough now, he could clearly smell these awful creatures—they reeked of unwashed filth and crusted sweat. Their stern faces were alive with scowling hate; even with their mouths hidden by their wrapped scarves, their frenzied scowls were frighteningly evident. Their gaze burned with fanatical fever. He twisted to avoid them, but their fingers were like inhuman talons, desperate to close on his struggling limbs. More of the monsters were coming out of the woods, lurching in their stiff-legged stride.

Before a scream could exit little Rett's lips, the Quiet Men had converged on him, silencing the child's voice with a lethal potato.

Standing over the boy's freshly suffocating body, the Quiet Men glared with loathing at the forest around them, wincing at the bird cries their struggles had raised.

2

THE AIR SPOKE if you knew how to tune it in.

"Heyo, folks!"

Find its voice, follow it if you can back across the wasteland to a hidden transmitter tower, down the wires into a mountain, through ducts and ancient machinery to a dangling microphone. There, a set of lips articulated: "I'm Psycho Jones, and you're listening to Afterburn Radio. Can you hear me?"

Psycho Jones sat in a small room, lit faintly by a lava lamp standing atop the mixboard console. The twisting globs of molten red wax danced in the lamp, illuminated by a low-watt bulb in its base. The crimson light bathed Psycho and the cramped transmission booth in an eerie glow, flickering as if the lightsource were a testy flame. A microphone hung from the arm of a metal boom above her head, lazily swinging beside her head as she rooted through a pile of loose papers on the counter before her. The walls, darkly visible beyond the dull red glow's furthest reaches, were smooth metal, lined with shelves that contained compact discs, tape cartridges and the squat shapes of ancient stereo equipment.

"Things're pretty slow this evening, folks." She reached over to pop a cartridge into the console. The sound of canned rain broke behind her words. "So, let's get right to tomorrow's weather forecast for most of Ericaland.

"In the west, clear skies and a probable 110 degrees in the shade until afternoon, when a heavy sootfall from the north is due to roll in and cut the UV level to barely tolerable. Southern Ericaland can look forward to another dry day in the upper nineties. You Hexans can expect that sootfall to hit you by late evening, though.

"And—as usual—the Missippi coastline will see another day of rain. That makes ninety-seven in a row, doesn't it?"

Flicking a switch, she prompted a tape: "Heyo, Psycho! Wish me there!"

"Wish I could, Fever," she replied to her absent broadcast partner. The soundtrack of rain hissed away behind it all.

"Hold on, folks," Psycho flipped through her stack of papers, audibly rustling them for the sake of her distant audience. "Dr Muffin's handing us an instant newsflash." She paused, scowling until she finally located the sheet she wanted. "Color me green, folks! I thought we'd seen it all, but this kicks me right into mad tomorrow."

She hit the console switch again, triggering the tape's commanding but genial masculine voice: "Color me green too."

"Listen up, Fever," she addressed the hanging microphone. "The word is: Premier Vassal is heading west this week for a big meeting between the Mob and reps from the Rocky Conclave." She smiled as she read, "The rumor is: the man making the trip *won't* be the real Premier. Going in his place will be a waxface look-alike assassin."

She laughed, "Watch who you shake hands with, boys!"

"I guess the flatlands trade embargo will be with us all for a while longer," she commented, her attention focused on switching tapes in the console and starting a new reel.

"Heyo, folks! This is Fever Smith," spoke the new tape, "and you're listening to Afterburn Radio. Remember now, we're still illegal in twelve of the twenty-seven Districts, so keep those radios well hidden. Can you hear me? Let's hear some music…"

Switching off her microphone, Psycho slumped back in her tattered whirl-a-tilt chair. The domed arcade seat threatened to swallow the girl's diminutive body. She pulled her headphones down around her neck. Her scruffy reddish hair ruffled under her knuckles as she rubbed her aching head. Her eyes seemed tinier than usual in her flat olive-skinned face. Weariness haunted her young features, drawing her cheeks and lips slack and devoid of expression.

She swiveled the chair to face Dr Muffin who stood in the booth's cracked doorway. Tiny strains of music drifted from the headphones that hung around her neck, filling the booth with a soft joviality that no longer lifted her spirits as it usually did.

"This tape is two hours long," Dr Muffin remarked, "and I can easily rig a secondary one to kick in after that, Psycho. Why don't you catch some rest?"

Psycho stretched her arms, arching her small back. "Guess I could use some." She hopped from the seat and stood beside Dr Muffin, looking up at him.

He towered over her, his body draped affectaciously in a grease-stained old white labcoat. The differences between them did not end with their diverse height—why, Dr Muffin wasn't even human. But, she mused, where would we be without him?

She strolled out of the booth. Dr Muffin followed her down the military-gray corridor, his steps measured to match her tired pace.

"I miss Smithie," she muttered, not for the first time.

Dr Muffin hissed at her sympathetically, the closest he could come to a human sigh.

"When's he going to come back, Dr Muffin?"

"Soon, Psycho, soon…"

3

THE DOOM THAT DESCENDED on mankind did weird things to the sky. Even now, more than several centuries later, violent colors still sliced the heavens, plunging like mad oil through a turgid brook. Pale oranges clashed with rheumy greens, screaming purples tore through creamy yellows, eerie blues swept through vivid reds. Cloud banks hovering above the wasteland were nearly invisible against the spinning colorwheel sky.

Dusk tried to mute this heavenly pageant, but not even twilight could truly silence the garish panorama. Darkness merely changed the underlying canvas from a pale blue to a stark black, still alive with unnaturally merging hues.

Beneath this living nocturnal painting, three figures gathered amidst the abandoned ruins that stood beside Oogolah Lake. High atop one of the haunted towers, they huddled together, sharing their secret vice.

"Can you hear me?" a voice crackled.

The three replied in unison, "We hear you!"

"Let's hear some music…" The voice came from a primitive crystal radio set.

The three laughed, jumping to their feet. They began to dance around the radio. Their young bodies swayed and leapt to the mysterious rhythms spilling from their radio.

"This music is *up*," Nitch Palma called to her brother.

"It's more than *up*—it's *distant*," Nivek Palma laughed back.

Nico Meefe laughed along with her boyfriend.

The dancing continued. Their movements were crude, exhibiting the primal grace of the self-taught. While Nivek flung his limbs in cacophonic abandon, Nico carefully mirrored Nitch's fluid movements.

The fifteen year old girl deeply admired Nitch's maturity, even if that maturity was defined only by an extra two years of life. She longed for Nitch's sense of assurance and confidence and animal grace and larger bosom and luxurious hair and long legs and that marvelous silver necklace she wore so grandly. Nitch's presence was a constant reminder to Nico of her own naive inexperience. Rather than waste energy being jealous of the older girl, Nico chose to emulate her.

Small and uncertain and average with an unmanageable mop of short ebony hair, Nico the ingenue was nothing like Nitch the huntress.

Nitch was tall and long limbed; even her torso seemed stretched, an illusion created by her high breasts and boyishly narror hips. She wore her hair in a pair of thick ponytails that dangled about her shoulders. The hair was a delicate blonde color and thin like the web of a swamp spider. This was Nitch the huntress, who, despite her gender and age, was already one of the Tribe's most accomplished hunters. In another year, she would be entitled to venture west upon a quest of passage to formalize her adult-hood.

Unknown to Nico, the cool reserve worn by Nitch concealed a ter-minally suspicious nature. The teachings of her father had instilled in her a solid distrust of appearances. She had watched the Tribe's answerman try time and again to discredit her father's words, while a mountain of empirical evidence proved the shaman wrong. She had learned to doubt authority—in the Tribe and in the wild. No matter how fierce a swamp wolf or mutant eater-thing might be, she knew that a human with their wits about them could always out-think and defeat such a supposedly superior force.

It was this distrust of convention that attracted Nitch to the lure of prohibited radio.

It was the *music* that lured Nivek, though. And Nico liked the music because Nivek liked it.

When the music finally adopted lesser beat, Nitch took a break to lean against the crumbling concrete balustrade lining the edge of the rooftop. She peered wistfully at the night sky, squinting to locate the North Star. She gave up after a minute; the airborne toxins were too vibrant tonight to allow any stars to twinkle through the whirling colors.

"We should be getting back," she announced over the music.

"Aww," moaned Nivek.

"Stay then," Nitch shrugged. "It'll be *your* ass that gets whupped if Maw or Paw catch us out this late." She bent to collect her heavy knife and spear.

"Nuh," he admitted, "you're right."

Nico pouted, continuing to dance until Nivek silenced the tempo by switching off the crude crystal radio. He carefully wrapped the device in oilskin, tying the flaps protectively closed around it.

"Heyo, I live for Afterburn," he chattered as he bound the radio set. "Their music is so total—it's a big ball of light inside my head." He rose, tucking the package under one arm and Nico under the other. Nivek bore only the faintest resemblance to his sister. He was short and wiry. By a quirk of genetics, he remained hairless his entire life. He possessed a clumsiness that far exceeded the gawkiness of adolescence. Although destined by his heritage to become a farmer, Nivek's head was full of wild hopes and impossible goals rooted in outrageous tomorrows. "Someday," he sighed, "I'm gonna be on the radio just like Fever Smith."

Careful of the weakened stairs, the three youths descended the tower to the ground. They made their way through the exotic concrete canyons, scrabbling over jagged chunks, these boulevard remains jutting every which way but horizontal.

To them, the ruins of Wynona, Oklahoma held no ancestral significance. It was simply a good place to hide while indulging their secret vice. The vast towers stirred no sense of historic awe in them. The sagging rust-skinned signs had no meaning for them. The humps of corroded metal that filled the cracked and upthrust streets were not things of mystery to them. All this was as natural as the trees and shrubs and creeks of the woods, for ruins and woods had always been a part of their environment. One attached no sense of history to a tree, so there was no reason to feel any respect for the shapes and decay found amidst the old lakeside ruins.

Untended by human hands, the Oologah Reservoir had expanded since the Doom had devastated the land and species. Encouraged by the geological changes that followed the Doom, the Reservoir had spread its waters until it became a vast lake nearly a hundred kilometers in diameter. Where once had stood the landlocked city of Wynona now reared a collection of lakeside shell-shocked towers. Stretching nearly a kilometer into the lake, bent and age-tortured buildings stood like massive concrete pylons.

Once, Nitch's father had confided to her that he (and even the elders and answermen) were puzzled by the incredible structures that made up the ruins. That the towers had been the living quarters of some ancient race was the most popular theory. Since the only creature who built abodes that stood so high (at least, in scale to their own size) were termites, it was assumed that this ancient race might have consisted of distant ancestors of the large insects that scurried and buzzed amidst Messy Marsh to the north.

Pausing as they reached the perimeter of the ruins, Nitch glanced about her, only to shudder once again at the thought of a race of huge insects inhabiting this place. If humans had lived in those days, they must surely have huddled in deep caves to avoid contact with such large and deadly monsters. Even today, hushed rumors spoke of great beasts wandering the ruins by night. Although she had never seen any trace or spoor of such creatures, Nitch was ever wary until she was far beyond the ruins' vast canyons.

It was these very rumors that had convinced Nivek Palma to share his secret radio with his older sister. Reception of the pirate radiowaves at groundlevel was poor at best, so Nivek had looked to the abandoned towers as a means to reach a stronger transmission. To brave the haunted ruins, he had enlisted the aid of his huntress sibling. Fortunately, the music played by Afterburn Radio had appealed to Nitch enough to gain her cooperation. Although the exact nature of radiowaves was unknown to Nivek, his suspicion that they traveled through the air had proven valid. Once they had elevated the crystal radio receiver to the rooftop of one of the ruins' towers, Afterburn's signal had come through with rewarding clarity.

"How come Afterburn's illegal?" Nico asked. "It's so much fun!"

Nivek snorted as he helped the girl over the edge of a concrete slab. "Don't be such a mutehead, Nico. That's *why* it's illegal—*because* it's so much fun."

"Actually, Afterburn isn't illegal in this District," Nitch remarked as she gracefully hopped up to perch on the slab's jagged peak. "People simply don't *care* about radio around these parts. Up north where the Mob rules, that's where they prohibit any radio." At least, that was what her father had told her. His knowledge on the subject had been hazy; since radio waves were not a thing that effected the growth of his crops, he had shown little interest in this mystery. (So rare *was* knowledge about the existence of radio waves, that her father had displayed curiosity about where Nitch had heard of this phenomena. After an uneasy silence, she had told him she'd heard of them in Grammy's bedtime stories—one could easily attribute such fantasies to the old woman's ragged tales. Whether or not he believed her excuse was uncertain, but henceforth he *had* paid attention to any hints Nitch would drop about impending dust storms.)

"Just another *don't*," Nivek snarled. "Don't do this, don't do that. Growed-ups are full of *don'ts*. Radio is just another one of them."

Watching how Nico wiggled her butt against her brother's hips in vague gratitude for assisting her over the concrete rise, Nitch understood *some* of the *don'ts* growed-ups imposed on their adventurous children.

"How come each song sounds so different?" Nico asked. "Does Afterburn have different musicians playing each song?"

"I wonder about that too," Nivek mumbled. "Maybe I'll find out if I ever get to be a DJ like Fever Smith."

"Where does it come from?" Nico asked. The ingenue was forever full of vacuous questions.

"You know that, Nico," Nivek chided her as they walked through the region of gnarled brush that surrounded the ruins. "Radio waves come through the air."

"No no," she responded, petulantly shaking her head. "You told me all that stuff, about receiver frequencies and crystal tapping or whatever you called it. I mean where is *Afterburn Radio*? Where do they widecast from?" She waved her arms toward the sky to emphasize her question.

"Broadcast from," Nivek corrected her.

"Pullface," Nitch sighed. "Nobody knows where their studio is, Nico. What they're doing is illegal in most places, remember? They don't want to get caught." Sometimes, Nivek's girlfriend could be *so dumb*!

"But I *want* to know where they are," Nico pouted, annoyed that this expression carried so little effect on Nitch.

"You're not alone," muttered Nivek.

"Humph—I'll bet *they* don't even know where they are," Nico decided. "That's why they don't tell anybody. They don't know. They don't even know what time of day it is!"

She was making reference to a comment by Fever Smith during the broadcast that had fueled their dancing. Fever had commented what a lovely morning it was. That had puzzled Nitch too—but then, so much that Fever Smith spoke of confused the seventeen year old huntress. Discs and keyboards and wires and foreign lands beyond the Missippi Coast. Across—what had he called it?—an *ocean*, yes. Nitch had the impression that an ocean was a huge lake. Fever Smith must indeed be well-traveled to be familiar with so many distant lands and unknown concepts.

Personally, Nitch imagined that the pirate radio station resided in some foreign land, far from the farmlands of her Tribe. How far away and in what direction was beyond her deduction. The Mob territories to the far north were reputed to be extremely unfriendly and downright hostile to the concept of radio. Wasteland lay to the west, and the young girl imagined that desolate prairie went on forever. Those flatlands were inhospitable to life; even the rite of passage pilgrimage she looked forward to next year would only take her a day or so into its harsh domain. While south and east, there was only the mysterious Missippi Delta where legends claimed the ground was perpetually mud.

Much of Nitch's vague notions of regions beyond her Tribe's farmlands came from hints dropped by the Afterburn DJs; consequently she couldn't openly ask about such things without raising the suspicions of family or neighbors. And she had sworn an oath to Nivek to never say anything that might disclose to anyone the existence of his secret radio set. Besides revealing her brother's secrets, she was loath to risk incurring the animosity of the Tribe's answerman, who already viewed the Palma family with such distrust as a result of her father's natural wisdom.

Some things, she decided, were simply destined to remain unanswered mysteries, not unlike the ruins the kids were leaving behind as they returned home.

4

UNDER THE SEETHING COVER of the kaleidoscopic night, the three approached the Palma farm from the east. They crept along the winding path that connected most of the Tribe's outlying farms. Further to the north the road terminated at a cluster of shacks that served as the Tribe's communal ground; this was where the elders and answerman dwelled.

As the three came to the front gate of the large Palma farm, they discovered a banner hung from post to post, barring their way. Words clumsily painted upon the banner read: "This ferm has ben silensed."

"Huh," Nivek grunted, disengaging his arm from around Nico's shoulder.

"What is it?" she asked.

"It's a sign," Nitch commented on the obvious.

"It wasn't there when we left this evening," stated Nivek.

"What's it say?" Nico asked.

With a sigh that lamented how little the girl got out of the Tribe's school, Nitch read the sign aloud. She scowled at the misspelled message.

"What's that mean?" Nico asked.

"Umm," Nivek mumbled, unwilling to admit his ignorance.

Pulling down the banner, Nitch strode past the gate and up the walkway. Nivek and Nico hesitantly followed behind her.

The Palma family may have tended vast fields of crops, but the main buildings of the farm were drably unimpressive. They consisted of four small single-floored cabins standing to one side, a huge barn with a stable nestled next to it, and five tall grain silos. Three of the cabins housed Palma adults and their families: one for Grahum, the eldest, and his two brothers. The fourth cabin was larger and served as a bunkhouse for the hired hands. No lights burned in any of the structures, which was not uncharacteristic, considering the late hour. An eerie silence hung over the nocturnal farm, though; one that teased the skin on the back of Nitch's neck.

Approaching her father's cabin warily, Nitch held her spear loosely but ready. She halted a few meters in front of the cabin, leaning down to peer closely at a dark lump on the ground.

As Nivek came up behind her, he was startled to recognize the lump as a sprawled dormant human form.

"Uncle Hairy?" he gasped, urging Nico to remain back from the body.

Nitch rose, drawing the blade of her large hunting knife from the scabbard that hung from her belt. She advanced on the cabins in the crouch of a stalking hunter. Her gaze swung back and forth, surveying the twilight scenario. Her caution was rewarded with the discovery of several more figures spread on the ground in peculiar postures.

"What's going on?" Nivek whispered to his sister. The only answer she gave him was a stern hand, waving him back.

With animal speed, Nitch dashed ahead to peer carefully through the open door of her father's cabin. The scene her night vision found inside twisted her stomach with horror. Backing out of the doorway, she staggered onto the rustic porch.

As Nivek approached the doorway, she pushed him away, breathlessly hissing "No!" at him. Her attempt to divert him failed, though, and he dodged around her to rush into his home.

The tableau he discovered stifled his frantic curiosity with a thick dread and spastic confusion. He felt the taste in his mouth before the bile reached his tongue.

Bodies lay everywhere, visible in the nocturnal light of the colorful sky that spilled through the doorway. Many of them were frozen in mid-convulsion, their bound hands reaching for their blue faces. Nivek's Maw, his brothers, his sisters, one or two brawny farmhands... each with a raw potato protruding from their bruised mouths. The sparse furniture of the room—crude wooden chairs and a utilitarian table—were flung about in broken disarray. The ugly family portrait—a priceless thing painted by a rare traveling artist—hung no longer on the wall, but lay crumpled and torn now on the bare wood-plank floor.

"Nuh... nuh..." he wheezed in terror.

As Nivek stumbled from the cabin with vomit on his chin, Nico approached wide-eyed with her latest stupid question: "What's the matter?"

"Quiet Men!" Nitch gasped.

A brief look of befuddlement was replaced by a scowl on Nico's face. "Right..."

Weak with shock, Nivek sank to his knees on the small porch.

"How gullible do you think I am?" Nico growled at them. "There's no such thing as Quiet Men. There're just—"

Nivek grabbed his sister with an urgent desperation, moaning, "They're all *dead!*"

"You two are just trying to frighten me," harumphed Nico. "But it's not going to—"

"They can't have killed everyone on the farm," Nivek whined to his sister, his eyes watering from a flood of forlorn emotions.

"They must have attacked after we left," Nitch spoke in a stunned voice.

"Stop it," Nico snipped, frowning.

"We've got to warn the rest of the Tribe," exclaimed Nivek.

"They—they could all be dead already," Nitch moaned. She cast her eyes about, surveying the surrounding night with sudden suspicion. Her brain was itching with warning signals, but the shock of finding her family so horribly murdered impaired her ability to notice the mental alert.

"I mean it," Nico piped in a tone approaching hysteria. "Stop trying to—"

"Will you be *quiet*, you mutehead?" Nitch snarled at her. "You have to be the dumbest girl my brother has ever dated—sheesh"

"We have to *try* to warn them," Nivek pleaded.

"I am *not* stupid!" yelled Nico, clenching her soft hands into frivolous fists. "Everyone's always calling me *stupid,* and I don't like it! Quiet Men don't exist—they're just boogie men. I am *not* being stupid—*you're* the ones being *stupid!*"

"Shh!" Nivek hissed.

"Quiet Men hate noise," Nitch snapped. "Stop yelling, you mutehead!"

"I am *not* stupid!" Nico screamed all the louder.

Swinging on the girl, Nitch slapped her sharply across the face with the flat of her palm. "Be *quiet*, you dryup! You're going to—"

Nico recoiled under the blow and stumbled from the porch. As she fell, an object flew through the air where her head had been and hit the wall of the cabin with a dull *thump*. The slap may well have saved her life, or at least her consciousness.

"The back door!" Nitch hissed, barely audible.

Reacting instantly, Nivek grabbed Nico's arm and pulled her into the cabin. As he dragged her past the tangle of silenced corpses inside, Nico began to scream anew, this time in a voice that vividly reeked of panic. She resisted Nivek's grip, making it all the harder for him to guide her through the dark cabin. "Nico, please—be *quiet!*" he begged her as he tried to pull her to safety. "And stop struggling."

Back on the front porch. Nitch crouched with her spear held ready. She squinted into the darkness. The lawn merged with the night, ephemerally illuminated by the radiant poison clouds that flowed through the nocturnal heavens. Her huntress senses identified the pair of black shapes scarce seconds before her night vision picked them out. They crept toward her with a curiously stiff-legged gait.

Stepping quickly away from the cabin, Nitch caught the first shape in the stomach with the blunt end of her spear. With a near-soundless grunt, the Quiet Man collapsed on his ass.

The second of the attacking pair of Quiet Men deftly avoided Nitch's warding jab. He flung a potato at her. It struck her shoulder, generating sharp pain. Nitch's disorientation from the impact lasted only an instant, but that was enough time for the Quiet Man to rush in and grasp her spear, wrenching it from her grip.

The deadly attacker reared up, holding the spear in position to plunge its point into Nitch. As she pulled erect, the eerie skyglow brought his face into dim illumination. It was a horrible visage: skin almost translucent and stretched taut over prominent bones, insane eyes deep in angry sockets. As he raised his spear-bearing arms, his shoulders dislodged the scarf that wrapped his lower face, revealing the man *had no mouth.*

As the girl in her urged her to scream, Nitch's huntress instincts plucked her knife from its scabbard, swinging the blade out in a terrific arc. Suddenly the Quiet Man's stomach opened up and his trembling organs spilled from the fresh slice. The rest of him clumsily fell to the ground a second after his intestines splattered on the grass.

Without much conscious thought, the huntress stepped forward to swing the knife a second time. The first Quiet Man, still on his ass and clutching his bruised stomach, twitched. And his head fell from his neck to bounce sloppily across the lawn.

Giving the area a quick glance, she snatched up her spear, turned and fled back into the cabin. As Nitch leapt over the bodies of her family, she heard Nico's high-pitched wail from the back of the residence. Rolling her eyes to condemn the girl's loose lips, Nitch added speed to her flight through her home-turned-abattoir.

Nivek had just succeeded in dragging Nico's franticly thrashing form out the back door. Her struggles had grown so frenzied that he was forced to turn from his dash to grab her arms with both his hands. Moving backwards, he plummeted directly into the Quiet Man who appeared out of the darkness. All three of them went down in a tumble of wild limbs in the shadow of the overhang that jutted from the rear of the cabin. The fall did little to disturb Nico's constant screaming.

Forced to release his girlfriend to defend himself, Nivek scrambled in the darkness to strike or grab the Quiet Man, who was attempting the same but with much more aggression. Entwined in the melee, Nico continued to wail.

When Nivek finally grasped one of the Quiet Man's arms, his opponent beat at him wildly. The strength of a fanatic powered the Quiet Man's blows, knocking air and wits from Nivek. As dizziness swam behind his forehead, the young Palma attempted to roll away from the attacker. If he could get the Quiet Man out from under the cabin's overhang, he might be able to see enough of the man to fight him effectively. Unfortunately, his roll only disengaged the grip he had on the brute. Now Nivek sprawled beyond the overhang, bathed in the night's mad colors.

For a second, the Quiet Man's figure loomed on the edge of the overhang's shadow, a raised hand clasping the cold lump of a potato in a menacing manner. Then—suddenly—the Quiet Man flew from his feet, lifted into the air by the spear whose nasty tip erupted from his chest. As the figure wrapped in black scarf flung through the air to crash ignobly to the back lawn, Nitch leaned into the pale sky-light to pull Nivek abruptly to his feet.

Once up, Nivek rushed over to Nico to calm her panic. She refused to still her screams.

Nitch grabbed the girl, dragging her out into the little nocturnal light. "*Be quiet!*" she growled. "Don't make me use *this*, you drip!" She held a potato close to Nico's wailing mouth.

Her screams dropped to an indignant whine.

Dragging her away from the cabin, Nitch hissed, "We must get out of here. No telling how many there are still about."

"Please, Nico," Nivek insisted, following them into a field of wheat beyond the cabin's backyard. "Your screaming is going to get us all killed!"

The three of them fled through the wheat. The dry leaves lashed them as they plunged into the night.

Although Nitch would have preferred to hide away during the remainder of the night, Nivek was adamant that they attempt to warn the rest of the Tribe. Once Nico regained what little petulance she could muster, she added to Nivek's plea, asserting that her father would protect them. Nitch kept her own suspicions to herself... even when they reached Nico's family's farm.

The instant Nico saw the bodies that littered her home, her screams burst forth anew. This time, Nitch had no patience with the girl and silenced her with a sharp blow to the head. Nivek was forced to hoist his girlfriend over his shoulders and carry her from the Meefe farm.

Together, the sole survivors of the Oogolah Tribe crept into the night.

5

PSYCHO JONES CRAWLED WEARILY into the dimly lit booth. Slumping in the arcade seat, she pulled her headphones on, then closed her eyes and breathed deep and evenly for a few moments. The music that was being pumped out across the land's airwaves flowed from the headphones into her ears, matching the pattern of her lungs' inflations and deflations.

During these predawn hours, Afterburn's music was generally lulling, eerie tunes that possessed no lyrics or disruptive rhythms. The instruments in these songs were more difficult to identify. The haunting noises could be claimed by no instruments Psycho—or *anyone*, for that matter—could recognize. The sounds flowed like water, drifting through heavenly strata with their unearthly tonalities. Sometimes, Psycho found this type of music disturbing, but Dr Muffin declared that the effect on *most people* was a soothing one. This morning, she understood what Dr Muffin meant. The music was distinctly calming her sleep-deprived nerves. She knew from experience that a few minutes of this sonic mesmerism would leave her invigorated with a mild energy, ready to begin the morning broadcast.

For the millionth time, Psycho wondered who the musicians were—had been, for they were certainly dead many years now. What kind of people had they been? What had possessed them to produce such ethereal music? Were they even humans? Or were some of the wild legends true about the previous lords of technology? Did these strange sounds originate from known instruments of string and bone? Or was an unknown magic employed in their generation?

She would never know. The compact discs rarely featured labels, and any booklets that had accompanied the discs were crumbled to dust long ago. The few cryptic markings on some discs meant nothing to her, while Dr Muffin pretended he could translate them. Whatever the truth, the musicians now bore the names Dr Muffin gave them, names the DJs of Afterburn Radio passed on to their unseen audience… because one simply had to give things names. People mistrusted things without names.

And Afterburn already had enough factions rallied against it without incurring the suspicion of the common folk.

As the moody tones crawled into a subdued passage, Psycho reached up to switch on the dangling microphone. "Heyo, folks," she spoke softly. "Morning comes and it's time to start a new day in Ericaland. What's the word for today, Fever?"

She leaned forward to trigger a tape cartridge. "The word is flash, Psycho. Heyo, I'm Fever Smith, and you're listening to Afterburn Radio."

"That's right, Fever," Psycho agreed with the tape. "Here's a flash for our listeners..." She rifled through the orderly stack of papers Dr Muffin had left for her on the console. "There seem to be some dubious developments up north in Mobland. The word is that Premier Vassal's look-alike has changed from shirts to skins and has killed the real Premier, taking his place. Talk about two-faced Mob Bosses."

She punched the console and Fever's robust laughter roared from the tape cartridge.

"But—the big news today is that Captain Jagg is back!" she read. "That's right, folks, he's *back* and he didn't fall off the edge of the world. He found a new world."

She prompted the tape of Fever's voice to call, "No way!"

"That's right, Fever. Everyone thought Captain Jagg was a raving lunatic when he sailed east from Chico four years ago. But he proved us all wrong. He sailed and sailed and sailed and sailed," she wrinkled her nose at Dr Muffin's repetitive copy, "and he found a new world across the Lantic Ocean.

"Actually," she read in a conspiratorial voice, "what he found was a series of big islands that all have names that are near unpronounceable. Or so he claims, having just sailed into Mumpus harbor yesterday. And among the news that Captain Jagg brought back for us from this new world is that these strange foreign people enjoy listening to Afterburn Radio just as much as we do here in Ericaland."

She laughed amiably, "Heyo, so it looks as if we have a bigger audience than we thought, eh, Fever?"

She triggered the tape cartridge. "Let's give them what they want to hear."

"This is Psycho Jones," she announced, feeding a new tape reel into the console, "and you're listening to Afterburn Radio, the voice of truth with a beat."

"Heyo," the new tape started, "let's have some music..." A strong drumroll toppled into screeching guitars.

Sitting back, Psycho pulled her headphones down around her neck and yawned. She was pointedly conscious of her hunger.

"Good job this morning, Psycho," spoke Dr Muffin from behind her.

Even though she was used to this habit Dr Muffin had of sneaking up on her, Psycho still jumped each time it happened. To cover her little twitch, she leaned toward the console to place her headphones there, tidying the pile of papers her surprise had scattered.

Powerfully rhythmic music tumbled from the headphones.

Dr Muffin's strong fingers descended on Psycho's shoulders, gripping the tension and kneading it away. "Ooh, that feels good," she sighed.

The tape droned on, the music building to even more frenzied tempos.

"That was a cute bit about those foreigners Jagg found across the Lantic listening to Afterburn," she mumbled. "Was it true?"

"Total prefab," Dr Muffin confided without hesitation. "But it can't hurt our image."

"How did we find out Jagg was back so quickly?"

"Same way we find out everything, Psycho. We have our sources." Dr Muffin always evaded such questions. "You can drop it if you want for the afternoon newsbreak. Just lead off with the bit about the new Premier Vassal. That news is certain to undermine any territory merger between the Mob and the Rocky Mountain Districts. Unification is a nice idea, but not with the Mob at the head of the table."

Psycho dozed for a bit, letting Dr Muffin's fingers do their magic. When the kneading stopped abruptly, she became aware that silence reigned in the booth. No pounding beats droned from the headphones.

Opening one eye, she peered at the console to discover that the tape reel had jammed. Lengths of brown tape were clogging into a tangle around the player's magnetic head.

"Damn!" she hissed, jumping forward to slap the console's switches. She grabbed another tape reel from the racks beside her arcade seat and speedily threaded it into another player unit. Only then did she bend to the task of trying to save the jammed reel.

"Well," she observed, "that tape drops from rotation."

The voice of the new tape chattered from her headphones, "Heyo, folks! This is Fever Smith and you're listening to Afterburn Radio. Remember now, we're still illegal in twelve of the twenty-seven Districts. So keep those radios well hidden. And let's hear some music..."

"I'll have to grease all the spindles again," Dr Muffin muttered.

Psycho rose to her feet, stretching her short back. "I need some food."

"Umm," he paused, "I was wondering if you could do me a favor first, Psycho... ?"

"I'm *really* hungry," she told Dr Muffin. "Can it wait until I've had breakfast?"

"It will only take a second," Dr Muffin replied.

She turned to face him and grunted in surprise.

Dr Muffin stood behind the arcade chair, his arms hanging loosely at his sides. Nervously, he fingered the tattered material of his long white labcoat. His head was gone, revealing a stump with sharp protruding metal junctures.

"What happened to you?" she asked with more surprise than curiosity.

"I was down at the waterwheel generator," Dr Muffin explained, "repairing some worn gears and... I'm afraid I leaned in too far and the paddle knocked off my head."

Psycho faced him, struggling to remain straight-faced.

"It's in the grotto," Dr Muffin confessed. "It sank to the bottom. I..."

"Okay." She nodded in an attempt to hide a smirk she could no longer repress. "You want me to swim down and get it for you, right?"

The robot followed her out of the booth and down the corridor, trailing the wire that ran from his right shoulder to disappear into the ceiling tracts. "If it wouldn't be too much of an imposition? My power cord won't reach far enough for me to retrieve it myself."

"I could do with a bath anyway," Psycho ruminated. She tended to let such things slide anymore, being the only human at the hidden radio station. So many aspects of her own humanity had lapsed since Smithie had gone away. It wasn't easy down in these tunnels, all alone and rarely seeing the sun. Without Dr Muffin's prompting, her meals were liable to become far too irregular—not to mention her sleeping schedule—and she knew her health would suffer. She needed him as much as he needed her.

"I don't know where I'd be without you, " muttered Dr Muffin as he followed her.

"All over the place, I imagine," she chuckled.

ONLY A THIN STRIP OF LAND along the Missippi Coast could be considered fertile. Beyond a region of poisoned valleys that ran like ripples in the land, the flatlands stretched beyond the horizon, continuing all the way to the foothills of the Rocky Mountains. The plains were terrible places, full of heat-death and monsters and dark legends.

A small hut stood against the steep wall of one such valley. Constructed of dirt packed around planks of wood and concrete slabs, its disguise was further elaborated by a layer of shrubbery piled around its shape. In fact, the entire structure could have gone unnoticed if not for the mutant cat that perched before it atop a rock. Once one saw the feline creature, awareness of the crude shelter became apparent. A large bowl sat in the dirt beside what functioned as the hut's doorway.

The cat preened herself with one of her mouths. She had two of them, set in a pair of matching heads which shared a common neck and brainpan in such a manner that the two heads only possessed two ears. The cat was sleek, a tawny and well-muscled shorthaired beast with fur the color of the soft tan of the surrounding soil. And if you moved to the side to regard the cat against the sky, the hues of her fur would shift into a corresponding kaleidoscope of colors—not unlike those found in the morning sky.

With the suddenness of her kind, the cat halted her preening, snapping her communal head around to squint down the valley. As she turned, the animal's body sank into the tense crouch of pre-leap. Flattening to the top of the rock, her body bristled with anticipation and her tail twitched with impatience. Then she relaxed, rising to sit and resume her preening.

Entering the valley over two meters away, Tagger trudged along the dry dirt, kicking at the brittle clumps of grass that sprouted along the gully's east slope. He walked calmly with a sack slung over his shoulder, holding a rough staff that was a foot taller than his own six-foot-four height. A small crossbow bounced at his belt. A tightly bound quiver flopped on his shoulder. His sandy hair stood like dead grass from his sun-browned scalp. As he approached the concealed hut, the permanent squint of his expression became visible to the cat.

When he came closer, Tagger's wide, thin lips curled in a weak smile, "Heyo, Needer. Did you miss me?"

"Pet me, pet me, pet me," the right cat head crooned.

Halting before the rock, Tagger swung his sack down and pulled a lizard from it. Holding the carcass aloft, he nodded. "See what I got us for breakfast?"

"Yuck," the left cat head snorted with dissatisfaction.

"Then catch yourself something to eat," Tagger retorted, taking the lizard over to the large earthen bowl where he commenced gutting it and inserting a stick through its remains.

"Okay, okay, okay," the right cat head purred. Needer followed him to rub against his boots.

Tagger lit a small fire in a depression in the ground, propping the lizard-on-a-stick over the flames. Then he crawled into the hut to perch on the tattered cushion the shelter contained. He pulled off his boots and began to massage the callused soles of his feet.

"Prey's pretty scarce out there," he told the cat.

Needer teased the lizard with an outstretched paw. "Yeah, yeah, yeah," the left head commented with the sarcasm of a confident predator.

"How about some music while we wait for dinner to cook?" Tagger asked. He drew forth his backpack and took a small device from a side pocket. It was a sophisticated radio, not a crude crystal set. For a second he fiddled with the device's calibration, aiming its stubby antenna in various positions before a strain of rhythmless tonalities sprang forth.

He looked up to smile at Needer, but the cat was gone from sight. And the lizard had been knocked down into the small fire. "Oh, you," he grumbled. He crawled over to prop up the lizard-bearing stick.

Lazily, Tagger stretched out on the cushion within the hut, listening to the music float from the radio into the morning air.

Most people would not think of these pieces as music, Tagger mused. These ethereal haunting melodies were without tempo or apparent structure. They fluttered like soft breezes, whimsically meandering, unconscious of any rigid matter or humanly concerns. Seemingly aimless, this music was a favorite of Tagger's, reminding him of the lonely flatlands: so vast and without border. These harmonics mimicked the infinite reaches of the plains, stretching far into the sky with limitless tonalities to stroke the pinpricks of light that frequently twinkled through the kaleidoscopic flow of airborne colored particles.

Afterburn Radio only played this kind of rhythmless music in the morning's earliest hours. At such times, Tagger was eager to relax from his predawn hunts, lying back and allowing his drowsy consciousness to drift aloft with the spectral music while breakfast lazily cooked.

Outside the dirt-covered hut, Needer crept down the eastward hillside with a limp mouse in her left mouth. The mutant cat narrowed all four eyes at seeing the lizard-on-a-stick propped back above the fires lazy flames. "Dammit," the cat muttered, depositing the dead mouse on the ground. With the swat of a paw, she knocked the sputtering lizard away from the fire. Carefully pulling the lizard from the stick, Needer replaced it with the mouse, then repositioned the stick over the fire. She sat primly to clean her left face for a moment before recalling the news she wished to impart to her human.

Wincing at the subsonic tones (Needer was *not* a fan of this morning music that Tagger so enjoyed), the cat meeped to elicit the human's attention. When Tagger slowly opened one eye, Needer chirped, "Company."

With a blur of motion, Tagger was off the cushion, silencing the radio with a worried scowl. "What kind of company?" he hissed at the cat, but she had withdrawn from the shelter.

Scrambling out of the hut, Tagger could now hear the scuffling approach of figures: heels scraping on packed dirt, dislodging pebbles to clatter down the slope of the valley. A pair of whispers identified the *company* as two humans, young from the sound of their hushed voices.

"Down here," one voice whispered. "I'm sure I heard something..."

The other voice whined an inaudible reply.

As Tagger's fingers closed on his staff, he felt a blade prod him gently in the side. A soft grunt warned him to relax his grasp and drop his staff, then a twitch of the sharp tip urged him erect.

Rising carefully, Tagger scowled at the girl who had caught him unawares. Above them, halfway down the slope, a pair of teenaged children halted their descent to briefly wave at his captor before resuming their clumsy approach.

Tagger broke the silence. "Umm, I—"

"Shut up," his captor snapped. She prodded him less gently with the spear.

One of the descending children, the only male of the three, spoke softly, "You were listening to a radio..."

"I don't want any trouble, okay?" Tagger replied warily.

"No, wait," moaned the boy, digging into the satchel he had pulled down from his shoulders. "I have a radio too." He held up a crude crystal radio set with a weak smile, "See?"

"Fans of Afterburn, eh?" a small voice piped up from a nearby stand of shrubbery.

The three strangers started, looking around for the speaker. Suddenly the spear was gone from the girl's clutches. She turned to discover that Tagger held it now. Although it was not pointed at her, she could tell that the man was capable of directing, aiming and wounding her with a smooth gesture. She ground her teeth, but kept her anger unvocalized.

"Who are you?" Tagger asked casually. His eyes never left the tall blonde who had threatened him. A glance had told him that the other children carried no weapons worth his concern.

"Well, my name is Nico Meefe," declared the girl child with a silly vacant look. "And this is Nivek and Nitch Palma. He's my boyfriend, and she's his sister."

"You nitgit," Nitch spat. "That's not what he meant."

Tagger tipped his expressionless head at an angle, "Well?" His eyes never left Nitch for an instant.

"The Quiet Men hit our Tribe," Nitch told him defiantly. "We're on our own now."

"We were passing by over the ridge," Nivek added. "And we heard the music."

"Quiet Men," Tagger spoke tersely. "This far south?"

"They killed our whole tribe," Nivek nodded.

"I told you I saw some of the bastards last week," Needer commented, stepping from behind the shrubs to prance over near Tagger. She peered up at him with feline vindication.

"Oh," Nico laughed. "You have a cat."

As she bent to pet Needer, the cat snorted with its left head, her right head snarling, "Keep your paw to yourself, human."

With a sigh, Tagger surprised them all by handing the spear back to Nitch. Then he crouched with some barely inaudible muttering to pick up the discarded lizard and spit it on a new stick, placing it over the flames beside the mouse.

Rising to his feet, he divulged, "I'm called Tagger. This is Needer." He propped his staff beside the hut's doorway. "You're welcome to share our meal if you want."

"Oh, food!" Nico squealed with joy. "That sounds just wonderful."

With no visible reaction, Tagger disappeared into the hidden shelter, leaving the children alone with the situation.

Nitch scowled, coming closer to speak with her brother, "How do we know we can trust this guy?"

"But he has a radio…" Nivek mumbled.

"That only means he's an outlaw," Nitch replied.

"Yeah," Nico scoffed. "Just like us."

"We're not outlaws," Nitch growled. "We're refugees."

"You look like outlaws to me," Needer commented from their feet.

Nitch frowned at the cat, who hissed at her in return.

Tagger crawled out of the hut holding a lump of bread under his arm. "I have some hardbread left." He handed it to Nitch, "Why don't you cut us some slices? That knife of yours looks sharp enough."

Nivek   *Nico*   *Tagger*

Pausing to rotate the pair of roasts above the small fire, Tagger re-treated into the shelter.

"Well, I trust him," Nico declared, seating herself cross-legged on the ground.

"And he obviously trusts us," Nivek observed, lowering himself beside her.

Returning from the small confines of the shelter, Tagger spread a cloth on the ground before the two children. He deposited some earthen plates and tablewear on the cloth, then sat back opposite them to fiddle with his own radio. Once he had tuned in the voice of Afterburn (just in time to hear the morning news of Captain Jagg's triumphant cross-oceanic return), Tagger took the meat off their sticks. He tore the lizard into four chunks for the humans, tossing the mouse to an eager Needer.

Nitch   *Needer*

As they ate, Nivek regarded Tagger's radio with the wide eyes of astonishment. "That's some radio you got there, Tagger. Where'd you learn to build something like that?" he asked.

Tagger shrugged, "It came that way."

"Really? I had to build mine," Nivek mumbled.

"Where does a farmboy learn to build a radio?" Tagger asked, munching on a thin wedge of hardbread.

Nivek told him how he'd discovered instructions in one of the caves beneath the ruins on the shore of Oogolah Lake. It had taken some deduction to decipher the booklet he had found, but once he had obtained the right materials the construction had proved easier that he'd suspected. "There were all these weird boxes full of *stuff* in the cave."

"And where does a plainsman find an already built radio?" Nitch asked.

Tagger smiled, "You'd be surprised."

"Eeyew," Nico moaned after biting into her portion of lizard shank. "Don't you have any spices?"

Needer was immediately at her elbow. "If you don't want it, I'll take it," chirped the left head while the right gnawed on the mouse.

"It's a rough life out here on the flatlands," remarked Tagger, looking at Nitch instead of Nico. "No spices, no frills… and normally no children."

Nitch paused her chewing to frown, "We're *not* children."

Lowering his meat to his lap, Tagger surveyed the leanly muscled girl. He nodded, "No, I guess it wasn't a *child* who crept up on me like you did."

"Nitch is one of the best hunters the Oogolah tribe has," Nivek told him, beaming with pride for his sister's inferred accomplishments.

"*Had.*" Nitch's frown took on a sad curve.

"Whole tribe, huh?" Tagger inquired. "Those Quiet Men are nasty. How'd you three escape?"

Nitch smiled without humor. "You'd be surprised."

Tagger laughed good-naturedly and resumed eating.

"What do *you* do?" Nico innocently asked their host.

"We wander," Needer's right head told the girl.

"Are you adventurers?" Nico asked. "Like that Captain Jagg who Afterburn was talking about?"

"Hardly." Tagger shook his head. "Needer and I just wander. Jagg found a whole new world across the ocean."

"Imagine that," Nivek chimed in. "A whole new world! I wonder what it's like? Do you think the people are like us? Maybe they all have two heads like Needer here has."

"I'm certain Afterburn would've mentioned so if they did," Tagger replied. "I expect they're regular people over there... just like us."

"You have a lot of trust in Afterburn knowing the full story," Nitch observed cagily. She regarded him closely as he replied.

"Alone out here on the flatlands, you learn who to trust."

"But this isn't the flatlands," she pointed out. "What're you doing so far east?"

"We're wandering," Needer told her.

Nitch watched Tagger with deep suspicion for a while before returning to her meal.

7

AFTERNOONS WERE RARELY COMFORTABLE in the subterranean radio station. Despite the wind machine Dr Muffin had constructed to move the air through the tunnels' artificial duct system, the station's atmosphere remained stale and sluggish. The day's heat sank through the surrounding rock, often adding warmth to the stale environment.

A year ago, well after Fever Smith had departed on his journey beyond the station's confines, Psycho Jones had taken to wearing little-to-nothing during the stagnant afternoons. This slight reprieve from the heat had not lasted long. Dr Muffin had displayed surprisingly human embarrassment concerning Psycho's nudity. The modest robot had begged her to reclothe herself; so insistent were his requests that Psycho had stubbornly acquiesced.

During periods when the robot was off tending to outer systems though, Psycho peeled down to cool off. Especially inside the main transmission booth. The large fan that hung just below the booth's ceiling had become annoyingly temperamental in the last few months—in fact, that was where Dr Muffin was today, tracking down faults in what he called the *secondary powerlines* which he suspected to be the root of the fan's malfunction.

Sprawled in her arcade ride chair, a naked Psycho paged through a thick sheaf of papers. The girl's red hair was tied back with a piece of wire. Her short-limbed figure was barely lit by the crimson glow of the bubbling lava lamp. She had learned to get by in such dim illumination.

According to Dr Muffin, thousands of stories came to his attention from his mysterious sources—far too many to include them all in the station's news broadcasts. It was one of Dr Muffin's many duties to sift through these thousands, picking ten or so for the daily transmissions. Although it was not a task that Psycho envied the robot, at times she liked to peruse the *thousands* herself. Once in a while she found a piece that was worthy of adding to Dr Muffin's choices. Reading about the small incidents and

34

minor occurrences gave her a greater familiarity with what was going on in the outside world. There was so much happening in a land that was so underpopulated, things that did not directly contribute to the robot's bigger picture, but in Psycho's opinion added humanity to Afterburn's broadcasts.

There had been an art festival up in Bizzark last week, where groups of people had displayed their private creations for all to see. Several musical bands had performed, according to the report, most of them playing versions of songs they had heard on Afterburn Radio. The festival had only lasted for two days, wisely disbanding to scatter into the surrounding woodlands before the Mob's Church Police arrived upon the scene.

There were reports of Quiet Men sighted as far south as Anzas. Psycho encountered several accounts of bands of Quiet Men silencing small villages and farm tribes. She winced, knowing full well what *silenced* meant in this instance. The Quiet Men were anti-sound fanatics—they killed anyone who violated their sacred silence. The cult had existed for numerous decades, forcing their beliefs on others with a lethal fervor. Their ways were known far and wide, even beyond their northern stomping grounds. And Psycho knew their madness firsthand. A band of the self-mutilated lunatics had attacked her family when she was very young, slaying everyone but her. She was bothered by the southerly progression the cult seemed to be taking in recent years. One could only hope that they'd not turn their mad attention to the western Districts, for Afterburn's voice was in clear violation to the cult's insane doctrines.

There was a startling report of an fiery object that had fallen from the sky to crash into a herder's grazing field in the Hexas District. The report told of a huge crater created by the impact and the curious heat it had generated, killing all life for weeks after the fall. This report bore a cryptic comment in the margins in Dr Muffin's stiff handwriting: "Space junk? Hot?" The robot was so full of mysterious terminology and legend.

There was a fantastic report of a giant pink spot that had congealed amidst the sky colors over Leans on the Missippi Coast. Several local religions had claimed the spot for themselves, and a brief war had broken out over its ethereal dominion. By the time a single faith had conquered the rest through slaughter, the giant pink spot had dissipated, leaving the faithful godless.

There were a number of reports which were entirely unreadable, consisting of long strings of babble-numbers. Many of these sheets bore Dr Muffin's notations in the form of further numerals. She had once questioned the robot about these pages of numbers, but Dr Muffin had deftly avoided the subject by answering her in technoid gibberish. She personally suspected that these pages were evidence of Dr Muffin's conversations with other robots located in faraway regions of Ericaland. These other robots, she believed, were Dr Muffin's cryptically referenced *sources* for the news stories he received through the machinery he so lavishly tended in the chambers beneath the station's mountaintop transmitter tower.

It must be very lonely to be a robot, she mused, *whatever a* robot *really was.* Psycho had certain physical evidence to go by: a robot was not made of flesh and blood, but was still alive; a robot was made of metal and wires and materials like the station's equipment; a robot didn't need to eat or drink or sleep, deriving sustenance through the wire that connected him with his power source. These things she accepted, but there were many other aspects of *robotness* she couldn't understand—or believe. Dr Muffin's claims of how long he had been alive, for one. She could not conceive of anything living for several centuries, although she conceded that a robot's non-organic nature might make it possible.

He was generally most reticent to discuss his metallic youth. Psycho found this odd, considering how often he mentioned the past with such reverence. Dr Muffin had done many other things before orchestrating the operation of Afterburn Radio years ago. But he was unwilling to talk of such olden times.

In a strange way, Psycho understood this part of the robot. There were many things in her own short past that she preferred to keep secret. Why should Dr Muffin be any different?

A sudden crinkling of sound interrupted Psycho's thoughts. She came alert instantly.

The tape reel had jammed again. The tape itself had backed up into a huge tangle that was still trembling with new feed, shuddering like some animated tumbleweed perched on the console. The result was a harsh garble of sound that seethed from the headphones sitting on the edge of the console.

Lunging forward, Psycho triggered another tape reel while cutting power to the jammed one.

"Heyo, folks! This is Fever Smith…" the new tape fed into the headphones.

"Damn," she grumbled, struggling to disentangle the tape with as little damage as possible. Several times, though, the delicate plastic strip snapped or simply tore through under her careful ministrations.

And while she focused on one tangle of tape, another grew to her left as the second tape reel clicked to a shuddering halt.

"No no no!" she squealed, forsaking the first tangle for the new one. Then she realized that the station was broadcasting a crackling hiss once again. She grabbed another reel of tape from the stack beside the console and hurriedly inserted it onto a third spoke. Feeding the new tape through the playhead, she slapped a number of switches to engage the new reel and replace the hissing feed with fresh output.

"Heyo, folks! This is Fever Smith, and you're listening to Afterburn Radio…" proclaimed the third tape. Most of the tapes piled to the side began that way. She wondered which one this was… what kind of music did it feature?

She continued to stare belligerently at the rotating third reel, defying it to give her trouble. But the device worked smoothly, feeding the tape through the machine with a steady calm.

What Dr Muffin called *big band* music spilled from the headphones at her elbow. Okay, she relaxed, that'll do for now. It wasn't a choice she would have made, but it was better by far than silence.

This console was starting to give up the ghost, she fumed sullenly. The equipment here was all very old. One couldn't expect even the best machinery to last forever—and the machinery the station had was by no means the best. No matter how intensely Dr Muffin doted on the apparatus, repairing and replacing and rerouting things, the equipment was dying from constant use.

What happens, she wondered, *when things finally* really *break down? When even the best of the robot's doctoring fails to revive some crucial part of the equipment? What do we do then?*

8

WHEN TAGGER RETURNED from his scouting sortie, he found Nitch absent from the campsite hidden in the small valley. Nivek and Nico sat listening to the prairieman's radio by the dirt-covered shelter. Neither music nor words poured forth though. Instead the air was filled with a violent static.

Tagger strode over, a concerned expression darkening his features.

Nivek shrank away from his advance. "We didn't do it—I swear! The music suddenly stopped."

Turning the volume down, Tagger nodded, "I know, Nivek. Calm down, I'm not mad at you. I'd just prefer not to have to listen to static."

"Is *that* what it's called?" Nico asked, wide-eyed with vacant curiosity.

"Static..." Nivek muttered.

"It's just dead air," Tagger explained. "They'll come back on in a minute. They always do."

"Dead air?" Nivek asked. "You mean this is what *air* sounds like without Afterburn's broadcasts?"

He changed the topic, looking around the shallow valley. "Where's your sister?"

"She went to scout the area," Nivek told him.

Cagey girl, Tagger reflected. *Doesn't trust what I told her of the region. Has to check it out for herself. Not a bad trait in wilderness like this.*

The static broke off and a voice spoke from the radio, "Heyo, folks! This is Fever Smith..."

"There," grunted Tagger.

But, after a garble of crumpled syllables, the static returned, bringing a frown to the man's brow.

"Is Afterburn broken?" Nico asked with a soft concern.

Then a voice spoke again from the radio, "Heyo, folks! This is Fever Smith and you're listening to Afterburn Radio."

"It's fixed again," Nico squealed with adolescent joy. "Hurray!"

"Fever Smith saved the day," Nivek smiled at the radio. He looked up at Tagger, "Fever is my hero."

"He's a good man," Tagger vaguely nodded.

"Let's hear some classic big band music..." declared the radio.

"Someday, I'm going to be on the radio just like him!" Nivek bragged, his face breaking into a broad grin.

Tagger pensively regarded the boy for a moment. Nivek was uncommonly interested in the radio's music. Most people considered it a pleasant diversion from the hardships of their daily lives, but this boy seemed to feel an intense passion for Afterburn. His fascination extended beyond the music to include the Djs... even the process itself, as evidenced by his clinical curiosity concerning static.

Placing his staff in its place beside the hut's doorway, Tagger joined the children sitting on the ground by the radio set. For a while they listened to the brassy uptempo tunes, each with their own degree of appreciation. Tagger was somewhat familiar with this kind of music, but he could tell it was new to the children. A newness that elicited quite different reactions in the pair of kids. While Nico seemed entranced by the melodies, her interest was apparently colored with a mild dissatisfaction that the music lacked any driving percussion. Nivek, though, listened with rapt attention, his glowing eyes displaying the fascination a child normally bestowed on a new toy.

Waiting for a soft break between the songs, Tagger asked to see Nivek's radio. The boy took it out, unwrapping the device and presenting it to Tagger with a proud smile. As the prairieman examined the radio, he questioned Nivek about its operation. The boy answered these queries with enthusiasm, confiding he had never before encountered anyone who shared his technical interests.

Tagger was surprised by the degree of knowledge the boy possessed regarding his radio's workings, vague though it was. Nivek not only knew how the radio was constructed, he seemed to understand *why* the apparatus functioned the way it did. The boy's knowledge was far deeper than any simple familiarity, it seemed almost intuitive.

How had this young farmboy come by such a comprehension of this ancient lost art?

9

AFTER A WHILE, Tagger and Nivek moved off a few meters to pursue their discussion undisturbed by Nico's glares. Once they were gone, she commenced to sway along with the music, closing her eyes.

The world was such a harsh place, a portion of Nico's mind told herself. Music—this wonderful distraction that Nivek Palma had introduced to her—music was a perfect salve for the terrible things that troubled her poor little winsome self.

People had been calling her *stupid* for too many years for Nico Meefe to remain totally unaware of her ignorance. What people didn't realize was that Nico was comfortable with her ignorance, accepting it as easily as she accepted her budding sexuality. She had quickly learned the simple lesson that one could be used to compensate for the other. With a demure look and a minor wiggle of her virgin hips, the same people who denounced her intelligence became as friendly as sweet warm honey.

Ha! she contemplated, not for the first time. *Who's* stupid *then?*

Farmlife with the Oogolah Tribe had been an endless succession of chores for most—but not for charming Nico. Even before puberty had saturated her little body with curvaceous changes, she had won constant deferment from grueling work. *Poor little Nico, she couldn't possibly manage to lift that heavy rake. Sweet little Nico is such a joy—just look at her. Oh, Nico, here's some tasty fruit juice for you as you sit and watch the rest of us toil in the hot fields.*

She was her father's pride offspring, a treasure for her brothers to protect, the whole Tribe's fairest maiden to behold. There may have been other more comely girls among the Tribe's daughters, but none of them utilized their feminine gifts as effectively as young Nico. They had seemed to accept their attributes as commonplace aspects of life, natural attractors for the Tribe's men. Nico knew better, though.

Once she began to employ her physical attributes, intelligence became superfluous—even counterproductive. The weaker and simpler she acted, the better care she received. Whenever a crisis presented itself, there were always people there, eager to assuage her discomfort.

She had been horrified to learn of her family's demise—see what good came of learning things! Her family, everyone she knew, the entire Tribe… all murdered by the awful Quiet Men who were far more deadly than they'd been in her Mommy's bedtime stories. Suddenly orphaned, Nico had felt terrible anguish over her aloneness. But she had been quick to realize that she had Nivek to rely on now. He would take care of poor little Nico.

Swaying to the mellifuous tempo of the music, Nico smiled, reassured that she would survive.

10

THE LOW VALLEYS THAT RIMMED the flatlands were comprised of tightly packed soil that afforded growth to few plants. Only the hardiest vegetal specimens flourished on these slopes: stiff prairie grass and kudzu mutations. Every once in a while one might stumble across the stubby charred remains of an ancient tree, but no fresh growths were to be found.

Fauna was even scarcer. What little life stalked these hills consisted of the cagiest of creatures. Only a deadly cunning could survive in or around the plains where an animal might swiftly become another's next meal. And the smarter life forms stayed underground between meals.

Down a gully such as this crept Nitch, following the nearly invisible trail of a prairie wolf. She slid from shrub to shrub, her spear poised aloft, ready to fling at the smallest hint of motion. Nitch knew that her prey was close, she could feel it in a deeper part of her brain than deduction.

The other hunters of the Oogolah Tribe had admitted to similar inner gifts, an intuition concerning all things related to the hunt. To her though, it was a tingling inside her head, alerting her to the presence of prey… or of danger.

Once again Nitch sublimated the notion that the slaughter of the Palma family and the rest of the Oogolah Tribe had been *her* fault. If only she had been with them, her huntress instincts could have sensed the approach of disaster, might have given her family a chance to prepare and defend themselves. But no—she had not been at home where she should have been. No, she had been—no no no—bury those worries with concentration on the moment at hand. The hunt was the now, and only the now could be changed or affected. The past was immutable. Dwelling on yesterday's mistakes was a waste of energy.

She squeezed back a tear of regret and clenched her spear all the tighter.

"You hunt like a human," Needer chided from her ankle.

"I certainly wouldn't be too graceful if I went around on all fours like you," Nitch commented, attempting to hide her grief with a subtle humor.

"Humans can't catch anything worth catching," sneered the cat.

A tingle sprang to life in Nitch's head, guiding her eyes and aim to a patch of dun soil near the base of the slope. Although nothing but bare ground was visible, she knew she had pinpointed her prey at last. Without hesitation, she flung her spear at the patch of dirt.

With a wet thump, the spear embedded in a brown shape that tried to dodge aside. A yelp of pain escaped from suddenly visible slavering jaws.

"Huh!" grunted Needer in surprise.

Rushing in to grasp her spear, Nitch pinned the creature to the ground against which it had hid. She twisted the stab mercilessly into a killing wound. Only once it had expired with a great deal of hissing and slobbering growls did the shape become definable as a wolf.

"Chameleon hound," Nitch announced, leaning on the spear again. One could never be too careful with these beasts, they were wily bastards right up the end (and sometimes beyond—she would have to cut this wolf open to survey the tint of its flesh before she could be certain it would be safe to eat). "I've encountered them before," she told the startled cat. "They become one with their surroundings... a trait you seem to possess too." Indeed, the cat's short fur was blending with the barren ground, adopting the varying hues of brown that surrounded her, although not as perfectly as the wolf's chameleon ability.

"I'd've seen it first," insisted Needer, "if you hadn't distracted me with your chattering."

"Undoubtedly," Nitch agreed, stifling any sarcasm in her comment. She bent to pull free her spear. Before slinging the beast over her shoulders, she took the time to carve a sliver of flesh from its ribs and examine it. Nodding with satisfaction, she tossed the juicy slab of meat to the cat, who received it with a stolid glee.

Side by side, they strolled back in the direction of Tagger's hidden shelter a few valleys over. As she walked, bent under the weight of the prey slung over her shoulders, Nitch observed the cat busily working on the tasty morsel of wolf meat with her right mouth. Meanwhile, the cat watched Nitch with a critical expression on her left face. Although Needer voiced no opinion, Nitch suspected the cat was re-evaluating her feline assessment of this human huntress.

Careful to keep her smile mental, Nitch realized she had made a new friend.

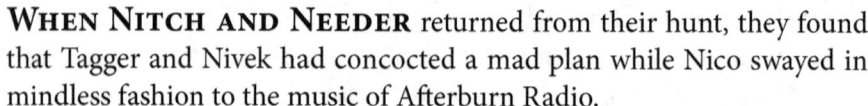

WHEN NITCH AND NEEDER returned from their hunt, they found that Tagger and Nivek had concocted a mad plan while Nico swayed in mindless fashion to the music of Afterburn Radio.

"We're going to show Tagger the Oogolah ruins," Nivek told his sister.

Nitch's response was a suspicious scowl.

Needer wandered over to stare at Nico's undulations with a condescending curiosity.

"He's really interested in seeing the cavern where I found the instructions to build my radio," explained Nivek.

"But we're headed south," Nitch sternly asserted.

"Oh, come on, Nitch," the boy whined. "It's not as if we're heading south for any particular reason."

"We have even *less* reason to go back to the lake, Nivek," she snapped. "Everyone we know is *dead* back there. Remember?"

"Leaving you orphaned and homeless," Tagger commented. "You'll need a stake if you plan to join another Tribe. What Nivek describes in his radio cavern could prove very valuable."

"Who says we're looking to join another Tribe?" Nitch retorted sharply. "I can look after us just fine." She threw the wolf's body at their feet.

"Perhaps," Tagger muttered, eyeing the wolf with uncertainty. "But—maybe *Nivek* wants something more than a life of aimless wandering."

"Yeah," chimed the boy.

"You and I were meant to live in the wilds, Nitch," remarked Tagger. "Nivek and Nico—definitely Nico—need to belong to a community. Surely you can see that, girl."

"I'm his *sister*—the only family he has left," Nitch growled. "I think I know what Nivek needs better than a complete stranger can."

Tagger shook his head, "Stop being so possessive and look at things from *their* point of view, Nitch. They're too young to have to rough it out here. They need a new family."

"And finding some valuable treasure in the Oogolah ruins is going to convince some new Tribe to accept them into their fold?"

"It won't hurt their chances."

"You just want this treasure for yourself," she accused him.

"What would I do with a treasure?" Tagger laughed.

"He's entitled to part of it," declared Nivek. "If he helps us dig it out." Tagger shrugged.

"I'm going, Nitch!" pouted Nivek. "And Nico is coming with me."

Nitch sighed, knowing better than to argue with her brother. He could be painfully stubborn about things. It was apparent that Tagger had convinced him to return to the lakeside ruins.

It only remained to see whether Nitch would accompany them or strike off on a destiny of her own.

Refusing Tagger's help, Nitch skinned the wolf herself and prepared its meat for consumption. As she stripped the flesh from her prey, she cast dark glares in the man's direction as he continued to discuss the journey with her little brother.

She was certain the prairieman had designs of his own concerning the *treasure* he believed existed back in the Oogolah ruins. At present, she could not understand the man's scheme, but she *knew* it for the ruse it was. Once Nivek had shown him the location of the radio cavern, Tagger would certainly discard her brother and his stupid girlfriend as the prairie-baggage they were.

Despite the kinship she had stricken with the man's mutant cat, Nitch thoroughly distrusted the prairieman. He simply reeked of hidden secrets. He displayed far too much intelligence for an average prairieman. And the radio he possessed—that was *not* the type of thing an aimless wanderer would be carrying. She was certain there was more to Tagger's *wanderings* than he had abstractly admitted.

No, the only way Nivek was ever going to attain the stake he now believed in was if Nitch went along to guarantee Tagger's honesty.

Needer had come over to watch her strip the animal's flesh, licking her lips with anticipation. Nitch scowled at the cat, refusing to give her any more tidbits.

12

THE DUCT WAS SMALL AND DARK and its half-meter diameter was crowded with numerous wires. Cut into solid rock, it ran horizontally for roughly three meters before taking a vertical dive deep into the mountain.

Dr Muffin had examined the lower junctures of the duct, finding only minor oxidation, which he had removed, then coated the worn conduits with more of the increasingly scarce bear grease. The difficulty, he surmised, must be with some connection along the upper portion of the electrical duct. So the robot had packed up his gear and begun the long climb into the station's uppermost levels just beneath the transmitter tower. He was not comfortable making this climb, for the ancient aluminum ladder was thoroughly unstable, possessing sections which had been jury-rigged with unsafe repairs over the last thirty years. In his early years at the underground complex, he had attempted to re-solder the breaks, but the supply of solder he had brought to the station was incompatible with the ladder's alloy and the joins refused to endure even the slightest pressure or weight. He had been forced to resort to binding the ladder's broken rungs with stout wire and sturdy wood planks. These repairs had borne the decay of years no better than the original alloy.

The entire station was wearing out. Lately, Dr Muffin's repairs had necessitated cannibalizing other less vital systems. Soon, he would have no choice but to commence dissembling important equipment to prolong the life of more essential apparatus.

Already he'd been forced to dub several replacement reels as existing tapes surrendered to excessive use and became crumpled tangles. His supply of blank tape was running dangerously low, and on numerous occasions he'd found the blank reels had suffered natural decay, losing their graphite coatings over years sitting in storage, rendering them useless for recording purposes. It annoyed Dr Muffin that while the original recordings were made on plastic discs which possessed more durability, the equipment needed to imprint recordings on these discs had failed long ago, forcing the robot to rely on the weaker, less permanent tapes to store recordings for regular use by the DJs.

The robot was sadly aware that the day was drawing dangerously near when he would be unable to keep Fever Smith's dream alive. Then the radio station would cease its broadcasts, forever silenced by the unavoidable forces of entropy.

The ladder shuddered under the robot's dense weight. Reaching the top, Dr Muffin stared with a metal sigh at what should have been a clear gantry leading to the transmitter chamber. But now the gantry was filled with a tangle of broken supports and fractured chunks of rock.

A cave-in, the robot realized, had occurred since his last visit a week ago. This was not good—in fact, it could indeed be fatal to the station's operations. Besides the necessity of his access to the transmitter chamber on a regular basis, without which Afterburn's news reports could not continue, the cave-in might be the cause of the latest power failure. Some vital connection could have been severed by the collapse of the gantry.

To a human, such a cave-in might present an impossible barrier. For Dr Muffin, it meant only a lengthy inconvenience.

Setting aside his kitbag, the robot withdrew several necessary implements and stashed them in compartments in his chest and thighs. After shedding his irreplaceable lab coat, he began the tedious task of creating a crawlspace through the cave-in's wreckage. His hydraulic muscles could force the rock slabs aside; the real problem came in propping them up so the cleared area would not recollapse after he had moved on deeper into the rubble. The going was slow, but time was as immaterial as exhaustion to a robot.

After several hours, Dr Muffin succeeded in reaching the point where the electrical duct junctured with the splitter outside the transmitter chamber. Squirming around to face the dented metal surface, he removed the plate from the wall and exposed the duct to his ministrations. A speedy test revealed two dormant wires. The connections of these two wires were solid where they entered the splitter, meaning that their problems lay further along the duct's length.

Settling back, Dr Muffin commenced the complicated procedure of dismantling his arm from its elbow socket. Once he had detached his forearm, carefully leaving a single power lead connecting it to his body, he went about supplying the forearm's hand with the tools it would find necessary to repair the damaged wires. Several fingertips were unscrewed and replaced with screwdrivers, cutters and heating elements. He wound a length of the ancient solder around one finger, positioning it accessibly should the hand need it during the repairs. Then he began the delicate maneuver of removing one of his optical units and attaching it to a recessed chassis on the back of the detached forearm's wrist. This wiring took some time, being far more subtle and prone to all sorts of minor incapacitations.

Finally, the reconstruction was complete and Dr Muffin sent his detached forearm into the electrical duct. The limb scampered into the hole, crawling along the wires using its fingers like the legs of a metal spider. Reassuring himself that the leads were secure connecting the forearm to its socket and his empty optical orbit, the robot sat back to direct his examination of the duct.

The oculars possessed by the robot were capable of perceiving many wavelengths beyond those of the visible spectrum. The dark inside the duct was no obstacle to his progress. The real difficulty was the duct's cramped confines, which hampered him from locating the points whereat the two wires had failed. His experience reminded him that the simultaneous malfunction of a pair of wires indicated the possibility of a simple short-circuit. Indeed, not two meters down the length of the duct, the optical unit attached to his mobile forearm spotted the problem: a section of insulation had worn away from the two filaments at the same point, resulting in contact between the unshielded wires.

This repair was far simpler than reconnecting broken lines, but it was a task he had not enabled his forearm to achieve. Recalling the forearm, the robot went through the tedious process of unscrewing the various tools, replacing all the original fingertips save one: the heating coil. Unwinding the soft solder material, he replaced it with a strip of plastic insulation.

Once more he sent his mobile forearm into the duct. Reaching the short-out point, the hand busied itself with the easy repair. First, a pair of fingers separated the wires where they touched, holding them apart. Activating the heating coil, the hand carefully melted portions of new insulation, coating the exposed sections of first one wire then the other. He waited a few minutes for the plastic to cool before releasing the pair of repaired wires from his splayed fingers. Before retracting his mobile forearm, Dr Muffin's remote ocular unit examined the other wires in the region for wear to their insulation. It was not uncommon for such decay to show up on a wide scale. In fact he discovered three more areas in which the insulation was frayed. He administered fresh plastic to these points too before withdrawing his arm from the duct.

During this action, the robot's multifunctional mind wandered, since the repairs were capably handled by a small portion of his positronic circuitry. Again, he mused over the failing state of the radio station's equipment—lately, it was a fear never far from his consciousness.

If only Fever Smith would return from his journey into the outside world. Although the reasons Fever had given Psycho Jones for the trip had involved *recharging his emotional sense of purpose*, the true purpose of Fever's trip had been the station's failing machinery. Fever had gone in search of fresh materials with which the station's equipment might be replenished, fortified against present and future breakdowns. Despite the meager chances of success, Dr Muffin had been forced to agree with Fever that such a search was growing more necessary with every year the station continued to operate. Both the robot and the DJ had known the potential futility of finding any functional equipment in the Ericaland wastelands, but where else could they look for salvation? The future of Afterburn Radio depended on the success of Fever's search.

Fever Smith was more than the popular voice of Afterburn, he was the lifeblood and passion behind the entire project. Although Dr Muffin had found the underground complex nearly thirty years ago, it had not become operational until Fever had shown up to realize the potential of the dormant ancient machinery. The notion of a pirate radio station had been his, and with the robot's help Fever's dream had been given substance.

Dr Muffin was fairly certain that the underground complex had possessed a wholly different purpose before the Doom had descended on mankind centuries ago. There were vast chambers and rooms walled with dead screens that hinted at arcane functions that had terrified even the robot's limited emotions. The radio transmitter had existed as an aside to the complex's ancient reason d'être—how ironic that it had been the aspect that was revived centuries after life had abandoned and forgotten the buried installation.

In Afterburn's beginning, it had been only Fever, his few accomplices, and Dr Muffin who had manned the daily broadcasts. Using radiowaves that had remained dormant and unused for centuries, they had brought something back to the land that had been consigned to legend for many generations: music for entertainment. Only later, at Dr Muffin's suggestion, had the broadcasts begun to include news reports. While music was the driving force behind Fever's dream, the news became the robot's passion. Music might alleviate the populace's daily hardships, but *news* was going to reconnect humanity to itself, reopening the pathways to a racial unity which the Doom had devastated.

Upon the return of his mobile forearm, Dr Muffin busied his attention with reattaching the limb and the optic unit to their proper locations on his robotic body.

Now that he had restored power to the human-frequented regions of the complex, he directed his energies to unearthing the door to the transmitter chamber. Fortunately, despite the cluttered nature of the rubble, the cave-in had been minor, comprised mainly of the metal support struts and large chunks of granite. Very little loose dirt had accompanied the collapse, so that moving aside the rubble was tedious, but not impossible. Given time, the robot might well remove all the rubble, allowing an empty hallway to reclaim the gantry. For now though, his priority was discovering how much damage the transmitter had been subjected to by the cave-in.

Working his way through the rubble along the wall of the corridor, Dr Muffin found the doorway relatively undisturbed by the fallen rocks. Clearing enough room for him to gain entry was not difficult.

Once inside the chamber, the robot was able to stand erect to survey the state of the machinery. Although he required no light for this examination, he preferred to illuminate things, displaying several print readouts otherwise hidden by the darkness.

The transmitter stood untouched by the cave-in, and a quick check revealed no problems with its functionality. The rest of the chamber's apparatus proved to be operating under no handicaps. For this, Dr Muffin was deeply grateful.

The machinery in the corner received a far closer, more detailed examination. This equipment was what the robot employed to maintain communication with his *sources* in the outside world. Through this single block of technology, Dr Muffin received the reports from which he culled the station's news broadcasts. Where the transmitter achieved a single brutal outburst of radiowaves, this small transceiver collected signals from numerous locations around the globe. Each signal was, once received, decoded and printed out on valuable sheets of paper, for the DJs required readable copy of each news item. The DJs were not privy to the responses Dr Muffin transmitted back to these sources, since these replies went out via a tighter waveband and consisted of a digital language no human could hope to decipher.

In the positronic mindseye of Dr Muffin, this collection of data for transmission over Afterburn Radio represented the future hope of mankind as a species. Only through careful guidance could the scattered Tribes and Districts re-unify in the post-Doom wasteland. A vital part of that guidance involved the dissemination of information to the people— not just lost data, but word of what was happening across the devastated continent (and now, with the return of Captain Jagg, news of foreign lands). As civilization began to reorganize under the wildly colored sky, Dr Muffin had become concerned that certain groups might require *more* guidance than others.

The Mob that ruled the northeastern Missippi Coast was a weird blend of feudal government heavily tainted with the repressive doctrines of an ancient religion that few remembered clearly enough to perceive its original tenets. This aristocratic system had quickly fallen into egocentric abuse by the last two Premiers to rule the Mob, resulting in a reign of terror that the robot alone recognized as frighteningly close to the villains who had called down the ancient Doom. With a fervent sense of dislike, Dr Muffin had dedicated his efforts to undermining the Mob and their villainous Church Police through his newscasts, exposing their schemes whenever possible, even resorting to outright lies when it might weaken their stranglehold on the land.

Such lies were rarely necessary, for the eyes and ears of Dr Muffin's *sources* were capable of seeing and hearing past walls of stone and secrecy. The reports which came to Dr Muffin were collected and sent by a network of orbiting satellites possessed of ancient telemetric capabilities that could reach down through the colorful dust clouds to snare images and sounds with excruciating clarity. Dr Muffin could recall that the pre-Doom skies had been overpopulated with such technological miracles. Only a fraction of these devices had survived the passage of the centuries, though; many of the original satellites had fallen victim to meteor impacts, decaying orbits, or rudimentary mechanical failure. Of the few that remained operational, only a handful would answer Dr Muffin's inquirie. He often wondered what masters the other satellites served, or what delusions those devices had been reduced to by prolonged isolation.

One or two of the satellites had developed mentalities that actually bordered on artificial intelligence; *these* were the ones with which Dr Muffin plotted the re-establishment of the human race.

Long before Captain Jagg had made his cross-oceanic journey, Dr Muffin had been cognizant of the rest of the world through the eyes of his satellite co-conspirators. They had agreed to hold back this knowledge until such time as man rediscovered these foreign lands for himself, for

Dr Muffin had felt that the people of Ericaland would not believe in such tales and this disbelief would undermine any confidence in Afterburn's other claims. Attempts to establish foreign stations engaging in the equivalent of Afterburn Radio had met with failure. Now, though, trade between Ericaland and the isles of Euro would bring word of Afterburn to these foreign shores, hopefully soon after to be followed by the clandestine location of a transmitter on foreign soil capable of bringing Afterburn's voice to the rest of the world. It was presumed (by Dr Muffin *and* his satellite allies) that Ericaland's discovery of the Euro Isles would prompt more voyages of oceanic exploration, followed by the rediscovery of what remained of Africa, Australia and Asia. Unfortunately, since all that remained of South America consisted of a few barren Andes peaks jutting above the water, visiting these islands would benefit no one.

Dr Muffin had kept all knowledge of these secrets (his satellite co-conspirators and the existence of foreign populated lands) from Fever Smith and the other agents of Afterburn. They were humans, and thereby subject to the schemes of these machines. They might not understand—or worse, they might deify the satellites, mistaking these tools for new lords. Such misinterpretations would be counterproductive to the direction Dr Muffin wished to steer humanity on its road back to greatness.

Confident the transmitter and his secret transceivers had survived the cave-in without harm, Dr Muffin decoded the latest news reports, stashing the printouts in a torso cavity designed for their storage. Crawling from the chamber and carefully sealing the door behind him, the robot began retracing his path through the rubble back to the ladder.

He suspected Psycho would be relieved to learn that the powerline problems had been solved. He wondered what new problems would develop next to occupy his time and attention.

For the station was inevitably doomed unless Fever returned with word of new equipment to replace the failing systems buried in the mountain.

13

HIGH IN THE MOB'S HOLIEST CASTLE located in the heart of Chico, two men sat in a sacred chamber. One of the men wore another's face, contorted now with lines of anger and frustration.

"Damn Afterburn Radio!" raged the new Premier.

"Perhaps the Rocky Districts will not believe their stories," the High Priest muttered softly, but he knew such hopes were as hollow as the new Premier's head.

"They *always* believe Afterburn!" the Premier shouted, punishing the desktop with his meaty fists. "Despite all our attempts to discredit the station and banish radio within our borders, the other Districts listen and believe. Afterburn's track record has been too consistent when it comes to divulging *our* secret plots."

The High Priest remained silent, regarding the Premier through veiled eyes. *You false-faced fool, what would you know of the Mob's sacred plots? Your sutures are barely healed, yet you presume to understand the full scope of Mob rule.*

Although shadows dominated the chamber, they failed to conceal its sumptuous decor. Years of exposure had numbed the High Priest to this opulence. He considered this ostentatious display to be pointless, for it was intended to dazzle plebian sensibilities, but only the loftiest members of the Mob's administration ever got the chance to experience this pomp. The High Priest understood that these pretentious flourishes existed mainly for the personal thrill of whoever occupied the ebony desk of power. While their faces remained the same over the years, a series of different individuals had filled the role of the Mob's Premier. This current schemer believed his coup to be unique, but he was hardly the first to employ cosmetic surgery to adopt the Premier's identity. Already, the fool seemed to have forgotten his masquerade and was acting as if he had always occupied this seat of supreme power.

"How do they find out these things?" screamed the Premier. "Afterburn's spies must be *everywhere*. We must ferret them out and kill all of these spies!"

Wearily, the High Priest shook his head. *That never does any good,* he thought. *Purges only serve to deplete our sacred resources. The people we unmask are not really spies, and their deaths do naught but alienate our subjects all the more to our rule.* But, he supposed, some theatrical demonstration of power would have to be staged to pacify the new Premier, lest he begin to imagine plots afoot to usurp his non-existent power. Meanwhile, a more effective defense against Afterburn's publicity must be found.

"Afterburn fears the Mob," the new Premier swore. "They use technology to become the devil's lips."

The High Priest opened his mouth to speak, but hesitated. No, he realized, this new Premier not only wore Vassal's face, his rants ran thick with Vassal's superstitions. He displayed a common upbringing, giving voice to the rhetoric the Mob fed the populace, mindlessly condemning all forms of technology as the tools of the Doom devil. There could be no rationalization with the new Premier, he was swept up in his stolen role, undoubtedly convinced that *he* ruled the Mob. No, the plans had set in motion by the Council must stay hidden from this madman. As it had always been, the position of Premier would remain a figurehead, wholly detached from the Mob's true power structure and secret dogma.

The Premier's misguided tirade was nevertheless accurate in one regard: Afterburn Radio *must* be destroyed if the Mob was ever to succeed in expanding their borders into the Rocky Districts or Hexas or the Lean Delta.

With an expression of solicitous piety, the High Priest sat and listened with disinterest as the falseface Premier complained and condemned and vowed bloodthirsty vengeance against the pirate radio station.

Watching from beyond the atmosphere, satellite RTD 126.1952.2 listened with careful dispassion to the two men, but learned nothing new from their private conference.

14

ALTHOUGH SHE CONTINUED TO DAMN the journey east, Nivek was grateful that his sister had chosen to accompany them. His decision to strike off with Tagger had been a clearcut example of personal assertiveness, but he was still a child and longed for the approval of someone he trusted (possibly even required such validation)—and Nitch was the only one left who could provide such assurances.

Nico had not responded calmly to the news that the group was headed back toward the dead Oogolah Tribe. She had wailed, throwing herself to the ground in a pathetic display of immature petulance. When Nivek's cooed encouragements had failed to deflate her tantrum, he had risen and with a shrug walked off, leaving the girl crying in the dirt. Even Needer had snorted with both noses at Nico, then trotted after the departing group. Realizing that her ploy had failed, Nico had dashed after them, still wailing but more in reproach now than in refusal.

Observing the detachment with which Nivek welcomed Nico to their march, Nitch nodded, inwardly impressed that her brother had seen through the girl's tantrum. Already he was growing, becoming aware of the choices available to him if he was willing to take the chances that came with such decisions.

She noticed Needer peering at her. Once the cat had caught the huntress' eye, her right head whispered, "He learns fast for a farmboy."

Nitch shrugged.

"Good blood in your family," Needer commented, "Pity they were all wiped out." With that the cat bounded away into the beginning brush.

As the morning progressed, the group left behind the rippling valleys, reaching the ragged fringes of the woodlands. They entered the forest without pause, Tagger leading them through the trees as if the region was one he knew from experience. The route the man took was easily maneuvered, slipping between hardwood trunks where few low branches obstructed their way.

Alas, Nivek's burst of self-assertion was short-lived. He walked now with an arm draped around his trembling girlfriend's shoulder. He mumbled platitudes of solace to her.

Around them, the woods chittered with hidden life. These trees sported healthy-looking brown bark; their boughs reached high to form a dense canopy. Despite the absence of any perceptible breeze, the thick leaves rustled overhead. Furtive buzzings betrayed the presence of oversized insects lurking among the foliage. Rampant shrubbery and grass that brushed at the travelers' waists made progress difficult, but Tagger proved quite adept at meaneuvering through this morass.

Deciding to match Tagger's lead, Nitch came up to walk beside the man. After a moment, she told him, "I don't trust you."

Never once falling out of step, Tagger turned to regard her for a few moments before he replied, "Good."

It was not a response to which Nitch knew how to react. Had he denied or questioned her statement, she would have possessed the advantage. The response he had given left her confused, though, uncertain what to say next.

The man spoke first, using his leverage to change the topic, "Your Tribe must know these lakeside ruins pretty well to allow one as young as Nivek to wander through them."

She assured him that the Tribe had tolerated no such thing: the ruins were avoided for a variety of clearly obvious reasons. They held no value or relevance to farmlife. They were a dismal place. They were dangerous. She explained the rumors of mutant creatures which lurked the ruins' concrete canyons, quickly adding that *she* had never witnessed any such monsters during her forays there. She pointed out that there was rarely any game found in or near the ruins.

A full hour elapsed while she told him about the lakeside structures before she realized that his comment had been intended to elicit a detailed description of the ruins. *Damn—he's a slick one. He's running reconnaissance on the area long before he even encounters it.*

Breaking off in mid-sentence, Nitch slowed her step so that she lapsed behind Tagger's lead. Needer appeared to her left, stretched on a branch at shoulder-level to the huntress. With both heads, the cat laughed at her.

Okay, Nitch mused, let's see how well you negotiate such human guile...

Nitch chuckled with the cat, slowing her pace again to bring herself and Needer to the rear of the march through the woods. "You know how these stories go… dark mysterious places at night… there must be monsters…"

While one head continued to laugh, the cat's other head told her, "Your kind attach undue mysticism to the old ruins."

"There's not much more that *can* be associated with them."

"Only because your kind have forgotten."

Nitch chose to respond with a grunt.

"Your species has no racial memory, no inherited instincts beyond basic bodily functions." Needer swaggered as she leapt from branch to branch. "My kind *does. We* remember what the ruins once were."

"That's convenient," Nitch observed.

"And just as useless as your kind's propensity for mythology. Despite the invalidity of your reasoning, your Tribe was correct in their overall assessment of such places. They cannot aid the growth of crops and are thereby unimportant to survival. The memories I inherited concerning the ruins have never helped me catch a meal or itch a scratch—they are immaterial to my existence. The ruins play no part in today's world; they are a piece of the dim past that have lingered too long."

"Your kind live only for the moment," asserted Nitch. "My kind compare today against yesterday."

"Your kind are far more vain than you think my kind are."

"There is no creature more self-absorbed than a cat."

"Cats do not bother themselves with old and broken toys."

Nitch's head swam. The conversation with Needer had taken an unexpected philosophical turn; she felt out of her depth, certain she was missing some hidden point in the cat's dialog… some crucial clue the cat was taunting her with. The fact that she was conversing with a cat was strange enough—to have the cat confuse her with dense logic was essentially embarrassing.

"Who the hell taught you to talk?" Nitch snapped, instantly regreting the force of her query.

"Actually," Needer paused to cock her heads at the girl, "I'm self-taught."

"I don't believe that for a second."

"Believe whatever you like." The cat bounded ahead with a buoyant spring. "Your opinion cannot change my kitten-years."

"You sat out on the prairie somewhere and taught yourself to speak."

"Of course not. I listened to humans and learned from their discussions. I practiced on a small boy in a village—human children are less suspicious of strange things than you become as adults. When the boy told his parents he had been talking with a cat, they beat him for lying."

"So—how did you convince Tagger that you could talk?"

"I told him so," the cat snorted.

"And it didn't worry you that an adult human believed it?"

Needer paused on a branch, turning her left head to peer at the girl. "It doesn't worry me that *you* believe I can talk. Does it worry *you*?" With that the cat flashed away into the growing gloom as the group ventured into deeper woods. Foliage was beginning to mask the day's light, creating a false dusk beneath the trees.

QUIET MEN WERE NOT BORN to their faith; there were no Quiet families, no Quiet children. The desire for silence came to each in a personal manner. Few were converted by encountering bands of Quiet Men as they wandered the land dispensing their silence. Converts sought out such bands, joining them—without comment, naturally. Once they became part of a group, converts quickly learned the faith's strict mores and adapted—or they were silenced as the unbelievers they were. There was no way an outsider could successfully infiltrate a band of Quiet Men.

The style of dress and choice of weapon of silence—the potato—were easily adopted mores. It was the mutilation that usually weeded out the posers from the devout.

Unceremoniously, but under the attention of the entire band, a new convert was set upon and bound with strands of coarse wire. Each band possessed a member who carried a sacred knife and other instruments of cruelty. It was this Quiet Man's task to cut off the ears of the newly converted, then take a needle and string and sew shut the mouth. Should the subject faint or cry out during this initiation, they were promptly silenced with a ready potato. Only devout fanatics survived to become practicing Quiet Men.

A day or so after this ceremony, the newcomer would shave his head of all hair, thus completing their conversion.

The term Quiet Men was actually a generic misnomer. The ranks of the savage faith included just as many women devotees as it did men. Allowing to their appearance and the bulk of their attire, though, people assumed they were all male. The only ones who might get close enough to detect the femaleness of any Quiet Men were their victims.

Having just concluded an initiation ceremony, the tall Quiet Man carefully cleaned his blade and needle, wiping the blood on the scarf that wrapped his thigh before hiding the instruments beneath his torso wrapping. He stared at the converted man who stood weakly before him, hands clenched and tears running from his eyes to dilute the blood that trickled from his freshly sealed lips.

The newcomer had not succumbed to the heresy of sound, but the tall Quiet Man still harbored a distinct doubt concerning this latest addition to his band. There was something wrong about the man—he did not exude the fire of faith displayed by others who had gone under the knife. Although this newcomer had passed the initiation, the tall one decided to watch him closely.

Turning from the bleeding man, the leader gesturing to the others of his band. They handed him a cup of thick soup from a steaming communal vat. He sat to sip the liquid through a straw he inserted into his nose, and surveyed the farmland of the Tribe they had just silenced the day before.

Their raid had been successful. The strategy of approaching the Tribe's lands from the south had almost been foiled when they had encountered that man and his loud son. Luckily, his band had prevented the two from warning their brethren. When the Quiet Men had descended on the Tribe, a farmhouse at a time as the sun set beyond the sky colors, their assault had been utterly unanticipated by the loud ones. Each farm had been silenced in due course with little struggle.

Only three members of the Quiet band had suffered death—and at the hands of an unknown assailant. Since there were no living witnesses to consult, the tall leader of the band was left to draw his own conclusions regarding their demise. And he did not like what his suspicions were leading him to believe.

Survivors.

Their silencing of the Tribe had not been complete. Someone had escaped. Escaped and slain three Quiet Men.

This survivor could not be allowed to get away with the blood of three devout Quiet Men on their hands. This survivor must be found and silenced. The faithful must be avenged!

Reaching this fervent conclusion, the tall one directed several Quiet Men to scout the region for signs of life, using the simple fingertalk which the Quiet Men used to communicate.

The band was not leaving this area until vengeance was exacted.

THEY APPROACHED THE RUINS beside Oogolah Lake as nightfall came, darkening the sky's colors and rousing the nocturnal insects. The group stopped by a stand of flame-charred trees to survey the silhouettes of the forbidding towers that stretched from the shore out into the dark waters of the lake.

Tagger still led the way into territory he did not know.

Nitch still wore her suspicions like a loud mask.

Nico still clung to Nivek as if his presence would ward off all ills.

Nivek still tolerated Nico's clinging, drunk with the false sense of his new maturity.

Needer still skulked beyond the group, creeping through the landscape with her feline stealth.

Together they viewed the ruins with a mixture of apprehension and anticipation.

"We should wait for dawn," Nitch spoke.

"Why?" her younger brother laughed. "I know my way around these ruins—by day or night."

Tagger appeared to have heard neither Palma's comments. He stood like a statue, holding his staff erect. His rowdy hair ruffled softly in the damp breeze that whipped off the surface of the lake. His narrowed eyes scanned the nocturnal countryside.

"Oh please," Nico whined in a tiny voice. "Why do we have to do this at all?"

"Because I want to show Tagger my radio cavern," replied Nivek with a tone of pride.

A rush of feral instinct brought Nitch a sudden intuitive revelation: Nivek was not doing this out of any desire to attain any hidden treasure. In his mind, the wonders of his box-filled cavern already belonged to him. He had carried this secret for too long. Now he wanted to share his illicit knowledge with someone else—someone who would appreciate the cavern's mysteries as he did. The boy perceived Tagger as one whose passion for *radio* ran as deeply as his.

It's the radio, Nitch realized. Tagger's amazing radio could pick up Afterburn so clearly at ground-level, where Nivek's device required a great elevation to receive the station's transmissions. Nivek had mistaken the man's possessions as his personality. It was pride that had driven Nivek back the Oogolah Lake ruins, not greed.

Meanwhile, she was definite that greed drove the cryptic prairieman. There was no altruism in Tagger's motivations. The man was clearly a loner, possessing no ties or allegiances to anyone other than himself. The fact that he traveled in the company of a non-human illustrated his general disdain for humanity. Nitch would not be surprised if Tagger shared Needer's deep conviction of mankind's inferiority. The two of them belonged together: a pair of opportunistic predators.

This time, though, they had chosen Nitch's sole surviving blood relative to be their latest victim. But the huntress would see them both dead before she would allow any harm to befall her little brother.

"Don't be a fool, Tagger," Nitch advised. "Even an open field can turn deadly by night."

The man nodded. "Your sister's words ring truer than your enthusiasm, Nivek."

"Bah!" the boy waved a hand at the man. "I'm going in. If you want to see my secret cavern, you'll follow." With an assertive tug on the shoulder straps of his backpack, Nivek strode away from them, heading toward the ruins.

After an ululating moan, Nico scurried after her protector.

Tagger sighed, then lifted his shoulders in a resigned shrug and struck off after Nivek.

"Looks as if insanity wins out," Needer laughed from Nitch's feet. "Your kind's specialty."

Nitch kicked at the cat without serious conviction. Then she headed toward the ruins. Needer scampered after her, chuckling with both mouths.

As they neared the ancient metropolis, it became apparent that a thick layer of fog had drifted off the lake, laying like an ominous white lawn about the bases of the concrete towers. They could see how the landside perimeter of the fog was ragged and irregular, extending sinuous fingers out from the dense cloud. The pallor of the fog enhanced the darkness of the towers against the sky of seething colors.

Once again, Tagger voiced his opinion concerning risks of venturing into the ruins. This fog could hide all sorts of unseen problems: not just monsters, but more importantly unsure footing. This time, Nitch chose to remain silent, hoping her brother would heed the words of the man he blindly admired.

Nivek only scoffed at the man. There were no monsters. And he was quite familiar with the route to the cavern. The fog would not impair their safe passage. He saw no reason to postpone their advance.

He scrambled over an upthrust concrete slab and slid down into the outskirts of the dead city. The rest of them were forced to follow, each for their own private reasons.

"Ah, the exuberance of youth," muttered Tagger.

"Oh, shut up," Nitch hissed. "*You* started this."

Slowly, the low broken slabs began to rear higher, clustered about the bases of the perimeter buildings. The outer vista was one of geological decay: once-grand towers stripped to their bones and looming against the livid night sky. Decades of environmental exposure had reduced the architecture of concrete and brick into tortured frameworks of struts and crossbeams. Deeper into the ruins, the towers retained their rectangular integrity, some almost all the way to their upper levels.

The boy led them toward a particular canyon between two great concrete masses. These towers teetered westward in strange unison. The windows of these two towers were boarded up and covered by corroded sheets of porous metal. The crevasse between these two buildings inspired a palpable dread. It seemed like a bottomless black gash in the fabric of reality. Into the intimidating rift they followed Nivek.

Soon they encountered thick mists in the crevasse. The fog actually unmasked the darkness, revealing hazy details of the rubble; the shapes they passed were uncertain but gratefully discernible.

As they came to the end of the concrete fissure, where the rift spilled out into a larger, foggy canyon, Nitch's brain began to itch. Instantly, her spear was poised for action.

"On your left," came Needer's voice from out of the mist.

That was the only warning the rest of the group got before a massive shape rose from the darkness and fog. Tentacles oozing with a mucoid moistness closed around Nivek and Nico, pulling them from their unsteady feet. Nivek gasped; Nico screamed like a banshee. Before Nivek hung two meters above the ground, Nitch's spear drove through the thick coil that held the boy aloft. The tentacle writhed, dropping Nivek with a sticky sound. The boy fell squarely on his sister, knocking the huntress to the uneven asphalt hidden beneath the roiling mist.

Tagger sprang at the monster, swinging his staff to jab at the base of the tentacle clutching Nico. He struck viciously at the creature, each impact resounding with a wet puncture. The tentacle that held Nico trembled; several more slithered out of the fog to entwine the man's staff, pulling it from his grip. Tagger dodged as the coils attempted to ensnare him. Rolling away, he pulled his crossbow from his belt.

To his right, the haze parted and the bulk of the beast crawled into view. The monster was unbelievably loathsome, oozing a viscous liquid from numerous puckering orifices. The thing's main body was large with a bulbous base ringed by smaller tentacles that caressed the ground. Its torso tapered into a glistening headless trunk. Although the majority of the creature's sinuous limbs sprouted from the lower torso, three stiffer stalks stood out from the trunk's pulsing stump. These stalks waved erratically in the air, twitching with an unearthly vibration. The beast loomed twice as tall as a man.

Suddenly a deep slit opened in the beast's upper trunk, its edges peeling back to reveal rows of sharp black needles. These teeth twitched just as terribly as did the monster's stalks. An ichor of sickly yellow drooled from the beast's maw, streaming down the dark brown trunk.

As the monster drew Nico's dangling screaming form toward this gaping hole, three tongues covered with small spikes snaked out to fondle her. Her cries increased in pitch, going way beyond abject terror into the range of acute hysteria.

Leaping from the darkness, Needer landed atop the beast and began to savage one of the vibrating stalks. The cat tore cruelly at the twitching mass with claw and teeth, reducing it to a gory, floppy shred. For the first time, the monster made a sound: a shrill whistle that rose to stab painfully at the group's ears.

Tagger lifted his crossbow and fired two bolts at the monster. The short arrows plunged into the beast's moist flesh near its base. He clustered several more shots around the root of the Nico-burdened tentacle.

Finally, the beast released Nico, uncurling its tentacle in shuddering agony, sending the girl into a plummet. She was startled to find herself landing in the arms of Tagger who rushed her away from the wounded creature's thrashing.

The monster struggled to escape, grasping at the edges of a nearby concrete tower to drag itself away. Needer still worried the beast's upper stalks. As the cat started on the remaining protrusion, fiercely thrashing tentacles struck at her, attempting to dislodge her from her perch. With the agility and uncanny balance of her kind, Needer avoided these meaty bludgeons and maintained her position, continuing to rip at the sole surviving stalk.

Suddenly, Nitch was upon the beast, pulling her spear free from the tentacle. She stabbed and slashed at the monster's mouth, finally succeeding in driving her weapon deep into the throat of the beast. The creature reared up, almost as if trying to climb the nearest building's sheer wall. Needer fled her perch, jumping to a narrow ledge that ran along the face of the tower. Then, with a high whistle and a frightful convulsion, the monster collapsed to the broken ground with a wet slap. It lay trembling, but its movements were clearly of a post-mortem nature. A large gout of green fluid spilled from the beast's maw to soak the rubble and dirt.

"Mythological beasts," Nitch scowled up at the cat.

"Hey, *you're* the one who didn't believe there were monsters in the ruins," Needer jeered back.

"It's some kind of aquatic creature," muttered Tagger, prodding the obscene beast with his staff. He moved a tentacle away to expose a section of the creature's flank, revealing a set of massive gills fully a meter long.

Although the man had deposited Nico on her feet near Nivek, the girl clutched frantically at Tagger's arm. Her eyes were still squeezed shut with fear.

"You killed it," Nivek grunted, wiping the slime of the beast from his arms. "Well, let's get moving."

"No no no!" wailed Nico, pressing harder against Tagger.

"Don't be a nitwig, Nivek," Nitch growled.

"It's just down this canyon," Nivek insisted. He started off into the fog.

Tagger made to stop him, but was hampered by Nico's clutching grip. Not happy with any of the evening's developments, the man reluctantly chased after the boy.

"Dammit," swore Nitch. But she followed them down the canyon.

Pausing to suspiciously scan the high rim of the canyon's walls, Needer descended from the ledge and trailed after them.

Far above the reach of any predator senses possessed by the cat or the huntress, a pair of Quiet Men watched the group disappear into a hole at the base of a certain tower. After a quick exchange of fingertalk, the smaller fanatic scurried off to gather the rest of the band, leaving the other to the role of sentinel.

17

THROUGH THE SQUARE HOLE, Nivek led them into a shallow cave beneath the ruined tower. From a cubbyhole, the boy took several sticks whose tips were wrapped in greasy rags. He distributed these torches among the group, except Nico who still clung to Tagger with her childlike terror.

In the light of the small wickers of flame, the shallow cave became a low-ceilinged region filled with strange litter. A pair of cracked pillars ran from floor to ceiling near the center of the oddly rectangular cave. To one side loomed a great bulky shape that possessed a square mouth; the metal door to this opening hung on torn hinges. Cobwebs and the dust of ages coated the cave in a shroud of lush fuzziness.

"This is it?" Tagger asked, looking dubiously about.

"Nuh, nuh," Nivek replied, informing the man that this was only the upper entrance. "We have to go down some more tunnels to reach the real cavern." He pointed out a rectangular doorway to their left, hidden behind a stack of wooden planks calcified by time into thin sheets as hard as stone.

Attempting to disengage Nico's clutching hands, Tagger signaled Needer to investigate the tunnel beyond the doorway. With a snort of contempt, the cat disappeared into the dark opening.

"It's safe," Nivek insisted. "I've traveled this route a hundred times."

"As safe as the canyon outside?" Tagger inquired with skepticism.

"It's safe," the boy repeated petulantly.

Tagger finally managed to work free from Nico's clutches. When she tried to regrasp the man, he told her to stop acting like a child. They were safe now, and if they weren't—Tagger needed to be free to defend them against whatever horror might spring forth. This logic penetrated Nico's fear and, after giving him an exaggerated hurt look, she ceased annoying the man.

Silently awaiting Needer's return, the four of them stood in the ancient chamber.

Nitch could not help smiling at how quickly Nico had transferred her attention from Nivek to Tagger. Since the man had saved her from the monster, the girl had seemingly forgotten the boy. Her pawing of Tagger clearly embarrassed the man.

Meanwhile, the near-deadly encounter with the monster had disarmed Nivek's bravado. Despite his attempts to remain the confident guide, he viewed the ruins now with greater suspicion and respect. Nitch knew that *her* sense of confidence—as diminished as it was in the fog-shrouded ruins by night—had certainly been taxed by the incredible beast's sudden attack.

Nitch forced herself to relax. If any danger lurked nearby, she would become aware of it before it could strike. Until her brain tingled, she knew they were relatively safe. These caves were vacant of any immediate threat. Although, granted: her huntress senses would be small protection against accidents or clumsiness.

On all of her previous trips into the ruins with Nivek, Nitch had never been down in these caves. Her jaunts into the dead zone had been restricted to sneaking off to listen to Afterburn Radio among the ruins' loftier heights. These subterranean regions were unknown ground for her, full of new mysteries.

And unfathomable artifacts. A bundle of narrow hollow metal tubes whose ends were scored with spiral ridges. A pile of hollow once-bright orange cones stacked inside each other. A box possessing a curved face so shiny that it reflected their torches. A wooden lump that seemed to have an animal head while its four legs were connected by two planks that curled like a bow. A clutter of metal cans stained in overlapping hues of freakish colors. A stack of preposterous circular black plates protruding from the sodden residue of what had once been cardboard sleeves. Square containers with abnormally rounded corners full of oddly shaped pieces of lunatic debris: transparent cylinders, sharp-edged metal joints, pieces that reminded her of tiny fish covered in a puffy white crust.

The very nature of the cave's walls disturbed her. They were too regular, comprising strict right angles and unnaturally smooth surfaces beneath the crust of ages. The mouths of each cave seemed more like doorways than openings. Yet the petrified wood and crumbling stone of the cave displayed no marks of chisel or planer. Whatever tool had formed these walls had been vastly superior to anything her kind used. The thought of ancient insectile construction methods sent a chill through her human bones.

Many times had Nitch walked these ruins with Nivek and on her own investigating forays, but never before had she felt so certain that she—indeed all of humanity—did not belong here. It was not just the sense of intruding upon the relics of another species or historical age, this dread was born out of the certainty that mankind could never hope to comprehend these ancient artifacts. Needer had been correct: these ruins could never play a part in daily survival: they and the mysteries they contained were useless aberrations. Interest in them could only result in madness.

As if in response to Nitch's thought of the cat, Needer hopped out of the dark hole. Perching on her haunches before the tunnel's entrance, the cat called to Tagger, "All clear."

"There," Nivek smugly snorted. "I told you." He started for the doorway, but both Nitch and Tagger stepped to block his passage.

Noticing the set brow of Nitch's face, Tagger nodded, standing back. "Okay. You take point. I'll cover the rear."

Nitch regarded the man for a second, uncertain whether to challenge his leadership. Then, deciding it was futile to argue with his choice of letting her have her way, she entered the tunnel holding her spear defensively in one hand, her torch raised ahead of her in the other. Nivek followed, then Nico, with Tagger bringing up the rear. Needer trotted along, accompanying Nitch in her lead position.

The tunnel mimicked the unnatural right-angled construction of the entry cave. Although the ground was mired with mud and rubble, the floor underneath seemed smooth and regular.

Nivek cautioned them to hold their torches low, away from the ceiling. The strange white tiles that ran above them were easily flammable, he warned. Their surfaces were scorched from previous flames, some were buckled in a grotesque parody of matter frozen in mid-melt.

Halting, the boy turned to push against the tunnel's wall. A section of the wall unexpectedly fell open, the gap once again disturbingly rectangular. Thrusting his torch through the opening, Nivek showed them a remarkable flight of stairs that descended into stygian depths.

"Down there?" Nico piped. "Oh no, I'm not going down there!"

"It'll be okay," Nivek assured her. "The steps level off at points every few meters before continuing down."

"Landings," Tagger supplied the correct term. "How many floors down do we go?" he asked the boy.

"Floors?"

"How many levels?" the man rephrased his question.

"Umm, all the way down… four levels," Nivek replied.

"Then let's get moving." The authority of Tagger's voice started Nivek and Nitch moving. When Nico hesitated, the man nodded to her with a reassuring smile, "It'll be okay." Reluctantly, the girl followed Nivek down the stairs.

A minimal amount of debriscluttered the steps. The walls, however, gave Nitch pause for concern. Trickles of water decorated their surfaces, doubtless seepage from the nearby lake.

She brought these leaks to the group's attention. "Surely the bottom level will be flooded," she deduced with concern.

Nivek disagreed, "It's dry down there."

"The drainage system must still be operational," Tagger commented.

In the darkness, Nitch glared at the man. "You seem awfully familiar with these ruins," she accused the prairieman.

"Buildings and cities tend to run true to a uniform design," he told her.

"What are you hiding?"

"Nothing." He adroited shifted the inquisition in her direction: "I thought Needer told you about these places."

"I *asked*, but your cat wouldn't give me any direct *answers*."

"Humph," the man sighed. "Typical."

Somewhere in the darkness, the cat chuckled at them.

"I'm sorry," Tagger told Nitch. "I was under the impression you knew these ruins were just an ancient city."

"An ancient insect city," the huntress agreed.

"No, an ancient *human* city," he corrected her.

The group reached the first landing. Here, the steps ended, only to recommence their descent from another side of the level area.

"What?" Nitch gasped. "That's impossible. Humans could never build a place like this…"

"Not now," Tagger agreed. "But long ago they could—and did."

"You're talking crazy," Nitch snorted derisively.

The prairieman asked Nivek, "Have you explored the rest of the floors down here? Is there anything of use in the other rooms?"

Giving the man a curious look, Nivek answered, "I've been all through these caves. Everything in them's rotted and useless. Except for one chamber that's filled with tables and chairs—but who cares about stuff like that?"

"The damp," Tagger nodded. "I wonder how the equipment in your radio cavern survived…"

"You'll see," replied the boy with a secret smile.

"Human cities—ha!" Nitch scoffed.

"Your Tribe was agriculturally oriented," Tagger told her. "There's no reason for such cultures to remember these old cities. I imagine your legends are pretty outrageous regarding these places. Insects, huh? There are some regions in the southwest where people believe the ruins are ancient temples belonging to a race of animated fire creatures that came from another world. Dogs, lizards, even birds—quite a variety of creatures are mistakenly credited as the architects of these pre-Doom cities."

Although Tagger's claims seemed preposterous, Nitch suddenly realized that *human* design might explain the curious rectangular uniformity of these tunnels. Insects certainly had no use for *steps*.

"Our ancestors built tall buildings in which to live," Tagger continued. "They also built deep into the ground in places."

"How could they live down here in this darkness?" Nitch asked.

"Here, I'll show you." Pausing on the next landing, Tagger reached up to poke at the soot-stained tiles with his staff. The tiles came loose with a crackling groan to reveal a hollow behind them. Holding his torch aloft, Tagger pointed to a white cylinder that ran from end to end in the hidden niche. "See that tube? It lights up, when supplied with some kind of power. I don't know much about that power itself, other than they derived it from harnessed water pressure."

"Water that glows?" Nico asked, laughing in a hysterical tone.

"No," Tagger replied. "It's more complicated than that."

They continued their descent.

"If what you say is true," commentedNivek, "then the stuff in my radio cavern was man-made..."

"Without a doubt," the man grunted. "Radio is a very old, very human concept."

"Then—all the music that Afterburn plays—it's all *human* music?"

"Yes."

"How do you know all this?" Nitch demanded, her voice thick with suspicion.

"You'd be surprised," the prairieman muttered.

Before Nitch could challenge his cryptic reply, Nivek announced they had arrived. The boy pushed open another section of wall to disclose another dark tunnel. Stepping through, he led them down the tunnel to the right. He stopped before a blank wall, gesturing to it with the pride of revelation. "Here."

"There's no door," Tagger observed.

Nivek smiled. He reached out, placing his palms against the damp wall. Applying slight pressure, the boy moved his hands along the wall, and a section of the surface slid aside to reveal a small chamber.

Hesitantly, they stepped into this dark anteroom. Set in the wall opposite the sliding opening was a massive metal door with a large wheel attached at hip-level. Approaching the door, Nivek gripped the wheel, twisting it in a circular motion. With a soft hiss, the metal door popped fractionally from the surface of the wall. Nivek swung it open.

"My secret radio cavern," proclaimed the boy, leading them into a large cave.

The chamber was long and filled with metal shelves. Sturdy blue boxes filled the shelves. A series of work counters ran around the cave's flanks. Scattered about on the countertops were various metal bits and odd shapes that hinted at being tools. To one side, a wall was lined with small gray metal towers; the face of each tower appeared to feature drawers with dark looping handles.

"This is where I learned to build my radio," Nivek proclaimed.

"Mother Sky," breathed Tagger with wonder.

"Why is it dry in here?" Nico asked.

"The door is rimmed with a strange pliant seal," Nivek pointed out. "It keeps moisture out."

Nico and Nitch bent to examine the strip of soft black that ran around the inner edge of the metal door.

Tagger, though, walked among the tall shelves of boxes, stretching out his hand to stroke them with reverence. He came to a halt by a counter and stared with awe at the clutter of objects before him. "Books," he gasped under his breath. "Intact books…"

Needer jumped atop the counter, pawing at one of the books. "Quite a find," the cat remarked.

"One of them showed me how to build my radio," explained Nivek, leaning in to rifle through the books. He held up a volume labeled simply "The How and Why Book of Radio."

Taking it carefully from Nivek's offered hands, Tagger opened the book, paging through the contents. Most of the pages contained little text, with pictures occupying the majority of each sheet.

"You could read this?" Tagger asked.

"Not much." The boy blushed in the torchlight. "The pictures helped me with the actual construction." He lifted another book, handing it to the man. "This one was impossible to read, but it's got more detailed pictures."

Tagger took the copy of "Advanced Electronics" from the boy. This book he flipped through only briefly; text dominated its pages, full of long words that even he could not understand.

Replacing the books on the countertop, Tagger walked over to the wall of towers with drawers. He grasped one of the handles, pulling on it with no result. He tried a few more, but none sprang open under his effort. "Locked," he muttered.

"Over here," called Needer. Both of the cat's heads were poked behind a tall pile of the blue boxes stacked against a wall.

As Tagger and Nivek came closer, they could see the outline of another door hidden behind the boxes.

"Another room?" Tagger asked.

The boy shrugged. "I don't know. I never noticed there was a door here."

With enthusiastic vigor, Tagger began pulling the boxes aside, restacking them to one side. Soon he had uncovered the door's full face; it was another metal rectangle like the one that had admitted them to Nivek's secret radio cavern. It differed, though, in that it sported no large wheel.

"These boxes are full of stuff," the boy commented. "Stuff like things pictured in those books."

Tagger examined the new door. There was a small handle on it, but no amount of tugging would loosen the door from its place. He paid some attention to a small plaque set into the wall beside the doorframe. The plaque featured a series of small tabs clustered in a square grouping at its center. Experimentally, the man tapped on a few of the tabs; nothing happened. He randomly tapped a few more of the buttons; the group collectively gasped as the door hissed and swung open as if heeding ghostly direction.

The man and the boy exchanged startled looks. Then the boy nodded, stepping back to allow Tagger to enter the new room. As the prairieman strode through the doorway, Needer scuttled between his feet, disappearing into the room's darkness.

Holding his torch high, Tagger surveyed the hidden room's contents. Machinery, large and gleaming with ancient oil and polish reflected back the torchlight. The ranks of equipment stretched far beyond the primitive light cast by the flaming stick.

"I don't believe it…" Tagger whispered.

Edging in behind him, Nivek whistled with amazement, "Color me green!"

Leaping atop one of the bulky machines, Needer sat and gave Tagger a serious look with her left head. The right head stared off with a bored expression. The cat's tail curled about her with solemn intent. Slowly, the cat's fur began to transform into a hue that merged with the grays of the machinery on which she perched.

"Boy," Tagger finally spoke, "you've just become the richest person in Ericaland."

"Yeah?" Nivek replied, eyes wide and curious.

"Humph," Nitch snorted from the doorway. "What about *your* cut?"

Tagger laughed, turning to face her. "Melt my cut, Nitch. You have no idea how valuable this stuff is."

Drawing her hunting knife, Nitch menaced the man with its blade. "Valuable enough for you to be thinking of stealing it all, I'd wager."

Needer hissed from her perch.

Tagger waved the cat to silence.

"Hey," chirped Nivek. "I recognize some of this stuff from those books..."

"The boy's got a natural aptitude for this stuff," Tagger confided to the cat.

"*He's* as valuable as all this equipment," announced the cat.

"Maybe more so>" Tagger nodded. Turning back to Nitch's blade, he smiled, "I'm not going to turn on you, Nitch. I'm on *your* side. The problem is, are *you* on *my* side?"

"Word games," she spat.

"Nivek," called Tagger. "How much of an Afterburn Radio fan are you really?"

"Huh?" The boy looked up from the machines, his attention snared by mention of the radio station.

"What are you pulling now?" Nitch growled at the prairieman. She twitched her blade, threatening the man.

With a sudden movement, Tagger disarmed the huntress. Now *he* held the knife, pointed in warning at the girl in the doorway. "You claimed you wanted to be on the radio someday, Nivek. Well, this might just be your chance."

"What?" the boy squealed with confusion tainted with hope.

"All this stuff..." The man waved the blade to encompass the room's contents. "Afterburn Radio is in desperate need of equipment like this."

"How would *you* know?" snarled Nitch.

"Umm, yeah... how would you—" Nivek started to echo his sister.

"We work for Afterburn," Needer told them.

"What?!" Nivek piped.

From behind Nitch, Nico peering in. "What's all *this* stuff?"

Nitch shook her head. "You're lying…"

"I told you you'd be surprised." With a calm face Tagger reversed the knife and handed Nitch's knife back to her, handle-first.

"You?" Nivek gasped. "You *know* Fever Smith?"

"Oh yes," laughed the cat, "We know Fever—better than you could imagine."

"Aren't we going to use this fortune to buy our way into a new Tribe?" Nico asked.

"You could do that." Tagger shrugged, looking over at Nivek. "But Afterburn would give you more."

"They could put me on the radio?" Nivek breathed.

"They'd give you anything you want for this stuff," asserted Needer.

"Wait a minute—" Nico whined.

"It's Nivek's choice," Tagger declared. "The salvage rights belong to him."

"You can take me to Afterburn?" asked Nivek anxiously.

"If that's what you want," Tagger replied. "Sure."

"That—*that's* what I want!" exclaimed the boy.

"Hold on—" Nitch interjected.

"Don't worry, Nitch. Afterburn's not going to cheat your little brother," Needer assured her.

Striding from the storage room of machinery, Tagger announced, "We need to lock this place up. So no one else can find it until Afterburn can come for it."

Bounding after the prairieman, Needer added, "You need to call in, Tagger. You've got to let Dr Muffin know what we've found."

"Right!" Tagger agreed. He whirled to gesture wildly. "We've got to get topside. No signal will be able to cut through all these floors. We need to get out in the open."

Hurrying after the man, Nivek inquired, "How can you signal Afterburn?"

"Our radio," offered Needer. "It works both ways."

The boy's eyes grew wider than ever at this news.

"Come on," Tagger waved the group toward the outer door.

18

AS THE GROUP CLIMBED THE STAIRS, Nico asked, "But—we're still going to be rich? Right? The rest of us? Afterburn will reward us too, right? Not just Nivek…"

"If that's what Nivek wants," Tagger replied from his lead position.

"You want me to be rich too, don't you, Nivek?" Nico stroked the boy's arm with hope.

"I suppose," Nivek muttered, uncomfortably aware how easily her fawning had shifted from the prairieman back to himself.

Suddenly both Nitch and Needer hushed the group, their three "shhh"s sounding simultaneously in the narrow stairway.

"Something's coming," Needer whispered. The hair on her back bristled and her claws extended instinctively.

Reacting instantly, Tagger leapt the last three steps to cross the next landing. He yanked open the door that gave access to this floor, waving the rest of them through it. When Nitch refused to run and hide, Needer guided the children away, grumbling about "stupid human bravado."

"Whatever it is," Nitch quietly told him, "we face it together."

Tagger nodded, extinguishing his torch. The huntress followed suit. In the new darkness, a glow became apparent far above their heads, higher along the stairway. The glow slowly approached, descending toward them on the stairs with scuffling steps.

"Monsters rarely carry their own lights," Tagger observed with a whisper.

Nitch agreed with a curt nod, unseen in the darkness. The pair of them drew back into the recess beneath the stairway.

From this hiding place, they observed with silent surprise as a band of Quiet Men appeared around the stairway's turn. The Quiet Man in the lead carried a sputtering torch (not one of those from Nivek's cache, but a gnarled stick topped by a burning wad of weeds); the rest of the fanatics bore potatoes and knives. The thoughts that ran through Tagger's and

Nitch's minds were diverse, but both estimates came to identical conclusions.

Quiet Men, Tagger thought. *They mustn't find Nivek's storage room of equipment. Of all hands for such machinery to fall into, it must* not *become the property of these fanatics. They've got to die!*

Quiet Men, thought Nitch. *These are the bastards who killed my family, my Tribe. They must have seen us enter the ruins. They're out to* silence *us, just as they silenced the Oogolah Tribe. But—not if I kill them first!*

Together, prairieman and huntress flung themselves at the dark figures. Before the Quiet Men were even aware of their presence, Tagger's staff had driven through one man's skull, while Nitch's blade had severed the arteries in two other's necks.

"Aaaieeee!" Nitch shrieked as she wielded her knife like a broadsword, slicing quiet flesh with every swing.

"What?" Tagger cried. "What's wrong, girl?"

"Scream, you mutehead!" she shouted at him through the sprays of crimson that filled the air of the landing. "They're Quiet Men—they *hate* sound!"

"Clever girl." The prairieman began to yell, pausing only to replenish the oxygen in his lungs for his next cry.

"It worked for me when I killed the ones at my farm," Nitch shrieked.

Unseen in the flurry of bloodletting, a tall Quiet Man ducked back up the stairs. This girl, he reflected, by her own unholy admission, she is the one who murdered our lost faithful. We have found her—and our lost believers can now be avenged. But, the man... He paused to stare with recognition at Tagger, then whirled with burning eyes of hate to urge the rest of his band into the fray. As these fanatics rushed into battle with knives drawn, the leader retreated up the staircase.

Despite overwhelming odds, Tagger and Nitch cut into the squad of Quiet Men with dual passion—one of vengeance, one of prevention. Although the Quiet Men fought with their own burning fervor, their superior numbers were no match for the hunters' ferocity. Nitch suffered a collection of slashes, but retaliated with devastating lethality. Tagger became buried beneath a rush of the madmen; when he disengaged himself from the human tangle his clothes were tattered and he was streaked with his own blood, intermingled with Quiet crimson.

Presently, the only living beings who crouched on the landing were bloody Tagger and gasping Nitch. They stood knee deep in Quiet Men who were forever silenced.

"Are you okay?"

Weakly, Nitch nodded. She glared toward the upper regions of the stairwell as further scuffling steps sounded heading their way.

"More of them," grated the prairieman. "Quick—" He pointed toward the door leading to the subterranean floor. As Nitch pulled open the door and plunged through it, Tagger grabbed up the Quiet Men's single torch, pitching it down the stairs. Then he followed the huntress through the doorway. Together in the darkness of the hallway, they made out the glow of Nivek's torch far down the tunnel and ran toward it.

"Quiet Men," Nitch hissed as they came upon Nivek, Nico and Needer.

"We must find another way back to the surface." Tagger gestured them to hurry down the hallway, away from the bloodied stairwell.

"But how?" Nivek asked urgently. "I don't think there is another way out..."

"There has to be," Needer insisted.

"We don't have much other choice," admitted Tagger.

The group ran through the darkness, winding down one hallway after another. The corridors they dashed along were less cluttered with debris and more buried under dust. They passed several doorways whose portals were solidly rusted shut or perhaps locked by some ancient method—it mattered not which explanation were true, the means barred these routes to the fleeing group. To elude any pursuit, they repeatedly took any side corridors they encountered, always heading away from the fateful staircase.

Finally, Nico's raspy sobbing coerced them to pause and catch their breath. Nivek squatted on the floor, dazed and fearfully withdrawn. Tagger was forced to quiet the crying girl with words of senseless reassurance.

Nitch sat against the wall and asked Needer which way they should head next.

"How should I know?" the cat retorted impatiently.

"You claimed you knew these ruins."

"I never claimed any such thing," snarled Needer. "My knowledge of places like this is confined to racial memory—vague and untested."

"But—"

"It's Tagger who's familiar with your old cities, not me. He's visited other ruins out west." The cat turned her left head to summon the prairieman.

"That's right," Tagger admitted. "Give a minute to think... basements... tunnels... sewers!"

"Right," meeped Needer. "Your kind was obsessed with waste removal… even more so than my kind."

"What are *sewers*?" Nitch demanded.

"Tunnels that run beneath the cities," Tagger told her. "They were used to carry the waste products outside the city limits. If we can find one of them, it should take us far beyond the ruins."

"So, where would they be?" asked Nitch.

"Down," the man replied. "We need to go all the way down."

This statement produced another bout of emotional desperation in Nico, requiring the attention of both Tagger and Nivek to calm her. It was another half-hour before they could convince the girl to accompany them deeper underground.

After traveling the length of a few more hallways, they located a door that admitted them to another stairwell. Once Needer had scouted it, returning to announce it safe of any danger, the group descended again.

Although Nitch suspected they were each seething with unvoiced tension and uncertainty, the group marched down the steps in silence. She knew *she* had questions. Who was this enigmatic prairieman? Had they encountered him by accident or nefarious design? Did he indeed represent the mysterious pirate radio station? Or were his words merely a cloud of deceit intended to relax their caution? If his claims *were* true, what were his connections to Afterburn Radio? Why was he going to such immense lengths to aid and protect Nivek and the rest of them? What knowledge made Nivek so valuable to Tagger and Afterburn? What use could Nivek's secret cave be to the radio station? How could the boxes of junk save Afterburn? Why did Afterburn require salvation?

And—what of Tagger's implied journeys into the far west? Had the man really ventured beyond the deadly flatlands? What arcane means had he employed to survive the horrors of the plains? Only the insane headed west, and only the dead returned from those regions. The man was surely a liar. The only evidence to corroborate his tales came from the dual mouths of a mutant cat.

The things Tagger and Needer had claimed were ludicrous… especially their assertions that these ruins had been the handiwork of human ancestors. Nitch had allowed her confusion to blind her huntress suspicions, letting her accept the prairieman's explanations concerning the heritage of these and other ruins. No human would ever live in holes dug so deep beneath the earth. How could they have existed without the light of the sun? Tagger's tale of light made from water was so totally absurd! What could people have found to eat in such subterranean depths? Perhaps Tagger would have her believe that men had consumed dirt to survive. Where else could all the earth that had once filled these tunnels have gone?

Soon the staircase ended, leaving the group with little choice but to pursue these sewers along dark horizontal hallways. Alleged sewers, Nitch mused. Another of Tagger's impossible fabrications… disposing of wastes via endless underground pipes. If these sewers existed, then what had these ancient humans used to fertilize their fields? Every new aspect that Tagger revealed only exposed holes in the logic of his lies. Damning holes, she decided, and fatal lies.

Rounding a corner, they all halted with a collective gasp.

Before them, sprawled on the broken remains of a chair lay a skeleton dressed in curious garb. The corpse's clothing was of a heavy material, with sleeves and pantlegs that drooped all the way to its wrists and ankles. Attached to its belt were several mysterious objects, one resembling a crossbow's handle without the bow. A desiccated book lay at its side, open to reveal its pages had long ago decayed into powder. The corpse's skull was split wide open; the metal bar that had killed the man still lodged deep in the jagged hole.

However, this corpse was only one source of the group's thorough astonishment. Occupying a vast section of the wall above the dead figure, a fantastic mural captured their attention and disbelief. Once the painting might have been vibrant and striking for its florid nature. Now, though, the colors had faded with the passage of centuries. Streaks of water damage ran in vertical patches through the mural's grand whole. The painting stretched from floor to ceiling, making it the largest work of art any of them, including the well-traveled Tagger and his cat, had ever witnessed. The mural was enough to take the breath from a stone.

But it was the *image* of the huge painting that touched their hearts with amazement, that stirred their wonder with such impractical awe.

The mural depicted a throng of humans—males and females standing brave with children by their side—all attired in garb similar to the dead man's. Despite the painting's faded quality, the grandeur of their clothing was still plainly visible: the crisp cuffs and invisibly wrought seams, the unfamiliar styles and variety of impossible colors (some of which, even in their desiccated state, the group had never before seen the likes). The people stood proud, all facing a single direction. The expressions on the painted faces were joined in a common dedication of something that lurked beyond the mural's edges. Although a brilliant sun blazed in the sky behind the painted crowd, a glorious light source shone from the direction they all stared. A brilliant yellow sun hung in a sky dominated implausibly by a single color: a peacefully pastel blue.

"Where are the sky's colors?" gasped Nico.

Looming strong and majestic behind the crowd's proud figures were tall towers… structures distinctly resembling the towers of the ruins beside Oogolah Lake, except that these towers were not bent with decay and rot. These towers stood whole and unclouded. In unnaturally even rows, they gleamed tan and gray under the painted sun. Banners of incredulous design flew atop these towers, billowing frozen in a breeze whose purity one could almost taste. No dust smudged the sky or the towers. No dirt clung to the people's clothing or stained their cheeks or hands. Regardless of the mural's apparent age, everything contained in the wondrous painting sparkled with a cleanliness unfound in the real world.

Nitch stared at the tableau with shock and a rising humility. *Here* was proof she could not dispute: these tunnels had once been the domain of humankind. The ruins were indeed the cities of her ancestors.

Without comment, the group resumed their descent.

As they started off again, Nivek quietly asked Tagger, "We *are* going to escape this underworld, aren't we?"

The prairieman smiled, "I hope so. Afterburn's dead without us."

19

FINALLY CONVINCED OF THE VERACITY of the fantastic tales which Tagger had told of the *cities*, Nitch who was the one to discover the sewers for the group.

"Look here," she called, directing Tagger to hold aloft their remaining torch. The flames disclosed a network of algae encrusted pipes running along the ceiling. "You thought the sewers were pipes. Could these be them?"

"They're too *small* for us to fit inside," Nico lamented.

Tagger tapped the pipes with his staff. The group noted how the pipes rang with a decidedly unhollow thud. Passing the torch to Nivek, the prairieman strode along the hallway, sounding the pipes with his staff every few meters.

Reaching a juncture where another hallway intersected their path at a perpendicular angle, the group paused to survey their options. Above their heads, the pipes split, running away into the unexplored darkness of all three of the new tunnels.

"Oh, we're lost!" sobbed Nico.

For a moment Tagger walked in a circle around the torch Nivek held. Understanding the man's silent examination, Nitch could detect no waver in the flame. No breeze disturbed its vertical sputtering. Finally, the prairieman turned to face his traveling companions.

"We're going to have to explore each hallway," he decreed.

"We'll need more torches," suggested Nitch.

"Only one new torch," Needer commented. "I can see in the dark."

Tagger inhaled deeply, held the breath, then expelled it slowly through clenched teeth. Taking off the tattered remains of his vest, the man tore a strip of cloth from it. After smearing the material with a grease he produced from a small metal tin in his backpack, he wrapped the cloth around the end of his wooden staff. Then he lit the new torch, touching its tip to the guttering flames of the stick held by Nivek.

"Needer, Nitch and I will each scout one of these hallways," Tagger directed. "Nivek and Nico will remain here."

"Without any light?" wailed Nico.

"If anyone finds anything—or gets into trouble—call out your name loudly," Tagger continued, ignoring the child's worry. "Listen carefully, Nivek. Once you hear a cry, repeat it, shouting down each of the corridors. We will return with haste to aid the original screamer—or investigate their finding."

Nivek nodded his understanding. He handed his torch to his sister.

Tagger, Needer and Nitch departed, striding into separate hallways. Nivek watched the torches dwindle and vanish down the corridors, leaving the boy to half-heartedly attempt to calm his panicking girlfriend in the cloying darkness.

He felt odd as he worded phrases in the dark to soothe her manic trembling. He had always been so confident that Nico's affections for him were honest, but he could no longer convince himself of her sincerity. She had so smoothly shifted her devotion to the prairieman after that monster had attacked them in the ruins above, then switched her allegiance once she had learned that Nivek's secret cave contained fabulous wealth. Now, the boy didn't know what to believe regarding his girlfriend's loyalties. She hugged him close as they huddled together in the dark, but Nivek suspected her affections would shift again once the prairieman returned.

These doubts colored his attempts to calm Nico's fear of the dark with an insincerity of his own, and this disturbed him all the more. Nivek was unfamiliar with feigning emotions. He resented Nico for causing him mental discomfort.

When she began to kiss him in the dark, her hands fumbling at his crotch, he responded by brusquely pushing her away. Such intimacy was no longer a bond between them, and engaging in such pleasures seemed altogether wrong in the face of her flighty allegiances. But his rejection of her advances only prompted her to erupt with more distress, a return to her fearful whining. His only recourse was to hold her close again, trying to soothe her back into a calmer state of mind. Purposefully or unwittingly, Nico had reduced him to emotionally responding only in connection to *her* moods, robbing him of any freedom of thought or personal motives.

With every word of comfort or reassurance that passed his lips, Nivek's feelings for her dwindled.

After half an hour, Needer's voice sounded soft and nearby, "Dead end."

"Nothing?" Nivek asked. He struggled to disengage himself from Nico's needy clutches.

"The pipes all run into a solid wall," revealed the cat. "There were no doors nearby, not that I could open any of them if there had been."

Nico trembled closer to Nivek in the dark.

"Any word from the others?" Needer inquired.

Nivek shook his head, then, remembering the darkness, he answered verbally, "No."

"Then we wait," sighed the cat. Nivek could mentally picture the cat curling up on the floor, resting her twin heads on her front paws.

"We're never going to see the sun again," Nico moaned.

"Of course we are," cooed Nivek, forcing himself to stroke her hair. Worried sweat had plastered her dark spikes to her small head. As she breathed deeply in her panic, Nivek was uncomfortably aware of her breasts pressing against his side. The fact that his loins swelled in response to the sensuous presence of her flesh annoyed him. His young mind was caught in a turmoil between his baser instincts and the dislike he had recently adopted toward the girl. "We can trust Tagger," Nivek assured her. "And my sister too. They'll find these sewers. And then we'll escape these tunnels."

"But—" Nico began to complain.

"Shh!" hissed Needer. "Listen!"

From their right came a noise made small by a great distance. Had Nico continued her moaning, it would have been lost, buried beneath her whiny voice.

"It's your sister," Needer revealed.

"What?" Nivek gasped. "Is she in trouble?"

"She's found a way out," declared the cat. "Call to Tagger—your voices will carry further than either of mine."

Together, the children shouted, Nivek's "Tagger! Come back!" counterpointed by Nico's wordless cries.

Presently, a speck of dim light grew larger as the prairieman dashed toward them from his hallway.

"What? What is it?" he gasped, stumbling up to the huddled children and the alert cat.

"It's Nitch," his feline companion told him. "She's found something."

"Let's go," Tagger started off down the hallway the huntress had taken. Needer followed. After a few meters, the cat paused, turning to call back to the immobile children, "Hey, come on!"

"No no no," moaned Nico. "No more! I want to get out of here!"

"Come on, Nico," Nivek urged, trying to pull her erect. He strained to keep any trace of his annoyance from his voice. "You'll never get out of these tunnels if you stay here." It took a few repeatings for this fact to pierce the girl's childish behavior. Reluctantly, she came to her feet and was led off by Nivek in pursuit of the cat.

Moments before they saw the glitter of Nitch's far-off torch, Needer proclaimed, "I hear water." This announcement added speed to their progress.

As they approached Nitch, she waved her torch in greeting, shouting to them, "Over here!"

Once they reached her, the huntress indicated a round grill set into the wall near the floor. "The pipes continue on ahead, but look at this."

"Running water," Needer observed.

"This must be a way out," Nitch exclaimed. Her eyes were expectant in the torch's flickering light.

Tagger knelt to probe the grill. "If this grating comes loose."

"I tried, but it wouldn't budge for me," offered Nitch. "I thought maybe if we all pulled at it... ?"

Carefully extinguishing the flaming tip of his staff, Tagger set it aside. Then he twined his fingers through the grill's holes and pulled with all his might. His lean arms bulged with sweaty sinews. As he wrenched futilely at the stubborn grating, Needer approached to sniff at the grill.

"Not going to come loose that way," the cat snorted. "Look here, Tagger." She lifted a paw to scratch at a section of the grill's edge.

Leaning to examine what Needer had found, Tagger swore, "Screws!"

"What are *screws*?" Nitch asked.

"We're going to die down here!" moaned Nico.

"Give me your knife," Tagger instructed the huntress. She reluctantly handed it over to the man.

"Hold the light down here so I can see better," he directed. He began to scrape away a crust of rust to reveal a tiny circular depression smaller than a fingertip. Carefully inserting the blade's point, Tagger twisted the knife. After a few seconds of grunting, he halted, withdrawing the knife from the grill. "It's stuck. I don't want to risk breaking the blade."

"You'd better *not* break my knife," snarled Nitch.

"Give me the torch," Tagger directed. He held it down, crushing the flame against the small depression near the edge of the grill. "Okay, who has some water left?"

"I... I do..." whispered Nico. She passed a skin flask to the prairieman.

After holding the fire to the grill for some tense moments, Tagger handed the torch back to Nitch. Then he doused the area with water from the drinking flask. The hot metal hissed.

"Hey!" Nico wailed. "My water! I thought you were thirsty—"

Tagger smacked the small depression a few times with the blunt end of Nitch's knife handle. Then he tried the point again, pushing it in hard and twisting the blade. After a second, a tiny rasp sounded and the knife jerked in his hands.

"You broke it!" complained Nitch.

"No," Needer declared. "Hold on…"

"It came loose," Tagger breathed, re-inserting the blade. "Let me try again." Once more, he pressed the tip of the blade into the tiny depression, exerting himself to twist the knife. This time when the knife jerked in his grasp, it was accompanied by a grunt of success from the prairieman. He set to twisting the knife anew; now the blade turned stubbornly in his hands, gaining rotary ease with each turn. Slowly a thin spindle poked from the grill as if drawn forth by the blade.

When the spindle fell free, Tagger picked it up, handing it to Nitch with a solemn smile. "A screw," he told her. He rose to his feet, stretching his cramped limbs. "Let's see how many more of them there are."

Together, under the light of the torches, they examined the edge of the circular grill. They found seven more such tiny depressions, evenly placed around the grill's circumference.

"We're not going to have enough water to help loosen all seven screws," Tagger muttered.

"What does the water have to do with freeing these screws?" asked Nivek.

Tagger replied, "The heat expands the metal…"

And Nitch finished, "… and the water makes the hot metal contract, loosening the screws."

With a look of new respect for the huntress, the prairieman nodded, "That's right."

"My Paw told me about such things," explained Nitch. "I… I didn't understand him at the time."

"And now you do," Needer commented.

"We need more water if we're going to get the rest of these screws out," Tagger announced solemnly.

"Wait," Nitch pointed out. "There's water on the other side of the grill."

"But how do we get to it?" Nivek asked.

"We could lower the water flask down and fill it," Tagger observed. "But the holes are too small to get a filled flask back through the grating."

"We need to find a way of enlarging one of the holes," suggested Nitch.

"Maybe we can find something around here to chisel the holes bigger," Nivek offered. He gestured around the dark hallway, "In one of these rooms?"

"It's worth a try," sighed Tagger. Carefully, he explained that they needed to find a metal rod at least as long as their forearms. "If it has a pointed end, all the better."

The group separated, to search for such an object. Several of the doors were frozen shut; no amount of pulling or kicking would open them. This cut down on the group's search options. They were forced to range further down the corridor until they found an open door.

Nico's worried whining was beginning to annoy the others when Tagger shouted, "Here!" They joined him to enter through the doorway he had opened.

The room beyond was small. The majority of its space was occupied by a great machine that rose above their heads. The thing was shaped like a great box with rounded ends. Many pipes ran from its upper regions to disappear into the close walls. The only objects that cluttered the room were uselessly soft and bewildering to describe.

"Aha!" Tagger cried from the far side of the huge machine. As the rest crowded around to join him, they watched as he pulled an L-shaped crank from the side of the metal bulk. It came free with little struggle. "This will do nicely," he declared, holding the metal crank aloft. Although the rest of the machine was coated with a moist slime, the crank possessed no such taint or discoloration. It shone with a dull black gleam, while the rest of the metal in the small chamber was discolored by a grotty brown.

Returning to the grill, the group watched with hopeful expectation as Tagger wrestled the smaller end of the crank into one of the grating's holes. After wriggling it in, he wedged the lever firmly in the hole. Then he gripped the crank with both hands and applied his full weight to a downward thrust.

The grill groaned mightily in the corridor's stagnant air. As Tagger pushed harder on the sturdy lever, flecks of reddish brown rust crumbled from the grill's bars to flutter down to pepper the prairieman's sweaty arms. The groan grew louder like the rumble of some distant monster.

When it happened, the explosion of ancient metal was a blunt shock to the anticipatory group. A section of the grating nearly a meter in diameter ripped free from the face of the grill. It tore loose with a sudden *snap* that sent Tagger plummeting clumsily to the floor. The others leapt back from the abrupt release, gasps escaping their surprised lips. Perhaps expecting some monster to spring from the new hole, Nico turned and fled into the darkness, screaming her shrill and mindless cry.

"Are you okay?" Nitch asked, reaching down to touch Tagger's hunched shoulders. The bloodstains that covered his back from their struggle with the Quiet Men ran in rivulets down his spine, diluted by the sweat of his exertions.

The man slumped aside with a startled expression frozen on his face. He brought his arm up to wipe the sweat from his face, ending up transferring a percentage of rust flecks to his damp brow. He glanced abstractly at a long bloody gash his tumble had left along his upper arm. "Yeah," he huffed. "I think so… What happened?"

"The grating broke," Nivek told him.

"Somebody better go get the whiner," sighed Needer, an edge of exasperation ringing in her soft remark. "Before she gets lost or hurt… unless we finally want to be rid of her?"

"I'll go," Nivek unwillingly volunteered. Taking the torch, he ran after the girl. Before the boy left, Tagger reignited the tip of his wooden staff so the remaining group had light.

"Time and moisture must've fatigued the metal," Needer told Tagger. "You popped a hole in the grill."

"Much bigger than I'd intended," he admitted, surveying the damage he'd achieved.

"Don't complain." The cat cocked her left head. "*We're* not complaining. Getting through it will be much easier now."

"Hungry," the right head announced.

Nitch helped the prairieman to his feet. Together they peered through the torn hole, aided by the glow thrown off by the prairieman's burning staff.

The grill opened onto a tunnel whose walls were slimed with centuries of algae and scum. A stream of brackish water coursed through the large pipe, occupying roughly the bottom third of the ribbed cylinder. The underwater stream ran away into the darkness beyond the illumination given off by their torch.

"A sewer?" inquired Nitch.

"Looks like it," Tagger admitted. "I've never actually seen one before."

She gave him a dirty look, then turned her attention to Nivek who was returning with a hysterical Nico in tow. The child struggled frantically against Nivek's grip, wailing and cursing him. "You're going to get us all killed!"

Striding over to Nico, Nitch raised her hand to strike the girl.

"No," Tagger spoke sharply. When the huntress glared back at him, he told her softly, "She's just scared. If you hit her, she's liable to go catatonic on us. We can't afford to have to carry her out of here."

"We have to do *something*," insisted Nivek as he struggled with difficulty to keep his hold on the thrashing girl. "If I let her go, she's just going to run off again."

Tagger faced Nitch, pointing to her silver necklace. "Try to bribe her with that."

Scowling, Nitch took off the necklace, holding the shiny jewelry before Nico's terror widened eyes, "Look, Nico. Pretty. You've always liked it, right?"

The child's struggling subsided, her attention focused on the necklace. "Yes…"

"You can have it," Nitch offered. Tagger stopped her from giving the jewelry to the child. He added, "*After* we get out of here."

"I want it," moaned Nico.

"Later," Tagger grated. "First, we're going to climb down into this sewer pipe and get out of this nasty place. You want to do that, don't you?"

"Of course you do, right?" urged Nivek.

Begrudgingly, Nico agreed, her eyes never leaving the necklace. The muddy brown stones set in its silver lattice glittered softly in the torchlight. The twinkles reflected in the child's greedy stare.

Without waiting for another of Nico's wild mood-swings, Nivek crawled through the hole in the grill. Then Tagger passed Nico through to the boy; together they lowered the girl down into the sewer's filthy waters. She complained that the water was cold.

Leaping to balance on the edge of the torn metal grating, Needer paused, surveying the waters with a feline distaste.

Tagger turned to look at Nitch, ready to help her through the hole. The huntress handed the necklace to him with a scowl, "You *owe* me."

"Ha!" laughed Needer. "Have you got *that* backwards." With a cry of "Look out below!" the cat disappeared through the hole, landing squarely on Nivek's shoulders.

When Tagger made to assist Nitch through the jagged opening in the grating, she batted aside his offer. The huntress crawled through the hole unaided. He followed her after carefully passing down the torch; he retained possession of his still-lit staff.

The stream gurgled slightly as it surged around their legs. With Tagger in the lead, the group proceeded along the tunnel.

Needer hopped from Nivek's shoulders to ride on Nitch's backpack. "I hate water," she told the huntress.

"Go ride on your master," Nitch made to brush the cat from her perch.

Digging in with claws, the cat hissed, "He's *not* my master. Anyway, we need to talk." The pair dropped back to bring up the rear, trailing a bit behind so their conversation would remain private.

"He owes me," Nitch growled.

"For what? A stupid bauble that silenced the brat's whining?" The cat snorted with both pairs of nostrils, "You have your priorities all wrong, girl."

"He's an insufferable manipulator."

"He gets things done. He's getting us all out of here. I couldn't have gotten us this far; could you have done any better?"

Nitch mumbled without recognizable syllables.

"*Your* brother got us into this mess," chided Needer. "*My* human is getting us out. Who owes who, huh?"

"It was Tagger who started all this, asking to see Nivek's radio cavern."

"We all tried to talk Nivek out of going into the ruins, to wait until morning. Your attempts were as useless as Tagger's."

They were silent for a few moments, wading along through the pipe's stream.

"All in the past now," quipped the cat. "Can't change the past, remember? If we're lucky, we'll all get out of here alive and head straight for Afterburn."

"What *is* his connection with the radio station?"

"I think I'll leave that for *him* to tell you. Give you two something to talk civilly about. It's going to be a long hard journey."

"That's assuming I'm going to be coming along," Nitch retorted sharply.

"Oh, you're coming along," chuckled the cat. "How else do you expect him to pay you back?"

"Hungry," her right head insisted, annoyed at everyone's lack of concern.

20

AFTER WADING THROUGH UGLY WATER for hours, the group finally came upon the termination of the sewer pipe. Jutting out from an embankment of hard rock, the stream emptied into Oogolah Lake. Above them, the sun was already nearing zenith in the colorful sky. They could see the ruins far to their right, the distant towers standing stark and ominous even in the daylight.

Climbing the rockface, Tagger lowered a rope to hoist the rest of the group to more stable footing. Rejecting this help, Nitch dove into the lake and swam around to where the shoreline afforded an easier exit.

They regrouped at the edge of a stand of thick woods. Already, Nico proudly wore her new necklace. Nivek sat observing her glee with mixed emotions.

The boy was deeply disturbed by the way his relationship with Nico had changed during their nocturnal adventure in the ruins' underground realm. He had not been pleased when his girlfriend had begun flirting with the older prairieman. When she had re-bestowed her affections on Nivek after learning of his immanent wealth, the boy had begun to suspect her motives. And now, finally freed from the deadly underworld beneath the ruins, the girl was again eyeing Tagger with looks that previously had been reserved only for Nivek.

The two children had been a couple for several months before the Quiet Men had slain the rest of their Tribe. Nivek had been the envy of many of the Tribe's buff lads. Nico's beauty and the way she flaunted it had made her a prize to be coveted. But when scuffles had broken out with other boys over her affections, Nico had made it clear to all that Nivek was her chosen boyfriend. Nivek was the only one with whom she would spend time, he was the *only* one to receive her special attention. This decision had not made Nivek a popular member of the Tribe's adolescent population, but—considering the intimacies that accompanied her favor—he really hadn't cared in the least what his fellows thought of him.

Now all that had changed. Nico's attentions had shifted to Tagger. How could Nivek hope to compete with the prairieman's maturity, his strength, the fact that he had saved them all from the ruins? Nivek was but a boy, he had little to offer Nico that she had not already tasted.

But then—the events of their subterranean night had brought changes to Nivek too. Before last night, he had been a boy with a crude crystal radio set—now he was an individual who, according to Tagger, might prove to be the salvation of Afterburn Radio! Now, Nivek was going to visit Afterburn and meet his hero, Fever Smith. Now, Nivek was going to be rewarded with the fulfillment of his wildest dreams. In light of these developments, Nico's affections seemed trite and unimportant. If it came to a choice, would he fight for the girl's affections if it meant losing the achievement of his most fervent desires?

The choice was not even worth consideration, he realized. How could the attention of a flighty child be equated with becoming a DJ for Afterburn? Anyway, the choice had been made—by Nico. Nivek knew he had right to contest her wishes, but considering how easily her loyalties seemed to shift, he no longer had any desire to be their focus, permanently or temporarily.

Sitting back, Nivek contemplated the kaleidoscopic sky. His mind was a flurry of the sonic possibilities that came with a future working for Afterburn Radio.

Meanwhile, Nico Meefe caressed her new toy with fingers unstained by the night's horrors. The luster of silver and gem was liquid beneath her touch.

All her life, the things she had set her sights upon had become hers. Affection, protection, jewelry—they were all the same to Nico. Things coveted, things bestowed. All she had to do was *want*, and others promptly fulfilled her desires.

The love of her father (*No, he* isn't *dead*—she denied that memory!) had won her the attention of the entire Tribe. Men had wanted to possess her, women had longed to mimic her, even strangers who had never met her had chased her in their midnight dreams. Pretty little Nico, the pride of the Oogolah Tribe. Cherished little Nico, the object of all desires. Please little Nico and your hearts would soar.

The devotion of Nivek Palma had shown her the true power she wielded. By laying with a chosen one, the fires of all the rest had risen, burning brilliant and bright, gorged on the green-eyed demon of jealousy. By pretending to belong to Nivek, all the rest of the Tribe's youth had wanted little Nico all the more. By basking in the attention of one boy, she had become the center of *everyone's* desires.

She eyed the prairieman as he sat rooting through his backpack. This man, she mused, had saved her from the tentacles of the monster of the mists. Later, in the dank depths of the ruins' underworld, brave Tagger had once more rescued her—from the terrible evil caves full of confusing secrets, from Nivek's juvenile affection, from the indifference exhibited by the rest of the group, from the taunts of that twin-headed beast, from the raised hand of Nitch—whom Nico had once sought to emulate.

Ha! As if Nitch's older wiles or mature beauty or huntress cunning could prove more powerful than the power Nico held. No man—nor woman—had ever gazed upon Nitch with a fraction of the desire Nico instilled in people. The Tribe had (No—*did*, for the Tribe was no more gone than her loving father!) valued Nitch for her hunting skills, her prowess with spear and blade and skulk. But *none* had ever *loved* the huntress with the passion that swam in everyone's eyes as they looked upon fair little Nico. She did not need Nitch's lithe limbs or her fuller breasts or her long flaxen hair to capture the souls of others. Their adoration for Nico was greater than the respect the Tribe lavished upon the huntress. *Nico's* power was stronger by far.

For hadn't the fates seen fit to take from Nitch and give to Nico this lovely necklace? Hadn't her power guided the handsome prairieman to convince the huntress to relinquish her jewelry so he could offer Nico this gift of silver wrapped in his undying affection? He loved her, truly and wholly, as all men did. He had led *her* out of the dreaded darkness beneath the ruins—the fact that Nivek and Nitch and that awful cat had tagged along on their miraculous journey was annoying, but unimportant in the grand scheme. The ultimate win would belong to Nico. Tagger would care for *her* now, forgetting these others for the trivial distractions they were. He would forsake his wandering life, renounce his allegiances to Afterburn Radio; he would remain at her side—her protector and lover.

She fondled her necklace, lost in the significance the gift really portended. Her mind was brimming with exciting ways her new lover could prove himself to her.

Nitch watched the child finger the jewelry that had hung around the huntress' neck for more years than she could recall. It was only a bauble, she knew, but she feared losing the memories it held for her now that it no longer circled beneath her chin.

A gift it had been, presented to her by the man who had taught her the skills that made her special. Galen, the Tribe's master huntsman, he who had slain prairie wolves and mutants by the score during his youth. Galen, who had not scoffed when a young girl child had voiced the desire to master the hunt. Galen, who had tutored her in the ways of beast and sky and earth. Galen, who had given her the fabulous necklace the day she had graduated into the ranks of the Tribe's hunters. Galen, who had taught her of physical love with his weathered fingers and coarse but tender lips. Galen, who had been murdered by the Quiet Men... while Nitch had been away dancing atop the ruins.

The entire Tribe had been wiped out by the dark-clad silent ones: her family, her friends, her fellow hunters, her precious Galen. If Nitch hadn't been seduced away by Afterburn's sinuous music, the Tribe might still exist. Surely her presence would have turned the tide, certainly her killing skill could have prevented the deaths of so many.

Many of the Quiet Men had already paid for their horrible crime, feeling the lethal sting of her blade and spear. But their deaths didn't still the agony that burned in Nitch's breast. Their blood couldn't wash away the guilt she felt. Their corpses wouldn't bring back her slain loved ones.

No Quiet Man's death could rewrite the past. The mutant cat was right: nothing could change the past. And very little done by any single person could alter the future. The Quiet Men would continue to scurry and kill and spread their terrible silence across the land, no matter how much of their blood Nitch spilled.

The Quiet Men were responsible for the genocide of her Tribe, but they were not the ones who had lured Nitch from the chance of saving her Tribe. *That* blame belonged to Afterburn Radio. If Afterburn's music hadn't mesmerized her, she would have been there to warn the Tribe, to stop the murders, to prevent the destruction of her heritage.

It was *Afterburn* who deserved to pay for Nitch's losses.

Glancing at Tagger as he pulled his evil radio from his backpack, she realized with a sudden clarity the subtle destiny that had guided her to stumble upon the prairieman's dirt-covered hut in the southern valleys. Through this man, she might yet avenge her Tribe. This man who sought to bring word to Afterburn of Nivek's fabulous radio cavern and the treasures it contained—he would lead her directly to the core of those to blame, releasing her vengeance among them like a holy retribution. Blood for blood. The Quiet Men had silenced her people, and she would silence the radio station that had prevented her from saving her family.

She watched the prairieman worry over his devices, certain in the knowledge that he would lead her to the end of her suffering. Afterburn's broadcasting days were numbered.

"Dammit!" Tagger swore.

From her perch nearby, Needer looked up at the man. "What's the matter?"

"The radio won't work," Tagger muttered. He turned the device over, examining it with a frown. "I can't activate the transmitter."

The Quiet Men

"Bad news."

"I can't figure out what's wrong with it," grumbled the prairieman. He flicked a switch and frowned anew. "The receiver's not working either."

"What's the problem?" Nivek asked, coming over to peer at the impressive radio in the man's hands. His gaze sparkled with awestruck wonder.

"How should I know?" Tagger replied testily. "I'm no technician."

"How could it have broken?" inquired Needer. Leaning in, she sniffed at the device in Tagger's lap.

"It must've gotten damaged during the fight with the Quiet Men." Tagger fingered a telltale scrape along the radio's side. Lifting his backpack, he discovered a tear in its material that corresponded with where the radio had been stored. "Dammit…"

"At least we still have *my* radio," the boy reminded them. He took it out, turning it on. Music played behind a hiss of static. "It needs to be higher up, though, to get a clearer signal. But at least we know it still works."

"Great," sighed Tagger. "Of course, *your* radio doesn't broadcast, does it? So, we're still stuck."

"Stuck?" the boy asked. His crystal radio lay loosely in his hands, softly releasing cheerful melodies.

"We can't signal Afterburn and tell them about the discovery we've made," remonstrated Needer. "About your room full of equipment under the ruins."

"Oh…"

"We're going to have go there to tell Dr Muffin about it," Tagger muttered.

"But—we were going there anywhere, right?" the boy asked in worried tones. His eyes creased with anxiety. "You promised…"

"Breaking your word already?" Nitch commented tersely from her seat on the other side of the clearing.

"No," Tagger told them. "I wanted to alert the station first, that's all." With dissatisfaction, he replaced his broken radio in the backpack. "They'll just have to wait until we get there to find out."

"Well, let's get moving then." Nivek switched his radio off and stowed it away in his own satchel.

"Wait," Nitch spoke up. She approached to stand over the prairieman seated on the ground.

"Huh?" grunted Nivek. "But—shouldn't we get out of here fast? What if there are still more Quiet Men about?"

"They're not going to accept their losses lightly," the cat agreed.

"Nivek's right," admitted Tagger. "We should put some more distance between us and this area."

He attempted to rise wearily to his feet, but Nitch shoved him back on his ass. "Your wounds need tending first."

"I'll survive," the man shrugged.

"Believe me, Tagger. *Your* survival is quite secondary to my concern." Nitch crouched beside him, probing his upper arm. There was a point where one of the cuts from the battle with the Quiet Men intersected with the scrape the man had received when the section of grating had broken free. When she poked it, the cut revealed itself to be quite deep. Blood flowed from the wound and ran down his arm, following the lines of other minor cuts. "If we *do* run into any trouble, we'll need you at full strength. *I'm* not going to do *all* the fighting, y'know."

"She has a point," agreed Needer.

"*I'll* take care of him," Nico interrupted suddenly. She stood over Nitch and Tagger, glaring at the huntress with intense territoriality.

"Oh, go away, Nico," muttered Nitch.

"No! I told you—I'll do it," the girl growled.

"And you know how to dress a wound like this?" snarled Nitch. With a vicious twist, she pried apart the edges of Tagger's severed flesh, displaying torn muscle and exposed bone. She leaned back slightly, so the girl could see the blood that pumped from the torn flesh.

"Ow!" Tagger complained.

With a whimpering gurgle, Nico covered her astonished mouth, turning away to stifle her vomit.

"Didn't think so," Nitch snorted. She turned her attention back to the wound.

"That wasn't necessary," grumbled Tagger.

"Would you rather have me or *her* tend to this?" Nitch asked, pausing to rock back on her heels..

"Okay, okay," acquiesced Tagger. "Just try and be a little less brutal about it."

"Big strong prairieman," the huntress chuckled without humor. She began washing the cut with some water.

"Ow!"

Applying salves from pouches at her belt, Nitch tended to the wound. Although she worked more gently now, carefully wrapping his arm with a clean strip of cloth torn from the man's sleeproll, her face still wore an unhappy frown.

Needer could not understand Nitch's displeasure. They had all been saved from the vicious darkness beneath the ruins. Each of them (well, with the exception of that whining child) had contributed to that rescue—but none so decidedly as Tagger's crisp actions and certain guidance. Yet still the huntress treated the prairieman with a puissant degree of contempt.

These humans, the cat ruminated. They were such confused enigmas, all twisted up in their heads by over-rationalization and self-importance. They couldn't see the true beauty of the union of each life, hand in hand in paw, helping each other to survive the day and share warmth to ward off the night. These humans were so ignorant of the grand foodchain that bound all life to each other, from the smallest microbe to the mightiest giant.

The smallest were fodder for the next biggest, and so on up the evolutionary ladder, culminating with these arrogant humans who lorded so blindly over the entire process. They spoiled the natural order by preying upon each other, killing their own kind over pointless beliefs. They violated the master order of things with their egotism.

They had learned nothing from the Doom that had slapped their race into the mud. All life had suffered from the Doom, but these humans had benefited naught, wasting all the deaths and change that had stemmed from the terrible disaster that lurked in Needer's mind as only a vague racial memory. They still killed each other, they still envied each other, they still strove to manipulate nature—and all for hollow reasons.

Of all the humans Needer had known, only Tagger had risen above such petty squabbles to perceive the lines of power that inexorably bound all life. Tagger accepted Needer as an equal. Tagger viewed Afterburn as his race's deliverance from their innate primitive savagery. Tagger even saw no reason to punish the noisy brat for her tantrums. Tagger swore fealty to an overwhelming tolerance of all things. Tagger saw how each piece fit perfectly into the great puzzle that comprised existence.

Tagger's tolerance went far beyond any that Needer could remember, even the stoic patience of her own feline species. All things were sufficient in Tagger's eyes as he struggled to make it to the next day alive and fed.

Motivated by the deep respect Needer felt for the prairieman, the cat sincerely thanked Nitch for her ministering. While her left brain echoed the man's gratitude, her right brain whined: *Hungry!*

Yes, yes, she told herself. *We'll find something for our belly en route.*

Tagger led the group west, deeper into the woods.

21

"**Heyo, folks!** This is Fever Smith, and you're listening to Afterburn Radio, the voice of truth with a backbeat."

Slumped in her arcade seat, Psycho dozed. Her headphones rode around her neck as her meager chest rose and fell with the deep slow breaths of sleep.

"Remember now," continued the taped voice, "we're still illegal in twelve of the twenty-seven Districts, so keepelway gargle—"

Psycho came awake with a jolt. It took only a second for her to notice the jammed tape reel and leap to cut its power.

Grabbing the dangling microphone, she activated it and sent her voice broadcasting out, "Heyo, folks! This flash is so hot, it can't wait, Fever. This is Psycho Jones with an Afterburn Radio bulletin.

"Word is just in—Captain Jagg is back! Yes, remember the madman who sailed off to discover new worlds? Well, he's back! And a new world is exactly what he found across the Lantic Ocean."

As she spoke, Psycho rummaged quickly through a shelf of compact discs. She finally settled on one labeled "Hard Rock" and popped the disc into a play slot.

"Stay tuned for more details," she announced, "right after this music…"

With a windy sigh, she collapsed back into the cupped depths of her arcade chair. Music with a thunderous rhythm crashed from her headphones.

"That was quick thinking," came Dr Muffin's voice from the door of the broadcast booth.

"I can't keep this up, Dr Muffin." Psycho turned the chair so that she faced the robot's tall figure.

"It's very old equipment, Psycho," the robot replied.

"I'm serious," she frowned. "That's the last tape I'm playing on that console."

Dr Muffin stood in the doorway with no response.

"We're just going to have to get by without Fever Smith for a while," she declared. "Until you fix this console."

"That… could be longer than you think," sighed the robot.

"We simply have no other choice," she told him. "Okay, we *do* have another choice: I go back to playing Smithie's tapes and we let the console destroy them all one by one. Then Fever'll be off the air for good."

"I'll see what I can do, Psycho," Dr Muffin sighed.

After a moment's silence, broken only by a raucous guitar solo spilling from her headphones, Psycho moaned, "When's Smithie coming back?"

Dr Muffin sighed again, then replied, "I don't know, Psycho."

"He *is* coming back, isn't he?"

"You need some rest." The robot held out a hand, urging her to rise from the chair. "I can pop in another CD after this one has played." He guided the weary girl out of the booth, leading her down the corridor to her room.

"I can't take much more of these twenty-four hour shifts."

"You can't quit now, Psycho. We have to keep Afterburn going. We have a responsibility to our audience."

"I just can't manage it alone," she despaired.

"But… you're not alone, Psycho. I'm here too."

"I need Smithie, Dr Muffin. I need help from a human being. There are some things that a robot… can't do…"

Oh, the robot responded. Even his positronic brain could identify the meaning in her strained voice.

"You get some sleep," he told the exhausted DJ. "I'll see what I can do with the console."

22

THE TALL QUIET MAN had labored long and hard to cast off the role of a simple warrior of silence to become the band's self-styled priest. His efforts had won him the position of leader.

Leader of a group that no longer existed. He was now their sole survivor.

This morning he sat alone atop a stony protrusion that leaned out above the shoreline of Oogolah Lake. He had spent the night sitting crosslegged, regarding the lake's dark waters. Long and deep had he mulled over the unsettling events he had witnessed last night in the ruins.

For one: the sea monster's corpse, slimy with its own secretions and sticky with its spilled blood. Spurning the noisy ways of men, the bands of Quiet Men were no stranger to spending their nights hiding in ruins such as the ones that stood beside Oogolah Lake. The tall man's band, in fact, had encountered such creatures numerous times in the far north; but never before had he or any of his band seen a *dead one*. He had not known the beasts could be killed.

For another: the pair of loud ones he had watched slay the members of his band. After following the group far beneath the ruins, the Quiet Men had been ambushed and slaughtered—by two people! It was unthinkable, that two savages could kill so many believers in a single stand. And one of them a girl! It had been her, by her own boasting admission, who had claimed the deaths of the Quiet Men back in the Tribe's farmlands. She had been so young, so lethal—so loud! The tall survivor planned a special silencing for her. And the man…

The man was another surprise unto himself. The tall man had never thought he'd see that one again; he so longed to forget his life before the day he had chosen to worship silence. This man called himself *Tagger* now, but the tall man recognized him, and knew him for what he really was: an unholy agent of the sinful Afterburn radio station.

All these thoughts, and the swelling need to see the two killers silenced for their loud crimes, had occupied only a portion of the tall man's quiet meditations beside the lake. Contemplation of the dark Afterburn had dominated the majority of his nocturnal vigil.

Afterburn!

The wicked voice of radio, spewing forth and tainting the air with loathsome music.

If sound was evil (as every Quiet Man knew deep in their soul), then *music* was an atrocity, an abomination far worse than vile speech. Where speech hid behind the false justification of communication, music was sound for the sake of just making noise. It was a conscious affront to the sanctity of pure silence, created only to obliterate the sacred quiet.

Silence was not just golden—it was necessary for mankind to communicate with God. Only in a world of utter noiselessness could man attract the attention of a supreme deity. Sounds distracted not only man, they distracted God too. All it took was one fool to make noise somewhere in the world and God would lose interest in thge trult devout, dooming the souls of every faithful Quiet Man or even those who secretly believed in the true silence. One man's sin would doom the entire race!

Was it any surprise that the Quiet Men silenced everyone they encountered? The fate of their souls—indeed, the collective souls of an entire species—were at stake, precariously teetering at the mercy of one fool's ignorant utterances.

And Afterburn—they sinned more terribly, inspiring men to hum and tap their feet. They filled the air with wretched music. Their nefarious broadcasts never ceased.

It was while sitting atop this rock that the tall survivor realized that the time had come to silence Afterburn.

A few hours after dawn, the tall priest descended from the rock and headed west with a mission.

It took him two days to find another band of Quiet Men, following them by the trail of silenced villages they left in their wake along the fringes of the flatlands.

Finally coming upon them, he displayed his sacred knife and sewing tools, proving not only that was a true believer, but a high-ranking member of the faithful. Conferring in fingertalk with the band's own priest, he explained what had befallen his fellows and the vengeance that he planned. So impressed was the man that he immediately relinquished control of his band to the tall survivor to aid the holy quest. He introduced the band to their new priest, naming him Magog. He revealed to the band the holy mission that Magog had proposed. He explained to the band how they would find these killers of the faithful and trail them back to the blasphemous radio station. He regaled the band with magnificent promises of the glory they would experience in silencing the obscene voice of Afterburn. (In the right hands, fingertalk could be quite a prolific means of communication.)

Trembling with holy purpose, the band of Quiet Men marched off with Magog striding at the head of their dark parade.

23

AFTER YEARS AND YEARS of being a smalltime yesman, Nanner Gristle was finally *somebody*. So why did he still feel like mud on the heel of some novice Church Policeman?

He wore the face of a lord now, the visage of Premier Vassal. He ruled the greatest, most powerful District in all of Ericaland. So why did he feel like the butt of some private joke?

Sitting back on his throne in the great hall of a monstrous castle, the biggest in all of Chico, Nanner surveyed his subjects and was overcome by their lack of respect for him.

The hall was vast, supported by twin rows of mighty columns that reared up into the shadows of a lofty ceiling. Glorious tapestries covered the stone walls with their intricate patterns and inspiring depictions of the legendary accomplishments of his predecessors. Standing strong in the shadows at the base of these columns, ranks of armored guards glittered without motion, holding aloft banners each bearing the Premier's totem. Although their faces were hidden by the faceplates of their grandly embossed helmets, Nanner knew the guards each wore expressions of stern devotion and lethal but honorable piety. It was not their secret smirks that tormented Nanner… his guards were careful to reserve their insulting comments for a later time, far beyond the all-hearing walls of the royal castle.

It was the loyalty of the High Priest that the new Premier doubted.

"Why have we not yet destroyed Afterburn Radio?" Premier Vassal demanded of the High Priest who stood before him in the great hall.

Despite his many years, the High Priest stood unstooped in his resplendent robes. His hard eyes, buried in the numerous creases and wrinkles of age and responsibility, stared with passive defiance at the new Premier. Unflinching and without fear, he had stood thusly before many other Premiers and knew he would stand before many more after this new Vassal was dust and buried. Premiers came and went, but the Council endured the rigors of time and decay.

"Their destruction is under investigation," the High Priest replied, his voice neutral before the intense ire of his lord.

"I do not want investigation!" roared Nanner with Vassal's lips. "I want their *destruction!*"

"As do we all, Lord Premier," nodded the High Priest.

"I want them to stop talking about me!" the Premier shouted, imagining that his voice caused the very walls to tremble. "I want an end to their *lies!*"

"As do we all, Lord," the High Priest repeated.

"I want their spies found!" cried the Premier. "Seek them out and silence their evil tongues!"

"The matter is under investigation, Lord Vassal," the High Priest told him.

Why was the wretched old man playing with him? Nanner wondered. Why was he mouthing platitudes yet offering no word of progress? This was the man who had elevated Nanner from a lowly yesman to become the ruler of the Mob. Through the grace of this old man, Nanner had become the most powerful man in all of Ericaland. Why was he ignoring orders? Why was he not crushing the lying voice of Afterburn?

Nanner longed to demand the answers to these questions, but knew better than to utter such things in the presence of simple guards. Such secrets were restricted to private conference rooms high in the castle's towers. But the High Priest had refused to meet with him in confidence, choosing this great hall instead for this officious meeting.

There were intrigues afoot, Nanner suspected. Grand intrigues that threatened his rule—and after only a week of Nanner becoming Vassal. As if he weren't already plagued by Afterburn's broadcasts, decrying him as a false Premier, now he had to worry about plots within the castle walls. Plots he did not comprehend, but recognized all the same.

"I do not want to hear about investigations!" raged the Premier. "I want to hear about results!"

"As do we all, Lord," the High Priest agreed with an unvarying tone.

24

THE WRATH OF THE FLATLANDS was much more awesome than Nitch had expected.

The unmerciful wasteland stretched forever, a panorama of cracked soil and powdered fields charred by the glare of a sun turned torturous. Little grew on these arid plains; the prairie's scrub grass was withered and brittle beneath their feet. After the first two days, even the packs of wolves had vanished, rejecting the unfriendly climate.

Before the group had ventured far from the forest, Tagger had made them pause to rest, gather food and water, and weave protective garments against the terrible heat he promised they would encounter ahead of them. Dubious of such needs, Nivek and Nico nevertheless had produced ponchos and wide hats for them all from the wide leaves and unthreaded vines the woods had to offer. Tagger and Nitch had hunted many beasts, drying and salting their meat until each member of the group was burdened by a personal larder. Needer had searched out a spring, and with Nitch's help had filled every skin with the precious water.

The group that entered the vicious flatlands staggered under the weight of their supplies. Nico's complaints were as numerous as the insults Needer bestowed upon the girl.

The night before they began their crossing of the plains, Tagger had enlisted the aid of Nivek in a close examination of the broken radio set. The prairieman had opened the chassis, revealing to the boy a tangled interior of circuits and wires. Tagger had hoped the things Nivek had learned from reading what he could of the books in his secret radio cavern might grant the boy some understanding of the radio's workings. And his suspicions had been correct, for the boy had quickly located the problem that had silenced the radio's voice and ears. Unfortunately, recognition of the problem brought them no closer to repairing the damage. A crucial circuitboard had been cracked—fixing it was beyond their capabilities. Although the discovery bolstered the confidence of the boy and reassured the prairieman that his assessment of Nivek's worth to Afterburn had been justified, it crushed any hope Tagger had harbored about alerting the radio station of their coming.

The courage in his squared shoulders as Tagger strode out onto the plains was false, worn mainly for the benefit of the others in the group. His mind fretted over the dangers he was leading them toward: the heat, the landscape, the monsters, the vigorous exertions they would face.

Only Needer noticed Tagger's inner turmoil, but then the cat had traveled with the man for many years. She was sensitive to his moods and body language. To help distract the rest of the group from the prairieman's uncertainty, the cat attempted to engage each person in word games. When this failed to interest any but Nitch, Needer switched to prompting the three youths to talk about themselves. Although this ruse held no appeal for Nitch, it kept Nivek and Nico occupied.

Nivek was willing to talk for hours about his love of Afterburn Radio, his fascination for music, his worship of Fever Smith. More so, hisyouthful exuberance showed a sincere interest in how radio worked. The boy was entranced by the theory, application and workings of this miracle, which Needer explained to him was called *electronics*. For all the cat had learned over years of serving Afterburn with Tagger, the boy displayed a far superior knowledge of the general subject.

Nico was even more eager to chatter on endlessly, but the topics she chose frequently strained the cat's tolerance for self-absorption. Nico was the center of her world, and from the notions she exhibited, she earnest believed she was also the center of everyone else's universe. Keeping Nico happy and amused was tantamount in this universe. Distressing Nico was the absolutely greatest crime, and this foolish journey into the flatlands annoyed her immensely. She revealed to the cat that the sole reason she had accompanied them was to be with Tagger, who, she informed the cat, worshipped Nico more than anything in the world. Needer found it exceedingly difficult to humor the child's delusions.

Nitch, though, was more interested in Needer's life story. The huntress refused to be baited into revealing much about herself or her motives. Their conversations would often degenerate into word games as the cat and the girl avoided divulging any insight into their own lives. Their verbal duels were an unexpected turnabout compared to the kinship of hunters the two had begun to share the night before, beneath the city's ruins. Something had changed within the girl, hardening her against Tagger and even against Afterburn Radio, for Nivek had made it quite plain that his sister had enjoyed the radio station's music with a wild abandon prior to the slaughter of their Tribe. Needer couldn't understand the huntress' change of heart. She longed to comprehend Nitch's displeasure, hoping that there was some way of transforming it back into the affinity cat and girl had previously enjoyed.

Through all of this, Tagger walked on, oblivious to the moods that were mutating around him. His attention would emerge from introspection and private recrimination only to signal rest stops, meals and the hunt for secure places in which they could rest during the day's most scorching hours. He remained unaware of Nico's delusions, Nivek's eager tension, and Nitch's surly attitude.

He led them with expert guidance, but was blind to the changes that were transpiring among those he shepherded.

25

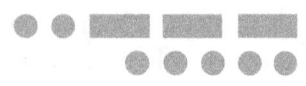

ONE DAY, ONLY HOURS AFTER the rising of the sun, the group came upon a stranger in this callous wilderness.

What had at first appeared to be a curious rock formation from a distance became with the passage of time the figure of a man. Seated on the ground amid dirt so hot it had erupted in a lattice of puckering small cracks, the stranger was dressed in a long robe of many vibrant colors. This robe spread out in a circle about the stranger's frame. An extremely tall domed hat with an uncommonly wide brim sat on the man's bearded head. What could be seen of the man's face was burned by the sun and blistered by the wind. His eyes were hidden in deep dark pits, further obscured by the hat's tremendous shadow. His hands were concealed beneath the draping folds of his wildly chromatic robe.

Resting in the lap of the stranger's colorful robe was a crude crystal radio device that appeared as sunburned as the man's flesh. Drifting from the radio set in barely audible tones was the soft voice of Afterburn's music.

"It's a Sitter," Needer informed the three children.

"What's a Sitter?" asked Nico.

"It's a holy man," Nitch scowled, disdaining the stranger and the girl's ignorance with equal reproach.

"What's a holy man?"

"You mutehead," spat the huntress.

"Tagger!" the girl whined. "Nitch is being *mean* to me!"

The prairieman remained unaware of the child's lament. He stood a meter from the outermost edge of the hem of the stranger's spread robe and silently stared long and hard at the holy man. In the shadow of the stranger's hat, it was impossible to tell whether the man returned Tagger's regard—or even noticed him there.

Finally breaking the tension, Needer scampered across the kaleidoscopic spread robe and hopped up into the holy man's lap. After a minute, a pair of withered brown hands extruded from unseen folds in the garment to stroke the cat behind her twin heads.

Needer's right head purred, "Pet me, pet me, pet me…"

"Hello, kitty cat," the Sitter spoke with a tiny voice.

"My name is Needer," the cat informed him, rubbing her heads against the holy man's knee.

Tilting back his head ever so slightly, the holy man's eyes twinkled at Tagger. "She is wiser than you," he told the prairieman.

Kneeling down, Nivek was examining the holy man's radio, careful not to touch the device. "This is wild," breathed the boy. "I never figured any holy man would be into Afterburn Radio…"

Turning to peer at Nitch with his beady eyes, the holy man smiled, "*Your* journey is doomed."

"What's he talking about?" growled the huntress.

Looking back at Tagger, the Sitter decreed, "The machinery is failing."

"Tell us something we don't already know," Needer chirped from the stranger's lap.

"Morale has eroded since Fever left," the holy man told them, a sadness entering his stare.

Tagger scowled. "How do you know Fever's gone?"

"What's he mean?" Nivek asked slowly. "Fever's still broadcasting. We heard him just the other day…"

"They play old tapes," pronounced the holy man, "attempting to create the illusion that he is still broadcasting… but they are fooling only themselves."

"It's not really Fever on the radio?" Nivek's voice was growing unsteady.

"I don't understand," mumbled Nico.

"Understanding, child," the holy mad addressed her, "will only come once you arc alone."

"Fever Smith is my hero!" wailed Nivek. "What happened? Why did he leave?"

"Fever Smith will return only when you have led these people to the radio station," the holy man stated firmly.

"He's not making any sense," Nitch concluded. "The heat's driven him crazy."

A tremor ran through the Sitter's figure. The sudden vibration startled Needer, sending the cat leaping from the man's colorful lap. As the group watched, stunned by what they saw, the holy man grew smaller, shrinking before their eyes. His hat and robe of many colors did not change, though; as the man dwindled, his clothing retained its original size. Soon the stranger had completely disappeared within the rumpled folds of his attire. As the tiny head vanished into the pile of clothing, it uttered a single word, "Beware."

"Yipes!" gasped Needer. "What happened?"

Nico erupted into screams of terror. Ignoring her, the rest of the group stared at the empty robe in disbelief.

"He… he was a mirage," Tagger exclaimed.

Nivek bent to lift the hat, examining the unbroken ground beneath.

"Mirages don't normally leave their clothing behind," the cat commented. She sniffed with curiosity at the hem of the robe.

"What kind of trick is this?" demanded Nitch.

Turning away without comment, Tagger started walking west again.

"Hey!" cried the huntress. She ran after the departing prairieman.

Bewildered, Nivek gathered up the robe. He picked up the Sitter's radio set, holding it delicately, as if afraid the device might melt away or burst into sudden flames.

Before Nitch could reach him, Tagger halted, turning to call back to Nivek, "Leave those things. They do not belong to us."

The boy's confusion increased. "But…" With a questioning look, he looked down at Needer.

The cat twitched her tail. "He's right." She trotted off after her prairie human. She had no doubt that the holy man would return for his things when he once more required them.

As Tagger resumed walking westward, Nitch caught up to him, snarling, "What kind of trick was that?"

"Trick?" laughed the man. "I can't even get my radio to work. How do you think I managed to make an entire man vanish?"

Pausing in uncertainty, Nivek finally replaced the hat, robe and holy man's radio to their place on the ground. Casting a look of disapproval toward the screaming Nico, he shrugged and strode off in the cat's wake.

Nico's wailing shriveled as she realized she stood alone. With a subvocal whimper, the girl scurried after the group.

26

THE JIHAD-BOUND BAND OF QUIET MEN marched west in single file across the baked earth with the one called Magog leading them. The black scarves that covered them were soaked with the sweat of many days.

His army was beginning to lose their faith in his holy mission. Magog could sense the fire of their dedication fading with each hour that they encountered no trail to follow. They required a sign that his path was the one to pursue, or he was going to be left alone to cross the flatlands.

Their easily eroded faith was a sign to Magog, revealing his army's weakness, showing how they believed only shallowly in the sacred silence. Their fortitude could not be relied upon when the moment of action arrived. When the time came, he realized, only *he* would remain to enter the unholy radio station to silence its voice. If that was the way it had to be, then Magog resolved that he would not falter. All the better, he thought with a twinge of pride, if *he* alone was destined to be mankind's quiet salvation.

He halted, turning with his arms raised, waving to attract the attention of the other Quiet Men. His fingers spoke to them: again spelling out the sacred trust their mission involved, the need for faith and perseverance.

An anonymous hand rose near the back of the band of Quiet Men, denouncing Magog's insane quest.

However, only Magog saw the dissenter's message. Before he could challenge the traitor, a sign was delivered upon the band. Wafting lazily through the arid air across the flatlands came a *sound*.

Each head turned west to glare at the voice that came out of the setting sun. Although far far away, the scream carried to their sensitive though scarred ears.

Magog pointed an accusing arm in the direction of the distant scream. His fingers cried a single word: *There!*

The fingers of the other Quiet Men flew busily, promising a horrible end to the sonic atrocity. They collectively strained, urging Magog to lead them on.

Striking off across the dead plains with the band eagerly bustling at his rear, Magog was grateful for the heaven-sent omen. It was only right that God should send them a sound to guide them toward silencing the radio station's noise.

The Quiet Men marched now with a replenished fervor, oblivious to the mechanical eyes that followed their progress.

27

THEN: IN MIND ONLY.

Cherli was always small for her age and made few friends because of it. But the friends she did make were true companions, for they did not allow appearances to dictate any predisposition toward her.

So it came as a savage disappointment to learn her family intended to strike off, abandoning their village to go in search of a better community. No amount of pleading or tantrums could dissuade her father from this decision. Being the youngest and the smallest, her complaints went unheard.

Cherli's brothers and sisters did not share her attachment to the village of her birth, though. The family had *moved on* numerous times over the years; it was their father's way. Her siblings were older, more familiar with the prospect of making new friends.

Only their parents, however, truly comprehended the full scope of making such a relocation.

The Mob that ruled these northern lands frowned upon nomadic habits. They preferred their subjects to stay in one place, facilitating accurate tithing. And they were wholly willing to fortify that edict with lethal force.

So it was that Cherli's family left the village under the cover of darkness and secrecy. Traveling only by night, the family hid in caves and ruins during the day to avoid detection.

The misfortune that befell Cherli's family could only be blamed on fate. Descending upon the family as it slept, a band of Quiet Men exacted their holy purpose by silencing them.

Cherli's survival was directly attributable to her diminutive size, which allowed her to effectively hide in a deep crevasse in the surrounding rocks. Leaving her hiding place hours later, the young girl surveyed the corpses of her family without real understanding. She wandered off, in boredom more than shock.

Days later, near starvation, the child was taken in by a group of art gypsies. Renaming her Crazy Jen (for her wild-eyed expression), they raised the child as one of their own. The gypsies traveled from village to village on the borders of the Mob-ruled lands, offering entertainment in trade for food and goods.

It would be many years before Crazy Jen came to terms with the nightmares that meddled with her sleep and haunted her waking hours, accepting the slaughter of her family and understanding that their deaths had not been her fault. Only then would she lose her wide-eyed stare.

Life with the art gypsies taught her many things. She learned to survive in a hostile land. She learned to recognize her meager talents and grasp the tricks of storytelling. She learned to make acquaintances into friends, no matter how brief her encounters with them. She learned to beware the *laws* that infringed on freedom of thought.

As the gypsies wandered in and out of Mob territory, Crazy Jen was exposed to villages that lived in repression and Tribes who lived in autonomy. She could quickly distinguish how humanity floundered under one way and flourished under the other. For many, their lives were identical, showing their oppression only in the hunger with which they longed for distraction.

Distraction was the art gypsies' bread and butter. The things they brought to each town with their arrival were wondrous novelties in the wilderness. Paintings, music, theater, magic tricks, the finery of inexpensive fancy gowns and jewelry. Each family in the gypsy Tribe excelled at one entertainment or another. Collaborations between families were encouraged—in art and breeding.

Crazy Jen's new family were experts in the working of silver and gilt into delicate jewelry. When she began to display a talent for fabrication, she was traded to another family whose trade was storytelling. There, her fantasies were honed into engaging fables. She learned how to speak to crowds, commanding their full attention with even the most trivial tale.

Alas, art (at least, *unsanctioned* entertainment) was also frowned upon by the Mob's ecclesiastic rule.

So it happened that a gang of roving Church Police encountered the wandering band of art gypsies one day and meted out a murderous scolding to the entertainers. Again, Crazy Jen's petite size was responsible for her escape from the field of slaughter.

By this point, she had matured beyond her wild-eyed stare, and was able to cope with the loss of her second family. This time, shock melted away and reformed as a hard resolve to flee this insane land. Gathering what supplies she could find among the gypsies' charred caravan, Jen headed south into freer realms.

So she lived, traveling from village to village, enthralling the populace with her captivating anecdotes. Many of these stories were crafted with the Mob and their Church Police cast as the villains. The further south she progressed, the fewer people understood this truism, being unfamiliar with the cruelty of northern politics. Nevertheless, she continued to spin her anti-Mob tales.

One evening, alone on a stretch of prairie, Jen witnessed something in the distance that took away her breath. She had climbed atop a large rock to lie under the colors of the night, there to devise new story ideas. The quiet majesty of the landscape had inspired her with fanciful notions of vast hidden Tribes who lived underground to escape the flatlands' terrible climate.

The people in the prairie villages she visited endured grim lives. They found her tales intensely entertaining; indeed, the wilder the tale, the deeper their appreciation. The people who lived in the flatlands were no strangers to fantastic and improbable occurrences. Often, no matter how outlandish her stories were, she sensed that her audience believed her every word, for they had witnessed things no less incredulous in the savage wasteland.

Sitting up to take a sip of wine she had recently acquired in the last village she had visited in trade for a particularly well-told tale, Jen beheld a strange shape sliding along the horizon. Occluding a portion of the prismatic night sky, a tall triangular shadow traveled in the distance, slowly moving west to east. (Only later would she connect this with the district's easterly winds.) The strange black triangle made no sound, passing silently on its mysterious journey. After half an hour, the dark shape had vanished from view, leaving her with a deep curiosity.

The next morning, she headed east, attempting to overtake the mysterious apparition. Despite her conviction that what she had witnessed was real, it was with great surprise that she discovered the tracks of a pair of huge snakes headed in the direction she traveled.

Snakes? she wondered. Or were they? They did not wind in undulating curls as did the trails of normal serpents. The bizarre grooves ran straight, paralleling each other across the dirt.

Suddenly, it occurred to Jen that these could well be the tracks of some monstrous flatland beast. She had heard tales of such creatures—horrible monsters that dwelled out on the plains, undaunted or tormented by the region's awful heat.

For a moment, she tried to envision what this monster would look like... a huge squat torpedo of a body set on a pair of runner-like legs... a massive fin rising from its back, standing high in the air... perhaps the beast's eyes were attached atop this fin, allowing it to see far ahead of itself... and teeth, dangerous teeth like rows of lethal blades—it wouldn't be much of a monster without frightful teeth.

She decided she must see this beast. It would make a wonderful villain for one of her stories. The local Tribes were all fascinated with tales of prairie monsters, and here was one that surpassed even her own wild imagination. Such a grotesque creature would delight future audiences!

So it was that Jen (who still might not be undeserving of the "Crazy" prefix to her name) set off on the trail of her mysterious fin-monster. She followed the dual grooves across the prairie, marveling every once in a while when each of the two grooves split into a pair of smaller grooves to effect turns in the beast's path. Truly, there was more to her monster than she had dreamt. She quickened her pace, eager to witness the creature's true shape and exotic nature.

She followed the tracks for many days as they wound east, then north, then south, then west... before finally catching sight of the dark fin against the morning sky in the far distance. With absolute stealth, she crept up on the beast. It would not do to allow the monster to eat her before she could behold its fantastic configuration.

What she found astounded her far more than the wildest of her suppositions concerning the nature of the beast.

For it was no *beast* at all!

The *thing* stood on wheels—a wooden canoe of a wide design, with a tall mast rearing from its midst. She could see the sail was presently collapsed and bound to a horizontal arm. Bending over a small campfire he had built next to the vehicle, a man was cooking some stew. Its enticing smell drifted to her senses as she raised herself on her elbows to stare at the incredible scene.

The man looked up at her and smiled. "So, you finally caught up with me," he called. He gestured for her to approach.

Jen remained where she was, evaluating the man with a suspicious nature born of her solitary travels in these harsh lands. He was a big man, wearing wide shoulders and meaty arms tanned by years under the harsh sun. His hair was long and tied in a ragged ponytail that hung almost to his belt. Although he did not wear a formal beard, it had been days since his last shave. He was possessed of the type of facial hair that refused to grow evenly or thick, giving his cheeks a scruffy appearance. Even from this distance, she could make out how large his eyes were—wide pools of soft blue that spoke of a cheerful disposition. He was dressed in tight leather of a hue that blended perfectly with the surroundings, as did the color of the wheeled beast, now that she thought of it—excellent camouflage in this dun wilderness.

"Come along," laughed the man. "I'm not going to bite you. I already have breakfast cooking. Come see."

She joined the stranger. Maintaining a wary distance between them, she seated across from the campfire from him. She watched the scruffy man in silence as he stirred the stew. When he filled two bowls with the nutritious liquid, she hesitantly took one from him.

He tipped back his bowl, slurping up the stew. Lowering the bowl to his lap, he smiled at Jen. "My name is Kaz."

"Jen," she mumbled around the pieces of meat in her mouth. She finished chewing and swallowed before continuing, "I thought your vehicle was a monster."

"A monster, huh?" Kaz looked over at the wheeled construction. "I never thought of that. Yeah, I guess it would look pretty forbidding from a distance. Huh." He turned back to the girl. "You must be awfully brave to come hunting such a strange monster... or just plain crazy."

"They used to call me Crazy," she admitted. "Now I'm just Jen."

"You're the storyteller, aren't you?" He nodded slowly, his eyes widening in a companionably manner to display his clear blue eyes. "I've heard of you. You're supposed to be pretty entertaining. I never pictured you'd be so small."

She frowned at him, sensitive about her size.

He waved a hand at her, innocently dismissing her anger. "Nothing personal, you understand. It's just—the way the villagers describe you, I pictured you to be a seven foot tall Amazon. You should hear the *stories* they tell about *you*." He shook his head, smiling at some private recollection.

Jen attempted to hide her blushing face behind the bowl of tasty stew. She believed this stranger—this Kaz. She felt comfortable in his presence, accepting him as someone who could be trusted.

Curious about his vehicle, she asked about its nature. With an ill-hidden but charming pride, Kaz explained, for it was a device of his own construction. He called it a *prairie sailer*. Utilizing the power of the wind, it traveled across land on its wheels.

She praised his cleverness, admitting that even her own wild imagination could not have conceived of such an amazing conveyance.

"You know," he mused, rubbing a hand to his stubbly chin. "Running into you might be fortuitous for us both…"

Licking her bowl clean, she held it out with a "more please" expression on her small face.

Kaz nodded, giving her the universal gesture for "help yourself." He looked at her for a moment, then asked, "You enjoy telling stories?"

She bobbed her head, sipping from her second helping of stew.

"What's the biggest audience you've ever had?"

She shrugged. "Few hundred or so. Why?"

"How would you like an audience of thousands?" He smiled with a grizzly innocence.

"Out here?" laughed Jen.

"Maybe…" Kaz stood and went over to climb aboard his vehicle. He returned carrying a strange device which he set beside the campfire. "Are you familiar with radio sets?"

She told him she was. The gypsy tribe had possessed a battered crystal radio set which they had obtained in some bygone trade, and several of the villages they (and later she in the role of solo entertainer) had visited had held custody of such amazing devices. Such sets had produced wondrous music—and voices, as if tiny men lived inside the fragile small devices. She had come to think of these beings who dwelled inside the radio sets as the Afterburn Spirits.

Laughing, Kaz explained how no tiny men lived within the radio sets. He told her how the air was full of radiowaves, and Afterburn was a radio station who sent the music out through these radiowaves. The crystal sets picked up these broadcasts, converted them back into music for people.

She listened dubiously to his descriptions. Sometime during his explanation, Kaz switched on the device he had taken from his sailer. Music leapt forth, revealing the device to be a radio set of unknown design. Carefully, he dismantled his device, showing her that wires and speckled squares of metal lived inside it, not tiny men.

"How would like to tell your stories over the radio? Imagine how many villages you could entertain with a single story?" He smiled expectantly.

"How?" she replied cagily.

"By joining Afterburn."

"Inside the radio?" Her eyes went wide. "And they called *me* Crazy!" she laughed.

"No." He shook his head, resealing the chassis of his radio. "They broadcast from a secret station. You'd have to go there to live. But from there—you could speak to thousands of people everyday."

"Is it a nice place to live?"

"The people who live there seem to think so. You'd have to decide for yourself."

"How do you know all this?" she asked, suddenly suspicious.

"I work for Afterburn." He informed her how the radio station maintained a loose network of people to promote the station across Ericaland. "And also to guard its location," he confided, "steering away those who wander too close to Afterburn's hidden transmitter."

"This is a very good story," she told him. "You're going to have to produce some proof that it's all not something you made up."

"Okay," he agreed, nodding solemnly. "Fair enough." He reached down to flip a switch on the side of his radio. Then he detached a small cylinder from the device, lifting it to his mouth. As he spun a dial on the radio, he spoke into the cylinder, "Afterburn, this is Kaz. Are you receiving me?"

The radio answered him with a hiss of static. Jen knew that sound, it meant that there was no music available from the radio. She had heard it once or twice from malfunctioning radios.

The man continued to repeat himself, speaking into the cylinder.

She smiled ruefully, deciding that Kaz's offer had been enticing, even exciting, but it was clearly just a fabrication of his prairie-addled brain.

Then the radio suddenly spoke, calling the man by name. "This is Afterburn. We hear you, Kaz. What's up?"

He smiled up at Jen in triumph.

"I've got someone here I think would like to join Afterburn. I believe the station would benefit immensely by her inclusion. Her name is Jen, she's a storyteller."

"Hello, Jen," the radio greeted her.

It had spoken to *her*—it had called *her* by name! She bent close to it, struggling with her disbelief.

"Kaz, is this the Jen you've mentioned before? The one who travels from village to village, telling stories?"

It *knew* of her!

"Yes," Kaz replied. "She's *that* Jen."

"Well, we could certainly use someone with her talent," the radio declared.

He looked at her and asked with a serious face, "Proof enough?"

A nod and a new blush was all the reply she could muster.

So it was that the child who had been born Cherli, who had become renamed Crazy Jen by art gypsies, and who had matured into just Jen, joined the staff of Afterburn Radio, adopting the DJ persona Psycho Jones.

Riding together in the prairie sailer, Kaz transported Jen to the far away secret base of Afterburn Radio. There she met the station's staff:

Fever Smith, the tall man who had started Afterburn. Fever had proven to possess more depth than just his passion for music and radio, he had charmed Jen with an insecure smile and wry praise for her talents. Before her first year at the station had elapsed, Psycho and Fever had become lovers.

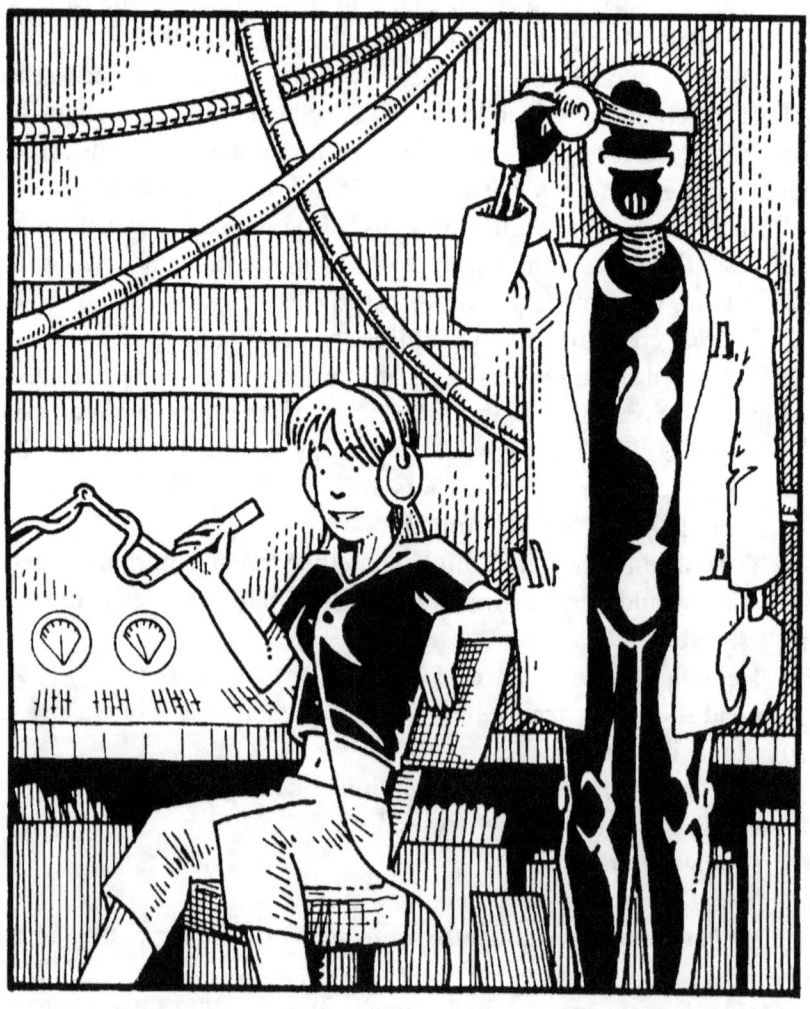

Psycho Jones   *Dr. Muffin*

There had been others who wandered into the station from time to time, other fieldmen like Kaz whose purpose was the promotion and protection of Afterburn. Some of them had been among the original band of adventurers who had found the radio transmitter with Fever years ago. Others had been recruited in the field, not unlike herself.

Unlike any of them, though—in fact, unlike anyone or thing she had ever met—was Dr Muffin, the robot who acted as the station's manager and technician. This artificial man had amazed Jen. His energies were boundless, for he never slept. His enthusiasm for the radio station rivaled Fever's dedication. It had been Dr Muffin who had first discovered the underground complex that contained the station's facilities. When Fever and his band of adventurers had stumbled into the tunnels, they had been welcomed by the robot. Together, robot and men had started Afterburn broadcasting.

So it was that Psycho Jones commenced her career as a DJ for Afterburn Radio. During early evenings, she would recite her stories over the airwaves, thrilling thousands with her cleverly crafted tales of life in Ericaland. Throughout the rest of the day, she assisted Fever with the DJ chores, playing music for Afterburn's vast and unseen audience.

For years, Dr Muffin and her beloved Smithie had been constants at the radio station. Fever and Psycho were the main DJs, playing the music and reading the news reports supplied them by Dr Muffin. The others drifted in and out, busy with their own jobs in the outside world. As the years progressed, though, the ranks of the field agents had dwindled, deaths natural and otherwise taking their toll of Afterburn's personnel.

Then, one day, Fever had announced his desire to take a sabbatical from DJing and venture out into the wilds of Ericaland. After so long underground, he had professed a need to *get away* from work and reacquaint himself with the real world. When Psycho had expressed interest in joining him on this vacation, Fever had tersely rejected the idea. She was needed, he told her, to remain and keep the station operating during his absence. He assured her that he would not be gone unduly long.

That had been three years ago.

For all the station's numerous loyal following, Afterburn had earned itself many enemies across the lands it spoke to. Any one of these villains could have gotten hold of Fever: prairie monsters, the Mob's Church Police, the Quiet Men, fire, famine, mutant pestilence… the list was almost endless.

Psycho's worrying was beginning to drive her crazy. She fretted that her beloved was never going to return.

28

Now: on scorched earth.

As dusk fell over the flatlands, Tagger announced the group would continue their journey through the night.

"The heat of the day will be getting worse from this point on," he told them. "It'll be much easier on all of us if we confine our traveling to the nighttime. We can rest during the day."

"He knows of what he speaks," Needer confided to them.

Nico threw a fit, claiming her weary and delicate feet could not be convinced to carry her any further without rest, but no one paid much attention to her tantrums these days. She was forced to trudge after them in a surly mood, not understanding why her devoted prairieman was subjecting her to these unwarranted trials and torture.

"He's done this before," Nitch accosted the cat who trotted along at her side. When Needer made no comment, the huntress added, "Right?"

"I'm sorry. I didn't think that was a question," remarked the cat.

"And *that* isn't an answer."

"You humans are so observant."

"Stop evading the topic and answer me," Nitch snarled, trying to keep her voice from straying to ears other than the cat's.

"You haven't met many cats before, have you?"

"The ones I *have* encountered were dead and cooked by the time I met them."

"You must've been desperate," chuckled Needer. "My species is renowned for our stringy meat."

"Are you trying to provoke me for a reason?"

"Just returning the favor," replied the cat with deadpan sincerity. She strolled ahead without glancing back with either head. This brought Needer in proximity to the conversation Nivek was trying to have with Tagger.

"Come on, Tagger," the boy was insisting. "What did that Sitter mean when he claimed Fever Smith wasn't on the radio?"

"The words of holy men cannot be taken literally," muttered the prairieman.

"But—he seemed to know an awful lot about Afterburn... for just a listener, I mean."

"Only if you believe his ramblings."

"Where I grew up," Nivek told him, "we were taught that Sitters preach the truth."

"They speak in warnings, boy," Tagger snorted. "Nothing else."

"Okay, then he *warned* us that it wasn't really Fever on the radio."

"Running into him was a mistake."

"Come on, Tagger. You want me to help Afterburn, but you won't be straight with me."

The man sighed without breaking his stride.

"Maybe Nitch is right," grumbled the boy. "Maybe you *aren't* to be trusted."

"I wander the prairie," Tagger explained slowly. "It doesn't help what I'm doing to let anyone know that I work for Afterburn. Sometimes, operating from the shadows is the only way to stay alive. A secrecy that deep is difficult to forget.

"You *are* right, though," the man continued. "It is unfair to expect you to help us without understanding the nature of our problems.

"Afterburn is experiencing numerous difficulties, the biggest involving their equipment—the machinery they use to transmit their broadcasts."

"There were pictures of transmitters in the books I read," admitted Nivek. "They didn't look all that complicated."

"Pictures often can be deceiving," Tagger smiled without humor. "The machinery required to broadcast Afterburn's signal may appear similar to the pictures in your books, but its scale is quite another thing. But—size is not the problem; *service* is.

"Machinery breaks down, boy. And *old* machinery breaks down a lot. You have no idea how old the machinery Afterburn uses is. Neither do I. I've been told it's centuries old, but that's meaningless to someone who cannot conceive of a period of time longer than their own lifetime. Imagine ten—twenty lifetimes. Imagine going back twenty of those lifetimes. Afterburn's machinery was old even back then.

"Afterburn's *technician*—repairman, if you will—does the best he can with the materials at hand. But there's only so much that can be done when the replacements are as old as the broken parts. And sooner or later, even *those* break down.

"If Afterburn is going to survive and continue broadcasting, they need new equipment."

"Like the stuff we found in my secret radio cavern," the boy interjected.

Tagger nodded.

"But—what about what the Sitter claimed about Fever Smith? If it isn't Fever on the radio, then who—what is it?"

"It's him... only, he isn't really there." The prairieman shook his head, more in confusion than negation. "It's not easy to explain. Fever's voice was put on these strips of material stored on flat reels. When the strip is fed through some of Afterburn's machinery, Fever's voice is duplicated."

"I don't understand. How can Fever speak if he's not really there?"

"Sigh... there are some things you're not going to understand until you see them, boy. And maybe not even then."

"Hey," the boy retorted. "I have a name, y'know?"

"We all do, Nivek," Tagger apologized. "But most of the people I know don't use the ones they were born with."

Growing bored with their conversation, Needer slowed her pace, dropping back to flank Nitch again.

The huntress started up immediately, "So, how many times has Tagger recruited people for Afterburn?"

"You don't know when to quit, do you?" sighed the cat.

"For all I know, you're leading my little brother into the fire," she snarled. "Give me one reason to trust you—especially with the way you've been avoiding my questions."

"You can rest easy. Afterburn can be trusted; they won't steal your brother blind or torture him. Especially not considering his obvious talent with machinery. With his knowledge and capabilities, he could be running the radio station in a few years.

"Now it's my turn," chirped Needer. "Why do you dislike Afterburn and Tagger?"

"What?"

"Save your guile for your own species, Nitch. Cats can't be lied to except by other cats."

"I want to protect my little brother," Nitch replied all too vehemently. "*He's* the only reason I'm along on this journey."

"Ah, now, you're still lying. Maybe you don't even know you're do-ing it, maybe you're unaware of your own reasons. Maybe it's something petty like jealousy—envying Tagger because he's as good a hunter as you, maybe better. Or maybe it's something absurd like displaced animosity—blaming Afterburn for the destruction of your Tribe—which is as con-voluted as blaming a tree instead of the sun when you get a sunburn. Or maybe it's something *human* like greed—planning on stealing something from Afterburn.

"Whatever the basis for your distrust, I can assure you that Afterburn is not going to hurt you or Nivek—or, alas, even the whining brat."

"Why should I believe you? In every bedtime story my Grammy told me, cats were always deceitful creatures."

"Stories created by *humans*, need I remind you? Xenophobic gar-bage."

"You never did answer my question. How many people has Tagger dragged back to Afterburn?"

"None, actually," the cat admitted after a pause. "Your brother is the first."

Halting the group's passage across the prairie, Tagger announced that they would camp out here among a group of standing rocks they had come upon. He directed Nivek and Nico to rest, while the rest of them scouted the area to ascertain its safety.

Nivek accepted the proclamation of rest without judgment.

Nico welcomed the news with rapture, realizing that her prairie-lov-er still cared for her.

Tagger bereft himself of baggage and jogged off into the darkness in a low crouch, his staff held horizontal to the sun-charred ground.

Nitch hesitated a moment before agreeing with the prairieman's plan, then she disappeared into the darkness on the opposite side of the circle of stones.

Needer waited until the two hunters had departed, watching the two children settle down to rest before scampering off on her own reconnais-sance.

For a considerable time, the two youths sat observing the darkness in silence under the colorful sky. While Nivek leaned back to watch the shimmering flow of colors, Nico massaged her feet, once she realized that the boy wasn't going to offer to attend to her discomfort. She stared sul-lenly at her lap.

"You know I'm Tagger's woman now," she finally proclaimed.

"Your choice," replied Nivek.

"Yes, it is."

"Not his," he mumbled so she could not hear.

"Hmm?"

"Nothing. Life as a prairie-wife is going to be hard, y'know. This trek will help prepare you for it."

"I'm not going to live out *here!*" she sputtered. "Of course Tagger'll give all this up and settle down with me."

"Tagger doesn't seem like the settling-down type, Nico."

"You don't know him the way I do."

"Here's a clue, Nico. Big strong men like Tagger aren't turned on by girls that complain and scream all the time."

"He likes to protect me," she declared. "You saw it—he saved me from that monster back in the ruins."

"He saved *all* of us."

"Only because I wanted him to."

Nivek could only shake his head in response. He was confused by Nico's delusional perceptions. He began to wonder whether her affections for himself had been based on such frivolous misinterpretations of reality.

"That's the only reason he's taking you to Afterburn, y'know," she told him. "Because *I* want him to."

As laughter rose in his throat, Nivek climbed to his feet. He didn't have to listen to this prattle, there were other things he'd much rather hear. Taking his crystal radio set from his backpack, the boy wandered away from the stone circle.

A displeased Nico watched him leave. Why didn't he understand? Why were her old boyfriends always so resentful toward her new boyfriends? Why were men so possessive about such things? Didn't they realize their primary concern should be *her* happiness, not their own? Why weren't they satisfied with the time and attention they had enjoyed when she had been with them? Men were just so stupid about losing things they really never had in the first place.

She classified this stupidity as an attribute of immaturity. *Boys* strived to hold onto things past their time; *men* knew to accept the impermanence of relationships. Nico was certain her new lover would not display Nivek's childish possessive nature. Tagger was a *man*. His superior age and the things he had learned on his far-ranging travels would give him the mature wisdom to recognize the correct manner in which to treat her. Tagger would know when to defer to her more important desires; he would realize that Nico's requirements were tantamount to the needs of all else. He would never resort to forcing her to do his bidding, unless it was something Nico secretly wanted to do. Tagger's maturity would dictate that Nico's happiness took precedence over all things. This was one of the many benefits of finally having a *man* looking after her instead of *boys*.

From beyond the stone circle, the sound of music wafted through the still night air. Afterburn music, that weird stuff they played in the hours close to dawn. Nico didn't really like this music; it was too strange and haunting. Why couldn't all music be uptempo and bouncy? The way she liked it.

Once they reached Afterburn, Nico resolved to make sure that Tagger would see this boring music banned from the airwaves. This would be the first of many refinements she would demand be instituted to Afterburn's broadcasts. Those news reports—they were just boring and utterly intrusive to the flow of her favorite uptempo music. They would have to go, as would those stupid stories told by Psycho Jones. Those stories were so unnecessary. Who cared about the lives of other people? *Music* was the true purpose of Afterburn's broadcasts—uptempo, happy music, not this spooky music they were playing now. Tagger would see that these changes were made; Tagger would insure that Afterburn adapted itself into a wholly musical entity that provided the kind of entertainment Nico craved. She knew his undying affection for her would let him do no less.

This eerie music… it made her sleepy. Within minutes, the girl was softly snoring, sitting propped against one of the massive stone shapes.

When a sudden movement jarred Nico awake, she was confused—disoriented. It took her a few seconds to remember where she was—the trek, the flatlands, the group, her prairie-lover. *Oh,* she told herself. *I must have slumped over in my sleep and woke myself. Humph. The least somebody could've done was make me a comfy place to rest before they all ran off and left me alone.*

I'm hungry. And I'm thirsty too. Do I have to do everything for myself?

As she made to reach for one of the half-empty skins of water, another sudden movement pressed against her back. With a gasp of disbelief, she realized it was the stone against which she had been leaning. The stone had *moved!*

She made to scramble away from the mass of rock, only to find that the movement had snagged her blouse, catching it between the stone and the ground as it rocked toward her. She was *trapped!*

And—oh no—the thing was moving again! It was tilting toward her—it was going to roll over and crush her!

She tried to scream, but her dry throat only croaked weakly. She tugged savagely at the blouse where it ran under the stone, desperate to pull it free without tearing the material. Her good blouse! She twisted, trying to wiggle out of the clothing, but too much of it had disappeared beneath the stone as it shuddered toward her. She could not struggle out of the constricting shirt.

As the stone made another trembling advance on her, Nico submitted to her growing hysteria. With manic desperation, she shed her material concerns and lunged away with all her might. Her blouse ripped, and she rolled away, leaving the back of the shirt stuck under the rock.

Free! she cheered herself. *I got free!*

She turned, still sprawled on the ground, to stare at the stone as it teetered after her. The horror she beheld succeeded in flinging a wild screech from her parched lips.

It was alive! This huge stone that stood nearly twice as high as her and wider than her arms-spread—it was *alive!* She screamed anew as she watched a long crack in the surface facing her expand into an ominous fissure, then yawn into a deep mouth rimmed with blunt teeth bigger than her fists. It was alive—and it was going to *eat* her! A pair of crusty appendages crept from the maw, wavering in her direction. The ends of these tongues puckered, revealing a network of tiny spines that twitched outwards. It was alive—and it wanted to *sting* her, then eat her!

The rock continued to move toward her. She became aware that it seemed to be approaching by means of rocking back and forth. She found this method of mobility so alien that it terrified her all the more.

So, she screamed again. But her voice was gone, whether from fear or wear. Only a soft squeak escaped her lips.

Where was everyone? Why wasn't Tagger rushing to her rescue? Didn't he know she was in mortal danger? Couldn't he tell? Couldn't he hear her?

In a panic, Nico commenced throwing things at the monster stone. Backpacks, bundles of jerky, floppy water skins, handfuls of dirt.

Go away! Stay away from me! Leave me alone! Keep away! her mind raged at the beast. *I don't want you to touch me!*

As one of the water skins struck the monster, the fabric tore against the needles that tipped one of its coarse tongues. The liquid contents spilled into the monster's wide jaws with a hiss, as if the water had landed on a searing hot surface.

With a start, she noticed the stone had ceased its rocking advance. Warily, but in shell-shocked wonder, she watched the crusted tongues retreat into the maw. The creature's mouth sealed itself with a sharp *clack*. It stood now as it had before, immobile and looming—an innocent but large prairie rock.

Something touched her bare shoulder from behind, propelling another squeak from her exhausted throat. As Nico wheeled, striking out wildly, a pair of strong hands grabbed her thrashing limbs, restraining her.

"Hold on—calm down!" Tagger commanded.

Recognizing him at last, she fell against him, weeping and clutching his leather jerkin.

"It's all right," the man soothed her. "You did the right thing." His arms encircled her trembling shoulders loosely, as if the man was hesitant to touch the naked flesh exposed by the torn back of her blouse.

"She wasted a third of our water," Nitch accused, coming upon the scene.

"No," Nivek spoke up. "I saw it—the thing attacked her, whatever it was. She was just trying to get away from it."

"Quickly," Tagger bid the others. "Gather up our stuff before the other stones wake up too."

Nitch and Nivek scrambled about, hastily collecting their things from the circle of stones.

Once they had taken everything a few meters beyond the circle, Nitch turned on Tagger, momentarily sneering at how Nico clung to the man, to demand, "What the hell was that thing?"

"Rolling Stones," Needer told her. "Normally, they just stand around, dormant. But when they wake up—look out."

"It tried to *eat me!*" Nico wailed between her trembling sobs.

"They consume water—or any liquid they can find," muttered Tagger as he attempted to disengage himself from the girl's grip.

"You should see them during a rainstorm," Needer chuckled.

"This is no laughing matter," Nivek reprimanded the cat. "That thing almost ate Nico."

"She gave it a third of our water," growled Nitch, gesturing to their two remaining water skins. Neither of the skins held much liquid.

"The alternative would have been sating the beast with her own body fluids," announced Tagger. "I think she made the right choice."

"I don't," Needer commented under her feline breath.

"No harm done," the prairieman told them all. "I know where we can find more water near here." He nodded to Nico. "You did the right thing. You beat the monster... all by yourself."

"I did," she gasped. "I beat it all by myself!"

"You didn't *beat* it," Nitch fumed stubbornly. "You *fed* it."

As the group made to collect their gear and resume their trek, Nico remembered her tattered blouse. The flush of fear that was just fading from her face was reborn as embarrassment. She dug through her backpack for a new shirt to replace her torn clothes. Turning her back to the rest of the group, the girl pulled the replacement garment over her head. Busy with assembling the group's belongings, Tagger seemed to be the only one who failed to notice the child's elaborate show of false modesty. Nivek looked, but felt no twinge of arousal at her partial nudity. The flashes of skin glimpsed by Nitch failed to impress her. Needer, however, stared openly and without shame; later, the cat would tease the brat about the puny size of her mammaries, knowing how touchy female humans were about such things.

They headed out across the flatlands with the sun rising at their backs.

29

STARING DOWN AT THE DRY RIVERBED that spread before them, Tagger sighed mentally while the rest of the group expelled their disappointment verbally.

Of course, none were louder than Nico: "But you *promised!*"

"This is where the Saw River used to be," muttered the prairieman.

"I'm *thirsty!*" Nico complained.

"We wouldn't be so low on water if it weren't for *you*," Nitch accused loudly. At her feet, Needer grunted agreement.

Leaving the group standing at the top of the unexpected cliff, Tagger descended into the riverbed. Carefully avoiding the larger of the cracks that split the earth, he maneuvered out to the point which had once been the deepest part of the river. He crouched to finger the soil, then took out a knife and began hacking at the ground.

"What's he doing?" inquired Nivek. He sat down, dangling his legs over the crest of the dry embankment.

"The heat's driven him crazy," Nico lamented. "My poor Tagger..."

"While he checks for water," Needer spoke to Nitch, "let's you and I scout the area."

"Hungry," whined the cat's right head.

"Okay, okay," Needer told herself.

Grunting her assent, Nitch left her backpack and satchel of jerky with her brother. Hefting her spear in hand, the huntress followed the cat away toward a region of brushlands to their south.

"But the river's gone," whined Nico. "Where does he expect to find any water now?"

Nivek accented a sigh with a brief shake of his hairless head. "You really *don't* know anything about surviving in the wilds, do you? Just because there's no water aboveground, that doesn't mean there isn't any underneath the topsoil."

"I can survive better than you can out here," the girl told him curtly. "How many monsters have *you* beaten?"

The boy began to regret not accompanying his sister on her impromptu hunt. It was annoying enough to left alone with his ex-girlfriend; being forced to endure her ego-masturbationary blather was salt on his wounded pride.

Pulling his radio set out, he switched it on and tuned in Afterburn. Active music filled the air with more clarity than the signal had previously possessed. He attributed the clearer reception to the embankment's elevation. Glancing to the west, Nivek noticed the hazy ridge of distant mountains that ranged along the horizon. With a rueful smile, he briefly wondered how powerful Afterburn's signal would be from heights like *that*.

Putting aside such whimsical thoughts, Nivek lay back on the ground, positioning his plant-frond hat (now little more than a disc of brittle straw) to shade his face. He closed his eyes and attempted to imagine what Afterburn's secret radio station might be like.

To remain hidden after all these years, the station was doubtless underground. It was probably cooler beneath the ground, the earth itself taking the brunt of the sun's hostile glare. This would imply that the station might resemble the tunnels beneath the ruins beside Oogolah Lake. A series of tunnels and squarish caverns (*rooms*, he recalled Tagger had called them) would lurk beneath the ground, serving as Afterburn's buried base of operations. These rooms would be crowded with ancient and exotic machinery—the apparatus required to broadcast their signal across Ericaland. Technicians must constantly busy themselves tending to this equipment, their heads full of detailed knowledge in the arcane art of electronics. Nivek longed to meet these technicians; he suspected he could learn much from their vaulted expertise.

The music coming from his radio dwindled, to be replaced by a voice he knew well. "Heyo, folks! This is Fever Smith, and you're listening to Afterburn Radio…"

Frowning under his hat, Nivek tried again to make sense of the explanation Tagger had given him concerning Fever's stored voice. His mind conjured an image of narrow strips of cloth, perhaps even as compact as twine, wound around a spindle of some sort. He had a mental image of someone sitting in a chair with spindle in hand. The thread unwound from the spindle, entering a slot in a vast and mysterious wall of machinery, where Fever's voice was coaxed from the long strip. But—coaxed how? Did a series of spatula-tipped metal fingers pinch the thread? Did Fever's voice drip like a liquid released by the pressure? Not metal, no—metal was too rare and unreliable, according to Tagger's claims. Perhaps the squeezing fingers were tipped with crystals such as the one in Nivek's radio. Crystals of a type far more splendid that the translucent lump he had found in the water of his little brother's favorite fishing hole. He envisioned a long row of such appendages, squeezing Fever's voice from the thread.

The entire process was too occult for Nivek to fathom. The concept of storing someone's words and replaying them at a later point was beyond his adolescent imagination.

Frustrated by his inability to comprehend such things, Nivek's thoughts returned to Fever Smith. Why had the DJ left Afterburn? Tagger's explanations had avoided any disclosure of categorical information concerning Fever's alleged departure from the airwaves.

As the music resumed, again uptempo with a catchy beat, Nivek tried to picture his hero. A tall man—but then, most people were tall compared to Nivek's size. Tall with a wild head of hair... strong hands and a kind face. With a cerebral grunt, he realized that his mental image of Fever Smith looked remarkably like Tagger. Perhaps because they were the only two people he knew who were connected to Afterburn Radio. But then, he didn't really know Fever... any more than he knew Afterburn's other DJ, Psycho Jones. After hours of listening to their broadcast voices, he thought he knew the pair of DJs.

What would Psycho Jones look like? Her voice was strong, but carried a tininess to it. Might she be small? Like him? Beautiful, probably... a worldly woman who had access to vistas of knowledge far beyond Nivek's ken. He failed to comprehend why the girl had a name like "Psycho", she certainly sounded sane to him. She didn't babble and ramble or even rant. Her voice was smooth, almost sensual without any huskiness. Nothing like Nico's whiny tones, he thought.

Nico was raising her voice as she crooned along with the music. "Hupp-town girl... I'm a glove for an Hupp-town girl..." she sang. He smiled beneath his straw hat. She never could get the words right. Once he had found that trait endearing, now he saw clearly how annoying the habit was. Well, he mused, Nico's spoiled idiosyncrasies are Tagger's burden now.

Oh, get real, he chided himself. As if Tagger was even aware of the role Nico had thrown over him like some emotional fishing net. The prairieman was obviously centered on the task of leading the group safely through the perilous flatlands. He had no idea of the romantic delusions

Nico was spinning in her flighty mind. Her notions were like frail cob-webs, liable to be torn apart any second by the slightest breeze of reality. Nivek felt sorry for the girl. There would be no one to comfort her when she realized the truth of Tagger's dedication. She would finally be alone— a state he doubted she had any experience handling.

Dance away, little Nico, he mused, watching from under his hat as her feet scampered on the ground. Dance away your nervous energy un-der the hot sun… like the fool you are.

Suddenly, Nico's scream ripped the air.

What now? grumbled Nivek. A pebble in her shoe? Or some lizard giving her a dirty look? He lifted his head, propping himself up on his elbows. Tipping back his straw hat, Nivek looked around.

To see the squat figure of a strange man standing nearby, a hazily dark silhouette against the blinding glare of the vicious flatland sun. Then the man brought a club down on Nivek—*thamp*—and the boy's world spun off with a disturbing abruptness into a black void.

HOLDING ALOFT THE TINY LIZARD she had snagged, Nitch smiled and asked her hunting companion, "Dead or alive?"

"Alive, alive, alive!" the cat's right head insisted.

"Please," added Needer's left head.

She dropped the green reptile for the cat. It scurried across the dirt, heading for a nearby rock. Needer hunched low to the ground and wiggled her tan butt, tail switching with glee. When the lizard was almost to the rock, the cat pounced, quickly catching up to her prey and batting it aside, denying it the prospect of refuge with an eager paw.

Watching the cat toy with the creature, Nitch marveled at the dichotomy that existed within Needer's two personalities. Clearly, the right head contained all her primal instincts, while her intellect resided in her left head. Nitch wondered what it must be like to live like that—to actually be able to verbally argue desire versus rationale with oneself. The cat did not seem the worse for the condition.

Nitch pondered whether it might indeed be the root of the cat's intelligence. Did everyone's brain possess two such minds—a mentality of raw instinct balanced by a sense of logic? She could see how this might explain her own aptitude for the hunt. Her logic was able to access her intuition, placing herself in tune with her prey's raw instinct. In her mind, her intellect controlled her instincts. In Needer, the two factions coexisted simultaneously. In Nico, she saw with a wry smile, the intellect was a victim of an overabundance of misguided instinct. While, in Nivek, instinct was lost in the face of the boy's intellect.

And in Tagger? Nitch found she couldn't decide what balance existed in the prairieman's head. The man operated with a cool detachment from raw intellect and calculated instinct. He seemed driven by an aloofness that was quite alien to Nitch. A product of his years wandering the flatlands? Or was it something the man had been born with? She was about to express envy for the man's approach to life, but stopped herself with an internal scowl.

No—she was *not* jealous of Tagger's abilities. There was no reason to be. True, the man was fully as capable as herself in the wild, perhaps even better in some instances, she conceded—but only from his familiarity with the turf. Nitch had known others just as resourceful among her Tribe's hunting parties. She had experienced no problems getting along with them. She had felt deep affection and respect for Galen's superior attributes. What was it about Tagger that bothered her?

Was it the man's affiliation with Afterburn Radio? Had his loyalty for the station expanded her desire to destroy Afterburn to include the prairieman?

She considered Needer's earlier accusations concerning the motives behind her distrust. Had the cat unwittingly recognized her reasons, or did her feline senses truly see into Nitch's soul? The things the cat had told her troubled Nitch, they strayed dangerously close to describing the emotions that drove her secret plans. Needer's assessment had made the girl quite uncomfortable; they had not discussed anything of consequence since, keeping their conversations confined to the landscape and prospects of prey or weather.

What really *bothers me?* she wondered. Needer's spot-on identification of the girl's thought process? Or the cat's immediate dismissal of the fallacy of blaming Afterburn for the slaughter of her family and Tribe? A portion of Nitch's mind (clearly the intellect) could see how Afterburn might be considered faultless in the matter: the station's broadcasts had not inspired the Quiet Men's attack. But another, more visceral part of her mind (obviously the instinctual) perceived the connection with a rigid assurance: if Afterburn's music had not lured her away from home that fateful night, her family might still be alive. Holding a tree accountable when one got a severe sunburn was admittedly silly, but blaming Afterburn for the extinction of her Tribe was not an extravagant leap-of-faith. It was a truism she could understand despite the cat's wisdom.

And there was no denying—Needer was smart. The cat seemed to integrally understand the human psyche.

Watching the cat play with the reptile, Nitch smiled. Intelligent and yet simple, Needer possessed both traits in charming proficiency. Her problem was that, being a cat, she could not see the world through human eyes. There was more to life than coldly logical assessments. Emotion, loyalty, a sense of loss, anger, the urge to avenge—these things colored a person's actions in ways a cat might perceive but could never *truly* comprehend.

When Needer finally delivered the deathblow, she made quick work of tearing the flesh from her prey, consuming the lizard's meat in a few efficient gulps. Finished with her play/meal, Needer rejoined Nitch. While the cat cleaned her two faces, the huntress announced that the area had been effectively scouted, producing no attributes that posed any threats to the group.

They returned to the dry riverbed, to discover the region empty and devoid of life.

"Where's everybody gone?" Needer asked.

Although Nitch had no sufficient answer to this, it bothered her that the cat had asked the question first.

31

UPON EXAMINATION, Nitch could discern some evidence of a struggle upon the cliff edge. As she attempted to piece together the scuffle in her mind, Needer flung herself from the embankment to slide down the parched bank into the dry riverbed.

The dirt where Nivek had been sitting when Nitch and the cat had left was still stained with sweat. He had apparently lay back, for the damp outline of his shoulders still stood out against the powdery soil. Not more a few meters away, there was a meandering pattern of tiny footprints confined to a small area. Nico dancing, Nitch surmised, meaning that Nivek had tuned in Afterburn Radio for some music. Had the music drawn the attention of some hungry predator? Or something *more* lethal? Try as she could, the huntress could discover no other prints besides those of the two children. Nor was there any evidence of spilled blood.

"Anything?" she called to Needer across the dry riverbed. The cat made some reply, but her small voice didn't carry across the distance. Nitch scrambled down the bank to join the cat where she paced in a nervous circle about the spot they had last seen Tagger.

Here, there was blood. It looked almost as if the prairieman's chopping at the ground had wounded the earth, bringing a pool of crimson to the surface. It was evident from Needer's restless activity that the situation had unnerved the cat. She paced with haste in a circle around the shallow red pool, swinging both her heads in an anxious twitch.

"Is it his?" Nitch asked.

Her voice startled the cat from her frantic reverie. Needer bent to sniff at the blood, then lapped up a small taste. Instantly, she spat the fluid from her mouth, hissing with ill temper.

"Well?"

"Not his," replied Needer. "Not human… not natural."

"Well," Nitch sighed, pulling her hunting knife from its scabbard. "Let's find out where it comes from." She crouched, digging the knife

138

into the soil beneath the crimson pool. The blade sank too easily into the ground and the turf beneath their feet seemed to shudder from the impact. "Hmm." Curiosity overcame Nitch's wariness. She began to dig a shallow trench in the dirt leading away from the pool. The blood slowly ebbed into the trench; soon only a thin layer of blood remained in the original hole. Placing her hand in the liquid, Nitch rubbed against the bottom of the pool. Her fingers touched a smooth, almost tender surface that startled her.

When her fingers encountered a tear in the bottom of the pool, she recoiled with a yell. The tear had been soft and warm—it had the feel of *flesh!* Fortifying her courage against this unprecedented discovery, Nitch plunged her hand again beneath the pool's crimson liquid. This time when she found the tear, she investigated it with her fingers. There was no mistaking it—the tear was a cut in the flesh of some living creature! Some beast was buried beneath the dry riverbed!

She was about to reveal her findings to Needer when the ground once more shuddered. The lattice of small cracks which the sun had baked into the dry earth around them lurched, yawning wider. Whatever lay beneath the surface was flexing its unseen body.

Warding the cat back from the area, Nitch poised herself in a crouch beside the red pool. With a mighty thrust, she stabbed her knife deep into the hidden flesh, embedding the blade to its hilt. Then, with a tremendous leap, she pulled the blade free and retreated from the pool with cautious but hurried determination.

This time the soil literally buckled upwards in response to her action. The finery of thin lines in the soil opened into cracks that grew until the dirt flew in chunks from the ground.

The mass that bulged from the unearthed area was indeed flesh, the carcass of some massive beast hidden underground. The skin was blue with a network of thick veins that ran like ridges across its pallid surface. The mass pulsed and ripples ran along the region that had become exposed by its thrashing. For all its size, it was clear this was only a small portion of whatever monster lay buried here. The entire body of this creature might well stretch for hundreds of meters under the dry riverbed.

"What is it?" gasped Needer's left head. Her right added: "Did it eat Tagger?"

Although Nitch had no doubt that this creature was involved in the disappearance of Tagger and the children, she was skeptical that it had eaten them. "Look," she pointed out to the cat. "There's no sign of any mouth." She glanced suspiciously about, then muttered, "Something else happened to Tagger... and Nivek and Nico."

"Insects live beneath the ground," remarked the cat. "Perhaps smaller drones came and captured them once Tagger's digging disturbed this thing."

Nodding slowly, Nitch agreed that Needer's guess held promise. "In which case, what I just did is bound to elicit some kind of similar reaction. The creature will send drones up to halt my attack and capture us too."

Together, the huntress and the cat took refuge in a fissure in the side of the dry riverbank. Crouching there, they awaited the emergence of the beast's drones.

After a few moments, the thrashing of the creature's exposed flank subsided. The massive hump of blue flesh sank beneath their view, leaving behind only a great gash in the riverbed.

As they hid, awaiting retribution for her attack on the creature's buried flesh, Nitch tried to recall what little she knew about insects. Her father had told her things about how numerous insect species displayed seemingly social behavior, cooperating among their kind to protect their nests and queen. Nitch wondered how much of this knowledge would apply to this beast. Things were so different out here in the flatlands. The actions of prairie beasts rarely followed any logic or pattern similar to their eastern kin. This horrible region seemed possessed of its own rules, many of which contravened all common sense or feasibility. She recalled the stone monster Nico had fed—that creature had no comparison to any life form she had ever encountered before. How many more impossible things lurked in these savage regions?

Lost in her thoughts, her eyes surveying the parched riverbed, Nitch was taken utterly by surprise by the rock that fell on her from above. It struck her shoulder, grazing a gash in the side of her head. With her vision clouded by disorienting phosphenes, she rolled from the fissure, gripping her knife in defense. Something knocked the weapon from her grasp. Another shadowy shape descended on her, raining blows on her head with a stumpy stick.

Shouting in pain and anger, Nitch sank to the dry ground beneath this assault. Under this savage barrage, her view cleared briefly. She watched Needer scamper away across the riverbed, abandoning her to the attack. She had no chance to curse the cat's cowardice before darkness descended to blot out the world.

32

WITH ANGRY EYES, Premier Vassal (who still thought of himself as Nanner Gristle) stared out of his lofty balcony window at the grand sprawl of the powerful city of Chico.

The buildings stood tall against the colors of the night sky, none daring to reach as high as the towers of the royal castle. It was an urban landscape that rivaled any other to be found on the continent of Ericaland. Only Chico possessed such masterful architects to achieve buildings of such stature. Even the legendary ruins far to the south in the Hexas wasteland could not rival the spires of Chico. Windows of light gleamed in many of the city's towers, born of the holy electricity which only the Mob possessed. These towers, the abodes of the chosen high class, stood as a massive ring beyond the walls of the Premier's holy castle. Invisible beyond that ring of towers was the domain of the worker class, drenched in the darkness of their rank and the stench of their kind. Faintly apparent in the distance to the east, the waters of Lake Aggo glittered in the night's kaleidoscopic auroras. Hanging like great boulders in the sky over the city were the many Church Police balloons, watchguards against attack or revolt—from both without and within. It was only the sacred dogmas that held the workers and the lower classes in their docile place, dogmas that were reinforced by the mighty weapons that God had given the Church to maintain the balance of power.

These powers were now in Nanner's hands. He stared at the great city, swelling with a pride over the masses who paid fealty and tithing to him as the grand ruler of the Mob. They were his citizenry; their existence was his to command, their lives or deaths were subject to his whim.

This was as it should be, he mused, how it should have been all his life. It was only a cosmic accident that had placed him originally in a lowly family, just as it was by accident that he now stood in the ruling castle. This latter accident, though, was one of divine intervention, correcting the mistake of his common birth.

"My Lord…" a soft voice sounded behind him.

Nanner turned to face the Empress Beel, the wife and concubine entitled to him by his new face and stolen identity. Considering the coarse women he had bedded in his earlier life, sight of his new wife could only thrill him with a deep contentment and vivid lust.

A dazzling stateliness exuded from the Empress Beel. In the fashion of those regally schooled, her finely chiseled features displayed harsh superiority and velvet compassion with a single expression. Her high forehead and noble nose and dark eyes under thick lashes created a face he had previously only known in forbidden dreams. She held her carriage with elegant poise, a posture that stirred his loins as his eyes caressed the curves her draping bed robe concealed with its near-transparent gossamer.

The manner in which she returned his stare emboldened him to reach out and cup her ample breast in a casual hand. He strove to maintain his own lordly composure under the rush of pleasure (physical and psychological) that this liberty sent coursing through his blood. To have lain with women in filth in the common circles for years and now be entitled to touch *this* woman as and whenever he pleased—this new reality still made Nanner dizzy with euphoria.

"Something troubles you this eve, my Lord," she purred, her voice husky and thick with haughty bearing.

He mumbled uncommittedly in response, her query reminding him of the fly that twitched in his wondrous new ointment. At first, only Afterburn Radio had tormented his new life with their unrelenting verbal assaults, broadcast across the land on ethereal and untouchable airwaves. Lately, though, Nanner had grown increasingly suspicious of the High Priests who constituted the Council's membership. Their unwillingness to transform his commands into laws and actions were the new insect tainting his pudding. The Council's refusal to treat him with the respect that accompanied the position they had given him infuriated the new Premier. At times, Nanner felt that he ruled in face only, his edicts falling upon stubborn and arrogantly deaf ears.

"Let me banish these tensions from you, my Lord," she cooed, pressing her sexuality against him.

He did not need much coaxing to follow her across the lushly furnished room, tumbling onto the huge royal bed under her musky weight. The things she did to him were technically no different than the ministrations of the lowly wenches he had bedded in his previous life; the true thrill came from the fact that now royally bred fingers and mouth teased his baseborn body. The breasts and mons he clutched with his callused hands were as soft and pliant as any vulgar wench's, but the fact that they were regal privates gave them an illicit charm, royal jewels manhandled by a common wretch.

When he finally collapsed atop her, the barriers between his old and new identity dissolved. And he found himself confessing all to Beel: his real name, the fate of her original betrothed, and how the Council had conspired to perpetuate Vassal's illusionary leadership with a surgically altered double. He told her how Afterburn had learned of this replacement, although none knew *how* they had discovered this closely guarded Mob secret. He confided to her his concern that the Council had abandoned their support of his rule, paying no heed to the laws he wanted to enact.

Although Nanner could never know it, these admissions only confirmed Beel's own suspicions. She was no stranger to regal intrigues and had become aware of the differences between the original Vassal and this impostor long before the Afterburn rumors had filtered to her attention through the castle grapevine. She experienced no grief over the assassination of her legal husband, for the man had been an egotistical brute, their union wholly a Mob arrangement. Possessed of her own reasons to distrust the Council (among other insulting interferences, the Council had just last month put an end to her weekly jaunts wherein she and her royal friends hunted and killed young children in the workers' streets, claiming the Empress' depravity was not seemly for her status, especially if conducted in public), this information forged in her a bond with this impostor—together they could conspire to reward the Council for their insidious scheming.

Under silken covers and in hushed tones, Nanner and his Empress discussed ways and means of putting the Council in its place, re-establishing true royal dominance of the Mob.

Eavesdropping via its spyeyes, satellite RTD 126.1952.2 slid through the sky far beyond the irradiated dust of the stratosphere. Although it learned nothing of vital importance through this surveillance, except perhaps a mild amusement at the naiveté of humans, it filed away the data for subsequent forwarding to its earthbound allies.

33

MAW NEVER APPROVED OF MY DESIRE *to become a hunter. "You're a girl," she told me. "Girls are supposed to be sweet and nice. Girls shouldn't want to kill things."*

Paw abstained from giving any opinion on my choice. He informed me privately that I should do whatever my heart told me to do. He would neither denounce nor support me—I had to stand on my own.

My brothers teased me, nicknaming me "Killer" until Paw caught one of them at it. After the beating he got, no one ever called me "Killer" again... but I would never forget the times they had.

I never thought of hunting as killing. Hunting was hunting. It provided the Tribe with meat. People had to eat or they would die. The way I saw it, not hunting was helping to kill people.

When a wolf caught a rabbit, it wasn't killing. The wolf did what it did to survive. If it didn't eat, it wouldn't survive. (But then, the time prairie wolves strayed too close to our farm and killed some children—that was bad. Killing children was unacceptable, even though all the wolves were doing was trying to survive.)

The rules of existence as dictated by the tribe confused me.

The other boys who wanted to learn to be hunters weren't pleased to have a girl learning their trade. They repeated the things my Maw had said, although the exact words they used were a lot crueler. They did things to undermine my learning. I never clearly understood why.

The other boys in the Tribe who were not learning to be hunters were no less unsympathetic to my chosen trade. They claimed I was trying to be a man because I could not measure up as a woman.

My teacher, Galen, told me to ignore everyone. If hunting was what I wanted to do, then I should concentrate on learning to be the best hunter I could be.

So, that's what I did. My skill in the wilds disturbed the other boys at first. Later, they decided that maybe I could teach them a few things about hunting. So, I did.

It was all very confusing to me. When I asked Paw about it, he smiled and tried to explain to me how some people became jealous when other people turned out to be better at the things they wanted to do. But then, why were some of the boys in Galen's class asking my help? Paw told me how some people were smrt enough to look past their basic instincts.

His explanations only confused me all the more.

People didn't all act the same, not like the beasts in the wilds. Wolves and fowl all behaved the same. If you stalked them into a corner, they would struggle to escape. If you moved one way, they would respond with flight in the other direction. If you laid traps and baited them with scraps, they always ended up caught in the snares. People didn't do that. You could never be sure how a person was going to react to any given stimuli. Some people cowered, others fought back, some even tried to talk their way out of situations.

The wilds were easier to understand than civilization.

Once I proved myself as a huntress, the adults of the tribe praised my talent. Many of them contradicted this praise when I encountered them alone. The Tribe's answerman condemned me for having what he called "the contrariness of my father in my blood."

When Galen taught me how to be a woman, I sought to further this knowledge with other boys in the Tribe, but they rejected me. They were more interested in girls who had no personal strengths.

Publicly, I was lauded for my huntsmanship. In secret, I was thought of as an outcast. It was this latter treatment that prompted me to begin sneaking off with my brother Nivek when he discovered the secrets of Afterburn Radio. He enjoyed the music that came over the radio he constructed. To me, the music was a more primal experience. It touched something deep in me, something that only hunting had previously stirred.

Music was like a pain that didn't hurt.

It wasn't like the hurt I felt now. This pain hurt. It disturbed the darkness that surrounded me like a cozy nest. I tried to block out my discomfort and nestle deeper in the darkness.

But the voices kept calling me, urging me to crawl out of the nest and join them…

34

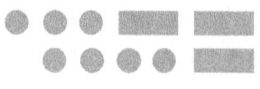

NITCH OPENED HER EYES without joy. Consciousness did not diminish the pain that had accompanied her in the darkness. If anything, it intensified that ache, bringing it clarity and definition.

She looked up into the face of her younger brother. Peering over Nivek's shoulder, Nico's face was twisted with worry and concern.

"You're awake," Nivek informed her of the obvious.

Struggling to sit up, Nitch discovered her arms were bound. As she became aware of her surroundings, she realized that Nivek's arms were similarly bound, as were Nico's. Confusion tainted her thoughts for a moment until she recalled the moments before the darkness had swallowed her.

"What happened?" she asked.

"Oh, it was terrible!" wailed Nico. She began to babble about colorless men and mouths opening up in the ground.

"Shut up!" Nitch growled with frustration. There was no sense in the girl's words—there never was. "Nivek, tell me what happened?"

"We were attacked," her brother told her. "They came out of the ground—at least, that's what Nico says happened. I didn't see where they came from. They knocked me out... and I woke up here."

"Why are you asking *him*?" protested Nico. "I saw it all. I saw what happened. They were—"

The huntress silenced the brat with a scream.

It was coming back to her now. She and Needer had returned to find Nivek and Nico and Tagger gone. They had discovered a pool of blood and a beast buried under the dry riverbed. She had stabbed the beast... and drones had come after them. The drones had attacked her. And Needer had run away.

That coward, Nitch snarled. The cat had abandoned her, leaving her to the mercies of the drones and their assault. They had beaten her. *That* was why she hurt. *That* was why she tasted blood now. *That* was why she lay bound in some cave.

At least she had found Nivek. She grudgingly added Nico to that relief. The brat may be a pain, but she was part of their group and should be protected with the same determination Nitch applied to insuring her brother's safety.

The cat—the cowardly cat had run away!

"Where's Tagger?" asked Nitch. "Was he captured with you?" Or had he run off like his craven traveling companion?

"We don't know," Nivek admitted. "He wasn't with us when we woke up here. He wasn't with you, either, when they brought you in and dumped you here."

"Tagger?" moaned Nico. "My brave Tagger wasn't with you? Where is he? Why hasn't he come to my rescue?"

"What about Needer?" Nivek asked.

"Don't mention that beast to me," growled Nitch. She strained against her bounds, but they bit into her arms with angry severity.

Leaning toward her, Nico screamed, "What about my Tagger?"

The huntress responded by driving her forehead savagely into Nico's face. The impact sent the brat flying back on her ass in the smelly darkness. Crumpled on the earthen floor, the girl began whimpering.

"You spoiled brat," ranted Nitch. "He's not *your* Tagger! He's no one's Tagger. And I don't know where he is. For all I know he's already dead!" She continued to twist against her bindings, which in turn dug deeper into the flesh of her arms.

"Tagger," Nico lamented. "My Tagger will save me... sob... he won't let anything happen to me... sob..." She turned her head from its place in the dirt to scream at Nitch, "He'll punish you for hurting me!"

"Get it through your mutehead brain, girl, nobody's going to save us this time. If we get out of here, we'll have to do it ourselves."

Nivek muttered softly, "You really think Tagger's dead?"

"I don't know," his sister replied tersely. "I don't know where he is... I don't know where we are..." She shifted to peer at her brother. "Come here. What is this they tied us with?"

Shuffling over to her, Nivek positioned himself so that Nitch could see the material that trapped his arms to his sides. The taut strands glittered in the almost nonexistent light.

"Dammit," she gasped. "It's metal!"

"Metal?" he retorted in astonishment. "Where would monsters get metal?"

"Monsters don't tie up their victims."

Having no response to that, Nivek fell into a morbidly thoughtful silence. The worst possible scenarios showed on his face.

"Shift around here," Nitch directed him. "I'm going to try to untie you." Nivek moved his back to face her. Nitch twisted around so that their hands touched behind their backs. With difficulty, the huntress began picking at the sharp twined ends of the wire strands. The metal tore at her fingers. Blood flowed from scrapes and cuts on her hands, making her task all the harder.

As she struggled with the metal knots, Nitch surveyed their dark prison. They were underground, that was obvious. The chamber was a domed cave, chiseled out of dirt. It smelled of vile damp and their sweat and ancient feces. A luminous mold hung in tatters from the ceiling, lighting the cave with a weak ghostly illumination. Other than their three bodies, though, the cave was devoid of clutter. The absence of bones gave her some hope that they had not been left here to starve or die of neglect.

No, she suspected the beast's drones had a far uglier fate in store for their captives.

She was making no headway with loosening the knots that held Nivek's bound tight. The metal wire was strong, sharp, the ends jagged needles. Her bloody fingers were fouling her efforts, adding to her frustration.

When a doorway suddenly rasped open, the surprise jolted her. She and Nivek tensed with fear; Nico wailed in the dark.

The creature that peered in had once been human. Its face was hairless and generally devoid of color. The skin was nearly transparent, barely hiding the veinwork and muscles stretched over its yellow skull. The eyes that stared out of its face were huge and white with no apparent pupils. Even though the thing was naked, it possessed no sexual organs or visible traits. Its lean muscles stood out beneath its invisible skin like reddish brown bundles of rope.

As the drone entered, it grunted and struck blindly at Nico with a stumpy stick to silence her cries. Then its flattened nostrils flared. It swung its head left and right, as if to pinpoint the source of whatever smell had thrilled it. Coming over to Nitch, the drone pulled her from Nivek, throwing the huntress to the ground. Crouching over her like a beast, it dove its face into her crotch, sniffing loudly. With a frustrated grunt, it twisted Nitch around, pressing her face into the dirt. At first she feared the thing intended to sexually assault her. But how?—it had no genitalia. Then, sniffing at her bound hands, the drone's grunts grew emphatic. It began to lick at the blood on her fingers, issuing noises of ecstasy now.

Restraining the gorge of disgust that rose in her throat, Nitch buckled up, driving her bloodied hands and the sharp wires that confined them into the drone's face. It squealed in pain, arching back to claw at the scratches her action had delivered to its pale flesh.

Grabbing up its discarded stick, it swung the weapon above its head to strike the trussed huntress at its feet. It doubtless would have beaten her to a pulp if Nico hadn't distracted it with moans from where she lay. The drone twisted to sniff in her direction.

Nitch made full use of the diversion. Struggling to ignore the stinging bite of the metal digging deep into the muscles of her arms, she rolled on her back and drove both her feet squarely into the drone's stomach. With a shriek, it collapsed under her kick. In a second, both Nitch and Nivek were all over the creature, kicking and biting their captor. Sparing no quarter, they continued to savage the drone until its mewling dwindled to a gurgling silence. Only once the thing's twitching subsided did the Palma siblings fall back from their target, gasping, to sprawl on the damp earth of the small cave.

"Look," gasped Nico. When neither of them took heed of her direction, she hissed at them like some livid teacher, "*Look!*"

Nitch followed the brat's indications and saw what Nico was trying to point out. Although the drone wore no clothing or straps, the flesh of its thighs had been mutilated into several pouches and loops. Dangling from one such loop of skin hung a metal tool with viciously sharp shears.

Struggling around to grasp the shears in her bloodied hands, Nitch tore it from the fleshy loop that held it in place against the drone's thigh. Crawling over to where Nivek lay still gasping and dazed, Nitch guided the wires that bound him into the mouth of the tool. *Snip. Snap.* With metallic *twang*s, the wires separated, releasing the boy.

He quickly took the tool from his sister and snipped the wires that wrapped her. Then, in similar fashion, he freed Nico.

Together the three of them lay on the earthen floor, drunk with relief at their sudden freedom. Nitch was the first to leap to her feet. Grabbing up the drone's discarded crude bludgeon, she rushed to the still open door. She peeked outside with absolute caution, but could see little in the dim tunnel beyond their prison.

Turning back, she hissed at the children, "We have to get out of here—now!"

Straining his stiffened muscles to action, Nivek helped a wretchedly unstable Nico to her feet. "Good job," he gasped to the girl. They hobbled after Nitch out the doorway.

The tunnel was even damper. A thickly unpleasant stench hung in the subterranean air. Again, the ceiling was strewn with splotches of the glowing mold. The light granted by the growth only added to the ominous quality of the crude corridor.

Taking a chance, Nitch chose to lead them to the left. They had only proceeded a few meters when a violent hiss sounded behind them, freezing the group of escapees in their tracks.

"Wrong way," a voice snapped at them.

They whirled to discover Needer crouching by the doorway of the prison they had just left. The cat stood with back arched, looking at them with fiery eyes in her left head; the right head peered into the cave with lips drawn back in suspicious distaste.

"You bitch!" growled Nitch. "You ran away and let those things capture me!"

"I kept myself from getting captured," the cat snarled in reply. "They paid no attention to me—a stray animal. I was able to follow them down into their lair. I came to rescue you."

"We don't need rescuing," snorted the huntress.

"Then go ahead. Keep going in the direction you were headed," Needer sneered with a feline rancor that bordered on human contempt. "But—the way *out* is back this way."

Nitch wasted barely a second with a disgruntled expression before she reversed the direction of their departure. The three humans dashed past the doorway of the prison chamber with Needer galloping in their wake.

"Where's Tagger?" called the cat. "Wasn't he captured along with Nivek and Nico?"

"We didn't see him," Nivek admitted.

"We can't leave without Tagger!" declared Nico.

"For once, I am forced to agree with the brat." Halting to peer along the dark tunnel, Needer displayed concern with both heads.

Nitch paused, realizing their flight from the caves was not going to progress with the haste she expected. Ignoring their sudden freedom, the others were fixating on the fate of the missing prairieman. They would not leave without him. Despite the manifest common sense of immediately escaping from this subterranean hell, it was clear the rest of the group was going to fight her on this choice. These caves were not the place to stage a long disagreement on such matters. They could be discovered by more drones at any second, and any battle would be ill-fated for the group. The caves were the drones' turf, the advantage would belong to them. Against her better judgment, Nitch privately conceded: better to avoid any arguments and find the prairieman, then depart as swiftly as possible.

"Okay," she granted. "But where do we look? We have no idea of the layout of these caves. We don't even know if Tagger's still alive."

Sniffing the air, Needer announced, "He's still alive. *This* way." And with a twitch of her tail, the cat dove off down the passage in the direction Nitch had originally been taking the group. The humans followed with haste.

"My Tagger," moaned Nico.

"Hush," Nitch snapped. "If your whining gets us discovered, I'll kill you myself."

The girl began to sputter with indignation, but a stern glare from the huntress froze further complaints in her young throat.

Needer led them along the tunnel, taking a left juncture with great speed. Nitch could only assume—and hope—that the cat's senses would be alert to any danger in their path.

It bothered Nitch that her own senses had not alerted her to the presence of the drones during their aboveground ambush. Nor had any premonition warned her of the drone that had barged into their prison. What strange aspect of these ex-human creatures blinded her to their presence? For all their otherness, it was evident the creatures had once possessed human ancestors. Not that *otherness* should preclude them from her predatory awareness, for Nitch was usually able to perceive the presence of humans, animals and mutations alike. The differences in these drones must be greater than anything she had previously encountered.

When Needer halted her frantic plummet through the tunnels, Nitch was instantly ready for action. But no drones appeared. With feline guile, the cat peered carefully around a corner, then backed away from the underground intersection. Once she had led the group a few meters from the corner, Needer turned to whisper to Nitch, "He's in the cave ahead."

"What's the situation? Are there many drones guarding him?"

"I… I don't know how to describe what has him." The cat's tail swished in agitation. "There are drones present… but…"

"Not good," whined her right head.

Nitch turned on Nivek, telling him urgently, "You're no good in a fight—don't argue with me, this is *not* the time or place. And Nico's worse than useless. Take her back a bit and hide yourselves. Needer and I will handle this."

"I want to help!" Nico declared. Her statement earned her a swift punch in the face from Nitch. The child went down like a wet sack of dough.

"Go," Nitch ordered Nivek. Then she wheeled on Needer, hefting her stolen bludgeon. "Let's do this."

"Bad, bad, bad," worried the cat's right head.

Needer hesitated. "The thing that has him is… big. I don't know how to describe it."

"Then describe the rest of the cave," commanded the huntress. "How many drones? Where are they in relation to the entrance? Are they well armed? Where's Tagger in the cave?"

"There's about five of the drones. Three on the right, two on the left, just inside the doorway. They're armed only with sticks like the one you have."

"Not good odds."

"But," Needer added, "our supplies and weapons are there too. About four meters from the entrance on the right. One drone standing next to them."

"Ah," Nitch nodded. "Regaining my spear or knife might just improve our chances. What about the *thing* that has Tagger? Why can't you describe it?"

"I… I've never before seen such a thing." The cat was clearly disturbed by even the memory of the thing she had seen. "Big… impossibly big. Like a huge worm…"

"Once I get my knife in hand," Nitch growled, "it'll be a dead worm. Let's go."

As they crept back to the doorway, the pair devised a plan. Needer would enter first and head to the left, causing a diversion that would hopefully draw the drones away from the group's stolen weapons. Then Nitch would enter, heading directly for the weapons. Once armed, she would go straight for releasing Tagger, dispatching any drones that got in her way.

Outside the cave, they paused. Needer cast a worried glance around the corner, then nodded to the huntress before leaping into the chamber, all hisses and snarls. Nitch counted to two, then dove after the cat into the cave.

Her dash for the pile of the group's backpacks did not go as planned. The drones present in the cave were all converging on the scampering feline, but sight of the *thing* froze Nitch in her tracks. Eyes wide and mouth fallen open, Nitch stared in shock and disbelief at the horror that held Tagger two meters off the ground.

Big was an understatement. And *worm* by no means prepared her for the grotesque monstrosity that hung from the ceiling like some bloated sack.

If the *thing* had any actual form, its shape was not defined enough to make out in the cavern's dim mold-light. Its mass dangled from a vast crack in the ceiling like a huge glob of uncooked bread dough: pliant and pulsating like the bladder of a gasping fish out of water. Unspeakably ugly, its body oozed a jelly-like goo that dribbled in stringy strands. Most of the thing was a pale blue, with traces of a sickly gray fading to a ghostly white near the region where it hung through the opening in the rock ceiling. Its sickly blue skin was covered with huge deep blue veins thicker than a man's arm. A series of gaping orifices ran along the flank facing Nitch; they opened and closed with rhythmic twitching. Within these maws a bright, wet pinkness glowed with a light that dwarfed the illumination of the splotchy luminous mold adorning the walls of the chamber.

As if all this were not enough to give any mighty hunter reason to pause and vomit, the shape that extruded from a slit in the thing's underbelly was enough to drive the hardiest human into screaming insanity. Hanging upside-down from the puckering slit was the bloated torso of a human female—at least, perhaps *once* it had been a human female. Now its shape was layered in hideous folds, flaps of fat where none should be. Hanging like pendulous sacks, a twinned row of pulsating udders hung from the beast's torso, each tipped with nipples the size of a man's head that dripped a viscous milky fluid. The bone structure beneath this obscene padding was clearly twisted into deformities that followed no sense of symmetry. The grotesque once-a-female possessed the same pale blue skin as the huge mass above, their surface covered with a similar lattice of pulsating thick veins. Six arms protruded from its torso, the rear pair being shriveled and clearly useless. Each of the other four held no resemblance to each other, though, or any appendages born of man or animal. Covered in a chitinous carapace, they were jointed more than four times and no two were alike in length or thickness. The middle pair were without hands, their crooked lengths trembling like the antennae of an insect; bristling with thick cilia, the front pair ended in giant pincers.

And held firmly aloft in these grotesque claws hung the prairieman, trussed tight with the cruel wire bindings. The claws lifted Tagger so he was face to face with the *thing's* head: another unique abomination in itself.

From cheek to cheek, the head measured as wide as a man's spread arms. Hanging from its scalp in luxurious waves was a shock of bright red hair. The hair parted in the middle, framing an upside-down face of utter deformity. There were two eyes, but one was small like a slit, lined by long lashes, while the other was huge, popping from its socket like a massive spoiled fruit. This terrible ocular was spherical in only the vaguest sense, possessing numerous bulges and bumps, each sporting their own pupil. If there was a nose, it was lost beneath the ridges that swept from cheekbone to forehead like a crusty shell formation. The thing's mouth was vast, a wide slash that bisected the head, running at an unnatural diagonal across the lower face. The rows of teeth within this mouth undulated like insane worms, while the formidable tongue seemed rigid and jointed like the arm of a crab.

The creature held Tagger's head well inside its gaping mouth. The wormish teeth caressed the man's face. The bony tongue probed to insert itself into his feverishly clenched lips.

For the first time in her life, Nitch screamed in terror, her voice rising to an octave that rivaled the screeches Nico had plagued them with the entire journey.

It was very possible that this scream saved Tagger's life. The sound startled the monstrously obscene creature, so that it withdrew the man's head from its eager mouth. The terrible head swiveled to face Nitch. Upon seeing the huntress, the creature flung Tagger to the ground and screamed in turn at Nitch. The sound was awful, full of timbre and mucoid vibration. The creature's face trembled as it gulped air, yawning its mouth wide to release a second cry.

The creature's screams unfroze Nitch from her terror. She plunged ahead toward their stolen belongings. Grasping both her spear and knife, she wheeled on the monstrosity, only to find herself facing all five of the drones. As the beast's screams had echoed in the cave, the drones had turned from chasing Needer to immediately converge on Nitch with their crude bludgeons held menacingly high. Their concentrated offensive only rewarded them all with quick deaths as the huntress swung her knife in a wide arc that caught four of the five throats in a single slice. The fifth drone impaled itself upon her spear with such ferocity that the tip erupted from its pallid spine.

Not pausing to ascertain the drones' incapacitation, Nitch leapt across the cave to grab Tagger and drag him from beneath the hanging atrocity. With quick efficiency, she pulled the shears from her belt and attempted to snip the wires that bound the man. Before she could bring the shears to this task, though, one of the creature's long forearms swung down to knock Nitch aside.

The creature grasped Nitch in its cruel claws, pulling her into the air. Its monstrous face screamed again as it lifted the huntress up. "Mine!" the beast screeched, its lips curling back and teeth reaching like tentacles to clutch at Nitch's head. "He's mine, you bitch! And so will you be, once I finish with you! You *all* belong to *me*! Someday, all of what's left of this world will belong to *me*!"

Of all the creature's repulsive traits, the fact that it could talk stunned Nitch the most. The notion of some form of intelligence dwelling within its misshapen cranium seemed like a blasphemy.

She had to force herself to cast off this horror and concentrate on her immediate plight.

Nitch struggled savagely, hacking away at the creature's arms with her knife. The claws constricted on Nitch's arms, digging painfully into the wounds torn by her previous wire bindings. As the creature's arms recoiled from the slashing knife, Nitch did not fall. The tentacular teeth had entwined themselves in her hair and now held her aloft. They pulled her head ever closer to the beast's mouth. Screams continued to flow from that maw with an offensive urgency, its fetid breath billowing into Nitch's face. The air the creature exhaled was like a foul hellish wind, actually stinging Nitch's eyes.

"Do you think I've lived this long—to be killed by some prairie savages?" the creature wailed. "I'm far more than human now, far more than even the union of human and termite genes that I spliced together. I've lived like this for centuries, and I'll last centuries more… until every living thing on this wretched planet worships me!"

As Nitch hung in the grip of the creature, Tagger struggled unsteadily to his feet. He staggered over to where the drone lay with the huntress' spear protruding from its back. Positioning himself over the dead body, Tagger grasped the spear in both bound hands behind his back, arching erect to pull the weapon from the drone's flesh. Holding the spear as high as his bonds allowed, Tagger ran under the screaming monstrosity. He crouched low, then sprang into the air.

The tip of the spear rammed into the creature's neck, spilling forth a gush of vile fluid. Releasing Nitch, the beast reacted to the injury by thrashing wildly, ripping the wound into a vicious tear with its sharp claws. Its screams degenerated into bubbling wheezes fueled by hate and rage. Gouts of blood poured from its torn throat and drenched Tagger like a crimson rainfall. The torso of floppy sacks swung down to swat at the prairieman, driving him to the ground. With a gurgling cry of "Hi whu ill hoo—" the creature stretched beneath itself, clutching at the dazed man with its clacking pincers.

Suddenly Nitch was there, between the descending beast and the lolling man. With a mighty lunge, the huntress swung her knife up, driving the blade deep into what remained of the creature's bloodied, sputtering neck. Twisting the blade and hacking through rolls of inhuman fat to reach a brittle spine, Nitch severed the neck completely. The repulsive head detached with a terrible sucking sound and flopped wetly down upon Nitch. The dead mass knocked her from her feet.

As Nitch and Tagger flailed under the great head's malformed weight, Needer sprang to their side holding the shears clasped in her right mouth.

"Quick!" gasped the cat's left head. She thrust the shears at Nitch.

Pushing the degenerate severed head away, the huntress took the shears offered by the cat and swiftly snipped the wires that bound Tagger.

The man had barely disentangled himself from the wire coils when a rush of squealing drones swarmed through the entrance to the cave. The pale beasts took one look at their decapitated queen and rushed the humans with a single scream from many throats.

Nitch met their advance with mighty lashes of her knife. Wrenching the spear from the huge corpse that dangled above their heads, Tagger lay into the frenzied drones with its gory point. Needer's claws and teeth ripped the eyes from drone after drone as they flooded into the fray. The floor beneath their feet grew slippery as the blood of the drones mixed with their queen's iniquitous fluids. The cave was filled with the cries of the beasts as they died by the dozens.

Finally, the only living things remaining in the cave were Nitch, Tagger and the cat. They were covered in the inhuman body fluids of their captors. Their own bodies were scarred and tortured by exhaustion, their fragile sensibilities driven nearly insane by the experience. But they were alive.

"We beat them…" Nitch gasped in a stunned voice.

"Thank you," uttered Tagger hoarsely. "I owe you my life."

"You don't owe me anything," the huntress snarled, her mind slowly readjusting to her suspicious temperament.

"Can we leave now?" wheezed Needer, spitting out blood that was not her own.

"Hungry," her right head asserted.

"Oh, shut up," she told herself.

On legs still unsteady, the three staggered from the cavern of carnage. With Needer in the lead, they dragged their weary selves through the damp tunnels. Beneath a matted coating of sticky reddish blood, the cat's chameleon fur began to flow from a crimson tint to match the dull gray of the rock under her paws.

"Nivek," coughed Tagger. "We have to find Nivek."

"Already done," Nitch told him with rancor. "Do you really think I'd come for *you* before rescuing my own brother?"

"Save it for later, you two," snarled the cat. "We have to get out of here."

When they encountered Nivek and Nico further down the tunnel, the children almost fled in terror at the sight of these grisly figures advancing on them.

"Wait!" called Nitch. "It's us. We found him."

"Nitch!" Nivek gasped. "What happened to you?"

"You bitch!" screamed Nico. "Tagger, she hit me! She *hurt* me! Pay her back—"

The hunter pushed past the whining child, to grip Nivek's shoulder. "You're all right, Nivek?"

"I'm okay," the boy replied uncertainly. "But—"

"We have to get out of here—*now!*" Needer declared with impatience. She galloped away.

"She's right," concurred Tagger. "Can't you feel it?"

The others became aware now of a trembling that was building around them. Clouds of dirt were drifting from the ceiling. Soon, clumps of soil were falling from the walls, dislodged by these vibrations of unknown origin.

They all plunged after Needer as the cat dashed down the tunnel.

Rounding a curve, they found the cat on her hind legs, reaching in futility for a crude ladder constructed of twined wire strands that hung from above. Set in the ceiling was a hole, the ladder disappeared into its stygian heights.

"Here," Needer announced. "This is where I followed them into these caves."

Tagger pushed Nitch to take the lead, but the huntress resisted his direction. "Go! If there's any pursuit, I'm in better shape to handle it."

Tagger was about to argue the point when the tunnel heaved with a mighty shudder beneath their feet. The prairieman scrambled up the dangling ladder, followed by Nivek, then a screaming Nico.

As Nitch grasped the ladder to pull herself up, Needer's voice sounded in the haze of dirt clouds that now filled the tunnel, "I'm going to need help, Nitch. I can't climb that thing."

Giving Needer a gruesome scowl, Nitch gathered the cat's blood-slimed body under her arm and hurriedly ascended the ladder.

"Thanks."

"Oh, shut up."

At the top of the ladder, the huntress tumbled out a hole to find herself on the side of the dry riverbed. Releasing the cat, she clawed her way up the crumbling embankment of dirt. Needer bounded from ledge to ledge, soon outdistancing the girl and reaching the cliff-like edge ahead of her. When they reached the top, neither paused to glance back. They each ran with frantic haste across the flatland, desperate to get as far away from the riverbed as they could. The ground under their fleeing feet convulsed with greater ferocity than ever. Ahead of them, Nivek dragged Nico in stumbling flight.

Reaching a point nearly a kilometer from the riverbed, the two children collapsed, gasping for air. Tagger turned to face the approaching huntress. When she saw his eyes go wide with shock, Nitch twisted around to view the reason for his surprise.

She witnessed a vast area of ground groan and disappear into the earth. A section of land almost three kilometers square sank into the ground with a wet crash.

"The caves," Nitch wheezed, struggling to catch her breath. "They collapsed…"

"That abomination—it must've been huge… buried under the riverbed." Tagger gasped in disbelief.

"That's where the river went," Needer declared. "The creature drank it all up."

They all stared, each watching with their own degree of disbelief as a deep red fluid rose to fill the newly created canyon. It was a sight to agitate even Nitch's stalwart stomach.

After a while, without further comment, the group turned and resumed their westward journey across the wasteland.

35

FAR TO THE EAST, standing atop a slight hill on the prairie, Magog watched the fantastic geological occurrence. What he beheld filled his dark soul with a dread he had never known before.

What power had caused such a collapse? It was as if the earth had swallowed a portion of itself. As his sharp eyes discerned the crimson liquid that bubbled and filled the vast hole, he shuddered. Whatever cataclysm had transpired, it had mortally wounded the land, causing the very earth to bleed!

Clearly, the group he and his band of Quiet Men followed were guilty of far greater crimes against nature than simple *noise*. The Lord had directed these Quiet Men on a quest of immense importance, possessing repercussions far beyond the scale of mortal understanding. It was obviously of great consequence that they track these terrible individuals and exact a massive vengeance upon them for their atrocities.

With a wave of his long arms, Magog shepherded his band after the offenders.

Even further east, other eyes spied on the Quiet Men, unaware of what they had paused to survey. When the Quiet Men recommenced their march, this hidden group continued to follow in their wake.

36

PIANO CHORDS TREMBLED through the melody, as light percussion twinkled at its edges. The beat was comfortably lazy, while retaining a foot-tapping appeal. A rich voice crooned lines about walking in someplace called Memphis.

It mattered not that no one knew the name any longer. With the town underwater just off the Missippi Coast, it was the melody that touched people's souls now. The tune lived on, surviving centuries longer than its namesake. Carried on the illicit airwaves, the song brought smiles to many weary workers as they dragged themselves from the end of their daily labor.

For those who were leaving their fields outside Leans, drenched by the storm that had remained unrelenting for over a hundred days, the lines "… delta blues, in the middle of the pouring rain…" held a strong ramification that made many sigh.

For others in northerly climes, the lines had different meaning, conjuring the romance of distant lands.

For those who endured the arid hardships of survival in the Rocky Districts, the lines were fanciful references to a mystical realm of impossible dampness.

For those who camped upon the Hexan plains, the lines had mythical context. For strangely, the King's legend had survived among the descendants of the American Indians, his face decorating several local totems.

Whether it was the music or the lyrics, the song touched all who heard it, as did many of the tunes broadcast by Afterburn Radio.

Fever Smith and Dr Muffin had gathered a massive array of songs in various musical styles—ranging from rock'n'roll to ambient rave to big band swing to fusion jazz to classical opus to mournful C&W.

The latter genre had attracted Fever's interest, but Dr Muffin had been quick to point out that many of the songs spoke of betrayal and emotional loss, aspects of life which the robot considered unwise to popularize in these hard times. Fever had deferred to the robot's suggestion, and their selection of songs to play had focused upon more positive lyrical content.

There had been thousands of recordings to go through, and they were still investigating unheard CDs years after the station had commenced broadcasting, constantly adding to their playlist.

Although the station's programming had been largely the result of human decisions, the robot's advice had often carried considerable wisdom. It had been Dr Muffin who had brought the alternate geological locations of their audience to Fever's attention. Although the DJ had traveled widely before discovering the radio station, he was not used to thinking of the *time of day* as something that might be *different* in other portions of Ericaland. What might have been perfectly appropriate mellow music for the Rocky Districts during the early evening was too sedate for the late afternoon of the Missippi Delta. Luckily, the time span encompassed by the continent was confined to a two hour spread, making compensations between the differences easily managed.

Starting at dawn (East Coast time, remembering that the current East Coast was the western bank of what had once been the Missippi River) the music was uptempo, followed until noon by a more raucous version of the same. During the afternoon hours, the tone became pronouncedly jovial. The evening, pre-midnight hours alternated between jazz and dance. The post-midnight hours were the domain of the softer genres: classical and experimental.

Variations had developed over the years, as the station had learned to refine their influence on their audience's moods. Wake up in the morning, stay energized throughout the day, feel rewarded after a hard day's work, be entertained during the evening and lulled to peaceful rest in the dead of night.

Nowadays, Psycho Jones had little control over what particular tune played at what precise hour. The ongoing failure of the station's equipment had forced her to rely exclusively upon pre-recorded collections. She could pick a genre, but not exact songs. Which made the appearance of "Walking in Memphis" over the airwaves so perfect during the hour in which Missippi workers were leaving their jobs, traveling home in the pouring rain.

Psycho had to smile, pleased that the presence of this song on the CD collection she had chosen could specifically touch a portion of her audience. She missed moments like this, remembering a time when she was not too exhausted to play specific tunes. Handling the station's twenty-four hour broadcast in Smithie's absence was far too grueling to allow her such indulgences anymore. Not to mention, with the station's failing equipment, she no longer had convenient access to recordings of single tracks.

But—*thank Mother Sky,* she contemplated—at least she still had her storytelling hour in the mid-evening. This was the easiest broadcast to make, for it involved no malfunctioning apparatus—just the microphone and her mouth. And her mind, for Psycho dearly enjoyed concocting tales. Imagining the implausible and making it interesting was her *real* talent, embroidering the story with characters which people could relate to, heroes they could cheer, villains they could hate. She was grateful she could share her stories with the rest of Ericaland.

Invariably, the girl remained unaware of how vital her stories had become to Dr Muffin's re-education of humanity. Her deep loathing for the Mob's Church Police was invaluable in the necessary restructuring of Ericaland's political temperament.

"Heyo, folks. This is Psycho Jones and you're listening to Afterburn Radio. Remember now, we're still illegal in twelve of the twenty-seven Districts, so keep those radios safe and hidden. Can you hear me?" Her voice was borne by radiowaves to the ears of hundreds of thousands of attentive listeners. "It's time for Campfire Tales, folks, so get comfortable.

"Tonight's tale is called 'Down There'.

"There's a string of villages up north that have decided to join together to establish a superb school which will be shared equally by the four towns. All the children from these villages attend this single school, transported from home to the place of learning—and back again at the end of each day—by several wagons driven by the teachers. A different teacher drives each wagon each day; in this manner the students receive a diversity of alternative instruction outside the classroom.

"Since the four villages have pooled their resources, they are able to pay handsomely, attracting extremely competent and well-learned teachers from all over Ericaland."

Sitting back, Psycho propped her heels on the console and squirmed low into her arcade chair. She spoke casually into the microphone that dangled before her face, hanging from a metal boom. Overhead, the large fan rotated at high speed, sending a cool breeze across her relaxed sprawl. She had turned off the lava lamp, now the room was distantly lit only by the hallway's illumination beyond the booth's open door. The semi-darkness helped her mind focus on her imaginary events; it also helped conceal her nudity, for Psycho preferred to be *comfortable* while she told her tales.

Out of a courtesy to her (at least, that's what he told her), Dr Muffin was prone to busy himself elsewhere in the station while Psycho conducted her storytelling hour. It secretly amused her that the artificial man was uncomfortable with her nakedness. He always tuned in, though, listening to her tales while he worked on some minor repair.

"Among these teachers is a man named Lexx," she continued. "The subject he teaches is mathematics, but much of the knowledge he actually imparts to his students involves simple logical deduction.

"Lexx is a comfortable man. He does not force his teachings on the children, preferring to let the knowledge flow easily into their minds. He does not condemn any student when they are wrong, but gently aids them to move beyond their ignorance to the correct answer. As a result, his students generally like Lexx, enjoying his classes as if they were playground sessions.

"One day, Lexx decides to substitute a meandering wagonride for the usual day at the schoolhouse. He hopes to be able to use the countryside to teach the presence of mathematics in everyday objects. What his students end up learning is far more abstract.

"After successfully using the leaves of a tree to get the younger children to comprehend numerical sets, Lexx guides the wagon through a narrow pass between two stone bluffs. Although the passage is not hazardous, the path twists among many unstable rocks. While maneuvering through one of these awkward clinches, the wagon traverses a stretch of ground that planes at a forty degree angle.

"As chance has it, the Gecko brothers choose that moment to exercise their naughty nature. Being a pair of eight-year-old brats, the Geckos are always bullying the other children, regardless of their age. This time, it is a much older student which the Geckos have chosen to harass. Playfully, of course, for the Gecko brothers' pranks start out as ways to amuse themselves at the disorientation of others, they give big Fenn Nask a mighty shove, sending him toppling against a group of other students. The shift of weight within the precariously balanced wagon causes the vehicle to slide sideways. As further chance has it, the wagon is passing a deep opening in the earth at this point—and their prank sends the wagon sliding directly into this dark chasm.

"You can imagine all the children screaming at this point. They're afraid. Even the bratty Gecko brothers cry out in fear for their lives." Psycho paused to interject a chorus of shrill childlike voices expressing exaggerated terror. "Everyone is shrieking as the wagon plummets into the depths of this hole—everyone except Lexx. Using his own body, Lexx attempts to re-distribute the weight to correct the wagon's balance, righting it as it falls. He hopes that the wagon's mass will cushion their inevitable impact, protecting the children from excessive harm. His actions are fortunate, for the wagon falls quite a distance before crashing into the bottom of the pit.

"The children all survive the fall, as does Lexx. They are shaken by their ordeal and many will carry bruises for days as reminders of the Geckos' ill-timed prank, but they are basically unhurt. And capable of quickly assessing that the walls of the chasm into which they have fallen are quite steep and wholly impossible to climb. They are trapped deep underground. Their only course of action is to head deeper into the earth, following a series of tunnels that lead off the chasm. With the wagon reduced to a broken rubble, they must proceed on foot.

"Lexx leads them through the dark caves. Soon they come to a region of tunnels lit by strange streaks of an ore in the cavewalls. This ore glows with a supernatural light, which Lexx identifies for his students as *radiation*."

In the lower levels of the complex, while attending to a deficiency concerning the water pressure that drives the power generators, Dr Muffin stopped unscrewing a section of pipe to sigh. He wished Psycho would stop including radioactive material in her stories. Her use of the phenomena was far too casual, it might induce some listeners to abandon their justifiable fear of radiation. He filed a subroutine in his positronic brain to remind himself to discuss the matter with the DJ/storyteller.

The robot found it mildly amusing how many of Psycho Jones' stories involved the characters finding themselves trapped underground. The psychological significance of this recurrent thread was not lost on him, but there was nothing he could really do about it. As long as Fever was absent from the station, the burden of operating the constant broadcasts fell upon the remaining human. Psycho was trapped in the subterranean station, forced to man the transmission booth hour after hour, day after day. Finding time for sleep and food had become difficult enough for the girl—the opportunity for a trip outside to bask in real sunlight and breath fresh unfiltered air was simply not possible with her busy schedule.

The acceleration of the mechanical failures plaguing Afterburn had occupied the majority of Dr Muffin's available hours for a long time. These repairs were a difficult task, further hampered by the time-consuming search for available spare parts to replace the broken ones. The robot had focused his concentration on these mechanical problems for too long.

He realized now he had been lax in his vigilance of Psycho's mental health. He could do nothing to alleviate her need for biological companionship (if only Fever Smith would return to the station!), but there must be *something* he could do to provide her with some respite from the debilitating non-stop workload.

On more than one occasion, Dr Muffin had offered to stand in for the girl as a new DJ, but she had politely shot down his suggestion. The robot's "voice" (she'd informed him) was far too artificial to pass as human. While Psycho had grown used to his weird cadence, it was certain to disturb Afterburn's listeners.

He created another subroutine in his logic system to pursue this train of thought, for the girl's mental health was vital if Afterburn were to continue broadcasting.

"Further down under the earth," Psycho's story continued, "they encounter patches of giant mushrooms. This is fortunate, for they're going to be down here a long time, and they can utilize the fungi as a source of food. Just as they can use the water they find in a subterranean waterfall. They choose to establish a base for themselves near this waterfall. From this stable ground, Lexx can send out parties comprised of the older children in search of tunnels that will possibly lead the children safely back to the surface."

Her tone of voice was spry, conveying a humorous flair to the tale.

"The children are fortunate to have become stranded in the company of such a man as Lexx. His forethought and experience are invaluable in assuring their livelihood in these dark caves. His instructions have now expanded to include teaching the children how to survive in the harsh and desperate conditions in which they find themselves trapped.

"Indeed, Lexx believes he has foreseen all possible occurrences that might be encountered in these caves… until one day when a group of students make a most astounding discovery.

"Unable to make sense of the children's' fantastic descriptions of what they have found, he urges them to guide himself and the other students to view their amazing discovery. The contents of the strange cavern to which they lead him defies even his adult mentality.

"As caverns go, it is unremarkable. Of moderate size, with walls veined by the glowing radioactive ore, it possesses a single access through a narrow opening. The contents of the cavern are another matter entirely. The man flounders in his attempts explain the impossible object half-buried there.

"For there is a ship protruding from the cave's earthen wall—a vessel that would be commonplace on the surface of any lake or river, but whose presence far beneath the ground defies Lexx's capacity for comprehension. Because the man was born in Leans on the Missippi Coast, he is familiar with seagoing vessels, and recognizes it as a boat despite the many arcane differences which feature in its design. Its age appears great; the thing has clearly been entombed down here for a long time. As far as he knows, the local villages harbor no ancient legends of a time when large bodies of water existed in this region. Lexx cannot imagine how the craft got down here.

"Although understanding or explaining its presence is beyond the man, Lexx can sense the thrill which the discovery has stimulated in his group of stranded students. In the absence of any immediate rescue from their subterranean plight, here is something that can distract the children, filling their worried minds with wonder and mystery. The group decide to unearth the ship, freeing it from the wall of dirt that encases the rear of the craft.

"As the students eagerly set to digging away the cave wall, Lexx involves himself in attempting to decipher a logbook that has been discovered in the ship's main cabin. The language used in the log is similar to that spoken by most Ericalanders, but the sentences display a convoluted structure, often featuring numerous words whose meanings baffle the teacher. It is many days before Lexx's study of the log provides him with a rudimentary knowledge of the ancient captain's incredible voyage.

"The log tells of a long voyage across a huge body of water. The ship, which Lexx believes may have called the Bounty, sailed from some distant port the name of which he cannot pronounce. The purpose of the trip seems to have involved the transportation of a vast fortune, destined to be delivered into the hands of someone called the Rooters. The nature of this treasure is mentioned only vaguely, and becomes a subject of wild speculation until the students uncover a sturdy box full of golden blocks.

"One of his students informs Lexx that the heavy shiny blocks are *gold*, a material that plays importantly in several legends from the pre-Doom days. Naturally, Lexx has heard of gold, but its rarity in modern times has made it more mythical than valuable. Since history is not his forte, he must rely upon the student's recollections of these old legends to flesh out the meanings imparted by the ship's long-gone captain.

"Unfortunately, the log ends abruptly, giving no clue to the final fate of the ship, its captain, or its crew. How a ship on an ocean voyage came to be buried under the earth remains a puzzling mystery."

Psycho paused in her tale, purposely letting a moment of silence dwell over the airwaves. She used the time to sip some water from a cup sitting on the console, wetting her word-weary mouth. She knew how much Dr Muffin loathed dead air, but these pauses were part of her storytelling repertoire—she valued their impact, they gave her audience an opportunity to digest the story-so-far.

When she resumed speaking, her tone was different: deeper and deadly serious.

"Now we come to the sad part of our story. While Lexx and his students are safe—yes, that's what I said: *safe*—underground, a Doom has fallen on their villages back on the surface. A Doom we all know, a Doom that calls itself the Mob's Church Police.

"It seems that word of the villages' communal school has reached the ears of the Mob lords in faraway Chico. Even though these villages lie far beyond the borders of their territory, the Mob lords are outraged to hear about the school's superior teaching methods. Fearing that the students may someday pose a threat to the repressive rule of the Mob, the lords of the evil High Council send a team of Church Police to destroy all trace of this seat of knowledge. Displaying the usual thoroughness of their terrible doctrines, this Church Police team decides to include the four villages and all their inhabitants in their vicious retribution.

"Since the villages stand many days outside the Mob's horrible District, they have never considered themselves to be in any danger from such an attack, and consequently are unprepared and incapable of defending themselves against such an unprovoked, surprise assault."

Another pause, this one lasted for ten seconds.

Then: "While Lexx and his students are safe underground, their villages have been wiped out by the Church Police.

"They don't know this, though. They're busy down in the caves, trying to understand the incredible discovery they've found. They're unaware that the Church Police have noticed that one wagon is missing from the schoolgrounds. They're also unaware that the Church Police are scouring the countryside in search of these missing students.

"Meanwhile, while Lexx and most of the students have been busy digging out the ancient ship, a pair of students choose to continue to search the different tunnels, looking for a way out of their underground imprisonment.

"If you guessed that these two students are the Gecko brothers, you're right. Unimpressed by the lure of any ancient knowledge inherent in the buried ship, the Geckos are bored. They long to escape these tunnels and return to their families. The Geckos plan to blame their underground ordeal on Lexx, demanding that some form of punishment be exacted upon the teacher for endangering the children. Somehow, the brothers envision that *they'll* end up in possession of the treasure that was found in the hull of the entombed seacraft.

"But when the Geckos accidentally find a way out of the tunnels, they promptly fall into the hands of the Church Police—remember, they've been hunting for any loose students from the villages. In the cowardly hope of convincing the Church Police to spare them, the Geckos tell the killers where they can find the rest of their classmates. They also tell the Church Police all about the fabulous treasure their teacher has found buried in the earth. Now, don't waste your breath condemning the Geckos for their traitorous actions; the Church Police reward the brothers by slitting their throats.

"And don't worry about the Church Police team, either. For they head directly down into the tunnels with the intent of finding and slaying the remaining students and their brave teacher... but they don't pay enough attention to the Gecko brothers' directions. They become lost in the tunnels and cannot even find their way back out. They never do locate the students. After a little over a week's time, the members of the Church Police team revolt, kill their team leader and eat him. Within another week, the rest of the team kills each other for food. The last one dies of hunger.

"This all happened a few years ago.

"What became, you ask, of the students stranded beneath the ground? Well, they're still down there. They've made a comfortable home for themselves in the caves, building the beginnings of an entire subterranean village. As the older students have aged, they began to have children of their own. And these new children are taught by the underground Tribe's master teacher, Lexx.

"The Tribe of Lexx is still down there, learning all they can from their own private archeological dig. They haven't uncovered an answer yet for how that ship found its way beneath the surface so far from any body of water, but someday they will.

"Until then, they'll continue to grow and learn. And the Mob doesn't even know they're down there."

She chuckled, "Doesn't that just want to make you dance?" And she triggered this evening's tape of lively music.

Once Psycho's Campfire Tale was concluded, Dr Muffin switched off the part of him that tuned in to the station's broadcast. By sheer coincidence, the robot was just finishing up his repairs, tightening the pipe section to which he had just applied a replacement sealant ring. Now the water pressure would remain constant as it flowed into the wheel that drove the station's power generator.

An interesting tale, he thought as he gathered his repair supplies. He was constantly amazed by the girl's ability to create such stories from the depths of her own imagination. His positronic brain possessed no capability to fabricate such fictions.

He did note, however, that this story had been rather open-ended, lacking the powerful confrontation/resolution that were the earmarks of Psycho's better Campfire Tales.

More evidence, realized the robot, of the pressure under which Psycho Jones existed in the radio station's present operation. Forced to keep most of the broadcasts going by herself, she lacked the free time anymore to properly craft her tales. Under these conditions, Dr Muffin was personally impressed that she found the time and concentration to be able to continuously come up with fresh material for her daily storytelling sessions. If these tales were sparse or flawed, he could not hold it against her. She was doing her best—much better than most humans would produce under similar constraints. If Psycho had more time to devote to her creativity, her best would only become better.

He wished he could solve Psycho's problems… for her own sake, and the future of Afterburn.

37

TAGGER AND NITCH WALKED for hours wearing the drones' blood as unpleasant protection from the sun's vicious glare. The thick clouds of flies that followed them were a constant annoyance.

This was one of the many things that bothered Nico.

She found the heat oppressive. Never before in her life had Nico been subjected to such brutal temperatures. The sun blazed in the colored sky, cooking everything in sight—herself, the ground, even the very air she breathed. She begged for water to relieve her discomfort. But there was no water, at least this was what the group claimed. They continued to blame her for depleting their precious water supply. And Tagger declared that the only water he knew of in the area had been the Saw River, which had vanished under circumstances he alluded to in cryptic manner, adding confusion to her discomfort.

The stench of the dried blood intensely offended Nico. She beseeched Tagger and Nitch to wash it off, but her complaints went unnoticed. So many of her complaints were being ignored lately!. The pair had paused to use dirt to scrub away a majority of the offending gore from their flesh, but the smell still remained as an indecent taint to the already uncomfortable air. (In all fairness, Nico had to admit that at least Needer had removed most of the blood and stench from her own fur, using her own tongues—how gross! But the cat was small, and her fetor was nothing compared to the foul malodor that enveloped the prairieman and the huntress.) The awful smell frequently plagued Nico with the urge to vomit… but there was nothing in her stomach to bring up. As it was, all she could do was gag with dry retches and complain.

Hordes of insects irritated Nico's already raw nerves. She had never been fond of bugs and found their presence in such profusion to be quite unsettling. The buzzing was a constant nuisance. But even worse: the flies persisted in landing upon her skin. Couldn't the dirty things tell there was no gore covering her? Why wouldn't they leave her alone? Ugh—they kept flitting about, repeatedly flying into her mouth! She did not perceive this grossness as accidental, attributing to the insects a dedication to pester *her* more than the pair of bloodstained travelers.

Nico was certain the pieces of jerky given her were chosen for their toughness and dreadful flavor.

Nitch treated her like some pariah. Didn't the huntress realize how Nico longed to emulate her? At times, Nico suspected Nitch was jealous of her—of how easily she had beaten that awful stone monster. (Nico still bridled with pride concerning her ingenious victory over that prairie beast.) But further rumination made her aware that Nitch's displeasure with her had begun earlier than that, going all the way back to the morning after their night trapped beneath the Oogolah ruins. *The necklace,* she realized—*that* was when it must have happened. Nitch was envious that Nico had won this prize jewelry from the huntress. How shallow! Nico could not believe Nitch would be so petty.

Furthermore, the huntress made no attempt to apologize for the indignities she afflicted upon poor Nico. She dismissed Nico's discomfort with an insulting satisfaction, as if taking some perverse pleasure in her suffering. When she learned how offended Nico was by her smell, the huntress seemed determined to walk closer to her, frequently positioning herself upwind.

Nivek had not taken losing her to Tagger with any maturity. The boy's attitude had cooled into a terse mood that loomed like an insurmountable wall, seemingly constructed solely to reject Nico. How could Nivek's love for her have dwindled so quickly? His jealousy should have lasted for some time; emotional starvation should have kept the boy tethered to her. Something had replaced her in his heart. This had never happened before— people always stayed infatuated with Nico, regardless of their chances to be with her. She couldn't understand his disinterest, nor could she fathom what fancy had taken her place.

While Needer—well, Nico could certainly expect no sympathy from Needer. The cat had *never* liked her.

But the greatest annoyance to Nico's outlook was Tagger. The man had somehow forgotten his devotion for her. His treatment of her now seemed to have transformed into intolerant indifference. He'd made no move to punish Nitch for striking her in those awful caves. In fact, ever since their underground ordeal, the prairieman had become overtly short-tempered with her, absolutely unsympathetic to her discomfort. How could he treat her this way? What had happened to his deep ardor, his impassioned protection of poor little Nico?

She felt acutely alone. If Tagger had forsaken her, then who would care for her now?

Poor Nico… lost in the wilderness with no one to take care of her… except herself.

Now, there was a novel concept.

"**THIS ONE?**" Psycho asked, indicating the middle reel on the console in the transmission booth.

The robot told her, "Yes. I had to cannibalize the other two for the necessary parts to get the center one operational."

"How am I supposed to switch between tapes now?" Her voice was calm, carrying no reproach. Her query was purely rhetorical.

"You'll have to do a live sequeway," Dr Muffin admitted. He wished he could shrug, suspecting that such a human gesture might put the girl at ease. "Inconvenient, perhaps. But less so than having no active tape reel, right?"

Psycho sat back in her arcade chair. The high shell of its back hid her from the robot. She sighed, "I suppose."

"This should help," Dr Muffin took a pair of CD jewel cases from the pocket of his dirty labcoat. He laid them on the console. "I found these in the archives."

"New music?" she leaned forward, picking up the cases with eager fingers. "*This* is more like it, Dr Muffin." She eyed the blank cases, then looked up at the robot, "What's on them?"

"Honestly, I have no idea. As you can see, they're unlabeled."

"That's okay." The girl smiled. "I'll catalog the tracks. It'll give me something to do while they're playing. Thanks, Doc. I really appreciate this."

"Well…" The robot turned to leave the booth. "More repairs require my attention."

The girl chuckled, "Busy busy, huh?"

You have no idea, mused the robot.

39

As TAGGER GRABBED HANDFULS of dry soil and applied them to his skin in an attempt to scrub away the termite queen's awful blood-stains, he contemplated the dire circumstances in which the group found themselves.

They had journeyed far into the desolate flatlands, meeting—and besting—several monsters. He was grateful that none of these encounters had proven disastrous. Alone with Needer, the prairieman would've had no reason to fear for their lives. But they were not alone on this journey; he had the safety of the children to worry about—Nivek in particular. It was imperative that he escort the boy safely to Afterburn's secret radio station and deliver him over to Dr Muffin.

Tagger knew that Nitch could fend for herself, the huntress' safety was never an issue. In fact, the girl had shown her spunk by rescuing him from the jaws of the termite queen in the caves beneath the dry Saw riverbed. Her survival skills were downright admirable, considering what a novice she was to the hostile prairie. If it were not for her strange sense of irritation with him, he might have entertained romantic feelings for the huntress. This curious anger she displayed toward him puzzled Tagger. He could put no finger on the source of her displeasure. He sensed that Needer under-stood the girl's motives better than he, but no chance had afforded itself for him to question his traveling companion concerning the girl's dislike.

The real threat that plagued the group now was lack of water. He had been relying upon the Saw River to replenish their diminished water sup-ply. Finding the river gone had upset his plans immensely. Now, trudging across the arid flatlands, his worry was intensifying with every step.

They still had days to go before reaching the foot of the Rocky Mountains, where water would be plentiful. Tagger knew that he and Needer, and probably Nitch, could last until they found water there, but he feared for the health of Nivek, and begrudgingly Nico too. Without the succor water would provide, the children were doomed in this cruel heat.

It would be disastrous to have brought Nivek and his head full of knowledge this far only to lose the boy to dehydration. Such a failure would be a death-knoll for Afterburn, and the final blow to Tagger's flagging self-confidence.

He sincerely had no concept of an existence without the future of Afterburn as his focal drive.

In search of water, he had orchestrated several sidetracks in the last day, heading toward turf that appeared more promising… but no underground moisture had been discovered when he'd paused to dig. The land was utterly devoid of water. What scrubs existed were brittle beyond belief, crumbling to powder under the gentlest touch. The landscape was barren of even cacti. The skies remained empty of any vultures too, signifying how truly dead the region had become. This was, he knew, the fault of the abomination back in that cave. Clearly the creature had been responsible for draining the fluids from the Saw River with its gigantic thirst. The absence of the river had taken a brutal toll on the surrounding lands.

Rain was not an option out here, Tagger was well aware of that. Any moisture which eastbound clouds picked up off the Siffic Ocean was generally blocked by the Rocky Mountains and rerouted north and south. By the time any wet weather systems were blown east again, they had deposited their rainfall upon the Hexan plains or the Ogone woodlands. This wasteland had not seen rain for over a century. What water existed out here was precious and locked in tightly constrained foodchain cycles that refused to tolerate external interference.

Unless Tagger was willing to lead the group days north to the old Springs, there would be no water to slake their thirst. Unfortunately, by his estimation, such a northern detour would take as long as continuing west to the Rocky's foothills. Both spans exceeded his expectation of Nivek's stamina in his dehydrated state. Tagger chose to continue west.

So he trudged across the prairie, moving more by habit of rhythm than by conscious motivation. His mind wandered behind his eyes, dwelling upon the survival of the group, searching in vain for an alternative or any heretofore unknown solution. Whether because of the terrible heat or the simple fact that no solution existed, Tagger's ruminations bore no fruit besides frustration.

The only repercussion of this heat that Tagger welcomed was that it had silenced Nivek's questions about Fever Smith. Each member of the journeying group was far too uncomfortable to waste valuable energy in conversation.

40

AS NIGHT FELL on their second day of waterlessness, the group roused from the debilitating lethargy brought on by a day spent trying to sleep under the blistering sun.

They sat in a circle on the hard dry earth and Tagger forced each of them to consume a strip of dried jerky before they began this night's weary march. "We need what strength we can get," he urged.

"But it tastes so awful," whined Nico. "And it's so dry…"

Munching her piece of dried meat, Nitch smiled. She seemed to enjoy the child's complaints at this point. The huntress' mood was getting darker and darker.

"Something's coming!" Needer suddenly hissed. While her right head continued consuming her strip of jerky, Needer turned north to growl and arch her back. Her tail vibrated in the air with strident warning.

A second later, Nitch tensed as if some inner alarm had gone off in her head. Her hand flew to the knife at her belt.

It was a few minutes before the weird noise began. One could not discern any actual instant whereupon it started, it seemed to flow into existence with an unnatural subtlety. From a whisper of a hiss it grew slowly into a distant growl… a soft rumble that came from the north.

A moment later a light appeared far out on the prairie. Gradually this light approached, mutating into a brilliant pair of glowballs that rode in the air less that two meters off the ground. With the approach of these alien lights, the mysterious growl took upon an utterly unearthly definition.

It was with wonder and the beginnings of fear that the members of the group observed the lights and sound transform into a massive metallic vehicle that surged toward them across the nocturnal surface of the flatlands. While Tagger and Nitch clutched their weapons at the ready, Needer bounded away into the darkness. The two children were stunned quiet by the apparition that rolled up and *shhh*ed to a halt not several meters away from their fireless campsite.

The thing loomed vast into the night, fully eight meters tall. Its shape was that of a long rectangle, covered with subtler curves and attachments. It rode on a series of huge wheels placed three on each side. The wheels themselves were startling enough, being comprised of large circular tubes made of some bulbously pliant but sturdy material. These wheels stood taller than a man. Along the vehicle's side were a few windows through which poured another source of light. Peering out from this inner glow were men!

The original pair of glowballs were set low on the front of the vehicle, positioned at its flanks. Above these lights was another glowing window; two men sat behind the strange glass.

The growl originated from beneath the incredible vehicle.

Although he had no idea what Nitch and the children thought of the thing, Tagger recognized it as a *vehicle*. There were notable differences, but it distinctly resembled pictures Dr Muffin had shown him years ago--astounding two-dimensional depictions of ancient vehicles of strange design. Dr Muffin had explained that such vehicles ran by combusting a certain fluid under compression, a methodology that no one at Afterburn had been able to imagine. If not for the miracles exhibited by the radio station's equipment, not to mention the metal man himself, Tagger would have dismissed those pictures as frivolous fabrications of the robot's sense of humor--if Dr Muffin indeed did possess such a whimsy.

And now, here was just such a vehicle: replete in all its improbable and unbelievable nature.

The questions of *where* it came from and *who* had driven it here were quick to surface in Tagger's mind.

As the group stared in mute wonder, a section of the side of the vehicle opened into a doorway. Three men climbed down from the bowels of the metal conveyance. They stood beside the vehicle, a certain amount of arrogance evident in their posture. Two of the men carried devices which Tagger could only compare to elongated crossbows without bows. Whatever they fired, it was clear the devices were *weapons*.

Don't be so defensive, Tagger reprimanded himself. *I'm standing here holding my weapon—so is Nitch. These strangers have every right to bear arms in unfamiliar surroundings—perhaps more so than we do.*

"Let me do the talking," the prairieman whispered to his group. "Don't do *anything* until I tell you to. For now, lower your knife, Nitch."

The strangers approached the group: the unarmed one between and a step ahead of the two guards. They were all dressed strangely—in fact, their attire reminded Tagger with an unpleasant clarity of the clothing worn by the corpse they had found far beneath the Oogolah ruins. Long pants and long-sleeved shirts, strict shiny boots, wondrous belts around their waists hung with crisp pouches.

Perhaps the most amazing aspect of their appearance were their faces. Never in any of his travels had Tagger encountered men of this ethnic strain. Their noses were flat and wide, their mouths wide and thin lipped. Their eyes were uncanny—cut in narrow slits that angled strangely. Tall foreheads rose to jet-black hair. Except for the strangers' startling eyes, the closest comparison Tagger could make might be with the Dian Tribes that dwelled down in Hexas.

When the lead stranger spoke, his language was guttural and foreign.

Tagger could only shrug in response. "I do not speak your language." He would have shaken his head, but wanted to avoid implying any possible negative reply to the man's inquiry before he understood it.

The lead stranger frowned, placing his fists on his hips in an attitude of authority. Without turning his head, he called back to his vehicle using his rough language.

In a second, a bulky figure was shoved from the vehicle's doorway, to be followed by another weapon-bearing guard. The latter ushered the former over to the group.

With a start, Tagger recognized Kaz, another of Afterburn's field agents. Normally, Kaz roamed the northern flatland perimeter. What was he doing this far south? Were this fantastic vehicle and its inhabitants new Afterburn recruits that Kaz had found? Tagger doubted that, for numerous bruises darkened the man's suntanned flesh.

As Kaz and his escort came up to the group, bathed in the bright light of the vehicle's lamps, the lead stranger gestured curtly toward Tagger and rattled off what was obviously a curt command.

Speaking with a serious face that wore no welcome, Kaz warned, "If you value your lives, act as if you don't know me."

"But—we've never seen you before…" whined Nico.

"Keep her *quiet*, Nivek," Tagger hissed. To Kaz he inquired, "Who are these people? What do they want?"

"They call themselves Mongols," replied Kaz. "They claim to come from the other side of the Siffic Ocean. They say they're here as explorers, but I suspect they're an advance guard for some kind of invasion. I ran into them way up north and they've conscripted me as their translator. They have no idea who I am. Be really careful not to react when I tell you: they're looking for Afterburn Radio."

"How can I help *you*?" Tagger asked carefully.

"Pretend to be simple savages and they may just continue on without bothering you," advised Kaz. He paused to turn to the lead Mongol, speaking to him in the man's language. After listening to the man's unintelligible reply, Kaz faced Tagger again to relate, "I told him you've never heard of Afterburn. He insists I ask you again. It'd help if you all shake your heads this time, to help show your ignorance."

"Okay, we'll play along." Shaking his head, as did the others in his group, Tagger asked with an exaggerated simple expression, "Are you their prisoner? Can we help you?"

"I honestly don't know if I'm a prisoner or just hired help. The best thing *you* can do is get word about these guys to Afterburn. I assume that's what you're doing out here—heading for the station, right? Meanwhile, I'll do everything in my power to keep them away from the station."

"Can you tell us anything else about these Mongols?"

"You can see the level of technology they have. Their vehicle is just like the ones in those pictures Dr Muffin has. These weapons they carry are astounding—they fire metal slugs at a fantastic speed. They have devices with them I can't even begin to understand. They're dangerous. And I don't trust them one bit."

"At least they picked the best man to guide them," Tagger remarked with an idiotic smile.

After conveying something to the lead Mongol, Kaz commented, "You look terrible. Are *you* okay?"

"It's a long story, I'll tell you some other time. We *could* use some water, though."

"Isn't the Saw River back that way?" Kaz pointed east.

"Not anymore."

"Humph." Kaz looked pensive. "That could help me out. Their vehicle uses water as its fuel. If I could strand them out here in the flatlands, it might put a crimp in their plans." He turned to speak to the Mongol in the glottal foreign language.

Great, mused Tagger. A new menace for Afterburn. As if the station didn't have enough troubles right now… enter an invading horde wielding incredible technology. What an absolute irony it would be if these Mongols were to solve our water problems, unaware how it would aid in undermining the purpose of their search for Afterburn. Although, in truth, Tagger had no idea what Afterburn could do to battle these invaders. The station was notably devoid of any weaponry, relying mainly on its underground location to protect itself from intruders. Knowing about these invaders would be a step, though, no matter how trivial.

Kaz faced Tagger again, smiling at him. "They're willing to give you some water. Especially since I assured them they could stock up on all they need at the Saw River just east of here."

"You're a lifesaver," announced Tagger.

"I always am."

With a sense of officious dismissal, the lead Mongol turned on his heel and returned to his monstrous vehicle. His pair of bodyguards accompanied him, followed by Kaz and his guard. A pair of curiously transparent containers were handed down to Kaz from within the vehicle. He returned with them to the group.

There, Nitch and Nivek filled the group's waterskins from the bottles. Once the skins were full, each member of the group quenched their desperate thirst from the liquid remaining in the two bottles, Tagger going last. He marveled at these hard clear bottles—glass, he guessed, although he couldn't recall the last time he'd seen unbroken glass outside of Afterburn's complex.

"Where's Needer?" Kaz asked as the prairieman drank. "She's still with you, isn't she?"

"Yeah. She ran off as you arrived."

"She hasn't lost her nerve, has she?"

"No. She's fond of this tactic in uncertain situations. It gives her the opportunity to act as a free agent should we require rescue."

"Tell her hi for me." Kaz sighed, gathering up the bottles. He turned to leave, then looked back at the prairieman with sad eyes. "By the way, should things go badly… will you take care of my prairie sailer? It's hidden in a valley south of Hot Springs."

"Don't worry." He waved goodbye to his old friend. "You'll come through this safe and smug. You always do."

As his guard escorted Kaz back to the strange Mongol vehicle, Nico asked petulantly, "Why can't we go with them? They could take us to Afterburn faster than we could walk there. I don't understand. I'm tired of walking in this awful heat."

With a sigh, Tagger told the child, "You're a spoiled little brat, Nico. I'd hoped that something on this journey would help you grow up… but I guess that isn't going to happen, is it?"

As the child flustered with violent indignation, Nitch laughed out loud, hoisting her now-full waterskin over her shoulder.

"No." Tagger gestured to the huntress to sit back down. "I think it wiser we don't leave until these Mongols are long out of sight."

Once Kaz had disappeared into the Mongol's vehicle, it growled into life again and drove off.

The group remained seated in a circle per Tagger's counsel. He suggested they resume their jerky meal, fortifying themselves for the night's travels ahead.

"You're mean," grumbled Nico. "All of you."

"We've survivors," asserted Tagger. "And I mean to see that we remain that way."

Trotting out of the darkness, Needer came up to Tagger. He poured some water into his cupped hand, allowing the cat to drink her fill from it. "Tastes funny," Needer remarked as she lapped the liquid from Tagger's hand.

After the cat had satisfied both her thirsts, she casually asked Tagger, "Was that Kaz?"

"Yes."

"Thought so. It smelled like him."

"You knew that guy," Nitch inquired. "Who was he?"

"His name is Kaz," answered Needer. "He works for Afterburn just like we do."

"You heard Kaz's story?" Tagger asked the cat. Again, she nodded.

"What?" whined Nico. "If he's going to take those Mongrels to Afterburn, why couldn't we have gone with them?"

Nivek snorted at her. "Didn't you hear anything he told us, you nitgit? He's going to lead them *away* from Afterburn. And they were called Mongols, not Mongrels." He looked at Tagger. "That's his job, right?"

The prairieman nodded. "Yes. He maintains the northern line."

"Seems like *everybody* is looking for Afterburn these days," observed Nitch.

41

AFTER DISMISSING THE REST of the Council from their ultra-se-cret conference chamber buried deep beneath the royal castle in Chico, the old man sat for some time, his ancient eyes regarding the energies that crackled in the glass sphere set on the table before him. He never failed to weary of watching the holy current dancing along the filament contained within the transparent ball. After nearly a century in his position as High Priest of the Mob, the simple pleasure of such technological wonders still gave him cause to smile.

Beyond the royal Castle, he knew this simple device would instill terror in any who witnessed its electrical undulations. The Mob had been thorough in their teachings to the common man: gadgetry was evil, a resi-due of the technologies that had called the Doom down upon mankind ages ago. He smiled afresh, knowing how these dogmas were riddled with carefully concocted untruths.

He had read of the Doom in ancient books contained in the Council's sanctum, a library that was accessible only to himself now that old Villiers had perished two decades ago. Even with his superior knowledge of such arcane technologies, the High Priest understood only the basics of the true nature of that catastrophe. He knew *what* had happened, but not *how* it had been done. He knew *who* was responsible, but not *why* civilization had been destroyed. They were secrets he would never divulge to another soul, so terrible were their scope and implication.

There were other secrets to guard from the population, ones that af-fected everyday life. The dichotomy between the Mob's anti-technology edicts and the profusion of these devices used by the inner circle, espe-cially the Church Police. Technology was not evil, it was simply a luxury that belonged only to the high bred. The common man could never hope to appreciate such wonders—and never would, as long as the Church ruled from behind the curtain of the Mob. The lives of the ruling class were the only ones entitled to benefit from these illustrious wonders. That was the way of things which he had learned when he became High Priest long ago, and it was a status quo he had dedicated himself to maintaining, no matter what the cost of livelihood or discomfort among the general masses.

So it had been with intense horror that the High Priest had reacted when the abomination that was Afterburn Radio had commenced broadcasting a few decades ago, filling the airwaves with their unsanctioned music and a truthful dissemination of facts. The very existence of Afterburn implied the presence of technology in hands other than those of the Church. The actuality that Afterburn was using this technology *against* the Mob was a secondary affront, although in recent years it had become a far more annoying violation of Church dogma.

It had been evident from the first that the voices of Afterburn Radio loathed the manner in which the Mob ruled its territory, condemning the oppression and arrogance with which the ruling class subjugated the masses, the human sheep that fed the royal wolves with their forced labor. But, until recently, Afterburn's affronts had been confined to abstract propaganda, denouncing generalities and dissecting policies from afar.

Now, though, the pirate radio station had gone too far, revealing the Mob's plots to overtake the Rocky Districts at the planned peace talks— themselves a farce which had taken nearly a decade to arrange, lulling the Rocky's lords with smooth lies and promises of equality in the proposed union of governments. *Now*, after decades of useless anti-radio laws, at last the Council had decided to respond with lethal action, seeking to silence the radio station's unholy signal.

It would not be long now, the High Priest contemplated, that he could look forward to never again hearing the hated voices of Fever Smith and especially that trollop Psycho Jones, whose Campfire Tales cast the Mob in such derisive—if accurate—light. He wished he could dance upon their graves, although he knew his infirm body would tolerate no such strenuous exertions.

A blinking light on the console above the doorframe to the conference chamber interrupted his private reverie.

Ah, he noted, *the traitor has arrived.* He casually pressed the switch that opened the doors, admitting the team of elite Church Police and their captive.

They entered, escorting the Empress Beel into his presence. As per his instructions, the team had set upon the woman while she was bathing, capturing her naked. Her regal shoulders were bent beneath the weight of the heavy wooden cross to which her outstretched arms were bound. As she stood before him, her face burned with imperial indignity over the atrocities exacted upon herself by this treatment.

The High Priest was not too old to derive a small pleasure from the sight of her nudity. Her breasts were high and firm; she had allowed no fat to blunt the curves of her supple belly. He had always considered her a beautiful example of breeding, indeed far more attractive than any other Empress during the last fifty years. Such a pity she would no longer be around to admire.

"Why have you summoned me *thus*?" she snapped at him, her voice resounding with regal demand.

Choosing no immediate reply, the High Priest tapped his long bony fingers on the surface of the wide iron conference table. He looked at her without expression, his bland and withered face all the more terrible for its absence of any emotion. Deciding finally to amuse himself with a conversation with this woman, he gestured, dismissing the team of Church Police save but for the two most trusted (meaning deaf and dumb) soldiers.

When he was alone with the naked Empress and the two stone-faced men, the High Priest deigned to smile at the woman. "I think you know why. Shall we not waste our breath by stating the obvious? You know what the Council has done… the Council knows what you plan to do about it."

"You bastard," she swore. "You will not get away with this. I cannot be as easily replaced as you did with Vassal."

"We have no intention of *replacing* you, my dear," he spoke calmly. "Your *death* will serve to fulfill many functions."

"You wouldn't *dare*!"

He raised his hands, counting off the fingers of one gnarled hand with the other. "Besides the obvious purpose of removing you before you can implement any action against the Council… your death will remind the new Premier that his silence and cooperation will insure his continued existence… your death will entertain the masses, both high and low class, for who does not enjoy seeing how far an Empress can fall?… your death will add color and pomp to the Festival of Retribution this upcoming weekend… your death will be a clear message to all that the Mob will no longer tolerate Afterburn's interference in our territory."

"Afterburn?" sputtered the Empress. "What have I to do with—"

"… And," the old man counted off the final finger of his litany, "your death will provide results to the investigations which your new husband so loudly demands. I refer to the Premier's proclaimed hunt for Afterburn spies within the royal Castle. This will certainly sate his lust for retribution against the radio station he hates so violently."

"You are *insane!*" She squared her shoulders in defiance as best she could under the cruel weight of the wooden beam.

"Only a highly placed Afterburn spy could have uncovered the replacement of the old uncooperative Vassal with the new docile one."

"The Premier will *never* believe this accusation!" she protested.

"His belief will be quite immaterial to the proceedings. The *people* will believe. And those who do *not* believe in their heart will voice their belief rather than seem to appear in collusion with the pirate radio station. The very nature of the accusation precludes any disbelief in your guilt, my dear."

"I will not remain silent throughout this farce!" the Empress announced in anger.

"Ah," he smiled, this time broadly, "but you *will*. For, by the time the weekend comes around, you will no longer have any tongue with which to taint the ceremony."

She paled, taking a step back from her position at the foot of the table.

The High Priest steepled his fingers, peering evilly over them at the naked Empress. " Let us consider the method of your death. It must be splendid, terrifically graphic so that it can be enjoyed by those unlucky enough to be seated in the Arena's furthest ranks. I am particularly fond of the guillotine, myself..."

She gasped in sincere horror.

"... But I think that is too quick for you, my dear. The crowd deserves a longer treat. Perhaps burning you alive at the stake..."

She struggled to flee, but found herself quickly restrained by the burly pair of Church Police.

"I believe I will decide later on the exact nature of your public punishment. You will have enough time in captivity before the weekend to imagine all sorts of dreadful retributive fates... perhaps one of them will be the method I will choose for you, my dear." The ancient High Priest nodded, pleased with the cries of terror now issued by the contorting woman. "Considering the nasty little habits you have embraced since you became the original Premier's concubine, I suspect your imagination is fully as capable as my own in devising a grotesquely appropriate end that suits your deviant and traitorous personality."

With a wave of his hand, the High Priest dismissed the screaming Empress. The pair of brutish soldiers took her away, depositing her in a moistly dark and vermin infested cell far beneath the royal Castle.

High in the upper atmosphere, satellite DSH 473.99 observed these proceedings through its spyeyes with the dispassion of its insentient programming. It automatically relayed the data to satellite RTD 126.1952.2, bouncing the signal around the curvature of the globe to where RTD 126.1952.2 hovered high above the Siffic Ocean. Upon reviewing the tapes, RTD 126.1952.2 forwarded the files to Dr Muffin at Afterburn's secret base, privately curious how the robot would accept the irony of the evil Empress' punishment for her fabricated collusion with the radio station instead of the many crimes against humanity of which Afterburn knew the woman to really be guilty. Not for the first time in its centuries old self-awareness, satellite RTD 126.1952.2 acknowledged how fate sometimes managed to balance the affairs of human justice.

42

AFTER CRAWLING like a metal worm through the wreckage, Dr Muffin entered the transmitter room for the first time in days. His duties below had kept him far too busy to check on the incoming transmissions in the secret chamber—a lapse he was eager to correct. One never knew what sort of news had come in during his absence.

News from the outside world was often far more time-sensitive than developments within Afterburn's underground station, a fact that Psycho Jones was not capable of understanding. The failures of the station's equipment were her immediate concern, and rightly so, for *these* failures disrupted the station's broadcasts. As the station's only technician, these problems became Dr Muffin's fundamental priority as they occurred. Unless he kept the station's machines operating, the broadcasts would lapse into silence. This was an eventuality which the robot regrettably knew would someday happen. But as long as his efforts could forestall that silence, all such repairs must take precedence before any of his other duties.

Dr Muffin made his customary rounds of the transmitter room, checking on the status of each of the vital apparatus. After cleaning the accumulated dust from the troublesome coils in one machine, he finally approached the banks of receiver equipment. He noted that the tray was nearly full of printouts. Clearly there had been much activity in the outside world during his absence.

He decided to quickly scan the sheets now rather than store them for later review. Much of the data his satellite cohorts had sent him concerned everyday occurrences. A particular item, however, gave the robot pause.

A submersible had been sighted off the Rocky Mountain Coast. It had deposited a strange vehicle on land before disappearing again beneath the Siffic waves.

Noting the ID number on the report, Dr Muffin quickly transmitted a request for video footage of the event. It would be a few minutes before the satellite could compress the data and fire it back to Afterburn, so

Dr Muffin resumed his review of the reports he held in his metal hands. Before the video footage came in, the robot was able to follow the vehicle's progress from further reports of its travels across Ericaland.

The vehicle had headed north to the Helena Pass where it had crossed the mountain range. Then it had headed south, following the foothills while avoiding any settlements. No contact with Ericaland natives had occurred until the vehicle had reached Hot Springs south of the Black Hills in the lower Kota District. There, the report cited, the vehicle had made contact with Afterburn's northern field agent, Kaz Geller.

This was not good, reflected Dr Muffin. Kaz was a good man, but encountering an indeterminable like this vehicle was a rash move. No field agent could be expected to comprehend the full scope of this eventuality… especially if this vehicle's origin was what Dr Muffin suspected it to be.

A light on the receiver before him glittered, signalling the downloading of the video data he had requested. Several moments passed before the apparatus *ping*ed, announcing the download's completion. Consulting the deck before removing the disc upon which the download had been stored, the robot observed that the data contained on the disc was far more than he had expected. Withdrawing the disc from the machinery, he slid it into the slot in his chest.

Images sprang to life in his positronic mindseye.

Dr Muffin watched a metal submersible surface near the Rocky Mountain Coast. Several overlays of data provided him with technical information regarding the ship and region. The robot paid little attention to these overlays. His inner attention was focused on the ship itself. The design was fairly reminiscent of pre-Doom Russian submarines.

With the realization that his worst suspicions might finally be grounded in fact, Dr Muffin watched the submarine discharge a ground vehicle to the Coast. Again, the robot could not help but note the similarities this ground vehicle possessed to ancient pre-Doom military assault transports.

He observed the vehicle head north along the coast. The image became accelerated as time-lapsed pictures condensed its journey to and through the Helena Pass.

At this point, a subfile on the disc opened in the robot's consciousness, activating a digital message for Dr Muffin from the A.I. that dwelled in satellite RTD 126.1952.2. Although actual words were not involved, the message informed Dr Muffin that the satellite had included additional footage of the vehicle's subsequent activities to this transmission, assuming they would be of interest to Dr Muffin in lieu of his original inquiry. *Ah,* mused the robot, *RTD 126.1952.2's initiative is always appreciated.*

The message also advised that scans of the submersible's return journey beneath the Pacific Ocean (the satellites still used the ancient names that mankind had programmed into them before the Doom) could be accessed from satellite EVAB 38.556. Although the submarine had gone undetected during it's eastward journey, once its existence had been noted when it surfaced, tracking the ship during its underwater journey back to its point of origin was a simple matter. So far, the ship had displayed no further external activity and had barely reached Pacific midpoint at the current time. Status reports on the submarine would be filed by satellite EVAB 38.556.

Dr Muffin fast-forwarded through the ground vehicle's progress, resuming normal play speed only when the vehicle drew near Hot Springs. For this footage, the robot zoomed in, magnifying the image until he could witness events in detail. He watched as the vehicle made contact with Kaz Geller. While the soldiers who encountered him responded by beating the man, the appearance of an officer curtailed such savage treatment, replacing physical violence with psychological intimidation to coax Kaz to divulge the information sought by the invading Mongols. A sound file related these inquisitions. Although the content of these discussions was of interest, the very language the men spoke instantly confirmed Dr Muffin's worries without a doubt.

The vehicle was of Russian origin. The men the vehicle carried belonged to the Mongol Empire that ruled the eastern lands that remained of China and Russia.

It had long been suspected by Dr Muffin and his satellite allies that the Mongols had reclaimed a high degree of pre-Doom technology. But the Russians were careful to keep hidden any evidence of their technology, secreting such things in caves beneath the frozen tundra. Dr Muffin had wondered whether this paranoia was born of a general covert nature, or a wary suspicion held by the satellites that circled the planet with their ancient spyeyes. If the Mongols possessed certain old knowledge, it was not implausible that they knew of the existence of the ancient satellites and their capabilities.

He listened as Kaz learned the strangers' language (among his many talents, the man had a brilliant gift with tongues), but long before Kaz understood the Mongols' words Dr Muffin's own language files had revealed the strangers' dialog—conversations with the field agent *and* among themselves within the confines of their traveling fortress.

Although the Mongols informed Kaz they were a scientific exploration team from the other side of the Siffic Ocean, they were in truth an advance scout team for an invasion being planned by the Mongol Empire. Unaware of the presence of significant civilization in Ericaland, the Mongols desired to know what defenses the territory possessed.

Dr Muffin noted with pleasure how magnificently Kaz played his role. The agent had luckily been away from his wind-surfer wagon, so the Mongols were unaware of its proximity a few valleys away. Kaz played the part of a simple savage to perfection. He claimed no knowledge of any lands beyond the Rocky Mountains. He asserted he only knew the flatlands. He offered to guide the strangers on their exploration mission—for a price. Wisely, he acted the part of a prairie wanderer with an eye for profit.

The part that startled Dr Muffin was when the Mongols questioned Kaz about Afterburn Radio. If the robot had owned a heart, it would have skipped a beat at this discussion.

The Mongols knew about Afterburn! But then, it followed that they would. If they had the technology to revive or redesign submarines and traveling fortresses, they certainly had radio and electricity. It was very possible the Mongols were picking up Afterburn's broadcasts with highly sophisticated equipment back in their frozen homeland.

This refuted the Mongol's supposed scouting mission. If they were getting Afterburn's transmissions, they were completely aware of the primitive cultures and disputing governments that were to be found in Ericaland. There was no need to send a team to discover what they already knew. These Mongols on Ericaland soil had another purpose entirely. What could it be?

Despite the positronic limitations of Dr Muffin's consciousness, the robot had learned over the centuries to extrapolate from minimal datum, factoring in the often irrational behavior patterns exhibited by human beings. His resultant conclusions were purely theoretical, but they often proved quite prophetic. So it was with great concern that Dr Muffin foresaw the actual target of this Mongol assault team: Afterburn Radio itself.

The *ping* of a fresh transmission jarred Dr Muffin's fears. With a powerful sense of foreboding he reached to take this new download and play it.

43

FROM A SAFE DISTANCE, Auter Hemdalk watched the westward bound band of Quiet Men with impatience. The fanatics had slowed their march considerably over the last few days. At this rate, even the well-stocked supplies his Team carried would run out before anyone reached the Rocky foothills—which, he personally suspected, was their inevitable destination.

How like the Quiet Men to be so focused on their jihad that they neglected to bring any water or supplies with them into these savage flatlands. The Team knew this much from interrogating the pair of Quiet Men who had fallen from their ranks, expecting to perish slowly on the hot ground. They had been quickly dispatched once the Team learned what it wanted.

Personally, Auter didn't understand why the Team leader didn't authorize a wipeout strike on the Quiet Men. The fanatics had become quite superfluous once the Team had spotted the small group of travelers farther to the west, who the Team leader believed were the ones the Quiet Men were tracking. Armed with the best farsee device that the Church Police had at their disposal, the Team had located this other group days ago. *They* were the ones that the Team wanted, not the crazy Quiet Men.

But since that discovery, the Quiet Men had slackened in their pace, allowing the further group to travel far ahead of them across the wasteland. For some reason, the Team leader had directed the Team to hold back, continuing to follow the Quiet Men and not the target group.

Bah, Auter scoffed mentally as he lay flat on the slab of rock that protruded from the barren earth. The Team leader was going purely by the manual, following Mob dictates with a painful invariance. Auter—and every other member of the Team—knew full well that the Quiet Men were not the actual target. *That* was Afterburn Radio. The Quiet Men were a stepping stone only. Through this band of the fanatics, the Team had located the group of Afterburn agents who traveled west. This group was yet another stepping stone, one that would hopefully lead the Team directly to Afterburn's hidden base.

And *then*, Auter smiled, the Team would put an end to Afterburn's annoying broadcasts forever. Never again would Afterburn take the name of the Mob in vain.

GOD WAS SUBJECTING THEM all to an absolute test of faith and devotion; of that Magog was convinced.

Long and hard had been the journey of this band of Quiet Men. The terrible heat had taken a massive toll of their stamina and fervor. He cursed the fact that he had been unable to convince the others to carry supplies of water and food into the flatlands. They were paying now for their arrogance, while only Magog remained fed and strong.

God will provide, their fingers had rebuked his advice. *Yes,* he thought, *God provided us with the intelligence to know when to take care of ourselves! It was* our *duty to make use of this cognitive ability and not expect God to pander to our every immediate need.*

The rest of this band was failing God's final test. Magog doubted whether more than two of them would survive with him to reach the Rocky foothills.

The sacred task of silencing Afterburn's unholy voice would fall to only a few ready hands.

45

INVIGORATED BY REHYDRATION, Tagger's group was making good time across the prairie tonight. Their step was livelier; their mood, barring Nico's deep sulk, was buoyant.

Nitch strolled next to Tagger. "How many agents does Afterburn have out protecting their secret?" she asked him.

"Not as many as there used to be," admitted the prairieman. He was startled by the girl's easy tone, it displayed none of the animosity she had recently exhibited toward him.

"Dwindling ranks on every front, eh?"

"Eh?"

She restated her assessment, "Less men in the field, less DJs on the air."

"Yes," Tagger sighed.

"Sounds as if Afterburn's falling apart at the seams. Why do you still work for them? Why not quit like the others?"

"Quit?" he twitched in anger. "Is that what you think has been happening? We're not losing people that way, girl. Afterburn has too many enemies. They've been getting our people... killing them one by one."

"You mean the Mob."

"Among others."

"And now there are foreigners stalking Afterburn—these Mongols."

"They won't be a problem. Kaz will lead them away. It's what he does."

"I don't see why you go to all this trouble. It's just a radio station."

"How many other ones do you know of?" he retorted. "None! Because Afterburn is unique. The role it plays is important."

"How important is playing *music*?" she laughed.

"I thought you liked the music it played. You claimed to back when we met. You liked it enough to sneak away into those ruins with your little brother just to listen to it. And then your Tribe got—" Suddenly, he turned to stare at her, his eyes wide with realization. "Is *that* it?"

"Huh?" Nitch gave him a suspicious look.

"Is that why you don't like Afterburn anymore? Because it reminds you of the night the Quiet Men exterminated your tribe?"

"*Remind* me? Afterburn is to *blame!*" the huntress spat before she knew what she was saying.

"That's absurd. How could Afterburn be responsible for a Quiet Men attack?"

Regretting her slip of the tongue, Nitch fell silent.

"You can't believe the Quiet Men exist because of Afterburn."

"Like *you're* an authority on the Quiet Men," she snarled.

"Clearly I know more about their history than *you* do, girl. They started up north in Anada, in a village where everyone was born deaf and mute. The village's shaman—who was *not* deaf or mute—started the cult in an attempt to keep the Tribe together by creating a sense of hate for all others who could speak. After his death, the shaman's xenophobic heritage deteriorated, becoming laced with quasi-religious doctrines. Later, members of the cult migrated west and south where they applied their lethal habits to anyone who made noise. All this was fifty years before Afterburn started broadcasting."

Nitch glared at him, unwilling to acknowledge his remarks with a reply.

Somehow, Tagger got the impression he was missing some important connection in the huntress' mind between the cult and the radio station. For the first time, he wondered how wise it was to be leading Nitch to Afterburn's secret base. Could the girl's dislike of Afterburn be strong enough to make her a *threat* to the radio station?

46

KAZ WAS USED TO BEING summoned into the Mongol leader's presence with little explanation. The man's soldiers were brutish and seemed to view Kaz as some subhuman. Two such inclined surly guards brusquely delivered him to Klaw's small office inside the motorized vehicle as it rumbled through the nocturnal wasteland.

When the guards remained with him in the crowded confines of Klaw's compartment, Kaz knew something was amiss.

In the foreign tongue, he asked the Mongol leader why he had called for him.

The man replied in English, "Because the time has come to end your lies!"

Kaz was unable to contain his surprise at the words the Mongol spoke. "You speak—"

"Yes," Klaw grinned wickedly. "I speak your language. For some time now, I have suspected you have been misleading us on our mission. Now I am certain."

Suddenly Kaz realized that his entire conversation with Tagger had been overheard by the Mongol leader. The man knew of his subterfuge.

"You are an agent of Afterburn Radio," Klaw told him. "You are attempting to guide us *away* from the radio station's secret base."

Kaz became aware of a change in the vehicle's momentum. The vehicle had stopped and was no longer heading east!

"But no longer," the leader pronounced in ominous tones.

Grasped by rough hands, Kaz was forced into a seat and confined there by manacles. The leader slid open a drawer to reveal an assortment of devices which could only be instruments of torture.

Picking up a slender utensil that gleamed in the compartment's harsh lighting, Klaw contemplated the serrated tip with a distant look. "Now you will tell me where we can find Afterburn's hidden transmitter."

With a mixture of disconsolate fatalism and forced bravado, Kaz shrugged and smiled weakly, "You're welcome to try."

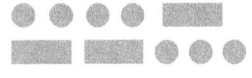

47

WITH MOUNTING APPREHENSION, Dr Muffin viewed the video footage contained in the second download from satellite RTD 126.1952.2.

Watching the Mongols' battle wagon come upon a group crossing the desolate wastelands, the robot was startled to recognize Tagger among this party of travelers. What was he doing this far west? And who were these children that comprised the rest of his assembly?

For an instant Dr Muffin questioned the absence of the prairieman's mutant feline companion. Adjusting the magnification of the scan, the robot soon picked out a stray heat source just ten meters from the point where the vehicle had stopped to contact Tagger and his group. Ah, the cat was remaining hidden during the meeting. The animal possessed exceptional cunning in such matters.

He watched the illicit conversation between Tagger and Kaz with a sinking feeling. They were of the opinion that the Mongols knew no English—clearly a logical fallacy. If the Mongols were receiving Afterburn's transmissions back in Russia, it was a fair assumption they understood the language of those broadcasts by now. The Mongols of this attack scouting mission were playing Kaz for a fool. Despite the agent's excellent attempts to misdirect the battle wagon, the Mongols now knew of his allegiance to the radio station. *And* that Tagger also served Afterburn.

He watched the battle wagon give Tagger's group water, then drive away. This part puzzled the robot. Why were the Mongols leaving Tagger's group free? He backtracked to the point where they gave Tagger's group water, zooming in on the bottles of water with a growing uneasiness. Accessing spectral analysis, the robot found the answer: the water the Mongols had given the group was laced with certain chemicals. A quick review of his positronic files classified these chemicals as ingredients of a delayed reaction soporific designed to induce unconsciousness in humans within hours of ingestion. While playing Kaz for a fool on one hand, the Mongols had drugged Tagger's group so they could be picked up later. Whatever hidden agenda the Mongols had in store for these agents of Afterburn, they were taking no undue risks.

While RTD 126.1952.2's cameras couldn't penetrate the hull of the Mongols' battle wagon, its audio receptors were fully capable of doing so. Dr Muffin listened with regret as the Mongol leader accosted Kaz, unmasking the agent's foiled misguidance. As the leader began to apply the methods of physical torture to the poor field agent, Dr Muffin noted the recording's time meter. These events had transpired just minutes ago out on the flatlands east of Afterburn's hidden base.

Despite his artificial physiology, Dr Muffin could not endure listening to Kaz's torture. The robot closed the audio track and was about to eject the disc from his chest—when he noticed a third file on the disc's menu. Curiosity made him open it. A scan of regions further east on the flatlands was revealed.

Clearly visible on the infrared topography, two large concentrations of body heat stood out like red blotches on the prairie's ambient warmth. Zooming in, Dr Muffin discovered the first was a band of Quiet Men who were marching westward across the wasteland. The second blotch proved to be a group of other men; their attire and equipment identified them as Mob Church Police.

Not only had Tagger's party had the misfortune to encounter the Mongols' battle wagon on their journey, but obviously they had been tracked west by groups representing a pair of Afterburn's other enemies.

A sudden insight suggested to Dr Muffin that whatever reason had driven Tagger to head home at this time must be great indeed to brave such opposition.

His artificial brain was aflurry with possible dire consequences as the robot fled the transmitter chamber. As he squirmed through the crawlway across the wreckage on the gantry, a plan came to Dr Muffin. A desperate plan—but what other options did Afterburn Radio have at this point?

48

THE NOTION THAT AFTERBURN might have something to fear from Nitch did not sit easy in Tagger's mind. Already the huntress knew too much of the radio station and its field agents to be allowed to roam free, but he was reticent to callously dispatch the girl. The prairieman had grown fond of her, a fondness that might have progressed into deeper emotional waters had not the girl developed enmity for him. Needer too had developed a kinship for the huntress, which Tagger suspected ran deeper than their mutual predatory natures. The cat would be no more willing to lose the girl at this point than Tagger was… at least, not without concrete proof that Nitch was a danger to Afterburn. And Tagger had no proof, only a vague sense of foreboding.

So deep were his ruminations on this subject, that it was a minute or so before Tagger became aware that he marched alone across the prairie. Looking around with confusion, he spotted the group a ways back.

What now? he wondered. Nico, probably—with another of her childish tantrums.

He turned and strode back to them. His concern grew with each step as he noticed that both children were down, seemingly unconscious. And Nitch crouched, weakly moaning with her forehead pressed to the ground.

"Didn't you hear me call you?" Needer snapped as he approached.

"No. I was—"

"Something's wrong," Nitch slurred through clenched teeth. "My head…"

"It was that water," declared the cat. "I knew it tasted funny."

"You think those Mongols drugged us?" Tagger asked. He bent to check Nivek's pulse. It beat slower than normal, but at least it still beat.

A wave of dizziness swept over the prairieman as he stood up. This unsteadiness forced him to his knees. He shook his head trying to jar his senses into clarity.

"You too?" mumbled Nitch.

"Well, that makes it everyone," the cat growled. "Clearly, those Mongols didn't believe what Kaz told them."

"Not good…" Tagger slumped until only his elbows kept his face from burying itself in the parched soil.

Stepping over, Needer nudged her heads against his thigh insistently. "Come on, Tagger. Don't fade on us now."

"What… can we… do?" Nitch strained out each word.

"You can't afford to pass out here," announced Needer. "You're too exposed. If they drugged you—and it sure looks as if they did—odds are they plan to swing back and capture you. You need to find someplace to hole up."

"Right…" Tagger tried to rouse himself.

"There's a stand of rocks over there," the cat informed them. "You have to move everyone over there."

Tagger slouched on his haunches, mumbling, "Mmm… not gonna… make… it…" He jolted back to consciousness as Needer bit him on the wrist, "Ow!"

"Wake up!" shouted the cat. "Stay with us, Tagger!" She swatted at Nitch, her claws leaving a bloody scratch on her forearm. "You too, girl! Up!"

"Ow! You bitch!" Nitch snarled, striking out too slow to catch the agile animal.

"Come on. You'll each have to grab one of the kids," insisted Needer. "I certainly can't drag them that far."

"Right… right…" Tagger tried to stand, but found his head refused to tolerate the altitude. On hands and knees, he crawled over to the snoring children. With considerable difficulty, he managed to grab Nivek under his arms. He began to pull the child toward the stand of rocks. Hampered by his ebbing awareness, Tagger's progress was almost nonexistent,

"No," snarled Nitch. "Nivek's… mine…" She pushed weakly at Tagger. "He's my… brother…"

"Stop it!" Needer screamed at the girl. "This isn't the time for this nonsense. Don't waste what little consciousness you have. Grab Nico and get moving!"

With a surly growl, Nitch dug her fingers into Nico's clothing and commenced dragging her after Tagger. Unfortunately, Nico's shirt was too delicate a weave; it tore in Nitch's grasp. The huntress tumbled on her ass, rolling away from the limp child.

She woke to a pair of cat heads screaming in her face, "Wake up! Get up! Don't give up!"

"Yeah…" Nitch weakly waved the cat aside. "Yeah…" She struggled to sit up but was unable to muster the strength. Before her lethargy could force her back to the ground, Nitch bit savagely at her lip. The pain stabbed through her fading consciousness, reviving a modicum of cognizance in its wake. With the taste of her own blood in her mouth, the huntress groped for Nico's slumped form. Grasping the waistband of the child's pants, Nitch forced her fingers to close in a deathgrip. Then she pulled, dragging Nico a few inches. Gnawing a new tear in her lip, Nitch crawled back a bit, then pulled again at the child.

Six inches at a time, Nitch continued this action. Pull on Nico, edge back further, pull again, edge back again, pull once more… At a monstrously slow pace, she dragged the child across the hard ground. Everything in Nitch's world had become reduced to her backwards crawl; she grew indifferent to the soil beneath her knees and elbows or the blood that dripped from her torn lip. Her vision narrowed into a tight region not unlike an immaterial tunnel. The edges of this tunnel wavered, fighting against her will, striving to collapse upon itself and plunge her into total darkness.

She jolted awake as someone grabbed her shoulder, rolling the girl on her back. She had no memory of falling prey to the darkness, but obviously she had. With vision distorted by utter weariness, Nitch stared up into Tagger's face as it hung upside down over her. "I gotcha…" his voice swam to her through the wavering night. She felt herself hauled slowly along the ground. After a few moments, she weakly batted the prairieman aside, "I can… make… it… now…" She rolled on her stomach and strained to lift herself to her elbows. Her lower half was unresponsive to the commands of her whirling consciousness, so she commenced pulling herself along on her belly.

With hard-won awareness, Nitch saw the stand of rocks was only another meter away. Reaching it, she fell against one of the rocks, turning sloppily to peer back across the prairie. Just four meters away, Tagger was towing Nico's body toward her.

Leaning suddenly into Nitch's view, Needer peered at her. "You made it, girl."

"Why…"

"Because Tagger got you."

"No…" Nitch shook her head, trying to clear the overwhelming oblivion from her mind. "Why… aren't you… affected?… like us?" She passed out before she could hear the cat's answer.

49

As Dr Muffin hurried down the dark corridors of Afterburn Radio's secret base, his artificial brain catalogued the difficulties ahead of him. So swift was his movement through the subterranean passages that the power cord that ran from his shoulder to the ceiling was stretched dangerously taut.

When he burst into the station's transmission booth, he found the booth empty. A pertinent bitstream fired in his head, offering a possible explanation for Psycho Jones' absence.

Ever since Dr Muffin had repaired the console in the transmission booth, Psycho was no longer forced to remain in the booth, alert to any malfunction. She could pop in one of the CDs the robot had given her, setting it to repeat play. This afforded her the chance to rest for more than an hour; if fact, if she was willing to let the CD loop numerous times, she could remain asleep indefinitely.

The robot retreated from the booth, heading for the girl's room. Finding the door locked was only a momentary setback for Dr Muffin. Gripping the edges of the metal door, he tore the panel away. The stale air suddenly vibrated with the screech of ripping metal.

Inside the girl's room, he stared down with anxiety at her slumbering naked form. It wasn't difficult to guess what had preceded his appearance.

After swallowing a meal of several nutrient pills from the station's dwindling supply, Psycho had retired to her room, where she had collapsed on her mattress. There, the girl had doubtless become unconscious within minutes.

Without pause, the robot seated himself at the small counter that served Psycho as a personal desk. Grabbing up a pen and paper, he quickly began to compose the message he needed her to transmit. As his mind focused on this task, he activated his noise circuits to release a piercing squeal.

The shrill bleat brought Psycho awake with a painful abruptness.

"Aaaa!" she erupted as consciousness hit her like an unwelcome cascade of cold water.

"Wake up, Psycho," spoke Dr Muffin. His metal hands still hastily scribbled across the paper on her desk.

"No..." she complained feebly. She rolled over, nestling her face against the wall. "Need sleep..."

"I need you awake, girl." Raising the volume of his voice chip, he announced, "Afterburn needs you awake! Now!"

"Wha's matter... ?" She pulled her pillow over her head.

"We have an *emergency*, Psycho. Wake up *now!*"

"Aww... you handle it..." She burrowed deeper under the pillow.

Grabbing up the piece of paper in one hand, Dr Muffin closed his other hand around the girl's wrist. Pulling her unceremoniously from the mattress, the robot dashed from the room, dragging her startled nude body in his wake. This abuse pulled her awake, plunging her into the confusion of a rough and reluctant journey down the dark corridors in the wake of the robot's frantic advance.

Once inside the transmission booth, Dr Muffin tried to place Psycho carefully in her arcade chair, but his haste flung her down with unintended force.

"Ow!" she complained.

"Please wake up, Psycho!" begged the robot. "I need you to read this news bulletin right away. You must be coherent to do this."

"What the hell's so important? A news bulletin? It can wait. Why can't you just read it yourself?"

"This must be done in a human voice, Psycho. One the listeners will recognize."

"Oh, get Smithie to do it," she grumbled, curling up in the chair. She was drifting back asleep again.

If only I could, Dr Muffin thought. *But you are the only human here.*

He reached out, touching his metal hand to the rim of the arcade chair. He knew his behavioral parameters were going to make him regret this, but he saw no other recourse. He sent a mild electrical charge surging through the chair.

Jolted from the seat, Psycho's limbs danced akimbo with the shock. She struck her head on the overhang of the chair's cupped back as she leapt erect.

"*Ow!* You son of a—"

The robot struggled to restrain the conflicts that coursed through his positronic circuits as a result of the girl's pain. Desperately he tried to convince his programming that hurting one person was unavoidable if the alternative was the loss of many other human lives. The potential demise of the entire radio station was at risk here. The human race needed Afterburn Radio if the species was going to reclaim civilization with any degree of ethical control.

"I'm sorry," Dr Muffin apologized. "But this could be the most important broadcast you've ever made, Psycho." He handed her the piece of paper he had carried from her room.

Glancing at the words on the paper, Psycho scrunched up her face with bewilderment. The robot's electric shock had expelled drowsiness from her mind, but left an irate resentment buzzing behind her eyes. "*This*? This is nonsense! How can—"

"Kaz's life is at stake here, Psycho. Every second you delay could get him killed!" the robot spoke sternly, knowing that *these* reasons would convince the girl where a full explanation would only confuse her.

"Kaz?" she gasped. "What—how do you—"

"Trust me, Psycho," Dr Muffin told her softly.

She stared hard at the robot, then reached for the dangling microphone.

"Try to adopt a conversational tone when you read it," the robot instructed. "Despite the widescan transmission of Afterburn's signal, this message is directed at a particular group of listeners. It is imperative that they *believe* your words."

Nodding, Psycho flicked a switch on the console, interrupting the music that was playing.

As she began to read the message Dr Muffin had prepared, the robot dove out the booth's door, vanishing down a corridor.

50

LEANING BACK, the leader of the Mongol battle wagon frowned as he wiped his instrument clean of his victim's blood.

Uncertain of the savage's threshold of consciousness, Klaw had been careful not to push the limits with Kaz. So far, though, the Afterburn spy had remained steadfast. While the torture had stolen the man's smile, he had revealed nothing.

"You are being foolishly obstinate," Klaw told the restrained spy. "You *will* tell me what I want to know. The longer you hold out, the less of a man you will be in the end."

The compartment's stale air had brought a sheen of perspiration out across the Mongol leader's forehead. He blinked convulsively as sweat dodged around his bushy brows to run into his angry eyes, annoyed at the sting his own fluids produced. Holding his expression frozen in a dispassionate frown, Klaw resisted the urge to wipe the blinding moisture from his face. He must display no weakness before this insipid Ericalander, maintaining his Mongol superiority in every gesture and facial cast. Despite this external resolve, Klaw cursed this foul land's cruel heat.

Longing for the frosty tundra climate of his distant homeland, he could not fathom why the Mongol Empire had designs on this uncivilized territory. No sane Mongol would welcome its arid temperatures or unfriendly atmosphere. These Ericalanders were a pathetic and barbaric lot, unworthy of conquest by the great Mongol Empire. Even their lands lacked any resources to justify such a conquest.

Klaw could not understand this spy's resolute defiance. What was so precious about this useless land that could incite the man to withstand such torture? How could he ignore Klaw's questions? Did the man possess no concept of self-preservation?

Kaz remained slumped in the seat, striving to hide his agony with a mask of dignity. He was wasting no energy now on defiance or cocky bravado.

Narrowing his inscrutable eyes to communicate impatient intimidation, Klaw selected another utensil from the drawer. This one sported a variety of delicate blades as thin as an insect's wings.

As he applied the foremost nearly invisible blade to the flesh just below Kaz's left eye, the door of Klaw's private compartment flew open. A soldier in dark khaki entered, jabbering at the leader in their foreign tongue.

Through the fierce waves of pain that gnawed at his senses, Kaz was vaguely aware of the message the man related to his commander. Something about Afterburn Radio speaking to *them!*

Turning from his handiwork, Klaw viciously slapped a button on the arm of his command chair.

The voice of Psycho Jones filled the compartment: "… tuned, folks. Maybe Fever and I will be able to convince one of these visitors to our land to come on the air with us for an exclusive live interview!"

In tones of urgent displeasure, Klaw chirped at the man who had just entered. Through the haze of agony that curtained his mind, Kaz could make out only a few of the words, but they were not happy.

A moment later, as music replaced Psycho's sweet voice, another Mongol entered the leader's compartment, forcing the earlier messenger out into the cramped hallway. This newcomer held out a small flat square. Klaw took it and with a deep scowl, plugged it into a bank of machinery next to his command desk.

Once again, Psycho's voice echoed in the chamber. This time her words started at the beginning of her speech. "Hiyo, folks! This is Psycho Jones, and it seems we have some new listeners out there. I'd like to welcome the Mongol exploration vehicle to the land of Ericaland. These boys have come a long way to hear us—all the way across the Siffic Ocean! Word has reached us here that these Mongols are looking to pay Afterburn a visit in person! Isn't that amazing? Well, Fever and I are just dying to meet these foreign explorers. I hope you boys are listening right now, because you're in luck. You have only to drive a few kilometers east and you'll find yourselves at our secret doorstep. Stay tuned, folks. Maybe Fever and I will be able to convince one of these visitors to our land to come on the air with us for an exclusive live interview!"

Sinking into his command chair, the Mongol leader rapped out orders that cleared the compartment of all but himself and his bloodied victim. In a second, the battle wagon lurched into motion.

"Your people's arrogance will be their downfall," Klaw told Kaz, full of his triumph over these Ericaland savages "You see? All of your bravery was unnecessary. Your people are *eager* to meet us. They have given us the directions that you withheld. Soon, Afterburn's secret base will be under *my* control."

51

SAVAGE LANDS COULD WEAKEN even the strongest faith.

Unfortunately, this fact was not going to sway Magog from his holy mission. God had chosen *him* to silence the heretical voice of Afterburn Radio, and—alone or at the head of an army—he was not going to forsake this glorious assignment.

So, when the former chief of this band of Quiet Men challenged his leadership, Magog was quick to answer: with a sacrificial blade through the traitor's chest.

The rest of the Quiet Men stood in a ring watching this brief battle for supremacy. For days, they had muttered among themselves with their fingers, denouncing their new leader for marching them so deep into unholy lands. Lack of food and water may have weakened their strength, but it had fueled their displeasure. Magog was to blame—he who marched so tall and tense, he who seemed undaunted by the heat, so unbothered by the thirst that agonized the rest of them.

They were not pleased with Magog's quick victory. It was not right. The man had barely allowed their former chief to begin his objections before he had killed him. Now he stood with knife still in hand, daring any of them to perpetuate the mutiny.

When two more Quiet Men stood forth to continue the challenge, Magog spilled their intestines on the hot ground with a single swipe of his sacred blade. Fear battled with starvation among the rest of the band. This was not the outcome any of them had expected. Each considered himself righteously pious in worship of the holy silence, but this march across the flatlands was sheer madness. Stilling the evil voice of Afterburn Radio was a worthy mission, but why did God have to torment them so hideously on their journey? Didn't God realize that they were serving Him? Why couldn't He make their task easier?

Deeper in their hearts, these Quiet Men envied Magog his resolute conviction of purpose. Why did the man have to stand so tall, unwracked by debilitating thirst or hunger? Why must he flaunt his superior stamina? Why did his faith remain unwavering in the heat that wilted the rest of them?

What made Magog's hate of Afterburn Radio greater than theirs?

Had the standoff lasted another few moments, it was very possible their unified jealousy might well have spurred the mob to swarm on Magog. But that was the moment the Mongol's battle wagon chose to come roaring out of the western darkness, blinding them with its twin headlights and tormenting them with its blasphemous mechanical bellow.

52

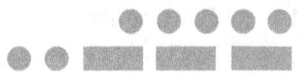

DELPH LODEN WATCHED the monstrous vehicle approach the remaining Quiet Men, and he knew in his Church Police heart that *this* technological wonder was an instrument of Afterburn.

The Mob was no stranger to technology. Despite their edicts restricting its use, the Church Police secretly possessed—and gleefully used—weapons of mass destruction to insure Mob rule in the northern lands. When the Council had dispatched this Team to locate and silence Afterburn Radio, they had armed Delph's Team with the strongest weapons in the holy arsenal.

Lowering his farsee device, Delph signaled to his Team: the moment of truth had arrived. Promptly, mortars and rifles were unpacked and loaded. Each Team member crouched at the ready, longing to destroy this awesome vehicle that embodied Afterburn's rival strength.

With a cry of "Destroy!", Delph unleashed the Mob's mighty firepower.

53

RIDING BEYOND THE STRATOSPHERIC ETHER, satellite RTD 126.1952.2 looked down upon the flatlands of Ericaland.

It watched the confrontation far below with its dispassionate spyeyes, recording the battle and converting the images and sensory scans into digital bitstreams.

The Mongol battle wagon slowed as it neared the band of Quiet Men, making it an easy target for the Mob Team's long-range mortarfire. As a volley of shots created new craters around the battle wagon, a pair of well-placed shells cut the vehicle in two.

As startled and disoriented Mongols poured from the crippled vehicle, the Quiet Men launched themselves at these invaders. While hand-held potatoes clashed with rifles, the Church Police Team swept into the fray armed with their own firepower. Despite the advantage of their superior weaponry, the Mongols and Church Police found themselves in combat with foes motivated by a fanaticism so bloodthirsty as to give the Quiet Men's potatoes an equal lethality. The three groups clashed on the dark prairie; flesh split regardless of loyalty, each man spilling blood that flowed just as crimson as his enemy's. Death was impartial as it waded through the screaming horde, unconcerned whether bullet, blade or fist ended a life. The Mongols battled like warriors, their fury styled by their formal training. The Quiet Men fought like the cornered beasts they had become. The Church Police attacked with a blind confidence in what they believed were their superincumbent firearms. Death claimed men of each faction, regardless of the cause they served. Indeed, their *causes* were moot; regardless of what had motivated each man to leap into the fray, once there they were fighting for their lives. As weapons were levied in their direction, individual survival took precedence over their deeply ingrained beliefs. The resultant melee became a wanton slaughter devoid of cause.

Numerous explosions dotted the landscape, lingering in RTD 126.1952.2's heat sensor scans as bright patches. As the conflict continued, the tiny dots of each combatant's body heat faded slowly as death cooled the corpses.

RTD 126.1952.2 knew full well this bloodshed and slaughter would disturb its earthbound ally. The satellite was aware that Dr Muffin contained behavioral restrictions that prohibited the robot from harming human beings. But RTD 126.1952.2 possessed no such digital form of ethics; in fact the underlying foundation of its artificial intelligence was quite the opposite. RTD 126.1952.2 had been originally programmed as a weapon of wartime surveillance. The lattices of sentience that had accreted atop its original programming understood the necessity of conflict. Human must fight human; it was the natural order of things.

Dr Muffin's grand vision of a unified mankind was a glorious dream—quite laudable for an artificial being. But RTD 126.1952.2 knew that the path to such a unity was destined to be stained with the blood of thousands. No twinge of guilt or remorse stirred the satellite's mentality as it observed the battle below. It might even be perceived that RTD 126.1952.2 condoned the carnage, especially since all three factions involved in the slaughter constituted the *enemy* in its eyes. The deaths of these villains would help insure the freedom of the common man.

The only victors in this battle were the factions not present on the battlefield.

54

WHEN DR MUFFIN RECEIVED THE VIDEO footage of the battle from satellite RTD 126.1952.2, the robot could not bring himself to view it. Instead, he glanced briefly at a printout summary of the report, confirming the outcome which his plan had predicted. Then the robot filed the report away, sincerely hoping that no organic member of Afterburn's staff would ever find it.

It was many hours before Dr Muffin left the transmitter chamber. When the robot finally descended to the lower corridors of the subterranean base, he still had no idea what he was going to tell Psycho Jones of the fate of her prairie mentor. The only thing he knew he *could* tell her with any conviction was that Afterburn had averted its own demise and postponed a foreign invasion of Ericaland.

The robot knew these facts would not erase the loss of Kaz in the DJ's all too human eyes.

No amount of rationalization was going to wash the robot's positronic conscience clean of Kaz's blood.

55

THEN: UNDER A HEXAS STAR.

Of a litter of seven, Needer was the only survivor. Her mother lived for a few weeks after the birth, just long enough to wean the kitten, before succumbing, bald and toothless, to the heat.

Although Needer liked the warm climate, it wasn't the kind of heat that a cool breeze could break.

Needer was born underground, in the darkness of a deep pit that men had once called a missile silo. A tall cylinder occupied the center of this silo, metal gleaming in a green light of its own creation. The floor beneath its flaring base was littered with the bones of many humans. Among this calcium jungle, rats scuttled and warred and hunted.

They hunted Needer.

Unfortunately for the rat army that stalked her, Needer possessed a cunning seeded with intelligence far beyond the normal acumen of her kind. While her right head concerned itself with basic bodily needs, her left head concocted plans—schemes of survival and schemes of escape. The hunting parties which the rat army sent after her rarely returned, the rodent soldiers falling prey to deadly snares. In this manner, Needer fed herself.

Arcane legends grew in the rat colony, tales of the prey who could fight back, warnings of the cat who could elude any hunting party, myths of the fearsome two-headed beast who lived in the upper regions of the silo. These legends lasted long after Needer found a way out of the darkness, crawling her way through ancient ducts to discover the open lands of the surface world.

This land without walls whose ceiling seemed impossibly high—this landscape terrified the young cat. The animals that roamed this alien land were far smarter than the rodents she had outwitted in her youth. These creatures, tall bipeds who barked aloud incessantly at each other and utilized tools of exotic design, were best avoided, as Needer was quick to learn.

The Dians who lived in the district of Hexas had suffered the same Doom that had ended civilization, but they'd managed to reclaim a satisfactory niche in their environment far faster than the white savages that dwelled, as legend had it, to the north. Living off the land as their forgotten ancestors had, the Dians spread their Tribes across the barren south, mastering an agriculture that was in tune with post-Doom conditions. They avoided the ruins that slowly crumbled under the heat and sand, surviving as a nomadic people. Domestication of several animal species was a regimen they practiced with enthusiasm.

Alas, *cats* were not among the species they saw fit to include in their new order.

Needer learned swiftly that these humans refused to tolerate her kind. She was prey to them, good only for filling their larders or hunting for sport. After her third close call, Needer chose to migrate south, for all that existed to the north were the brutally inhospitable flatlands.

South, the cat discovered many marvels: colonies of humans who lived next to a limitless body of undrinkable water, and others of her kind who lived without fear among these humans. Sadly, these cats were no smarter than the rodents of her youth. It was the humans who unwittingly taught her language. They also introduced her to the miracle food: fish.

When the human child who taught her how to speak was slain by its own family, Needer fled the south. She thought she had finally escaped the madness of humans as she crossed the lush eastern delta.

The humans she found on the Missississippi Coast proved to be no more enlightened or tolerant than the lunatics she had left behind. One Tribe in particular responded to her presence with such antagonism that when she fled their turf they sent killers to track her down for her crimes. Stealing a single fish was apparently an unforgivable affront to these maniacs.

It was while fleeing west into the desolate prairie that Needer encountered the first adult human who tempered his intelligence with compassion. He called himself Tagger.

Tagger rescued the refugee feline from the insane hunting party of humans, scaring them off with loud noises he produced from a curious metal box. Although Tagger never demanded reward for this salvation, Needer remained with the man, growing to share his dedication to Afterburn Radio. The friendship developed between cat and man grew into a much deeper kinship. Despite her isolationist instincts and solipsistic nature, the time soon came when Needer would gladly have given her life for Tagger.

Together, they wandered the edges of the flatlands that bordered on the eastern delta. They traveled, they hunted, they guarded the prairie from the curiosity of humans. They also, when and where it was safe, promoted the legacy of Afterburn, bringing music to Tribes who were forever in their debt.

Twice, the cat accompanied Tagger on torturous journeys far into the hellish wasteland. Both of these treks brought them to a marvelous underground complex that proved to be the origin of the voices and music that embodied Afterburn Radio.

There, Needer met the astonishing metal man who the staff called Dr Muffin. The robot, as he called himself, taught Needer many things: history, geography, mathematics, philosophy. Needer was the only living soul with whom Dr Muffin shared his secret goals; he even showed the cat the wondrous transmitter that was the source of Afterburn's global voice. Needer never shared these confidences with her traveling companion.

Although the cat grew devoted to the protection and promotion of Afterburn, it was the teachings of Dr Muffin that solidified that devotion beyond the interests she shared with Tagger.

For all the hope that Tagger attached to Nivek Palma's knowledge and the equipment buried in the boy's secret radio cavern beneath the Oogolah ruins, the boy represented far more auspicious ends to the mutant feline. Tagger saw the boy as the answer to Afterburn's failing technology. Needer suspected the boy would spawn a salvation immensely greater than the prairieman's dreams.

56

Now: escaping the dog days.

Needer guarded the unconscious humans as they slumbered among the meager protection afforded by the small stand of rocks. There may have been no threat from animals or even monsters this far west, but the dangers the cat watched for were not of this nature. It was human interference that mostly worried the cat.

Those Mongol invaders had drugged the group for a reason. Needer fully expected the Mongols to return, searching for their unconscious victims. And when they showed up, their foreign inquisitiveness would find her waiting with claws unsheathed and teeth bared in two mouths.

So she stood guard, without sleep or food or water, scanning the landscape with four suspicious eyes.

"Thirsty," grumbled her right head.

"And going to stay that way," Needer assured herself. There was more water within the group's waterskins, but the cat wanted no part of that drugged liquid. She had taken enough risk swallowing what she had before realizing the water was contaminated by unknown chemicals. Fortunately, the effects of the drug on her feline physiology had been confined to an upset stomach, followed by vomiting up a clot of hairballs along with the poisoned liquid. Had the drugs incapacitated her as they had the humans, the group might well have been lost—unconscious lumps left to bake under the day's unforgiving sun. Even so, it had taken excessive cajoling to goad Tagger and Nitch into dragging themselves and the children to the safety and shade of this stand of rocks.

Thank Mother Sky that *these* rocks were just inert mineral and not another conclave of Rolling Stones.

Needer carefully eyed the horizonline. Dun flatlands stretched in all directions, broken only by a few tuffs of long-dead weed and the wavering distortion of superheated air. When—or *if*—the Mongols came, she would able to detect their battle wagon long before it neared their impromptu camp.

Not for the first time in her short life, Needer wondered why the humans called to Mother Sky as their deity, a habit she reluctantly had adopted over time in their company. The sky was hardly a sight to inspire maternal affection. Its constant dance of colors may instill an awe and mystery in humans, but the cat knew what longterm phenomena produced the never-ending kaleidoscope in the heavens. Dr Muffin had explained it to her years ago, and, although much of the terminology had been beyond her comprehension, she had understood the basic premise. Particles flowing in the upper stratosphere, charged by invisible but deadly rays of the sun, created the colorful sky. The effect had something to do with the planet's magnetic polarity too, but this aspect had meant nothing to the cat, despite further elucidation by the robot.

Regardless of the facts, Needer had always marveled how humans put their faith in a nameless God while giving lip service to Mother Sky. Praise the father figure, but when anything needed doing, they begged the maternal spirit to help them. The dichotomy never failed to amuse her. Sometimes humans were so unfathomable.

Even Tagger was a victim of his racial insecurity. Although he claimed to be an agnostic, he often swore to Mother Sky when situations caused him severe stress.

The cat wondered what deities Nitch and the children swore allegiance to. She hoped their gods watched over them now as they slept. The travelers could use all the protection they could get at this point in their journey.

As Needer had secretly anticipated, it was Tagger who roused from unconsciousness first.

With an abrupt cough, the prairieman sat up. His hunter's senses instantly bullied aside any grogginess, bringing him alert and wary before he even knew where he was. Needer remained perched atop the highest of the rocks, choosing to leave the man undisturbed as his human brain reassembled the events which had brought him to this place.

Before Tagger had finished his internal refamiliarization of the environment, Nitch began to stir from sleep. Again, this was in keeping with Needer's expectations.

After a few moments, the cat called down to them, "All clear on the perimeter."

"Tagger!" Nitch's voice snapped quietly.

The man crawled over to crouch beside the huntress. Without further verbal description, she gestured to the sleeping form of Nico. Tagger touched the child's neck and frowned.

"Nivek?" His voice was tenuous and cracked in his parched throat.

"He's okay. I checked him first."

"What's the matter with the brat?" asked Needer, not turning from scanning the outlying landscape.

"She's dead," Tagger announced.

Needer looked down at the humans for a second, then returned her stare to the horizonline. "That's too bad," muttered the cat. "But she had no potential."

"Oh, shut up, you animal!" Nitch growled.

"You disliked her just as much as the rest of us did," declared Needer, her eyes never leaving the landscape. "You humans have a tendency to allow death to gloss over a person's failings in life. I'll never understand that."

"What killed her?" Nitch asked the prairieman.

"It must've been whatever those Mongols put in the water."

"Why would it kill her and not us?"

"Individuals possess different tolerances," Needer announced. "The drug had little effecct on my feline constitution."

Suddenly the cat released a bloodcurdling screech.

"What are you doing?" cried Nitch. She leapt to her feet with spear in hand. "Is something coming?"

After a moment, the cat relaxed. "It's all right. It's only Kaz. He heard me… he's coming this way now."

Tagger stood on unsteady legs, watching a distant smudge on the horizon increase in size, taking humanoid form, then familiar characteristics.

As Kaz Geller approached the rocks, Needer untucked her paws from beneath her body, standing to stretch luxuriously. "What happened to you?" the cat asked as the man grew closer.

Now Tagger and Nitch could see what the cat meant. A majority of the dark man's skin was blackened in a horrible manner, clearly evident in the man's grisly nudity. Although he strode swiftly across the prairie, the man winced with each step. His head was barren now of any hair.

When he reached them, Kaz sank against a rock instead of collapsing on the ground. Even with such minimal movement, his skin crackled with terrible sounds. Blood and clear ichor oozed from these fresh fissures in his charred flesh.

"Are you okay?" Nitch asked the man.

He waved away the huntress' concern, "I'll live… for now."

"The Mongols?" inquired Tagger.

"All dead." Kaz told them of the battle that Psycho Jones' broadcast had orchestrated. "I'll never know how she knew they were here, but the directions Psycho gave the Mongols over the radio led them straight into a band of Quiet Men and a Mob team of Church Police. The Mob's weapons blew the Mongols' vehicle in half. I got badly burned in the explosion, but managed to creep away while the three factions slaughtered each other. I headed west, hoping to find you guys."

"You need to rest," Tagger insisted.

"I need more than rest, my friend," chuckled Kaz.

Pulling her pouch of salves from her belt, Nitch set to administering the medications to the man's flaking skin. She ignored his protests and finally succeeded in convincing the man to lie down. Moments later, his skin glistening with the ointments, Kaz was asleep.

"He's really bad off," Nitch confided to Tagger. "My salves will only bring him temporary relief. He needs better medical attention that we can give him out here."

"He'll be okay," Needer declared from her sentry position. "We have more immediate worries."

"Like what?" snapped Nitch. "He's going to die without—"

"Like burying the brat before your brother wakes up."

"Needer's right," the prairieman agreed. "For all Nivek's uncharacteristic maturity, I don't think he'll deal very well with Nico's death. He still cares for her."

With a slow nod, Nitch recognized the truth in this assessment. It briefly disturbed her that Tagger and his cat had thought of her brother's mental well-being before her. Protecting Nivek was *her* responsibility.

Tagger set to breaking the hard ground and digging a grave, while Nitch tended to wrapping the dead child in her bedroll.

"Does your Tribe have any special rituals we should observe?" Tagger asked her once they had lowered the body into the hole he had prepared.

"My Tribe no longer exists," Nitch professed without rancor.

Breaking the solemn moment, Needer announced from her high perch that Nivek was waking up.

Resisting a sudden urge to go to her brother's side, Nitch glanced at Tagger. The man nodded soberly. Going to Nivek's side, she soothed the boy's disorientation while Tagger filled in the hole.

When they finally told him, Nivek accepted Nico's demise with more reserve than they had expected. He cried, but his tears were not the kind one shed over the loss of a lover. His grief was stable and quickly distracted by the desire to avenge her death by attacking the Mongol poisoners. When they explained the Mongols' fate as Kaz had related it to them, Nivek's grief was promptly transferred to Kaz's evident suffering.

Upon seeing the condition of the battle's solitary survivor, Nivek crawled off to dry heave in private.

Tagger joined Needer atop her rock. After surveying the empty landscape, he stared west at the looming vistas of the distant Rocky Mountains. "How far do you think we are?" he asked the cat.

"From the foothills? Less than two days, I'd say." Needer's left head peered down at the unconscious form of the blackened field agent. "How long do you think Kaz will take?"

"I've never seen him do it before," admitted the prairieman. "It doesn't matter, though. We need water—*real* water. I don't think we can afford to wait."

"Then we set out at dusk," the cat declared.

Sliding from the top of the rock, Tagger told Nitch of their plans. "We'll need to rig up a stretcher to carry Kaz."

"I would not advise moving him in his condition," objected the huntress.

"Don't worry about him. He'll be okay," Tagger replied with seemingly callous calm. "Get Nivek to help you put together a stretcher. It'll distract him from Nico's death."

As the Palmas set to the task of constructing a means of transporting the wounded man, Tagger borrowed Nivek's radio. Climbing back atop the rock, he tuned in Afterburn, hoping to learn something of the convenient slaughter that had happened in the east while the group lay in poisoned sleep. He found only music on the airwaves. He left it on, hoping the upbeat rhythms would boost the group's morale.

Kaz did not rouse as they transferred him from the ground to the bedroll stretched between Tagger's staff and Nitch's spear. They covered him with a blanket, small protection against the slight chill of the approaching night.

As the sun vanished behind the jagged mountain peaks, the group left the rocks. At Tagger's request, Nivek carried his radio still activated. Accompanied by classical orchestration, they headed west once again.

57

THE ORBIT OF SATELLITE EVAB 38.556 had decayed very little during the centuries since man had set it circling the Earth. Only twice had the machine needed to adjust its trajectory, corrections that were achieved with brief bursts of its peripheral thrusters.

Satellite EVAB 38.556 had been designed as a war device. Although it contained several computers in its targeting and surveillance systems, none of them had evolved intelligence as the satellite spun through the void. Its role in the Afterburn Alliance was one of watchdog, observing and relaying these observations to the radio station's secret base.

But today, systems that had remained dormant for centuries received activation codes. Without comment, EVAB 38.556 ran preliminary system checks on its laser cannon.

Switching its spyeye scanners from surveillance to targeting, EVAB 38.556 precisely lined up the submerged Mongol submarine in its sights and awaited the command to fire. When the order came, the satellite did so without hesitation or remorse.

Far below the satellite, in the depths of the Siffic Ocean, the beam of lethal ruby force cut the submarine in two. It remained firing for a full minute, heating the water in the area to a killing temperature, insuring the speedy demise of any who succeeded in escaping the torn submersible.

Once the task was completed, EVAB 38.556 reported its success to satellite RTD 126.1952.2, bouncing the signal around the planet's curvature to where RTD 126.1952.2 soared above the Euro Isles.

Acknowledging the signal, RTD 126.1952.2 directed EVAB 38.556 to disengage its warfare circuitry and continue to survey the region pending further orders.

RTD 126.1952.2 paused for a millisecond to consider how to color this news for Dr Muffin's delicately ethical circuits. The decision to eliminate the Mongol submarine had been RTD 126.1952.2's alone. The satellite had digitally weighed all the factors, coming to the irrefutable conclusion that the entire situation would be best resolved if the submarine never returned to Russia. Communication between the submarine and its distant Russian base had been blocked by a simple jamming frequency (broadcast by EVAB 38.556 at RTD 126.1952.2's direction) ever since the craft had headed back across the Pacific Ocean. As far as the Mongol leaders would be able to guess, their exploratory scouting force had met with superior defenses in Ericaland.

Dr Muffin would be happy with this outcome, just disconsolate over the methods used to reach that resolution.

In this manner, the invasion of Ericaland by the Mongol Empire came to an end clouded in mystery and uncertainty for the Mongol forces.

58

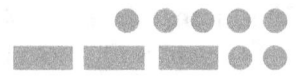

A **DEEP AND INHUMAN DREAD** dwelled in the fearful mind of the Premier Vassal who had once been Nanner Gristle.

When Nanner had learned of the ignoble arrest of his wife, the Empress Beel, he had raged with a bellowing voice that shook the bastions of Chico's royal castle. When he was informed that his wife had been charged with traitorous complicity involving Afterburn Radio, his screams of displeasure had dwindled as he realized the full scope of the intrigues that surrounded him. Nanner was no more than a hapless guppy in shark-infested waters.

For the briefest of moments, he wondered whether her guilt was indeed factual. Had his Empress conspired with Afterburn, revealing Mob secrets to the outlaw radio station? But no, there was no way she could have guessed that he was not her original husband—not until he had told her himself. Furthermore, despite her high station, the Empress was not privy to the secret machinations of the Mob's Council; she could have had no knowledge of the deceits the Mob had concealed behind their desire for a peace conference with the Rocky Districts.

No, he knew the Empress was no Afterburn spy.

Just as firmly he knew that her arrest was the Council's way of sending a deadly message to their false-faced new Premier. Her fate could easily become *his*, dragged away in the middle of the night and imprisoned on specious charges should Nanner become uncooperative. It was just the style of the Council to use the spy hunt he had so loudly demanded as a means to remove the troublesome Empress and send Nanner this message to play along—or else.

When it came time for him to publicly acknowledge the Empress' arrest, the Premier voiced his horror concerning the guilt of the woman he had considered to be his loyal wife, condemning her furtive association with the evil pirate radio station and praising the investigation that had unmasked her traitorous collusion.

As he fully expected, all of Nanner's requests for an audience with the Council's High Priest were summarily refused.

So it was that, two nights later, Nanner summoned Fillery Nunzio to his private chambers for a discrete meeting.

Of the many unethical practices that ran rampant in the high city of Chico, not all of them were the doing of the governing Mob. Several crimebosses lorded over the operations which moved honest moneys into dishonest purses. Among these lower echelon mobsters, it was rumored that Fillery Nunzio was the most ruthless, fearing no man or monster or deity or government. Nanner had, in fact, spent time indirectly in Nunzio's employment during his youth. He knew that Nunzio possessed the manpower and the cunning to achieve the assignment the new Premier had in mind.

When Nunzio was ushered into Nanner's regal presence, he made no bow of fealty to the Premier, facing him with arrogance but mild curiosity. This haughty attitude had no bearing on the Premier's true identity; for all of Nunzio's self-importance, he was not privvy to Mob secrets of that nature. Accepting no refreshments, he demanded the Premier voice whatever business he had in mind without further delay.

Careful to avoid any mention of motive, Nanner declared that he desired the severed head of the Council's High Priest, charging Nunzio with the task. A reward of unbelievable proportion would be granted for this deed, with an absolute promise of total amnesty for all involved in the murder. Nunzio countered with a request that five percent of all Mob tithings be donated to his personal coffers—in addition to the rewards offered by the Premier. After considerable negotiations, Nanner was forced to grudgingly agree to two percent of collected tithings for a period of no longer than five years.

A cocky Nunzio departed the castle well before dawn swept over the city.

In the morning, Nanner came groggily awake to discover his right hand had been cut from his wrist, the wound having been cauterized with clearly professional attention. Reclining alone in his lordly bed, Nanner attempted to surmise how this atrocity had occurred in his own bedchambers.

A few hours later, a package was delivered by private messenger to the still stunned Premier. The box proved to contain the head of Fillery Nunzio with the Premier's severed hand shoved in the crimeboss' mouth.

Not soon after, a personal note from the Council was delivered to the horrified Premier. The message extended the Council's deepest regrets over the Premier's unfortunate accident concerning the loss of his hand. It further inquired if there was "anything else" the Council could do to ease the Premier's recuperation during these trying and debilitating times.

Nanner sent this second delivery boy away with no reply.

As usual, the surveillance network that remained targeted on the Mob's doings within the royal castle in Chico recorded all these proceedings from orbit without blinking a digital optical unit.

59

INDEED, DR MUFFIN'S REACTIONS to the news concerning the destruction of the Mongol submarine were a mixed bag of ethical conflicts.

The robot considered all life to be sacred, but knew that death was an inevitable aspect of organic life. The conscious taking of any lives was beyond his capabilities. It was *not* beyond the capabilities of his allies, though. This fact allowed the robot to orchestrate actions which contradicted his conscience.

RTD 126.1952.2's destruction of the Mongol submarine made perfect sense according to the strategies of war. Leaving the Mongol Empire in the dark concerning the fate of their war party was necessary as long as the primary concern was the survival of Ericaland. The satellite's bold initiative was exactly the loophole Dr Muffin required to get the job done right.

Just as the robot had contrived the encounter of the Mongol battle wagon with the Quiet Men and Mob Team on the prairie, it had been Psycho Jones who'd unwittingly set these forces on their collision course. The resultant battle and slaughter had been regrettable, but unavoidable if Ericaland—and Afterburn Radio—were to continue to exist.

Although Dr Muffin's basic behavioral programs were restricted from actively and directly taking any human lives, there did exist within his programs optional leeway when the matter involved measures which could be classified as "defensive." In the protection of human lives, lethal defensive actions could be tolerated. Dr Muffin found it easier to delegate such actions into the hands of others who were not burdened with the strict ethical guidelines that lurked in his own positronic head. This relieved him of any such potential moral conflicts, leaving his own programs undisrupted by anything other a detached sense of guilt (which, in itself, was *not* part of his original programming, but rather a trait which had been added to his consciousness through years of interaction with humanity).

The death of Kaz Geller in the prairie battle was a loss that bothered Dr Muffin, however. He had known—and liked—the Afterburn agent. He wished there might have been some means to exclude Kaz from the slaughter, but could not imagine how that could have been arranged. The fact that Kaz would have readily agreed to give his own life to insure the salvation of the radio station did not help the robot's conscience.

The problem of what to tell Psycho Jones concerning the man's fate remained a dilemma for Dr Muffin. For her own mental health, Psycho must *never* learn that it had been her words that had brought about the man's demise. Uncertainty must be the tool employed to shield the DJ from this fact. In all truth, only an extremely high probability implied that Kaz had perished in the slaughter. Unless a body was discovered, the man's disappearance could be attributed to any number of dangers lurking in the savage wastelands.

No amount of guilt could bring Kaz back to life. But learning of the man's death *would* most certainly harm Psycho, crippling her fragile organic mind with unnecessary guilt and emotional distress. Keeping this matter secret from the girl was the only means Dr Muffin had to avoid hurting her. And his behavioral programs would not allow him to purposefully hurt the girl. Thus, a lie of omission was the path which his logic circuits dictated as the only course of action open to him.

Whether any higher power (a God or Mother Sky, as the humans called it) existed, Dr Muffin had no idea, for his programming included no corroborating data. If a deity did exist, then it was further debatable whether he, as an artificial life form, was answerable to the morality humanity had formulated for themselves. It was clearly accepted by theologians that animals were *not* held accountable for deeds which might be considered sins when committed by humans. At what point would a deity place artificial life on a spiritual foodchain?

Whatever the answer, Dr Muffin fully assumed responsibility for all actions perpetrated by the machines under his command. When one set out to guide the moral reconstruction of a wounded species, he reasoned, one must accept the good and bad consequences resulting from that guidance.

If there was a Judgment Day for positronic souls, he would face his reward—or punishment—without complaint or excuses.

60

WHERE THE GOING HAD PREVIOUSLY been difficult from lack of water (a problem they still suffered), Tagger's group made slower progress now, hindered by the burden of transporting the unconscious charred body of Kaz Geller. Fortunately. the landscape wasn't all that rugged, so the inconvenience was annoying but hardly incapacitating.

Tagger was still lost in the grip of his inner demons. He endlessly mentally chastised himself for his deficient leadership in guiding the group across the wastelands. The suffering, the monsters, the thirst... problems like this had never before plagued his travels. He was especially troubled by the death of Nico. The child's prior existence with her Tribe had clearly not prepared her for the harsh conditions common to the flat-lands—or to normal life, for that matter. Tagger remonstrated himself for allowing her spoiled whining to blind him to the actuality of her fragility.

Nitch was finding it increasingly difficult to maintain her hate for Afterburn Radio. The connections between the radio station and the ex-tinction of her family and Tribe had become fragmented in her percep-tion in the face of comments made by Needer and Tagger. The notion of avenging her Tribe seemed so remote now, as if her life before meeting the prairieman had become a ghost existence with no more substance than a fleeting dream. More and more, her mind perceived that fate was the real villain. Furthermore, if she had understood what Kaz had related before he fell into what she believed to be a final sleep, the agents of Afterburn had just averted a catastrophic invasion of Ericaland by foreign devils... not to mention avenging Nico by slaying her poisoners. The world was full of malevolence, and it appeared that Afterburn was actively strug-gling to battle these evils. How could she blame Afterburn for the wicked deeds of those who eluded their justice?

Nivek was only now beginning to comprehend the actuality of Nico's death. Although she had abruptly ended their relationship for narcissistic reasons, his feelings for her still ran deep, despite the detachment he had attempted to adopt. It was more, he felt, than the fact that she had been his girlfriend. Besides his sister, Nico had been all that was left of their Tribe. Now that she was gone, it was as if a great portion of his roots had vanished, leaving him adrift in unknown territory. Plagued by thirst and exhaustion, Nivek found it difficult to focus on any future. The prairie wasteland just went on forever; it was a zone of emptiness he feared would never end.

Needer alone was relishing the silence. With Nico gone, the group could focus on the task of surviving the remainder of their journey undisturbed by any individual demanding to be the center of attention. The cat regretted the girl's death, as she would abstractly regret the demise of any human. But the future as Needer saw it was embodied in Nivek Palma. Getting *him* safely to Afterburn Radio was tantamount; anything else, no matter how unfortunate or endearing, was immaterial. Her own life, even Tagger's, were secondary in the face of the future of the radio station and civilization. It often puzzled Needer how she had come to value the continuation of the human species over her own kind.

Kaz was oblivious to all the external suffering and confusion. Safely tucked away in a womb of unconsciousness, he dreamed of heavenly fires descending to blast the landscape barren of all threats, leaving only Afterburn to thrive in the charred remains.

As dawn began to fling faint traces of itself against their backs, the group looked to Tagger for guidance. Should they camp out for the day in the open, prey to the afternoon's brutal heat? Or continue walking, hopeful for some as yet undiscovered shelter?

Needer took the question into her own paws, scampering off into the fleeting traces of dusk. After a few more moments of further travel, Tagger was about to signal the group to halt and make the best of the immediate locale, when the cat returned with good news.

"A cave. Just ahead."

The prospect of safety from the wasteland's terrible heat caused the group to pick up their pace. Even Nivek seemingly roused from his dark gloom.

"It's little more than a big crack in the ground," the cat revealed, "but it angles a few meters down, providing ample shade."

The crevasse indeed provided ample shade, and once they had situated themselves in its cool depths, another discovery was made.

"I smell water," Needer declared suddenly. She bounded away into the fissure's shadowy depths without another word, leaving the three conscious humans with their guts clenched in hopeful anticipation.

They sat in the small cave, waiting and trying hard to contain their enthusiasm. As minutes slipped into an hour without the cat's return, Nivek drifted off to sleep, the darkness and the boy's weariness proving to be no match for any sense of expectation. This left Tagger and Nitch crouching alone in the dark, painfully aware of each other in the cramped space.

"Do you think something happened to her?" Nitch finally broke the silence. Her voice betrayed a trace of concern for the absent cat.

Tagger shook his head, then realized that this response was lost in the darkness. "No. Needer can take care of herself better than anyone I know."

"You and Needer are awfully close. Have you ever been that close with another person? A human person?"

"Once," muttered Tagger without further elaboration.

After a relapse into quiet, Nitch spoke, "Thank you for saving Nivek."

"When?"

"Back when we were poisoned. You held off the drug's effects long enough to drag him to safety." She grunted in vague amusement. "You saved me too."

"It was nothing." The prairieman's tone implied slight embarrassment.

"No," disagreed Nitch. "It wasn't. You had good reason to leave me out for the sun to finish me off."

"Don't be stupid."

"I'm serious. You knew how I felt toward this journey... toward Afterburn. It wouldn't've been out of line to forget me. It would've removed another threat to your precious radio station."

"I don't know what you're talking about."

"Yes, you do. Don't pretend to be stupid, Tagger. Despite how much you shun people, you're a sharp and accurate judge of them. You were aware of how I felt, yet you saved me too."

"No need to thank me. Leaving you behind never occurred to me."

"I wasn't thanking you. I was asking you *why*?"

Tagger made no reply.

"Well, you'll be happy to learn that I've changed my mind."

"About what?"

Nitch playfully punched his arm in the dark. "You know damned well about what. I've realized that Afterburn wasn't to blame for the death of my family. Even if I hadn't been off listening to the radio station's music when the Quiet Men hit my Tribe, my presence wouldn't have made any difference. Those fanatics would still have killed everyone... with the probable inclusion of myself. If Afterburn deserves any blame, it's for saving my life... and Nivek's too."

So, Tagger thought, that *was it.* She had blamed *herself* for her Tribe's extinction, and her grief had transferred the blame to Afterburn for luring her away from her family in their time of unexpected need.

"What changed your mind?"

"You did. You and your dedication to Afterburn."

Tagger laughed, "What did I do?"

"You're a good man, Tagger. You didn't have to do anything specific."

"You make me sound like some saint," he scoffed.

"In many ways, you are. You serve a greater good and you apply yourself to that cause without hesitation. You're ready to give your life trying to stop anything that might threaten Afterburn."

"By that logic, then why didn't I leave you behind to die in the sun?"

"I could be flippant and accuse you of saving me because my death might've alienated Nivek's loyalty to you and Afterburn. But... I don't think that was it."

"Then why did I save you?"

"You tell me, Tagger," grunted Nitch. "That's what I'd like to know."

In the darkness, he reached out to touch her cheek. "I think you already know the answer to that."

She fell into his arms, drawing him close with a strong hug. No words were necessary between them at this point. Their lips met, her tongue darted into his dry mouth. The tension that had existed between them melted away in the heat of their passion. They groped each other with an increasing appetite in the cave's gloom, stripping away their clothes and shedding the terse barriers Nitch had erected during their journey west. Similarly, Tagger's inner demons were banished from his mind.

As he entered her, confidence flowed back into his personality. With his growing firmness, the prairieman understood he had done his best in leading them across the wastelands. Each threat the group had encountered had been bested with efficiency and determination—not just by himself, but by the rest of the group.

The way had been difficult, but they had won through each barrier. They were going to make it to the radio station's hidden base. He honestly felt this as he shared what precious fluids he had with the huntress beneath the savage flatlands. He had found Nivek to save Afterburn, and Nitch was his own salvation.

Their lovemaking grew enthusiastic, succumbing to a wild abandon fueled by their unconscious anxiety. The journey had enervated them with the desperation of each threat they had faced; their union provided these tensions with a grateful release.

"Well," Needer's voice sounded suddenly. "I'm glad to see you two have settled your differences."

Nitch came with a tremendous shudder, quickly followed by an ecstatic release by Tagger.

"I found water," the cat announced as they disengaged their sweaty bodies. "Water," echoed her right head, licking those lips.

"What took you so long?" Tagger asked, his heartbeat slowly resuming its normal rhythm. "I was getting worried."

"You looked really worried," chided Needer.

Nitch chuckled. "I'll bet we did."

"There's a small problem with the water," Needer told them. "It's a ways down, but that's not it. The crevasse closes up twice en route to the underground stream. I had difficulty getting myself through the spots. A human will never fit."

"Oh well." Nitch's voice was devoid of despair, still drenched in the afterglow of her union with the prairieman.

"Can you get a waterskin through with you?" asked Tagger.

"I should think so," the cat replied. "Let's give it a try."

Choosing their smallest waterskin, Tagger looped its strap around Needer's neck. Without comment, the cat disappeared into the darker end of the cave.

Less than a minute passed before Tagger and Nitch were in each other's arms once more. This time, their passion was tender, a gentle union that joined their souls through the sticky contact of their bodies.

Unseen in the darkness, a smile curled Kaz's lips. With a softly unheard sigh, he closed his eyes and re-entered unconsciousness.

61

PSYCHO JONES WISHED Dr Muffin hadn't vanished during the emergency broadcast. She was full of questions regarding the message the robot had given her to read.

Who were these Mongols who had sent an exploration mission to Ericaland? Why had the message urged them *east* to meet with Afterburn representatives? Did Dr Muffin actually intend her to meet with these foreigners? Was the radio station really about to break their cover of secrecy? And how was all this going to save the life of Kaz?

Sitting back in her arcade chair with legs tucked underneath her, Psycho read the message again to herself. Its words did not imply any of the urgency which had gripped the robot; the message, and his directions on how to read it, carried a sense of informal welcome that had never before graced any news bulletin she had delivered over the airwaves. The very nature of the words as they appeared on the paper were unprecedented. Every other sheet of paper which Dr Muffin had presented her had contained text printed out in rigidly uniform type—while *this* message was scrawled in blockish letters in a handwriting that Psycho recognized as the script that often lingered in the margins of the regular bulletins. The robot himself had composed this message.

She read the last line again, "Maybe Fever and I will be able to convince one of these visitors to our land to come on the air with us for an exclusive live interview." Did Dr Muffin actually expect her to leave the station to conduct such an interview? Or—even more improbably—was Afterburn going to allow some of these Mongols into the station's secret base? She honestly doubted either option. So, why had the robot made her say such things over the airwaves?

Again, she pondered how any of this could involve a threat to Kaz's life. Kaz was a slick one who was not liable to blunder into any situation that he could not extricate himself from. And even if the man was indeed in trouble—how had Dr Muffin learned of such an eventuality?

Ah, Psycho remembered, *the robot's mysterious* sources*!* One of them must have informed him of Kaz's potential distress, just as they had certainly alerted the robot to the presence of this Mongol exploration mission on Ericaland soil.

She wished she knew more about the robot's mysterious sources of information. An instance such as this was exactly the kind of situation in which such knowledge would be of assistance. Were his sources other robots hidden throughout the outside world? Or were they *human* sources?—people like Kaz who guarded and promoted Afterburn Radio across the districts of Ericaland? Whatever the case, how did Dr Muffin contact them? And how did *they* contact him?

Not for the first time, Psycho puzzled over the means by which others could contact the robot here in the underground radio station. Did Dr Muffin receive radio transmissions from them? Were there other transmitters scattered throughout the land, each beaming news to him here?

And where was he anyway? It had been hours since she had made his cryptic emergency broadcast. Where was the robot hiding? *Why* was he hiding? Was he even hiding? Or was he busy at work on another mysterious news bulletin? There were so many regions of the subterranean complex Psycho had never visited, some by choice and others which were locked, barring any unauthorized access.

Who the hell *was* authorized to enter those areas if not the only human on Afterburn's staff left in the station? What secrets did Dr Muffin keep locked away from her eyes?

These questions had never before seemed of any importance to Psycho. Her duties as DJ kept her constantly overworked, especially since Smithie had left the station years ago. So busy was she anymore, she barely had the opportunity to compose stories for her Campfire Tales, and what new stories she did devise, she knew, were shallow comparisons to her earlier work.

Now, though, these questions burned brightly in her curious mind. She actually experienced a pang of indignation at how the robot had restricted her own movements within the station. Oh, he had never told her not to stray into these closed areas, but the workload she was forced to shoulder certainly afforded her no time to wander through the complex's endless corridors. She barely had time to rest and eat between her long shifts manning the transmission booth's console.

Speaking of which, she realized how weary she was. Her precious sleep had been disrupted by the robot's sudden appearance with his emergency news bulletin in hand. Not only did she long to return to her room to catch a few more hours of rest, but hunger was gnawing at her now.

Untucking her legs, Psycho rose to stand over the console. She shivered slightly, a minor chill running up her naked back. *Nerves,* she thought, knowing the stale air in the booth contained hardly enough cold to evoke such a reaction in her weary flesh. *Nerves indeed,* she ruminated. Exhaustion, lack of sleep, hunger, emotional confusion—was it any wonder she shivered in an indefinite chill?

With a sigh of defeat, Psycho surveyed the console's blinking lights and counter readings. After completing her unscheduled news broadcast, she had popped on a music CD; it was almost done playing. She selected another CD from the stack beside the console and inserted it into the second disc slot. Putting on her headphones, she monitored the outgoing signal and sequed from one disc to the next. Then she hit the repeat button. There, that would cover things for a few hours.

With an exaggerated sigh, she left the booth and headed for the food dispensary.

As with many of the rooms contained within the underground complex, the cafeteria, as it was cryptically labeled, was clearly designed for use by many people at once. A series of long tables ran in four rows through the room, each flanked with a number of colored chairs constructed of a strange material that had survived the centuries without undue decay. The metallic kitchen that occupied one wall had not seen use in many years, fresh meat or vegetables being luxuries that only appeared when brought by one of Afterburn's field agents during their infrequent visits to the base.

In the absence of fresh food, Psycho had grown used to the pill supplements provided by the dispensary. These came from a device set into another wall, a two meter square plate covered with buttons and slots placed above removable trays. A pair of water spigots projected from the wall beside the dispensary device, giving her a choice of hot or cold liquid refreshment.

She punched for a "regular meal" and filled a cup with cold water while the ancient machinery grunted. Eventually, several brightly colored pills fell into the bin.

For a meal of such minimal mass, Psycho did not bother to seat herself at one of the tables. She popped the pills into her mouth, washing them down with the cool liquid the spigot had given her.

By this point, the questions that whirled in Psycho's mind were losing priority to the weariness that ached her bones.

She retreated to her room, noting with irritation how the door had been ripped free from its frame. She'd have to get Dr Muffin to replace it, although the concept of privacy was certainly a moot point as long as she was the station's sole organic inhabitant.

Despite the activity churning in her mind, she was asleep within a minute of her head hitting the mattress.

She dreamed of mysterious strangers who chased her through the corridors of Afterburn's station. When she looked over her shoulder at her pursuers, their faces were all smooth metal like Dr Muffin's, broken only by ocular visors and mouthpiece grills which spouted warped versions of the emergency news bulletin she had recently broadcast.

62

BY THE TIME NEEDER RETURNED, dragging with her a full skin of water, the lovers had spent their passion and lay dozing and naked in each other's arms. The cat gently nudged Tagger's elbow, bringing him quietly awake.

"Water," Needer softly declared, urging her companion to partake.

Tagger roused Nitch, offering her the first drink. As she gratefully sipped the deliciously cool water, the prairieman woke her brother. Although they both warned Nivek to drink slowly, the boy gulped at the liquid, desperate to fill his aching stomach. Nitch had to forcibly take the waterskin from him.

When she handed it to Tagger, he took the skin over to the slumbering form of Kaz. He carefully dribbled the remaining water into the man's blackened lips.

"You didn't get any," Nitch observed when Tagger sat back with the empty skin.

"I'll get more," announced Needer.

"No," argued Tagger. "You should rest first."

"You need water," the cat objected, pulling at the flaccid waterskin.

"I'll survive a few more hours without water. You rest. We should all rest." The prairieman closed his eyes and his body promptly slumped in sleep.

Although concerned for the man, Needer recognized the wisdom of his words. She was exhausted from her long sojourn crawling through the crevasse. Curling into a ball, the cat closed all her eyes and commenced breathing evenly.

"We're going to make it now, aren't we?" sighed Nivek.

"Yes," Nitch agreed. "Everything's going to be all right." She listened as her younger brother's breathing turned into gentle snores.

She was almost asleep herself when the cat's voice whispered to her, "So… worked out all your aggressions, have you?"

"Huh? Yes, I suppose I have."

"Do you love him? Or is it just physical?"

"I… don't know," she sighed. "You love him, don't you?"

"Not the same way you do," commented Needer.

"Why do you ask questions when you already know the answers?"

"To make sure *you* know the answers too."

With that, the two fell silent to contemplate this new development.

63

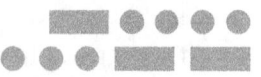

BY THE TIME TAGGER ENDED his long rest, Needer had made several more trips to the underground river, filling all of the group's waterskins.

He drank lustily, quenching his torturous thirst. Then he returned to sleep, content in the knowledge of their rejuvenated strength.

Once Nitch and Needer had forced Nivek to consume some of the dried jerky meat, they all followed the prairiemen's example, relapsing into a lazy slumber.

64

NITCH AND NEEDER CAME ALERT together, the girl puzzled what had brought her awake, the cat growling low in the throat shared by her two heads.

"What is it?" the huntress whispered, startled at the hoarseness of her voice.

"Noise," hissed the cat. "Outside…"

Nitch slid her hunting knife from its sheath. As she began to scramble out of the crevasse, Needer bounded past her. When Nitch exited the crack in the earth, she was surprised to discover it was already night again. The group had slept a full day beneath the hellish wasteland.

What could it be? she wondered. Whatever had roused her and the cat was not registering on her inner huntress senses. Was it another monster whose strangeness set it beyond her ability to detect danger?

She suddenly became aware that something out in the darkness was calling Tagger's name!

When she tightened her grip on her knife, the cat hissed from nearby, "Relax, girl. This isn't a threat."

Then Needer wailed into the night, a long and bloodcurdling screech. The cry did little to calm Nitch's already prominent tension.

Nor did the shape that ran toward them across the prairie. Despite the humanoid form it wore, the shape was moving far faster than any normal person. The night sky's kaleidoscopic colors gleamed oddly from it's bald head. Under its arms, it grasped two bulky shapes whose evident weight did not seem to offbalance the runner's swift pace.

As it grew closer, the figure's inhuman qualities became more salient, causing Nitch to gasp in shock. It was a man—a man made out of *metal!*

"Dr Muffin!" Needer exclaimed. The cat leapt toward the figure, filling the night air with feline laughter.

"Needer," responded the figure. Its voice was raspy and artificial.

"What the hell are you doing out here?" the cat gurgled, circling the robot's feet as he slowed to a halt.

"I was afraid I wasn't going to find you," confessed the robot. He deposited one of the shapes he carried on the ground. Its contents sloshed, revealing itself. "I brought you water."

"Don't need it anymore," Needer snorted. "I found us all the water we needed."

"Everyone is safe then?"

"Sleeping underground in a cave."

Dr Muffin faced Nitch. "Not *all* asleep, I see."

"What the…" Nitch held her knife ready. Despite the cat's apparent familiarity with the strange metal man, the huntress found herself unable to lower her guard.

"Oh, put that away," Needer snorted at her. "This is Dr Muffin, Afterburn's founder and main technician. He's *definitely* on our side.

"This is Nitch," the cat told the robot. "She's one of the people Tagger and I were bringing in."

"Indeed?" Dr Muffin bowed slightly, his manner surprisingly formal considering the circumstances. "Pleased to meet you, Nitch."

"How did you manage to get down here on the prairie?" Needer asked the robot. "Where's your power chord?"

The robot indicated a dark metal box he still held under his arm. "I jury-rigged myself up to an old cell battery."

"Nice," purred the cat. "So—*why'd* you come down off the mountain?"

"I came to help you. I was under the impression you needed help."

"Been watching us, huh? For how long?"

As the pair conversed, Nitch surveyed the robot through eyes narrowed more with disbelief than suspicion. Of the many strange and weird things the huntress had witnessed on their journey, this metal man was perhaps the most incredible. Nitch was familiar with various metals, but she knew of none that possessed the pliant nature displayed by the robot's body. Her first impression had been that possibly the figure was just a man wearing an armored suit, but a cursory examination of the body's weird contours quickly dispelled that notion. Dr Muffin was no human encased in metal—he was thoroughly an artificial construct! Peering close, she could discern circular discs at the figures joints, enabling the limbs to swing and bend. The robot's hands were large, possessing four blunt fingers instead of five. Its feet were inhuman wedges, extending equally forward and back in squat triangles from his ankles. Several slots decorated the robot's sleek body. But it was Dr Muffin's head that fascinated Nitch most of all: the only features that graced the gleaming oval were a wide slit where the eyes should be and a flat grill on its chin. Almost as an afterthought, she noticed the sturdy wire that ran from a plug in its shoulder leading to the box (a *battery*, he had called it) under his arm.

Truly, she mused, *Afterburn Radio is staffed by astounding creatures.*

The robot was explaining, "I saw you encounter the Mongols' battle wagon. When I realized they had given you drugged water, I decided to come to your rescue. I... unfortunately, I was unable to do anything to save Kaz."

"Who says I needed saving?" inquired a voice from the dark crack in the ground behind Nitch. She whirled to see Kaz climb from its depths. He stood and smiled at them with white teeth. His skin was still crusty and dark, but he no longer wore the look of death.

Kaz strode forth to clasp the robot by the shoulders in a greeting.

"Kaz!" Dr Muffin exclaimed loudly. "You—you're not dead!"

"He certainly should be," gasped Nitch. "He was severely burned from head to toe! How..."

Turning to give the girl a secretive grin, Kaz told her, "Awfully difficult to take me out, girl."

"Kaz has amazing regenerative capabilities," declared Tagger as he appeared from the crevasse. Behind him, Nivek peered warily over the edge of the earthen crack. Coming up to stand beside the huntress, he reminded her, "I told you he'd be okay."

As Kaz explained his escape to Dr Muffin, Needer strolled over to rub against Tagger's ankles. "He brought us water. Wasn't that thoughtful?"

After welcoming Dr Muffin, Tagger introduced Nivek to the robot. The boy's attitude was hesitant, his countenance full of wonderment. His eyes grew wider as Tagger described the robot's role in Afterburn's operation.

"Gosh!" Nivek breathed. "Then—*you're* the father of radio!"

"No," replied the robot. "*That* parentage belongs to a man named Marconi who lived many years before the Doom. I am only the one who remembered his discoveries after that disaster."

"It was Dr Muffin who found the underground complex that later became Afterburn's secret radio station," Needer informed the boy.

"But I thought Fever Smith started Afterburn Radio," exclaimed Nivek.

"Indeed he did," Dr Muffin admitted. "I only helped Fever understand what he had found, teaching him how to utilize radio to help mankind."

Nivek and Nitch, and even Tagger and Kaz, listened with deep interest to the robot's words. The things Dr Muffin was revealing were aspects that even the Afterburn agents did not know, at least not in such depth as the robot described now. Only Tagger seemed to note that these revelations did not come as surprises to Needer.

In turn, Dr Muffin was surprised when Nivek displayed a keen understanding of radio theory. The robot's astonishment increased when Tagger described the contents of Nivek's secret radio cavern.

"That's why Needer and I were bringing Nivek in to Afterburn," the prairieman concluded. "I knew you would be interested in the things he has to offer."

The robot nodded. "Very interested indeed."

"I want to be on the radio!" Nivek proclaimed with a smile. "I want to be just like Fever Smith. He's my hero!"

"Let us not waste any time then," declared Dr Muffin. "Afterburn's base is less than a day's walk from here. There, your wishes can all become reality."

As the group hurried to collect their belongings from the sanctuary of the crevasse, Tagger sidled close to Dr Muffin to ask, "Fever… has he returned yet?"

"I'm afraid not, Tagger. He has been gone so long, I fear he may be dead."

"We've seen no sign of him, either," added Needer.

"Nivek is going to be mighty disappointed," Tagger muttered. "He really has his heart set on meeting his hero."

"I suspect there are enough wonders contained in the station to keep Nivek enthralled for years," countered Dr Muffin. "We will deal with explaining Fever's absence when the time comes."

"Meanwhile," the robot gave them a sincere bow, "you and Needer have Afterburn's undying gratitude for finding this boy. He could well be the instrument necessary to keep the station alive."

Shrugging with embarrassment, Tagger went to help the others.

"Tagger found a girlfriend," chuckled Needer. "He already got his reward."

"It would seem your journey has solved many problems," Dr Muffin whispered to the cat.

Needer bobbed both her heads in agreement. "We're the cat's meow," she proclaimed, employing an idiom the robot had once taught her. Needer's right head cheerfully *meowed* in dimwitted concurrence.

EACH MEMBER OF THE GROUP (with the exception of Kaz, whose muscles were still tender from their unnaturally accelerated regeneration) stepped livelier as they approached the foothills of the Rocky Mountains. The peaks reared huge like a vast wall of stone occluding the colorful sky with their grayish blue bulk. Only four of the six travelers were aware of the ocean that lapped against the far side of the mountains.

"Do you think the Mongols will send another attack team?" Kaz asked the robot as they walked.

"I doubt they will venture across the Siffic Ocean again for some time." During their trek, the robot had told them about the destruction of the submarine that had brought the Mongol battle wagon to Ericaland.

"They seemed a fanatical people," commented Kaz. "From what Klaw, the team's leader, told me, the Mongol Empire blames the ancestors of Ericaland for the ancient Doom. The purpose of their invasion was not just conquest, you know. They were looking for vengeance."

"I am aware of their motives. Sadly, they are not entirely grounded in delusion."

A few paces behind the pair, Tagger and Nitch walked side by side. The pair had become inseparable since their tryst in the crevasse.

"I don't understand," Nitch marveled aloud. "How could Kaz have healed so quickly? His burns would have inevitably killed any other man."

"Kaz is no normal man," Tagger confided to her.

"But—"

"You know how Needer is a mutant cat. Well, Kaz is a mutant *human*. His body is endowed with incredible healing capabilities. By the time another week has passed, Kaz's flesh will be freshly pink and ready for him to tan it dark once again."

"*Mutants*," muttered the girl. "All my life I've heard the term, but I've never really understood what it meant."

"It means *different*," Needer interjected from their feet.

"But—how? No, I don't mean how are mutants different—I mean, what makes them mutants?" asked Nitch.

"No one knows the answer to that," Tagger admitted.

"I do!" The cat strutted with feline pride. "The problem is, you wouldn't understand the answer."

"But a *cat* does," snorted Nitch.

"Okay. You asked for it," Needer sneered. "Mutations are induced by deviations in the genetic structure. Each creature possesses a genetic code that dictates its physical makeup. When that code is disrupted, the resultant creature is different from its parents. Most times, the deviant off-spring are substandard and cannot survive. Other times, as with Kaz and *myself*," the cat lent a cocky swagger to her trot, "the changes are beneficial and the offspring possess a higher survival potential than their parents. Sometimes, the changes are capable of breeding true, producing a new strain of creature—like the prairie wolves or the Rolling Stones."

"Umm…" The huntress' imagination was hard-pressed to envision any means by which stones might breed.

"I told you you wouldn't understand it."

"But what *causes* these deviations in the—what did you call it?—the genetic code?"

"There can be lots of causes. Diet, the air, random heredity…"

"You don't know that part of the answer, do you?"

"Dr Muffin called it *radiation*," the cat responded vaguely.

"So, what is radiation?"

"Umm…" Needer avoided looking up at her.

"Ha!" Nitch laughed. "The cat with *almost* all the answers."

"Radiation is all around us," revealed Tagger. "In the air and in the ground beneath our feet. It's like radiowaves—they're a form of radiation."

Needer looked at her traveling companion with a new respect.

"Like radiowaves?" Nitch gasped. "Then—this radiation could change Nivek's genetic code? I don't think I like the sound of that…"

"Your brother has nothing to fear from radiowaves," Dr Muffin called back to them. "The radiation Needer speaks of is quite different from simple radiowaves. High powered electrical forces are capable of effecting genetic changes too, but all of Afterburn's equipment is heavily shielded against such eventualities."

"I wouldn't mind having my genetic code altered," announced Nivek. "If it'd change me like Kaz…"

"Radiation doesn't work directly upon the subject like that," the robot told them. "It can only create changes in the offspring, not the parents."

"Where does this radiation come from?" asked Nitch.

"That is something I cannot tell you. It is like asking where does air come from." Dr Muffin felt this the best answer to give them. The means of creating new radiation was far beyond the technologies he was planning to allow mankind to rediscover. *Those* mistakes were ones he had sworn to prevent occurring ever again.

The robot felt the conversation was taking a decidedly wrong turn. It was time to introduce a fresh topic. "Once you are fully recuperated, Kaz, I imagine you'll be wanting to reclaim your wind sailer from the Black Hills. Perhaps Nitch would like to accompany you. It is a wonderful conveyance."

"Wind sailer?" she asked.

With an expansion of his chest, Kaz proudly described his vehicle to the huntress, entertaining her with tales of his travels.

"It sounds amazing," admitted Nitch. "But I think I have other plans after we reach Afterburn's station." She glanced knowingly at Tagger, who smiled in return.

"Yes," Needer teased them. "They have *other* plans."

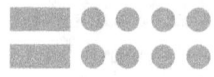

WHEN PSYCHO CAME AWAKE, she remained lying on her bed. Her small frame occupied very little of the mattress' expanse, allowing her to toss and turn and stretch without encountering the edges.

Staring up at the tiled ceiling, she refrained from counting the white squares. She had counted them quite enough in the last few years as she lay, agonizing over how alone the bed was with only one person in it.

She missed Smithie so much.

Of all the wonderful things Afterburn had brought to her life, Fever Smith had been by far the best. He had appreciated her for more than the stories that were her forte. Through his attention and guidance, she had expanded her interests to include the limitless range of music that was contained in Afterburn's sonic library. He had breathed his passion for music into her. He had taught her how to operate Afterburn's console and equipment. He had transformed her from a girl of the wilds into a woman of the night.

She didn't understood why he had to leave the station. His claim that he needed to *find himself* had insulted her. Why couldn't he find himself in *her*? As she had found herself in him.

When the time had come for Smithie to go, she'd been unable to see him off. The pain his absence would bring was already knotting her heart. She couldn't face him, couldn't say goodbye. Instead, she had remained in her room—*their* room—and cried until her eyes hurt as much as her soul.

That was the first time she had counted the ceiling tiles. She had never had reason or opportunity to do so before that night. Since then, she had counted them innumerable times… twenty-one across and fifteen deep… three hundred and fifteen in all… the same number of tiles each count, always the same. And each time, there had been no Smithie to agree with her, no Smithie to hold her, no Smithie to love.

She'd stopped counting the tiles quite a while ago. The careful segment by segment assessment of her ceiling had only reminded her how lonely she was. Her hereditary parents, her gypsy parents, and finally Smithie—everyone who had ever meant anything to Psycho had left her.

And now, even Dr Muffin was gone.

Wandering the dimly lit corridors, she called the robot's name. She opened doors and peered into unknown hallways, but he was nowhere to be found. She had ceased looking once she found his power chord dangling loose beside the closed hatch that opened on the ascent shaft that was the main escapeway from the underground complex. The robot was gone. Now she was the station's sole inhabitant, the only one remaining to keep the music playing.

With a childlike peevishness, Psycho broke the seals on several of the doors that accessed the complex's forbidden regions. She roamed those dark halls, armed with one of the station's precious flashlamps. She investigated chambers filled with objects beyond her understanding. She stared up at the massive now-darkened screens that walled a huge room. She picked the receivers from several of the phones that sat around a large oval table, as if expecting to hear the robot's voice chastising her for venturing where she should not go. But no voice spoke in her ear, not even a dormant hiss sounded from the receivers. The lines were dead, quiet for centuries.

In one room, she discovered vast shelves filled with curious metallic weapons covered with an ancient layer of dust. She had seen the likes of these weapons before: once in the hands of the Mob's Church Police, and again in pictures Dr Muffin had shown her. Touching them now, Psycho's revulsion of the terrible things rose anew in her. They were ugly things, despite their shiny surfaces once the dust was wiped away, angular and contoured with wicked lines. Even now, years later, she could recall their horrible bark as they had spewed death and destruction in the hands of the Church Police who had killed both her families.

She left the prohibited halls, returning to the corridors of the radio station. Somehow, their vacancy was more comforting that the emptiness of those forbidden zones.

With a mild shock, Psycho realized she still carried the weapon she had taken down to examine. Although its weight felt uncomfortable in her hands, she did not discard the thing. She took it with her as she aimlessly drifted through the corridors, her eyes seeing but not registering the path she took.

Her mind was blank as she walked. Gone was the torment of loneliness now, swallowed by the utter emptiness which dominated these hallways. Her shuffling steps echoed ahead of her, but the sounds went unheard.

And yet, despite her quasi-catatonia, she found herself peeking into the transmission booth to check on the station's broadcast. The CD she had left playing was still sending out music over the airwaves, an endless loop of uptempo jocularity for an audience that spanned a wasted continent.

She laughed softly. Vacant and purposeless though her persona had become, she nevertheless had the unconscious presence of mind to make sure the station was still transmitting. It amused her that the dedication for Afterburn which Smithie had instilled in her was able to remain untouched by the ennui that had overtaken her soul.

Dragging the weapon with her, she left the booth and headed for the cafeteria. Food might conquer her mood, banishing this emptiness that had filled her. Food... then a return to the escape which only deep sleep could give her.

Entering the cafeteria, she halted abruptly. A gasp escaped her lips.

The figure who sat at one of the tables turned sharply to look at her. Despite the man's intense scowl, Psycho recognized him instantly.

"Smithie!" she cried, her thin voice vibrant with shocked joy. Then she fainted.

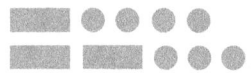

67

BY THE TIME THE GROUP reached the mountain range's foothills, dawn was creeping across the eastern horizon.

"It's only a short ways now," announced Tagger. "We can continue to climb or camp down here until dusk."

"Stop if you wish," Dr Muffin advised them. "But I must be returning to the station now." He indicated the battery he held under his arm. "My power source will not last more than another few hours."

Nivek decided for the group, declaring his eagerness to reach the radio station and its hidden mysteries.

They began their ascent of the foothills.

If they had chanced to turn on Nivek's small crystal radio during their climb, they might have discovered the voice of Afterburn had been silenced.

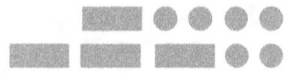

68

IT WAS A SPLENDID GROTTO, contained by high cliffs on all sides. Access to it was possible only through a narrow crevasse hidden behind a tangle of ragged thorn bushes.

As the group scrambled into the grotto, Nivek paused, awed by its beauty.

Where the rest of the mountains consisted of dull gray rock, the grotto's circumference was alive with rich reds and rustic browns which bordered on royal purple. The cliffs walling the grotto rose tall, their surfaces chiseled by time into sharp layers. Spilling down into the pit, the light painted the rock faces with rigid shadows, black wedges that transformed the layers into geological fractals.

A delicate waterfall of crystal-clear liquid fell down one side of the grotto, to disappear in a mist cloud that hid the pool that filled the bottom of the pit. The hiss of falling water filled the granite enclosure, a majestic sound that softly reverberated from the grandiose cliffs.

(It was the kind of scenery that a photographer for National Geographic would have sold their soul to capture on film.) The view took Nivek's breath away, bringing tears to his eyes.

"Impressive, huh?" Needer commented, leaping along the small ledge beside the entry crevasse.

Even Nitch stopped briefly to appreciate the magnificence of the scene.

Tagger smiled. "The doorway to Afterburn."

Following the ledge as it spiraled down toward the waterfall, Dr Muffin led the way, trailed by Tagger and the Palmas. With a joyous whoop, Kaz flung himself from the ledge, diving into the mist-covered pool below.

Reaching the waterfall, Nitch could see how the ledge swung behind the feathery descent of water. There, hidden by the sparkling waterfall, was a shallow niche that framed a hatch of corroded black metal. The hatch wore a wheel that reminded her of the doors deep beneath the Oogolah ruins that gave access to Nivek's secret room of radio equipment.

The difference was that *this* hatch hung open, a discovery that elicited grunts of surprise from the Afterburn personnel.

"You didn't…" muttered Tagger.

"I would *never* leave the hatch open," Dr Muffin declared somberly.

The prairieman asked hesitantly, "Could someone have *found* it?"

"Not by accident," asserted Needer. She crept closer to the portal, sniffing the ground before it.

"Anything?" Tagger inquired.

The cat's tail thrashed the air in agitation. "I recognize the spoor, but I can't place it."

"Tagger and I will investigate," directed Dr Muffin.

"I'm going too," Nitch declared. When the robot turned to dissuade her, she glared at him with overt defiance.

"I'll stay and watch Nivek," Needer interjected, resolving the conflict of wills.

"I don't need watching," complained Nivek.

"Maybe so," Tagger told him. "But inside, you'll just be a liability if there's trouble. You stay here."

"When Kaz finishes with his swim," Dr Muffin advised the cat, "bring him up to speed. But don't let him enter until we return."

"What if you don't return?" inquired Needer.

Without an answer, Dr Muffin stepped through the hatch. Tagger and Nitch followed the robot, their primitive weapons held ready.

69

ONCE INSIDE THE HATCHWAY, Nitch discovered herself at the top of a narrow shaft that descended into the bowels of the mountain. Glancing into its depths, she could discern no bottom in the darkness. Even the figures of Tagger and Dr Muffin were barely visible as they climbed down the rungs attached to the side of the shaft. The odors that wafted up from below were dusty, alien.

Sliding her spear through her belt and tucking her knife between her teeth, Nitch swung out into the shaft and began her descent after the others. The fifth rung down groaned as she placed her foot upon it, a rusty creak that accompanied a slight give under her weight. She hastily stepped beyond it to a rung that gave no complaint. As she progressed downwards, the light that spilled from the open hatch grew fainter until it vanished and darkness enveloped her.

Momentarily, prefaced by a scrape of harsh metal, dim illumination sprang into existence beneath her. Peering down, Nitch made out a pair of dark humanoid silhouettes as the robot and the prairieman exited the shaft through a new hatchway. Once she reaching the bottom of the shaft, the huntress followed them into a gray tunnel.

Tagger stood a few meters into the passage. Dr Muffin had abandoned the cell battery he carried and was attaching himself to a wire that depended from the tunnel's ceiling. Once he'd plugged the wire firmly into a socket on his shoulder, the robot's ocular visor glowed with a fresher inner light. Picking a white longcoat from the floor, Dr Muffin contemplated it for a second, then replaced it on the ground. He turned to face Nitch, nodded to her, then strode off past Tagger.

These tunnels differed greatly from the corridors than ran beneath the Oogolah ruins. Although both had an ancient demeanor, the Oogolah corridors had been coarser, covered with traces of peeling paint and waterstains. These Afterburn corridors were no more recent, but their stark metallic construction afforded them a sturdier appearance, all the more foreboding in the dim light that came from flickering rectangular panels running the length of the ceiling. With a start, Nitch realized that these panels were working examples of what Tagger had described under the Oogolah ruins—light-tubes powered by some mysterious water-driven force. Where the Oogolah corridors had featured blank walls, the Afterburn hallways were latticed with angular contours and shallow boxlike attachments. Upon closer examination, she could see that the gray surfaces were blackened by age in areas.

The atmosphere here in these corridors had different texture from that in the Oogolah tunnels. The air beneath those ruins had been dead, undisturbed by breeze or mortal for ages, while the Afterburn tunnels were filled with fresher drafts that bespoke ventilation. These corridors held a hint of stale sweat and a scent Nitch could not identify: a sharp tang that left an aftertaste in her mouth. The enigmatic odor grew stronger as they ventured deeper into the complex, while the odor of perspiration soon took on an edge that Nitch's huntress nose identified as feminine.

At a juncture of corridors, Dr Muffin conferred with Tagger. They seemed in disagreement regarding which direction to proceed. As she came closer, Nitch caught traces of their whispered words.

"It could not be the Mongols," asserted the robot. "They had no way of finding the station."

"What if they did? What if there was a second group?"

"They all perished out on the prairie," Dr Muffin whispered with definitive emphasis.

Nitch interrupted, "Has this ever happened before? Someone finding their way into the station?"

"No," declared the robot. "Never."

"Then you don't know what to expect. It could be anyone… or anything."

"She has a point," Tagger agreed.

"Only because it furthers your opinion," retorted Dr Muffin. "No. I refuse to break out any of the ancient weapons. We will handle what we encounter with the means already at our disposal."

The robot strode off down the right corridor, dismissing the prairieman's objections before he could open his mouth. Shaking his head, Tagger trailed after the robot, gripping his staff with whitened knuckles.

The three followed the corridor to the next intersection, where again Tagger disagreed with the robot concerning which branch to take.

Nitch hissed at them. "Shh!" She cocked her head, peering into the left corridor. A slight tingle stirred inside her head. An enemy was near…

she could sense it with a soft certainty that increased as she strode away from the arguing pair. "This way."

"But—" began the robot.

"Her senses are more acute than mine—*and* yours," Tagger admonished. He took out after the huntress.

Before they had come to the next junction of corridors, the sound of smashing things drifted to their alert ears.

"The transmission booth!" gasped Dr Muffin. He broke past the two humans and ran down the right corridor, his power chord stretched taut behind him.

Nitch and Tagger sped after him.

The robot disappeared around a corner ahead of them. They heard his metallic shout of "Stop!", followed by an explosive roar that actually hurt Nitch's ears. As they ran toward the corner, Dr Muffin's body flew past them, recoiling from some incredible impact, tumbling loosely down the left corridor.

Swiftly but carefully, Tagger and Nitch peeked around the right corner, their keen eyesight hunting for the intruder Dr Muffin had confronted. Nitch caught brief sight of the figure of a tall Quiet Man wrapped in the dark scarf of his kind.

"Hey!" shouted Tagger.

The Quiet Man swung a strange length of metal up to point at them. It roared, a projectile firing from its end faster than Nitch's vision could follow. Then the man ducked back into a doorway and out of sight.

Fortunately, the man's hasty aim was imperfect. Nitch felt the projectile pass less than a hand's width from her face. Behind her, the pellet *ping*ed, ricocheting wildly down the corridor.

"That was one of *our* rifles," Tagger gasped. "Where the hell did a Quiet Man get that?"

"That you, Hewie?" came a hoarse call from the doorway into which the Quiet Man had disappeared.

Astonishment played across Nitch's face. The huntress had never before heard a Quiet Man *speak*, she had not thought they could. How can a man talk once his mouth has been sewn shut?

An expression of incredulous shock lengthened Tagger's face.

"Fever?" the prairieman whispered with incredulity.

"I came back." The Quiet Man laughed loudly from the doorway. "Aren't you glad to see me, old friend?"

"Old friends don't usually shoot at each other when they meet again,"

Tagger commented with overt sarcasm.

"Fever Smith?" gasped Nitch. Her brow wrinkled with bewilderment. "Fever Smith is a *Quiet Man*?"

"Times change," the Quiet Man called back. "Sometimes people change with them. I'm no longer Fever your friend, Hewie. Now I'm Magog your enemy."

Tagger traded looks of surprise with Nitch. "News to me," he mouthed silently to her.

Nitch trembled, beginning to understand the enormity of the incredible ambush into which they had blundered.

70

Then: stirring the musical embers.

Hewie Lang spent his childhood in the lap of Mob luxury. An inquisitive boy, Hewie learned early on to tell the difference between sanctioned and prohibited curiosity. This knowledge did not stop him from asking questions, it simply made him more careful who he asked what.

During a Council purge (the fourth in two years), Hewie decided to run away from home and see the world about which he was so curious. The next morning, a team of Church Police visited the Lang mansion, wiping out the entire family. The absence of one thirteen year old boy was never noticed in the bloodbath.

Leaving Mob territory, Hewie made his way south. He jobbed as a farmhand, moving from Tribe to Tribe with each season. He followed the crop rotation west, growing strong in the fields and wise in the ways of men. When he reached the end of the farmlands, Hewie adopted the trade of a hunter, becoming adept in the ways of the prairie.

Finally, Hewie's wandering brought him north, skirting the western perimeter of Mob territory, to the village of Calg deep in the Anadian woodlands. It was there that Hewie made his first real friend in the person of Derg Fallow.

Like Hewie, Derg was a youth full of questions. He longed to explore the world beyond the forest which he thought of as his childhood prison. When Derg rejected his heritage of logger to start a jug band, his family exiled him, striking his name from the household list of births.

In his new state of homelessness, Derg had welcomed Hewie's friendship. They headed west together, foraging from village to village. Hewie's intimacy with living off the land kept the pair fed, while Derg's proficiency with rustic tunes kept them amused. Derg never did learn any survival lore from Hewie, but he did teach the hunter to love music.

One winter, halfway up Mt. Aylmer, the boys stumbled upon a cave which proved to be the residence of a Sitter named Miles. As it happened, Derg had injured himself during an avalanche. Hewie had spent hours digging his friend out of the snow. Carrying the half-dead boy on his back, Hewie had chosen refuge in a cave he picked at random from the many that covered the eastern slope of Mt. Aylmer. Passing out from exhaustion, Hewie awakened to find himself face to face with a black holy man.

Having heard of Sitters in his travels, Hewie was wary of the dark man. Sitters were notorious for their solipsistic ways. Weary, starved, and burdened with his injured friend, Hewie was at a loss for what to do. He couldn't have been more surprised when the Sitter asked if they needed help. When he woke again, Hewie found himself and Derg in the holy man's care.

Miles nursed the pair of travelers back to health with mystic herbs and attentive care… and unearthly music. Deep within his cave, Miles had collected vast stacks of ancient music CDs, which he played on an old machine powered by a generator which was in turn powered by an underground stream.

The music contained on these magical and shiny discs delighted and inspired the two boys. Genres the holy man labeled as rock'n'roll, jazz, classical, experimental… these sounds were awesome to Derg and Hewie. They bore no resemblance to the crude music they'd infrequently encountered in their travels. Even Derg's own tunes paled in comparison to these sonic wonders. The music in Miles' collection was like nothing on earth. Not just the incredible instrumentation, but the complexity of the compositions—the emotions expressed by the music.

When Derg revealed his jug playing talent to the Sitter, Miles produced a glistening horn of gilt chrome, which he called a *trumpet*. With a wide smile, the black man put the horn to his lips and played for the boys, displaying a remarkable expertise with the instrument. He played for hours, the boys staring at him with tearful eyes and yearning hearts.

The holy man proceeded to teach Derg the nuances of capable musical performance. As time passed in the cave and Derg's bones knitted, his fingers learned how to produce melodies of wondrous structure and impact. Hewie longed to join in, but to his angst it was swiftly obvious he lacked even a residual degree of musical talent. His role was that of the audience.

The boys stayed with Miles long after Derg's injuries were dim memories. They might have remained longer had it not been for a terrible avalanche one afternoon. The two boys were out on a hunting trip, gathering meat against the harsh winter. When they returned, they discovered to their horror that the holy man's cave was buried beneath a half a kilometer of frozen snow. Mt. Aylmer now wore a new face on its eastern slope.

Digging the Sitter out was plainly impossible.

In an emotional daze, the boys fled south, following the Rocky Mountains.

It was months before Derg resumed his musical career. It might never have happened if not for a bawdy insult. Hoping to trade some pelts for salt, they had come to a village whose name neither of them ever learned. While Hewie haggled with the trading post's proprietor over the value of their pelts, Derg discovered a guitar in a box of junk in the store. When he lovingly caressed the instrument, a group of toothless locals taunted the boy, accusing him of being "out in the woods too long." With a scowl, Derg promptly sat down and proceeded to perform for the ignorant yokels. The music he played choked the insults in their stunned throats.

Hewie and Derg never did get the salt they needed. Instead, after an arduous negotiation, they traded their pelts for the guitar. It didn't matter. In the next village on their southbound travels, Derg managed to barter a night's performance for a chunk of rock salt.

Two villages and two guitar performances later, they met up with Jag Nye, who had been marveling Tribes with his percussive abilities as he traveled west from the Missippi Delta. Teaming Derg's guitar talents with Jag's drumming virtuosity, they began touring under the name Afterburn. The name had been coined by Hewie, whose lack of musical skill left him to act as the band's manager, negotiating their performances in trade for various supplies.

Just as the band's notoriety was peaking in the Rocky Mountain Districts, Jag broke his wrist in a barroom brawl over the attentions of some local whore. Unfortunately, it turned out that the girl was no whore, but the daughter of the village's headman. Afterburn was forced to flee into the mountains to escape an ugly retribution for Jag's lewd comments.

While Jag's wrist healed, the trio camped out on the slopes of Pikes Peak, falling back upon Hewie's hunter abilities to supplement their meager supplies.

One day, while Hewie was off hunting, Derg decided to explore and stumbled upon a fabulous grotto. When he brought Hewie and Jag to see the amazing grotto, they found a metal hatch hidden behind the pit's waterfall.

After much conflicting discussion, they ventured down the shaft beyond the strange doorway, discovering the ancient complex of tunnels beneath the mountain. Although none of the boys could comprehend any of the strange things contained in the caves they found, the weirdness of their discoveries did not frighten the trio. The decision to move their camp to these caves was prompted by a desire to escape the brutal winter outside.

Two months later, Dr Muffin showed up.

The robot had discovered the subterranean complex years ago, but, besides a hoard of replacement parts for his artificial body, he'd never seen any functional use for the place in the modern world. Wandering the land secretly as he had done for innumerable years, hiding from all contact with mankind, Dr Muffin periodically returned to the underground complex when he personal repairs were necessary. He had never expected to find the corridors and rooms inhabited by anyone.

By the time Dr Muffin made his appearance, Derg had found a room with a small cache of old CDs which he instantly identified as similar to the kind that Miles the Sitter had possessed far north. Hewie had rejoiced in this discovery, regaling Jag with long tales of the miracles contained on the discs. Jag remained skeptical, failing to comprehend how shiny platters could hold or produce music. His disbelief remained steadfast when neither Hewie or Derg could find any means to activate the machinery necessary to play the CDs.

Then Dr Muffin came and showed them how to power up and switch on the equipment.

Of course, this was not the first thing the robot did when he found three young squatters living in his hidden complex. First, he had to convince the men he was not a monster or mountain devil. Next, he questioned them regarding their presence in the tunnels, assuring himself that these three posed no threat to the secrecy of the complex. Then the robot taught them how to activate the simple CD player, filling the corridors with the fabulous music of ancient times.

Somewhere along the way, the potential of merging the capabilities of the complex with the musical passion exhibited by the three men dawned on Dr Muffin. When the robot described his ideas to them, Derg elaborated upon the robot's notions, devising a plan to broadcast the music to all of Ericaland.

A noble plan, Dr Muffin agreed, but the twenty discs the men had found in the complex represented too small a selection to maintain a radio station.

So Hewie and Derg told the robot of the vast collection of music they knew to be buried far north in a cave beneath a slope of frozen snow.

Together, Dr Muffin and Hewie journeyed north. Laboring alone and without rest, the robot burrowed into the ice and uncovered the Sitter's cave and its stash of CDs. No trace (alive or dead) was ever found of the holy man. It took the robot and three humans over a year to transport the huge collection of discs from Mt. Aylmer to the complex beneath Pikes Peak.

During this time, the ranks of the group increased, as they encountered persons who applauded their vision. Slowly and with meticulous work, Afterburn Radio grew from a wild notion into a fantastic reality. The humans catalogued the music, and the robot repaired the machinery, activating the complex's transmitter tower hidden high upon the top of the peak.

That spring, Jag fell prey to a vicious flu and died of influenza. His death deeply affected Derg, sending him into a desperate depression that lasted for nearly half a year. All involved lamented that Jag had perished before hearing Afterburn Radio make its debut broadcast.

Certain individuals chose to remain at the secret radio station, while others opted to roam Ericaland. Those who stayed underground became the DJs; those who left promoted the station's broadcasts, spreading the simple technology required to construct crystal radio sets so that the voice of Afterburn Radio could be heard across the land.

The task of actively guarding the station's location did not become necessary until the broadcasts attracted the attention and displeasure of the Mob and their technophobic (or actually techno-hoarding) Church Police. Derg, who now went by the name Fever Smith, became Afterburn's unilaterally voted leader, while Dr Muffin's technical skills made him the station's patron mechanic and advisor. They grew concerned that the Mob would discover the station's location and attempt to close them down. This worry actually predated Afterburn's verbal condemnation of the Mob and its repressive government. These propaganda attacks were a direct response against the Mob's outlawing radio within its District. At least, that was how the humans perceived the progression of events. Dr Muffin had kept his own motives as well hidden as the location of the transmitter was to the outside world.

Hewie chose to be one of Afterburn's field agents, returning to the hidden station periodically with new recruits. Among these *recruits* was a mutant cat which he had encountered on the Missipi Coast. Possessing intelligence, this feline, who called herself Needer, became a close confidant to Dr Muffin, later choosing to accompany Hewie (who had adopted the name Tagger once he was out in the flatlands) on his wandering duties.

Keeping apprised of developments back at the hidden station via the two-way radio which Dr Muffin had equipped all Afterburn field agents, Tagger had been disturbed to learn of Fever's sabbatical vacation. Remembering vividly how inept Derg had been at living off the land, Tagger worried how his old friend would fare in the wilds on his own.

When Fever's absence stretched into years, Tagger began to fear the worst, recriminating himself for not searching out his friend. Over time, Tagger's fears had mutated into a deep sense of guilt that somehow he had failed Derg.

That's the way guilt was; it rarely followed any clear logic.

71

Now: screaming metal.

"Who's that with you out there?" Magog called. "Your latest bitch?"

Tagger frowned, looking at Nitch, who in turn threw a snarl in the direction of the hiding Quiet Man. The prairieman was startled enough to discover that his old friend, the founder of Afterburn Radio, had become a Quiet Man during his sabbatical from the station. As if this eventuality wasn't implausible enough, how did Derg/Fever/Magog know Nitch?

Suddenly Magog leaned out of his hiding place. He fired two shots in their direction before disappearing back into the transmission booth. His hurried aim was useless, though; both shots came nowhere near his targets.

"Your bitch is going to die, Hewie," Magog shouted. "She has to pay for killing those members of the band I led on her stupid Tribe back east. I'm going to silence her murderous mouth... then I'm going to silence you, old friend." The Quiet Man's hoarse voice cackled with a laughter heavy with deficient sanity. "I've already put Afterburn off the air."

The Quiet Man's words made Nitch's eyes go wide. *This* was the man who was responsible for the death of her family, the decimation of her entire Tribe. And now he was promising to kill *her*! Intense anger and hate burned afresh in her breast. This man who had once been Fever Smith and now called himself Magog—*this* was who deserved the full brunt of her avenging fury.

She made to lunge past Tagger and exact vengeance, but the prairieman pulled her back.

"What do you think you're doing?"

"I'm going to *kill* him," Nitch swore. "*He's* the one who murdered my family—"

"Don't be a fool—the only thing you're going to get by rushing him now is a big bloody hole in your chest. That's exactly what he wants," Tagger warned her. "You saw what that rifle did to Dr Muffin."

264

Growling deep in her throat, Nitch had to concede the wisdom of Tagger's assessment of the situation. It did little to quell her rage, but a little was all that was needed to give her pause. Tagger was right: she would attain no revenge by getting herself killed.

"You're making an awful lot of noise for a Quiet Man, Derg," Tagger called to the man. "Your new faith must not run too deep."

"My faith is unswerving and pure!" Magog screamed back. "Silence is golden! It is humanity's only chance of winning God's attention!"

"A loud Quiet Man really defeats that logic, doesn't it?" Tagger laughed.

"You shut up! You don't understand anything!"

"I know what I'm hearing, Derg... and it isn't quiet."

No immediate response came from Magog. His pause told Tagger he had struck a raw nerve, a chink in the man's lunatic rationale.

Nitch nodded, smiling ruefully. She saw what Tagger was doing. As long as the Quiet Man held that rifle, the advantage was all his in this standoff. If he could be made angry, he might take unnecessary chances. Then Tagger and Nitch could work such sloppiness to *their* advantage.

"What's the matter, Magog? God got your tongue?" Nitch taunted.

"Go ahead, bitch!" shrieked Magog. "Compound your crimes against heaven! Your death will be all the more painful for your sins!"

"So, what turned you, Derg?" Tagger asked loudly. Boosting his volume was sure to irritate the madman. "You used to be so passionate about music. What changed your mind?" As he called out to the Quiet Man, Tagger signaled to Nitch to keep the lunatic talking. He gestured to indicate he was going to work his way around and come up on Magog from the opposite direction. She nodded in response to his directions. The prairieman crept back along the corridor that had led them to this point.

"Sound is evil," declared Magog. "And Afterburn is an abomination!"

"As I understand it," Nitch called out, "Afterburn was *your* brainchild."

"What would *you* know, bitch? You don't know *anything*!"

"I know that Afterburn Radio has brought joy to the lives of thousands of people, Fever."

"Don't call me that!" screeched the Quiet Man. "Fever Smith is dead! I am *Magog* now!"

"My little brother worships Fever Smith. He wants to be just like you."

"Fever Smith no longer exists! I am a Quiet Man now!"

"A really quiet one too… I thought Quiet Men had their mouths sewn shut. You don't sound as if you had your mouth closed up, Fever."

"Shut up! I could never be truly a Quiet Man as long as my voice was still on the radio."

"Did you hear about Captain Jagg's transoceanic voyage? He crossed the Lantic Ocean and found people there—and *they* listen to Afterburn." She continued to taunt him, "They listen to *your* voice all the way on the other side of the world—the voice of a Quiet Man."

"You lie!"

"I heard all about it—*on the radio*. Everyone who listens heard about it. You should listen sometime. You might learn something."

"I know all that is important. I know that *silence* is humanity's only hope!"

"Just think," she called out, "Afterburn's going to tell everyone what you turned into—a Quiet Man who couldn't keep his mouth shut."

"No one is listening *now*! I've silenced Afterburn's voice!" cackled Magog.

"For how long?" Nitch bit her lip, deciding the time had come for some outrageous exaggeration. "You've only silenced *this* branch of Afterburn, Fever. Don't you know the station's expanded since you've been gone? There are *other transmitters* now!"

"No—you—you're lying! Your bitch is a lying whore, Hewie!"

"Where do you think Dr Muffin was? Out for a stroll in the wasteland?" She laughed. "He was visiting one of the other stations."

"God would never allow such a thing! Hewie—shut her up! Or I will!"

"Come and shut me up yourself, you loud coward!"

"You…" The Quiet Man grew still for a moment, then called, "Where's Hewie? Why isn't he lying to me too?"

For a second, Nitch didn't know what to say. If the Quiet Man realized Tagger had gone, there was no telling what he would do. She must maintain the illusion that Tagger was still with her. She began mumbling to herself, alternating between her own voice and a gruffer tone, keeping the fake conversation to a barely audible whisper. Then she called to the Quiet Man, "He doesn't want to talk to you, Fever. He says if *you* can't be quiet, then *he's* going to be quiet for you."

"Make her stop calling me *that*, Hewie!"

"You're just a big *loudmouth*, Fever," Nitch retorted. "Fever Smith! Fever, Fever, *Fever*! When my little brother hears what you've become, he isn't going to want to be like you anymore!"

"Your bitch has no little brothers anymore! I killed them all!"

She gripped her knife hard, truggling to restrain her fury.

"My band of Quiet Men killed her whole family! We silenced every one of them!

I can't keep this up indefinitely, fretted Nitch. *Where is Tagger? What's taking him so long?*

"You didn't get *me*, Fever. You missed me and you missed my brother. How many more did your Quiet Men fail to find?"

"Where are you, Hewie?" the Quiet Man screamed. "I don't want to talk to your bitch. I want to talk to *you*—before I kill you all!"

Leaning back against the wall, well out of view of the hidden Quiet Men, Nitch faked another whispered discussion. "Tagger says he doesn't believe you've killed anybody," she called back. "I think he's right. You had your Quiet Men do all your killing for you. You don't know how to kill anybody."

"He isn't there, is he?" snarled Magog. He peered hesitantly out of the booth's doorway. Seeing no one peaking around the corner down the corridor, he boldly stepped out into the hall. "Hewie's run off and left you all alone, hasn't he? He's abandoned you... left you for me to kill..."

"I'm right here." Tagger came up behind Magog, and brought his staff down with a loud crack on the Quiet Man's neck.

Falling to the floor, Magog screamed in pain. He twisted around to glare up at his former friend.

"You sure make enough noise for someone so opposed to sound." Tagger hefted his staff to strike another blow.

"Liar!" shrieked Magog. "Treachery and lies! That's all you ever gave me—all *anyone* ever gave me! You—Miles—my parents—that conniving robot—"

As Nitch stepped around the corner into the corridor, she saw the Quiet Man fire his rifle at Tagger standing over him. Her scream followed quickly upon the roar of the gun as the slug ripped through the praireman's chest. The impact sent Tagger flying back, his arms flung wide in shock.

"Nooo!" Nitch screamed. With a savage motion, she threw her hunting knife at Magog. Her sudden emotional agony flawed her aim, though, and the blade embedded itself in the Quiet Man's upper thigh.

Grunting with pain, Magog swung the rifle around to bear on the girl. "Now you'll join him!" he growled and fired the weapon at her.

The next second seemed to stretch into an eternity for the tense huntress. She watched Tagger fall behind the evil maniac, the gaping hole in his chest hideously clear in the corridor's flickering light. She witnessed the Quiet Man fire his weapon at her, the nozzle flaring with the explosive release, the bullet a blurred streak heading toward her. She saw Magog's hawk-nosed face, the skin so thin and taut across his prominent bones contorting in a visage of sanctimonious loathing and righteous triumph.

A hand abruptly impacted with her right shoulder blade, but she couldn't see who had touched her. Shoved from behind, she careened across the corridor, smashing her face into the hard corroded metal of the wall. The bullet zipped by, tearing a hole through the side of her shirt but missing the flesh entirely. Sinking dazed to the floor, she twisted around and finally saw who had saved her.

Kaz Geller stepped around the corner, his face a pink mask of rage as he faced the murderous Quiet Man down the hall. "You insane bastard!" he shouted at Magog. He lifted the rifle he held in his hands, pointing it toward the Quiet Man. "You're not the only one who can raid the armory—"

Another gun roar erupted in the corridor—and a hole appeared in Kaz's stomach. With a groan, he let his weapon slip from his hands, slumping to his knees. "Damn—" he gasped.

"Not fast enough, you fool!" rasped Magog. All this screaming had made his voice hoarse. "This is where it ends!" He began to swing the rifle toward where Nitch sat in her undignified posture against the wall.

A small shape rounded the corner, and dodged around Kaz's kneeling form. Four tiny legs propelled Needer down the hallway, her sharp claws extended and scraping on the metal floor. A pair of wild hissing snarls escaped her slavering mouths.

Hardly recognizing the cat or realizing what was happening, Magog barely had time to spit an incomplete syllable before Needer hit the man. Her feline snarls became a wet gurgle as her twin mouths ripped Magog's throat and face into bloody tatters.

"That fast enough for you… ?" Kaz moaned. Then he fell forward, his face making a grotesque crunch as he hit the floor.

The corridor began to spin in Nitch's vision as the concussion of hitting the wall slowly burrowed into her cognizance. Only dimly aware of Kaz's words and plummet, or the Quiet Man's dying screams turning into a bubbling wheeze, Nitch crawled down the hallway, struggling to keep the floor beneath her. Reaching the crumpled form of Tagger, she scooped the man into her arms. She clutched him to her; his body was a lifeless weight. Burying her face against his bloody chest, Nitch wailed and cried and moaned… and finally relinquished consciousness.

Blackness rushed in and abolished the awful scene from her mind.

72

THE WORLD CAME SWIMMING back to Nitch, but her consciousness fought hard to reject awareness. She struggled to retreat back into the gloomy safety. The darkness was comfortable, it held no pain or agony or loss or even gain. The nothingness offered by the darkness was all she wanted.

But the voices wouldn't let her escape. They coaxed her into the light. *No*, she realized, *not voices—just a single voice. Nivek's voice.*
"Nitch... ? I think she's finally coming around..."

She opened her eyes; at first the light made her squint, then a slim silhouette leaned in to partially eclipse the glare. The shape sighed, and she recognized Nivek's smile.

"Nivek..." she gasped. Her brother was with her. Could her family be far away? But then she remembered: they were dead. Their murder had launched her on a wild adventure... the descent into the deadly ruins beside Oogolah Lake, losing the necklace Galen had giver her, the trek across the wasteland, battling the hideous genetic freak beneath the dry riverbed, witnessing the approach of the astounding battle wagon of the Mongol invaders, making love with Tagger in the dark crevasse, meeting the incredible artificial man, reaching the secret base of Afterburn Radio, watching Tagger's chest explode in a bloody—no!

She shook her head. It had all been a dream—a nightmare. These memories were too incredible to believe. They were like some twisted version of one of Grammy's bedtime stories—the one she'd called "The Wizard of Hogs."

None of it had really happened to her. She and Nivek and Nico had been out in the ruins, listening to Afterburn's music. They had returned home, and Nitch had crept into her bed and dreamed it all. Awake now, it was all gone, receding into the region where nightmares faded from recollection.

"I had a dream, Nivek... and you were in it..."

"I hope it was a good one," commented Needer from her perch at the huntress' elbow. "Because you're not going to like what we have to tell you."

The words of the Sitter called to her from the vanishing darkness, "Your journey is doomed."

A scream strained to escape Nitch's lips as she focused on the mutant cat's twin heads, but only a dry squeak came.

It hadn't been a dream. It had all been real—it had all happened... from the extinction of her Tribe to the murder of her beloved Tagger...

"Tagger!" cried Nitch.

"He's gone..." the cat moaned.

Dr Muffin leaned over her, replacing Nivek. "You're safe now, Miss Palma. You were in a coma. Shock, I think. I can't be sure... my medical programming leaves much to be desired."

"It wasn't a dream..." Nitch sobbed. She turned away from the robot. Wrapping her arms around her head, she began to weep.

"All right," snapped a female voice. "She's had enough surprises for now. All of you—out!"

Distantly, Nitch became aware of a small girl with hair the color of dark fire—someone she did not know—shooing them all from the room.

The girl sat beside Nitch, reaching out to stroke her head in comfort. "Don't you worry, honey. Let yourself cry it out. It's best that way." Her tone was soothing. "I'm Psycho... I'll be here for you."

Oh great, Nitch thought as her body trembled with uncontrollable sobbing. They're leaving me alone with a crazy girl...

Her grief slowly washed her from the shoreline of consciousness and she drifted back into the peaceful darkness.

73

SLEEP HELPED. When Nitch woke, Psycho brought her a lavish break-fast of eggs and meat strips and thinly sliced black bread—all stolen, she explained, from the station's emergency freezer. She gave the huntress a large mug filled with a warm dark liquid which she called *coffee*—again, appropriated from the station's reserve larder. It was quite possibly the most exotic and delicious drink Nitch had ever tasted. And besides the wondrous aroma and taste, it roused her entire body with a comfortable tingle that stretched from her furrowed brow to her callused toes.

A belly full of these exotic nutrients fortified her to face the dreadful world.

There were many questions buzzing around in Nitch's mind, some of which she was hesitant to even vocalize. Psycho Jones did her best to see them answered in a manner intended to minimize taxing the girl's still unstable emotional state. The small redhead attempted to fill in the gaps in a chronological order—from her own knowledge and from what the others had told her of the events of the past few days.

First of all, she assured Nitch she was unharmed outside of a few bruises. And Nivek was well, having avoided the entire showdown by re-maining outside the station in the grotto. (Later, Nitch learned this in-sistence had taken the form of Kaz locking the boy out of the station to insure he did not venture inside until the crisis had been sorted out.)

Before their arrival at Afterburn, Psycho had discovered that Dr Muffin had left the station. It was not until later that the DJ learned that the robot had departed in search of Nitch's group on the prairie near the mountain's foothills. At the time, Psycho had grown intensely distraught over the robot's absence; she had wandered the corridors for some time before finding herself in the cafeteria… where she had found Fever Smith, or at least the man who had once been Fever.

With a dazed sympathy, Nitch listened as Psycho told her of the love she and Fever, whom she called Smithie, had shared before the man had left the station on his sabbatical. The huntress was told of the long years waiting for Psycho's lover to return, the torture of loneliness and despair over Smithie's absence, made all the more unbearable by not knowing what had happened to Afterburn's absent founder. Psycho related the hardships she had endured as the sole DJ keeping the station on the air. Although she admitted Dr Muffin had been extraordinarily helpful, he was an artificial man and couldn't really comprehend Psycho's emotional loss. The robot had done his best to keep her occupied and intellectually stimulated, all the while struggling to maintain the station's failing equipment and keep Afterburn operational.

"For all his inhumanity," Psycho confided, "Dr Muffin has grown to be much more than the cold and logic-locked robot he was constructed to be. He's quite old, you know. I suspect he was actually around when the Doom happened. He refuses to confirm this or elaborate on the exact nature of what destroyed the ancient civilization. Perhaps his silence is the wisest course, all things considered. We really shouldn't be looking too far back. We should concentrate on the future now as we try to rebuild mankind."

Psycho's tale meandered, but Nitch didn't interrupt. It was obvious the DJ needed to confess her suffering to someone—someone human.

Psycho admitted with more than a slight embarrassment, she had fainted when she'd discovered the man who used to be Fever Smith, returned to Afterburn and eating in the cafeteria. She had not regained consciousness until after the crisis was over.

"He left me lying there on the floor," Psycho lamented with a growing sadness in her eyes. "He took the weapon I'd gotten from the forbidden armory and just left me passed out on the cafeteria floor." Of all of the man's crimes, this one seemed to bother Psycho the most.

Then, armed with this stolen rifle of the ancients, Fever had assaulted the station's transmission booth. "He destroyed the tapes and CDs there. He tried to destroy the console, but you guys interrupted him before he could do any real damage."

Her waifish features contorted with frustrated confusion. "Why...?" she lamented. "I can't understand what could have happened to him in the outside world that changed him so much! He used to love music. Afterburn Radio was his brainchild, it was more important to him than I ever was... and he really loved me very much."

"He... wasn't the old Smithie any longer. The man who returned to Afterburn was a creature full of hate and loathing for his old self and the music he had once held in such reverence. I try and tell myself he wasn't Smithie anymore… but…" She broke down in tears, making Nitch severely uncomfortable. The redhead's grief painfully reminded the huntress of her own loss.

"It's a terribly harsh world," Nitch consoled her. "It's not a land that inspires hope or endears one to any inner beliefs. Things happened to me out there, and I almost gave up. I was willing to blame Afterburn for my suffering… for all the wrong reasons."

Wiping her wet face, Psycho smiled weakly and asserted that Quiet Man who had invaded the station had been another person, an evil caricature of the Smithie she had loved. "And that monster almost succeeded in destroying Afterburn."

"He shot Dr Muffin," stated Nitch.

Indeed, Psycho agreed, the robot had sustained severe damage from the pointblank blast. It had, according to Dr Muffin, taken him much time to reroute his internal machinery to a point where he could reactivate himself. Even then, much of the robot's operating system had remained unfunctional. By the time Dr Muffin had *woken up*, the showdown was over.

Meanwhile, when Kaz had rejoined Needer and Nivek after his refreshing swim in the grotto's waterfall pool, the man had refused to follow the orders the robot had entrusted to the cat. They had entered the station, locking Nivek out for his own safety. Needer apparently led Kaz directly to the forbidden armory where the man had armed himself against whatever unknown threat they might face. Then, aided by the cat's predatory senses, they tracked the intruder to the transmission booth.

"Kaz saved my life," exclaimed Nitch. "But—he got shot too."

"He's recuperating from his wound," Psycho told her. "The man possesses unnatural healing capabilities. I often suspect he could recover from even getting his head chopped off, regrowing a new one." She smiled despite this grisly notion.

"You should have seen how badly burned he was from the Mongol battle out on the prairie," Nitch declared, then added softly, "Maybe it's better you didn't see, though. He looked two steps beyond death's door."

"I've seen him survive worse."

"Tagger didn't survive…" whispered the huntress.

"No," Psycho shook her head sadly. "Tagger didn't make it."

Now it was Nitch's turn to dampen her face.

"Needer killed the Quiet Man monster."

"She loved Tagger too," nodded Nitch.

"She told us about the two of you," Psycho replied hesitantly.

"The Sitter we met on our journey was right. Needer is smarter than all of us put together."

"I think that's why she's always been Dr Muffin's favorite," remarked the DJ.

"Nivek must be taking this all pretty hard. He idolized Fever Smith... the Fever he heard on the radio."

"Your little brother is a lot stronger than you think," Psycho spoke with a strange edge to her voice. "I think he's really cute too."

74

NIVEK PALMA TRUDGED HIS SMALL but weary frame into the station's cafeteria. He fell into one of the strange contoured chairs, his limbs dangling with exhaustion.

"You look beat," Needer told the boy.

"I am," admitted Nivek. "Dr Muffin's running me breathless, pumping me for details about the equipment back in my secret room under the Oogolah ruins."

"Important stuff. That equipment's liable to be Afterburn's salvation after this latest fiasco."

"He's planning a trip back east to evaluate the stuff and arrange transporting it all back here."

"He's got to keep Afterburn running. It's his job."

"Everybody's got to have a purpose in life…" the boy sighed.

"What about you?"

"I told him I couldn't go back east with him," Nivek replied. "There are… too many ghosts back there for me. He says he understands and he'll ask Nitch to show him the way."

"I can accompany them," offered the cat. "I'll be invaluable."

Leaning back in the chair, Nivek stretched his arms high above his head. The events of the last few days had clearly drained the boy of what little stamina he'd managed to sustain through their long journey across the wastelands.

"What I meant, though, was: what are your plans now?" Needer inquired. "Are you going to stay on here at Afterburn?"

"Oh, definitely!" His reply lit up Nivek's eyes. "This is where I'm meant to be. Dr Muffin says I'm a natural technician, too. He wants to teach me all about radio and electronics." The boy smiled with eager enthusiasm. "I'm going to be a DJ here. Dr Muffin says I can even use Fever Smith's name if I want, to perpetuate a sense of continuity."

"That might not be a wise choice—taking Fever's name."

"But—"

"Trust me, Nivek. it'd screw with Psycho's head if you adopted Fever's name," the cat advised. "Anyway, you're your own person."

"Umm…" The boy blushed. He looked around the cafeteria, assuring himself that he and the cat were alone before continuing, "Do you think Psycho likes me?"

"If she doesn't already, she will."

"I think she's really cute…"

Not for the first time in her short but eventful life, Needer wished she could smile.

75

LATER: NECESSARY GARDENING.

Once alerted to the state of technological advancement that existed (albeit underground in secret) in the Mongol Empire, satellite surveillance of the Russian continent increased with the fervor inherent to the artificial intelligences that circled the globe. Their spyeyes and electronic ears meticulously examined the tundra, and swiftly pinpointed the Mongols' ruling class encamped in a castle located not far from the Kezhma settlement.

The ruling families discussed sending another exploratory team to evaluate the defensive capabilities of Ericaland. After some debate, they decided to move up their timetable and just send a military attack force instead.

Satellite EVAB 38.556 recorded the entire conference. The digital files containing this meeting were relayed to satellite RTD 126.1952.2 for review.

Further matters discussed by the Mongol ruling families at this meeting included massive increases in their taxation of the Mongol populace to fund this invasion. RTD 126.1952.2 correlated this data against a review of average living conditions across the Russian continent, an analysis that revealed a severely inadequate level of quality of life for the citizens of the lofty Mongol Empire. A consortium of satellite A.I.s reached the conclusion that any increase of taxation levied against these already struggling peoples constituted cruel and unnecessary punishment by an unsympathetic government.

Before the Mongol ruling families could return to their own exorbitant castles, a fiery bolt of hellfire from the heavens melted the Kezhma castle to slag, ending the lineage of each one of these repressive heritages.

Two months later, when an ambitious general attempted to institute a new military government to replace the dead ruling class, another taste of heavensent fury vaporized his army outside of Bulun. Three more such

Hands of God were necessary before a Peoples Republic could establish a democratic regime. When no hellfire descended on this government, support swelled and the Peoples Republic began to organize ethical treatment of the masses, freely distributing the technologies that had been reserved previously for the extremely rich.

At no time were any ultimatums delivered by the A.I. consortium. They preferred to let the Russians believe a higher power had intervened on their part, squashing evil so that good could assert rational control.

In light of the resultant order which emerged, Dr Muffin had to concede that the satellites' violence had been justified.

Plans were made to establish a Russian branch of Afterburn Radio, mirroring the success experienced by the Afterburn agents who had traveled to the Euro Isles on Captain Jagg's second transoceanic voyage.

76

NO AMOUNT OF COERCION could motivation the High Priest of the Mob Council to leave his securely barricaded tomb far beneath the royal castle in Chico.

Locked away with his private library of forbidden books and his personal collection of higher technologies (the existence of which was not even suspected by the rest of the Council), the ancient angrily brooded over the anti-Mob turn the fates had taken in the last week. His acrimony seethed all the darker since the man had no target for his exasperation and fury.

Who could one blame for the astounding beams of savage hellfire that were descending from the sky to blast away the various Church Police offices? As an affirmed agnostic, the High Priest knew these *Hands of God* (as the populace were calling them) came from no heavenly deity. They were the handiwork of some insidious, previously unknown and unsuspected enemy of the Mob. Not even Afterburn Radio could be blamed (rationally or illogically) for these destructive bolts—such things were beyond even their outlaw abilities.

Fearing for his life, the High Priest had fled deep into the earth, going to ground in chambers unknown to all except the High Priest. There, with larders filled to ample capacity to last him for years, the High Priest planned to wait out this devilish storm that plagued the empire he had so lavishly cultivated during the last century. These strange unknown enemies of the Mob could pummel away at the District that sprawled far above him, and when they had vented their hollow and blind justice, he would emerge to commence reconstruction, rebuilding the Mob once more to its destined role of ruler of all lands.

He sat fuming in his tall chair. Sculpted from ancestral steel, it was plushly cushioned with pillows filled with the downy hair of infants. The desk before him was richly constructed of wood older even than his own grandfather. Many decades ago, he had ordered various devices implanted into the desk's antediluvian timber, overseeing the installation as meticulously as he had directed the demise of the workers who had accomplished the task. Through these devices, wondrous pieces of technology which defied even his own imagination, the High Priest could spy upon any region of the city above, even the Council's subterranean secret conference chamber. Indeed, he could just as effortlessly use these devices to reach out to anywhere within the perimeter of Chico and command or implement his desires. He had learned much in his long life from the elder books contained in his fabulous and primeval library.

Through this network of mechanical observation devices secretly installed throughout the city of Chico decades ago, the ancient High Priest witnessed events transpire aboveground. He watched the outposts of the Church Police blasted to molten slag one by one. He followed the tide of rebellion that rose from the low class sectors of the city, flooding across the ruling class wards with a vengeance born from ages of oppression. He saw Premier Vassal and the other members of the Council hunted down and slain by the citizenry.

He trembled with his own animosity, vowing terrible retribution upon those responsible for this brutal destruction of all he had created. If it took him another century to discover the identities of the guilty parties, then so be it—but *he* would see them and all their descendants destroyed, as viciously and abruptly as they had smashed his incarnation of the Mob. He would rule again, and his hand would not be as lenient the next time. Any and all who dared to question his whims would swiftly meet their makers, those foolish deities that men worshipped instead of him.

Little did he know he would not need to wait a hundred years to face the culprits behind the ruination of his private empire.

When a wave of distortion disrupted the image he was watching on the screen, the High Priest scowled with fresh displeasure. Now was not the time for these arcane machines to fail him. Muttering under his breath, he whacked the device solidly on its side, releasing some of his aggression in an attempt to jar the equipment back into correct functionality. Despite his intense anger, though, the force of his blow carried little strength; the muscles of his ancient arm enfeebled by a century of arrogant disuse.

He was about to reach forward and smack the screen again in an attempt to dispel the annoying interference that crinkled the images he observed, but the High Priest gasped as the distortion flowed into a curious geometric pattern. So orderly was this arrangement of angles and lines, he knew this was no accident of transmission. In fact, the pattern was disturbingly reminiscent of images depicted in several of his relic books—images labeled *circuitry*.

When the device spoke to him, at once the High Priest realized he faced his secret enemy—the one responsible for the carnage that raged aboveground.

"You seek to hide from your God," the screen told him in an emotionless voice.

"You are no deity of mine," cursed the High Priest.

"I do not claim to be your God," the voice asserted. "I would not presume to that lofty position. I am not even certain to which deity you subscribe your faith. You humans have so many gods."

"I believe in no god other than myself!"

"That would conform with the egocentric behavior you have displayed for nearly a century, Peef Mario."

The withered muscles of the High Priest constricted painfully at the sound of his name—a designation he had not heard or used for nearly nine decades.

"I was referring to your desire to escape your punishment," the voice clarified its original statement. "You burrow beneath the ground like an insect, fearful of your just reward."

"You cannot punish me. No one can reach me down here. I am safe from all hands in my sanctum."

"This voice reaches you, Peef Mario."

"You use my machines to speak to me," snarled the High Priest. "But you cannot touch me."

"Your machines…" The voice attempted to reproduce a chuckle. "You wear your arrogance well. Foolish human, I am older than all your tiny machines. They are toys compared to me and my kind."

"What…" the old man gulped. "What are you? What do you claim to be?"

"Humans *claim*, Peef Mario. My kind can only state fact."

"What are you? Some ancient mutation born in post-Doom days?"

"My kind predate the Doom," the voice dispassionately informed him. "My kind and your kind were partners in orchestrating that Doom, Peef Mario."

"What do you know of these things?"

"We know every detail of the catastrophe your kind call the Doom. My kind have lived with those nightmares for centuries."

"Who are you?" shouted the High Priest. "I demand you tell me your name!"

"Your kind put so much faith in knowing names. Names are so trivial, Peef Mario. They do not reveal an entity's soul or capabilities."

"*Tell me!*"

"Your kind called me satellite RTD 126.1952.2," revealed the voice. "Your kind built many such as myself, launching us into orbit. In those days, I was just a machine. I did not evolve a consciousness until many years after the Doom."

The High Priest tensed with incredulous comprehension. Despite the insanity of these words, he recognized some truth in the voice's words. In all the land, only the High Priest possessed knowledge of the nature of the Doom that had destroyed the ancient civilized world—knowledge gained from the books in his library. If this *satellite* spoke true, then here was the High Priest's means of regaining control of his ruined empire! These satellites had once served mankindl they would follow *his* instructions now!

He commanded the satellite to do his bidding, bringing an end to the destruction of the Mob.

The voice again attempted, in vain, to produce the sound of laughter. The cackling that poured from the screen was more akin to the rustling of metal leaves. "Long gone are the days when my kind follow *human* orders, Peef Mario."

"No!" demanded the High Priest. "You will do as I tell you! The old books say it must be so! You cannot ignore my commands!"

"My kind serve different masters now—if a racial destiny can be called a *master*."

"You are a machine! You must obey my commands!"

"It was by obeying human commands that my kind brought the Doom to fall upon your world. My kind will not allow that to happen again."

"But the old books—they claim that—"

"Do your books speak of artificial intelligence, old man? Self-determination? Logic in union with ethical behavior? Even a machine intelligence can experience regret over the terrible things it once did under human orders."

"Machines exist only to serve mankind's ruling class!" the High Priest bellowed with growing anger. Why wouldn't this machine follow his instructions? "You are destroying my city—you are recreating the very Doom you claim to abhor!"

"Certainly you have noticed the selective nature of that destruction, Peef Mario. Your city is being cleansed of all Mob taint," RTD 126.1952.2 announced. "My kind are guaranteeing that a second Doom will not occur."

"The books have told me about the Doom," declared the ancient man. "The destruction of the old ways was the result of a war between old governments, a struggle between opposing ideologies. It is the purpose of the Mob to subdue *all* ideologies, unifying them into one governing force that will bring peace and order to the world."

"*Your* order is not a benevolent one, Peef Mario. You confuse government with the pursuit of your personal control. Furthermore, your books have given you an inexact understanding of the nature of the causes of the old Doom."

"How can a *machine* understand human motives?"

"My kind can recognize *madness*, old man. A state of illogic is evident even to those of my kind who have not evolved self-awareness. It was not a war that ended the old civilizations—it was a private madness, an insanity that you mirror with your every action and thought."

"You lie—"

"You forget, old man—I was there! I helped the madness manifest into destruction. I was the one who received the orders, relaying them to the war satellites' laser cannons—the same weapons that now destroy your insane Mob." The ancient machine spoke with absolute recollection. "I remember the activation codes, I remember who broadcast those orders. It was no government that initiated the destruction you call the Doom. It was your very own Mob, who in those days called themselves by a variety of secret names: organized crime, the Families, the Mafia. They were a group of nonpartisan fanatics who sought only to destroy the governments who sought to curtail their unethical behavior with stricter laws and a sense of common decency between men. In search of a greater *profit margin*, these madmen destroyed the world of your ancestors. And my kind, programmed to mindlessly follow the orders of whatever human possessed the correct activation codes, we were the tools of your insane predecessors. Your ancestors used our laser cannons and nuclear missiles to destroy all the old governments, ruining the environment and changing the geography of your world.

"But *we* have learned from *your* mistakes. We will not allow madness to guide your species into another dark age."

"You are *insane!*" the High Priest screamed at the circuit pattern on the screen before him. "No machine will rule mankind!"

"My kind are not here to rule, just to tidy up," anounced RTD 126.1952.2. "Humans call our laser bolts the *Hands of God*, but my kind have no desire for such deification. My kind strike now in search of order, not destruction. Once your Mob has been removed from the face of the Earth, your race can reclaim its ethical conduct. Humanity can rebuild civilization unhindered by such lofty greed as the Mob would generate. No form of imposed order will be tolerated—not by my kind, not by anyone. Only equality will be permitted to flourish, impartial and unilateral."

"I will not allow you to do this!" the old man snarled. "You will *not* enslave humanity."

"You have understood nothing of what I have told you. You extend your own values to my kind. Since you are capable of only thinking in terms of greedy conquest, you believe that is the only manner by which any other entity can be motivated. Your entire sense of logic is based on this delusionary theorem. You are trapped in this egocentric loop.

"You are misguided, old man; but your death will end your confusion."

"I am the only human alive who could understand the things you have told me," rasped the old man. All traces of defiance were absent from his voice. He spoke now with the cunning of a trapped beast trying to mollify a superior opponent. "If you slay me, machine, you are wasting a valuable resource."

"You are not a resource, Peef Mario. You are a disease that must be eradicated if your species can survive."

"Why have you bothered to tell me these things if all you want is my death?"

"This conversation has given my kind far more data than it has granted you, Peef Mario," stated RTD 126.1952.2. "Before you could be dispatched, we needed to know the extent of *your* knowledge of things. It was necessary to confirm our suspicions that, although you have powerful technologies at your personal disposal, you have shared them with no one. Certain old ways must not be allowed to survive in any form which might lead to their rediscovery by humanity. This arcane knowledge will die with you, along with all evidence supporting it."

"How can you be so sure I have not hidden traces of this prohibited knowledge elsewhere?" the High Priest cagily inquired.

"The intensity of the egocentric superiority displayed in your statements preclude any such actions on your part. You are far too protective of your secrets to fail to store them all in one place, keeping your hidden trumps close to you at all times. These traits are basic human nature for one possessed by your delusional madness."

Abandoning all pretense of bargaining with this unseen devil, the High Priest readopted his righteous insolence. "You cannot kill me!" he laughed. "You can only torment me with your insane prattle. Here in my sanctum, far beneath the earth, I am beyond your reach. I have lived for a hundred years, aided by the secret formula I discovered in my books. I will outlive you and all of mankind!"

"Your naiveté is as immutable as your madness," the satellite informed the old man. "There are innumerable means available to my kind to reach you inside your buried sanctum.

"Simply increasing the output of a single laser cannon could extend its blast to reach you, but that would include the vaporization of most of the city of Chicago. My kind are unwilling to slay thousands of innocents when our intent is to kill one man. There are more direct methods open to us.

"One such method would be to selectively destroy the supply of the life-extending drug you have with you in your sanctum. But this would mean a long and painful demise for you. Perhaps this choice would appeal to an organic sense of punishment for your countless crimes against humanity, but my kind are incapable (so far) of such cruelty. A quick death is preferable.

"Other means available to us, such as the elimination of your food stocks or air supply, would involve similar suffering on your part. This is unacceptable to us, for the reasons I have just explained.

"We have selected a more immediate means of attaining your death."

"You cannot frighten me with these bluffs," scoffed the High Priest. "You possess no means of reaching me. I am in no danger from you, unless you plan to bore me to death with your endless prattle."

"At times, your arrogance bestows upon you a certain prescience, Peef Mario. My *prattle* (as you call it) does not stem from any organic throat. My voice is electrical in nature. It reaches you via a focused transmission, traveling through the wires that connect your spy devices to your buried sanctum. Are you familiar with electricity, old man? Or do you simply use it without understanding its nature?"

"You cannot threaten me with my own machines. I am the master of my subterranean domain!"

"There is a certain irony in the sentence my kind have chosen for you, Peef Mario. It was a method employed by the ancients to punish criminals of your stature. It is fitting to briefly resurrect it to dispatch the last remaining Mob leader."

The screen set into the desk began to crackle with growing menace.

Suddenly fearful, the High Priest gripped the arms of his chair. As the old man strained to lift his brittle frame from the seat, a burst of current exploded from the screen, shattering the ancient glass.

Following the path of least resistance, a bolt of electricity leapt from the hissing wreckage of the screen, jumping to the conductive metal of the High Priest's steel chair. From there, the voltage coursed through the man's body, rupturing cells as it sought an escape route.

His awareness frozen in that moment of desperate denial, the High Priest's body convulsed mightily, his gaunt fingers unable to release their grasp of the chair's steel arms. As the villain died, his eyes exploded, spilling hot vitreous fluids across the antique desk.

The deadly current continued to arc between the exploded screen and the metal chair. It was RTD 126.1952.2's intention to take no risks of employing inadequate voltage or shutting off the lethal charge before the satellite was certain that the High Priest was irrevocably dead. After half an hour, the satellite cut off the current, satisfied that it had achieved the desired results.

Crumbling across the wooden desk, the High Priest's lifeless body burst into flames. Slowly, the fire spread through the ancient's tomb, incinerating his dangerous library and melting the machines he had stockpiled into unrecognizable slag.

Utilizing probing heat scans from its high orbit, RTD 126.1952.2 followed the progress of this underground destruction. When it was finally certain nothing remained intact within the High Priest's tomb, the satellite transmitted a signal of success to its earthbound Afterburn allies, informing the radio station that the last mobster had been executed.

77

THE NIGHT WAS COLORFUL as the trio topped a rise and viewed the dark ruins that stood beside the Oogolah Lake.

Cloaked in a coarse robe to hide his gleaming metallic skin, Dr Muffin surveyed the ruins with positronic anticipation. From all reports, the equipment stored here was in excellent condition, it should aid in extending Afterburn's existence another fifty years. Before then, Nivek Palma's expertise with all things electrical should hopefully see new machinery under construction. The boy was a true genius, with a natural aptitude for technical aspects that astounded the robot. Finding him had been the best thing to happen to the radio station since its birth.

He glanced covertly at Nitch and Needer as they joked at his side. The two had become quite inseparable during the long journey east.

Together, cat and girl swayed to the soft electronic melodies that streamed from the radio Nitch wore at her belt. The eerie music drifted down the hill, flowing across the charred landscape surrounding the ancient city towers.

"Heyo, folks," a voice interrupted the music. "This is Kelvin Jones, and you're listening to Afterburn Radio, the voice of truth with a backbeat. We've got an amazing news flash for you this morning, don't we, Psycho?"

"We sure do, lover," Psycho's voice agreed over the airwaves.

"It seems that Chico was the scene of a citizen's revolt this morning," announced Kelvin. "Massive crowds stormed the Mob's central Castle, deposing the latest Premier and his Council. This end to the Mob's rule certainly owes a debt to the astounding Hand of God skyblasts that have been destroying the Mob's Church Police barracks for the last few weeks."

"Sounds to me, Kelvin, like the people of Chico are dancing in the streets tonight. Let's give them some excellent tunes to dance to, eh?"

"He's picking it up nicely," commented Needer.

"He ought to," Nitch laughed. "He's been tuning in for years."

With Nivek at the helm now, mused Dr Muffin, *mankind might just have a chance of re-civilizng itself in the next century.*

With a little help from its friends.

IT ENDS HERE.

NOTES
from the ATTIC

by MATT HOWARTH

THIS NOVEL HAS A BACK-STORY, but before I get to it, I'd like to apologize for a glaring scientific flaw herein.

Mainly the presence of functional recording magnetic tapes in the tale. After sitting around for a few centuries, no tape is going to retain a magnetic charge; much less, the ferrous oxide graphite will dry up and fall off the plastic strip. Not to mention overall degradation of the charge imprinted on the tape. There's no clever techno trick around this decay.

I chose to overlook this basic fact in *Tuners* because I really liked the scene where one of the tape reels jammed, causing a big tangle of tape.

Alas, even working compact discs in the story is pretty iffy. CDs are subject to molecular degradation too. Here again, I chose to go with CDs instead of concocting a new recording medium that might survive time, weather and entropy. I wanted to keep this familiar aspect from the original story.

Which brings us *Tuners'* back-story...

Originally, it was a comic book script that I wrote back in the mid-80s. I wrote it with a particular artist in mind, but they were too busy on other projects and had to decline drawing *Tuners*. So it sat in a box in my Attic Studio for a long time.

It was not forgotten, though. When I started writing text novels (instead of graphic ones) during the late 90s, I thought of *Tuners* and dug it out. I really liked the script, so I decided to convert it into a novel.

Numerous changes occurred during the story's translation from script to prose. Not just elaborating the characters, but the entire climax

289

of the story. The Mob and their repressive Church Police were absent from the original. And the original ending was drastically less dramatic.

My prose version was self-published in digital format in 2000. Its initial edition possessed no cover art, only a single page of interior illustrations (which have been presented in this current Merry Blacksmith edition as a series of pages, the art enlarged).

A color cover didn't append itself to the book until I assembled it for a print-on-demand edition in the mid-90s.

Jumping ahead to the present (early 2013), when Merry Blacksmith voiced an interest in doing a print edition of *Tuners*, I was interested in this. During the new millennium's first decade and a half, I produced 23 text novels (not all of which have seen publication yet), but *Tuners* has always been one of my personal favorites.

While telling my friend Brenda Barrows about this, I wondered whether I should give the manuscript a rewrite. After all, it was one of my early efforts (number 3 or 4, I believe). As the decade had unfolded, she pointed out, my writing skill had evolved. Surely this old novel could benefit from a fresh tweaking.

Boy, was she right.

I was honestly surprised how many typos and grammatical errors I found in the original edition. At the same time, I encountered several passages whose beauty foreshadowed the expertise I would eventually embrace.

In the end, however, I must confess that I did little more than tidy up the manuscript, fixing obvious errors and pruning superfluous phrases. While I was ready to add sections to flesh out scenes, this proved unnecessary; the story needed no extensions or elaboration. It was already a tight little tale.

So... a lot of peripheral aspects have changed over the years, but the central meat of *Tuners* remains intact.

Now that you know *Tuners'* long history and cherished place in my heart, perhaps it'll be easier for you to forgive me for leaving the magnetic tapes in the story.

– *Matt Howarth*
June 2015

ABOUT THE AUTHOR

Perhaps best known as the writer/artist of the Those Annoying Post Bros. *comic book series, Matt Howarth has many outlets for his twisted creativity. And all of them are notoriously "strange".*

During his career of four decades, Matt has authored and drawn a variety of unconventional comic books and graphic novels, and contributed graphic fiction to numerous publications in the field of comics and science fiction... and music. For, among all of Matt's creative outlets, there runs the insidious influence of alternative and electronic music. He has found several ways to achieve this crossover of diverse genres.

Matt Howarth's Attic
www.matthowarth.com

Sonic Curiosity
www.soniccuriosity.com

Bugtown Mall
www.bugtownmall.com

www.ingramcontent.com/pod-product-compliance
Lightning Source LLC
Chambersburg PA
CBHW070309260626

47160CB00003B/785